No Choice But Freedom

A Novel of Treachery and Triumph in Colonial America

High Country Publishers

Ingalls Publishing Group, Inc
Boone, NC

No Choice But Freedom
A Novel of Treachery and Triumph in Colonial America

by Pat Mattaini Mestern

High Country Publishers

Ingalls Publishing Group, Inc
Boone, NC
2006

High Country Publishers is an imprint of Ingalls Publishing Group, Inc., 197 New Market Center, #135, Boone, NC 28607

Visit our website at: www.highcountrypublishers.com

Cover design by James Geary

Library of Congress Cataloging-in-Publication Data
Mestern, Pat Mattaini.
   No choice but freedom : a novel of treachery and triumph in Colonial America / by Pat Mattaini Mestern.
        p. cm.
   ISBN 1-932158-76-6 (trade pbk. : alk. paper)
   1. Virginia—History—Colonial period, ca. 1600-1775—Fiction. 2. North Carolina—History—Colonial period, ca. 1600-1775—Fiction. 3. Africans—England—Fiction. 4. Merchant mariners—Fiction. 5. Women immigrants—Fiction.
I. Title.
        PR9199.3.M446N6 2006
        813'.54—dc22
                                                        2005022190

First printing: March 2006

Dedicated to
Charlie Mattaini
who during his life
bridged many gaps

Acknowledgements

I am indebted in many ways to a number of people who made their private collections of documents, journals, diaries and books available for research. The more I became immersed in relevant primary source material, the more respect I had for the individuals, some now deceased, who had the foresight to preserve what may have seemed at the time, unimportant trivia of the 18th century. Today, their collections are priceless. For fear of missing a name, I will state that you all know who you are and how much I value your counsel. Thank you!

I must in particular thank Jeff Marshall Craig for his input and encouragement, Albert A. Bell, Jr., Senior Editor of Claystone Books of Ingalls Publishing Group, Inc., for his direction and schuyler kaufman, Associate Editor of High Country Publishers, for her wonderful sense of humour, diligent editing and absolute knowledge of the 18th century.

Judith Geary, Senior Editor at High Country Publishers, has done a stellar job of editing, keeping the project on track and bringing *No Choice But Freedom* to successful fruition.

Many thanks are extended to Barbara Ingalls, Executive Editor and Bob Ingalls, Publisher of Ingalls Publishing Group, Inc. Without their unflagging dedication to the publishing industry, books such as *No Choice But Freedom* would not be made available to discerning readers. Of course, a final thanks must go to dedicated readers for purchasing this book. Enjoy!

Ingle Ken'lt "Hearth Rekindled"

From the northern white of the winter's snow -
From the eastern blue of the spring's new moon -
From the western red of the summer's sun -
From the southern gold of the autumn's leaves -
Come coals from the hearth's flame,
Entrusted to the hands of friends.
Though the fire has died in the ancestral home,
Its spirit remains alive.
When touched to wood in the new laid hearth,
The warmth is rekindled again.

For warmth is friendship,
And friendship is love,
And love is bestowed upon all.
Let the door fore'er be open -
Let the cawther run free.
It is sung far and wide,
That this ever may be.

The home is the hearth.
The hearth is the flame.
The flame is the spirit of love.
Let all know, from whence they came,
They are warmed by this hearth and this flame.

Pat Mestern
c1984

I am now a shadow that worships the wind -
But my spirit lives in the river -
When it reaches the sea it will travel -
Until it touches the shore of my homeland
Then I will be free.
        Ndamma
        Slave 1753

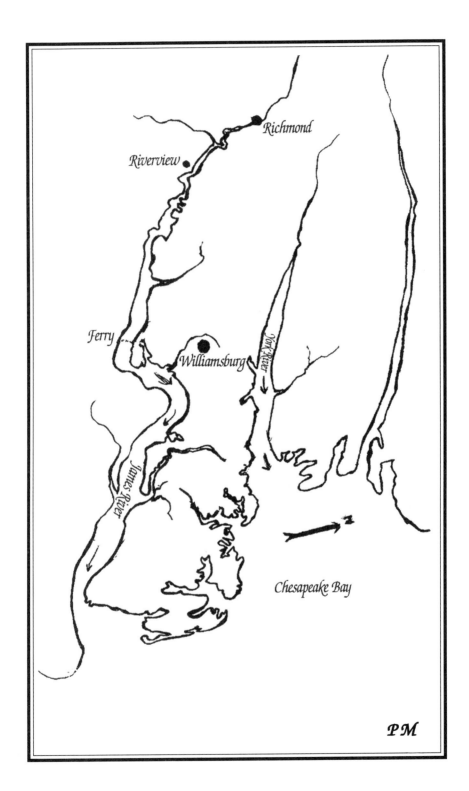

NO CHOICE BUT FREEDOM

CHAPTER ONE
WILLOWBANK, ENGLAND
November 1750

THREE men shared the hearth in Charles Turnbull's lair on this raw November day, their chairs drawn up before the crackling blaze. They held glasses high in toast.

"To your son," said Charles Turnbull, nodding to the man across from him. "'Tis unfortunate the date is not auspicious for his birth. Nevertheless, we must make the best of all we have."

"My son." Talbot Showcroft took a drink.

"Your son," echoed Timothy Bushnell.

"To Joanna," proposed Turnbull.

"Joanna," said Talbot, and took another drink.

"Showcroft, you appear less than overwhelmed at fathering of my first, and only, grandchild," Charles Turnbull said.

Talbot glanced up from his brandy. "I am thrilled, Sir," he said without feeling. "You must remember we endured a gruelling two months at the mercy of the Atlantic and are not yet recovered from the voyage."

"The passage was rough," admitted Bushnell. "We lay at anchor in the harbour at New York for some days awaiting a favourable wind, then lay over at Nova Terra riding out another storm."

"All the more reason for Joanna to join you in the Colonies, as she is determined to do," Charles said.

"Why so?" Talbot asked.

"You have visited Joanna but twice since you married her four years ago. 'Tis not right that man and wife should live an ocean apart. The crossing to England takes two months with favourable winds, and the return to the Colonies takes no less. You are not attending to either your wife or your business affairs."

"The Colonies, especially the Carolinas, are no place for a refined lady," said Talbot.

"Neither is England for Joanna without her husband," Charles barked. He got up to push aside the rich draperies and peer out at the river and hills beyond, land he owned as far as he could see. "I'm certain she will soon grow accustomed to life in America. I will, of course, provide her with comforts befitting a Turnbull."

"Such elegances come dear, especially in the Colonies." Talbot looked toward Timothy who remained silent, nervously fiddling with his brandy glass. "I should wish her to live near Williamsburg. A good plantation in coastal Virginia is not easily found, and costly when it appears."

Timothy stopped playing with his glass, and watched the adversaries.

"I insist that whatever will ensure my daughter's comfort shall come from my pocket," Charles said turning from the window. "I will not tolerate my daughter living in a hovel when she is accustomed to – this." He gestured at the window. "Arrangements can be discussed and a letter of terms for purchase drawn up before you leave."

Talbot joined Charles by the window. The parterre with its statuary, pools, pathways and cozy nooks spread like an elaborate tapestry over nearly an acre beyond the window. The ornate, twelve-sided doocot glittered like a massive diamond in the sunlight. "I believe it was you who wished her to stay at Willowbank after our wedding."

"That is true. Joanna is my only child. I shall miss her, and she will miss her home. However, she wishes to be in America with her husband."

Talbot responded, his gaze lingering on the scene outside the windows. "I shall need to prepare a proper home. 'Tis early November. Crossing the Atlantic in winter is hazardous. I propose to leave at once for the Colonies. Joanna may follow in the spring."

"Nay, but you've just arrived," Charles protested. "And Joanna cannot make the crossing alone."

Talbot raised his hand to silence his father-in-law. "Sir, you know well the dangers of a winter passage. 'Tis practical that she stay here until spring," he said. "I've a sugar crop to oversee. I cannot waste time in England; especially if I've to travel to Virginia before I return to the Carolinas."

"Why can Joanna not join you in the Carolinas? Is the climate not better there?"

Talbot turned from the window and watched Bushnell's reaction to his words. "The Highlanders who backed young Charles Stuart are emigrating from Scotland to the highlands of Carolina. They're scattered throughout the mountains, rebellious as ever. They wear the tartan openly and obey no laws but their own."

"Come now, Showcroft. You exaggerate."

"Not at all, Sir. I am acquainted with a few of them. Believe me. The Carolinas are no place for your daughter and grandson."

Timothy, squirming under Talbot's scrutiny, nonetheless stared at the boldness with which the man wove his web of deceit.

"Perhaps then Mr. Bushnell would remain here, and escort Joanna and the child." Charles turned his attention to the quiet guest. "Pray accept my hospitality until spring, Bushnell. While you are here, I might seek subscribers for that ambitious project of yours. I am sure I may find more than a few gentlemen of means who would be pleased to back a book of artistic renditions of ... the flora and – er – etched rocks of America."

Timothy's eyebrows shot up in surprise. He glanced warily toward Talbot. "What a generous offer, Mr. Turnbull. I thank you from my heart, Sir. But I have ... pressing ... business in America, specimens to collect ... sketches to –"

"You seem reluctant to accept my invitation, Sir." Charles had missed neither the guard Timothy had set on his response, nor the play of looks between the artist and Talbot.

"Why, Sir, 'tis sudden. I had not looked for such a charge, far less such an offer." Timothy nervously stroked his chin, collecting his thoughts. "In the face of your generosity, I'd be a fool to refuse your kind offer." He sketched a bow to his host. "I should be honoured to stay at Willowbank."

"Then all is settled," Talbot said. "I shall leave within the week."

"If I may say so, Turnbull," Timothy said. "Some situations in the Colonies might conflict with Mrs. Showcroft's rather ... eccentric beliefs. To be blunt, I mean her objections to the keeping of slaves."

Charles reached for a bell cord. "My daughter has weighed the consequences of both voyage and move. She will attend to such questions in her own way. She's a head-strong woman; she'll not change her mind. Aye, I'll miss her, but I won't beg her to stay."

Talbot bowed. "Begging has its advantages; 'tis a recourse you should consider, Sir."

"Begging is no recourse for me," Charles said.

"Whoever owns the recourse, it might be wise to contemplate it," Timothy said.

"Why so?"

"America is a hard master, Sir. It holds many surprises, slavery being only one of them." Timothy felt Talbot's eyes on him.

"Ah, but my Joanna is a firm mistress. Yes, Burns," Charles addressed a liveried butler who had slipped quietly into the room. "I believe the weather has cleared sufficiently for a ride?"

"Indeed it has, Sir."

"Gentlemen, we can either take the horses out for an hour or join Joanna for tea in her sitting room."

"Your pleasure, Sir." Timothy rose from his chair and stood behind it. The chair stood like a rampart between himself and Talbot.

"Perhaps we should allow Joanna to rest." Charles said. "Burns, send word to the stable to saddle up three of my best hunters. Shall we say on the half-hour ... at the north portico? That will give us time to change into riding gear."

Timothy, his hands still firmly gripping the chair he had chosen as a shield, cast about in his mind for a harmless topic as Charles left the room. Instantly the memory of Charles' determination that the wedding between Joanna and Talbot take place on the first of May, 1746 emerged. Its numbers, added together, were divisible by twelve. Charles' earlier comments about the inauspiciousness of his grandchild's birthday alerted Timothy to the importance of the number. Everything about Willowbank, from the twelve-sided doocot, and pavilion, to the number of stairs and windows in the mansion itself, seemed based on the number twelve. "What is Charles Turnbull's fascination with the number twelve?" blurted Timothy.

"Insane codswaddle. One of his ancestors made his first guinea on the twelfth of December, in 1614. Generations of the whole damn family have found meanings in it. Charles is as stupidly eccentric as his father. He would never knowingly break the chain."

"And Mrs. Showcroft? Does she hold the number twelve to be lucky?"

"I don't know, and to say truth, I don't give a damn. See here, Bushnell, I must be certain you know enough to guard your tongue and your actions during your stay here. You know what I must do before my wife arrives in America."

"I am well aware of your circumstances," Timothy said. "But I mislike being a party to deception."

"Well, you'll have to like it. I've no desire to lose my share of Turnbull's money merely because I care nothing for his daughter," Talbot said. "My wife's determination to come to America means that I must now tend to the Carolina situation."

"The lady is your wife!" exclaimed Timothy. "You went into the marriage with your eyes open."

"You need not remind me," Talbot said. "I am painfully sensible of the fix I am in. I have encumbered myself with both a mistress in America and a wife in England. But remember, Bushnell, Joanna is a very wealthy English wife. The Carolina woman is ... expendable. You had better also remember while you are dawdling here that you are indebted to me. Without my support, your comfortable little world will collapse around you, Bushnell. To me, you are as insignificant as that fly on the wall. Need I say more?"

"You offered to underwrite my book. I thought you believed in the worth of the project, in cataloguing new Carolinian plant forms."

"Don't parade your stupidity, man. Monies were given to buy your loyalty, to ensure your silence." Talbot paced before the hearth, pounding one fist into the other. "To the devil with your artistic endeavours. I expect that while you reside here, my *patronage* had damn well better ensure both your continued loyalty and your silence."

Timothy stood out of Talbot's reach. He knew too well that the man was violent enough to order him killed on the slightest hint that he posed a threat.

"Why are you so mumchance? Your silence is beginning to grate." Talbot said.

Keeping a wary eye on Talbot, Timothy ventured, "You are by all standards very wealthy. To allow Turnbull to buy a plantation for his daughter when you could well afford to do so, seems greedy in the extreme."

"That warrants no response," Talbot said. "What is your decision, Bushnell?"

Timothy retrieved his brandy glass from the table and drained it slowly, allowing time to think. It would be difficult to maintain silence about Mairi MacKinnon. But to refuse Turnbull's generous offer was lunacy. Painting was Timothy's passion – his life. Perhaps by spring, enough patrons could be found to rid himself of Showcroft by paying off his debt. "If I have one quality I can state positively I possess, it is that I keep my word," Timothy finally said. "I shall tell no tales. Permit me to say, however, you ought to render your marriage vows more respect."

"By God, there is no need for lecture!" Talbot turned his back to Timothy. "Enough chatter. We'll be late for our ride. It would be imprudent to keep the old man waiting."

Willowbank – The Gazebo

JOANNA was not in her sitting room waiting for the gentlemen to arrive for tea. Nor was she resting upon her bed. Wrapped in a warm woollen cloak, she sat in a remote gazebo on the north hill, watching clouds on the wings of a strong west wind, scudding across the sky. As the clouds passed in front of the sun, their shadows danced across the river valley's landscape, alternately bathing the great house in bright light, then immersing it in deep shadow.

The display matched Joanna's mood. She had made her way to the gazebo because she needed time to think, away from the menfolk, the baby, the bustle of the manor house and gardeners wintering plants in the parterre. She was not entirely alone. John Melrose, the head gamekeeper, placed an inlaid wooden box on the bench beside her, and retreated to a discreet distance, waiting patiently for his orders.

In the quietude of the gazebo, Joanna opened her lap desk with its bottles of prepared ink and array of pens, opened her diary to a fresh page and wrote:

November 3, 1750 – This day I did say to my Husband, that I am going to America, and that under no circumstances would I change my Mind. I should have thought Talbot would show pleasure at the announcement. He exhibited such a Sour Disposition, that I was quite taken aback, but refused to spar. Father reminded me that I took the man for the Good, the Bad – and the Marriage Agreement.

I cannot help but think of my dear Harrison. Had he lived, we would have married this Month, seven years ago. It was his wish to journey to India to become acquainted with Turnbull holdings before assuming their care, though I did endorse that Undertaking, to my Profound Regret. Curse the fever that led to his Demise so far away from Home! I shall never forget his gentle nature and kind way.

Joanna dusted the page with sand from the shaker, tipped it onto the ground and closed the book. Across the hillside her father, her husband and Timothy Bushnell rode toward the east pastures and hunt grounds. Each had his own posture in the saddle; each his own temperament in discussion and debate.

The past cannot be retrieved, Joanna thought. What's done cannot be undone. I must be all reason now. I have a husband and babe. 'Tis my consenting to marry Talbot Showcroft has put me in a pucker. What reasons stood during our courtship may not now hold true. Mother anathemized him for a coxcomb and worse, woefully unsuitable as a husband. Granted, he is not a man of delicate scruple, but I have never seen a predicament I cannot make something of. The man will not be easy to live with – or as Father says, to outwit. He is handsome, intelligent – and, yes, perhaps *dangerous* for want of a better word. And he did present himself at a time when I had really begun to seriously contemplate the question of an heir.

Indeed, there were many circumstances in our courtship that I question now. Will living in America provide answers? In truth, who can say with certainly what will transpire in this great adventure, I am about to undertake? *All the world's a stage, And all the men and women merely players; They have their exits and entrances. ...* Shakespeare, her favourite playwright did pen a quote *à propos* to any situation, Joanna thought.

"Ma'am?" Melrose interrupted Joanna's thoughts. "The time is just on the hour."

"Ah, thank you Melrose. If I am to have my hour with baby Luke before high tea, we should begin our walk back."

"Yes, Ma'am. May I say, your husband rides as well as you, Ma'am."

"So he does, Melrose."

Melrose, his shooting piece slung over his back, assisted the Mistress down the steep hill to level ground. He retrieved the lap desk and walked a distance behind her.

CHAPTER TWO
WILLIAMSBURG, VIRGINIA
February 1751

TALBOT stepped into the taproom of the Raleigh Tavern, removed a clay pipe from the rack by the door, broke a small piece off the stem and looked around for Matthew MacGregor. He made his way through the candle-lit, crowded room and sat down at a table in the corner, opposite the bearded sinewy Scotsman. Stretching his legs, Talbot filled the pipe from a small pocket pouch, tamped the tobacco down firmly, then handed the packet to MacGregor.

"How's MacGregor tonight?" Talbot touched a slender wood splinter to the candle on the table. He took his time, lighting the pipe while looking around the room to see who was at the inn this evening.

"I've had word that you wished tae see me," said MacGregor.

"That I did," Talbot replied. "I understand you want to sell Riverview Plantation. Is that true?"

"Aye," said MacGregor. "For the right price."

Talbot glanced around the noisy room. Catching the barkeeper's eye, he held up two fingers. "I rode past the place today. You're well situated to the west. The property backs onto the James River so crops can be river-shipped."

"Aye. That's one beauty o' the place."

"Why are you selling?"

"My wifie wants tae tak' the bairns an' join the kinfolk doun sou'. To tell ye the truth, 'tis tae bloody English aroun' these parts. 'Tis better tae rekindle our hearth near kin."

The barkeeper placed two pewter tankards of ale on the table. Talbot reached into a pocket and handed the man several coins. "What is included in your price?"

"Do ye wan' the slaves?"

"How many have you got?"

MacGregor thought for a moment. "Seven fer the hoose an' eighteen fer the fields – not counting the little ones. Mollie's expecting. Twenty-five adults, two tobacco hauling vessels an' a thousan' acres of the best Virginee soil tae be had."

"When can you move?"

MacGregor took a swig of ale, wiped his mouth on his sleeve and said, "We are awa' in two months. We're nae takin' much wi' us. There's furniture tae be left in the hoose."

"I heard you had trouble with some of the slaves."

"Sukie is a good'un. She keeps t'other slaves in line. She be good with the slave-bairns and cooks too. 'Tis her husband might give you trouble. He an' Flanagan are always tae each other's throats. Flanagan says I should sell him, but he's useful tae have aroun' the place. An' I don't hold wi' breaking up families like the former owner. He sold all of Sukie's bairnies awa' fra' the plantation just afore I bought it." MacGregor picked up his tankard, but put it down without drinking. "Why do you want tae be a tidewater planter, Showcroft? You own hundreds o' acres doon Carolina wa'."

"My wife is coming from England, and I want to locate her in Virginia."

"Ye're married?" MacGregor's tankard stopped mid-air. His eyebrows rose up in surprise. "'Tis strange indeed –"

Talbot cut him short. "'Tis not at all strange for a man to marry. I took a wife four years ago. Recently she chose to join me in America."

"Aye, if you say." MacGregor took a stiff drink, and held his tankard up to indicate he wanted another. "'Tis nae fer me tae question."

"I'll buy Riverview," Talbot said, "including the slaves, the vessels, the animals, with a promise you'll put in this year's crop before you leave."

"Ye dinna' e'en ask ma' price!" exclaimed MacGregor.

Talbot pulled a folded sheet of vellum from his pocket and tossed it in front of MacGregor. "Read this. The terms are listed. I want Riverview. 'Tis elegant enough to please my wife and her father. I'll see my notary and have all the necessary papers drawn up, if you are agreeable with the terms. They are to be signed by my wife when she arrives. I am staying at the Wetherburn. You can send word to me tomorrow."

A disturbance caused heads to turn toward the door. "He can't come in here," someone protested.

"Are you man enough to stop us?" came the reply. "Out of my way."

A ruddy giant of a man stepped into the tap room, followed by a well-built African, his mirror in ebony. The room seemed smaller with their presence.

Talbot waved. "Makem! Over here!"

Makem grabbed a tankard from the bar and strode through the room, followed by his shadow. He sat down heavily, his back to the wall. The shadow stood behind the chair, arms folded on his chest. "Innkeeper chews about Caliganto. He's a free man and I'm not asking that he be served at the same table as these scurvy lads." Makem waved his arm around the room.

"He is imposing," Talbot said, glancing at the burly black. "How are you, Makem? Do you know MacGregor? Master MacGregor, this is Captain Anthony Makem."

Makem nodded at MacGregor. "I'm tolerable. I never feel right without a deck under my feet. I sail again with the morning tide on the second of March."

"Business good?" Talbot caught the barkeeper's eye again and held up three fingers.

"Would be better but for the season," Makem said, making himself comfortable by putting his feet on a nearby chair. "I am signed and chompin' to take the cargo to England. What are you doing in these parts? I expected to run into you in the West Indies."

"He wants tae become a member o' the Virginee gentry," MacGregor said. "He is buying Riverview tae please his English wife, and her pa."

Makem masked his surprise by quaffing his ale and smacking his lips. "Barkeeper, wherever you be," he thundered. "You had better bring another round of keg-swale for this table, if you please."

CHAPTER THREE
WILLOWBANK, ENGLAND
April 1751

BETWEEN the attentions of the gamekeeper Melrose and Mr. Bushnell, Joanna never managed to be alone on her daily walks. This day was no exception. She wanted privacy to read her letters but Mr. Bushnell, a pleasant enough guest, accompanied her to the parterre. When she asked a few minutes' leave, he retreated to a respectful distance and spoke with one of the gardeners about an old wrought iron gate in the high stone fence that had captured his artistic eye.

Joanna's first letter bore Talbot's red wax seal. Eagerly, she broke it and read the page. "He awaits my arrival," she said aloud. "But he has not asked after Luke or his father-in-law." She reread the letter, put it in her reticule and examined a second envelope closely before opening it. She didn't recognize the seal, the imprint of a cat's paw. Frowning, she read the letter's contents. The handwriting was delicate, that of a woman, but the signature was bold – that of a man. "Mr. Bushnell," she called. "Would you come here a moment?"

Timothy hurried to the pavilion, leaving his footprints in newly laid sawdust footpaths.

"Do you know this person?" Joanna handed him the second letter.

Timothy read and stammered, "MacKinnon from the Carolinas ... yes, he is ... one of your husband's friends."

"Well, he seems to have mistaken my circumstances," Joanna said. "He congratulates Talbot on the birth of his son in America."

"Yes ... Yes. He has – perhaps – been misinformed."

"But if he is a friend of my husband, surely he knows there is no baby in America?"

"'Tis ..." Timothy faltered over his answer. "You must understand, Mrs. Showcroft, that miles and mountains separate Virginia and the Carolinas. MacKinnon has not visited your husband to see that the baby is not there. He has very likely only heard the good news, and assumed ... yes, assumed you ... and Luke ... were in America."

"I see," said Joanna. "If distances are as great, and travel as difficult as you say, that would be an understandable error on the part of Mr. MacKinnon."

"It would," Timothy said, fidgeting with his cravat. "It would. ... Are your trunks ready for transportation to the dock? We board the ship in three days."

"I should hope so, Mr. Bushnell. Katie did assist Hetty with my list."

"Hetty?"

"Hetty Melrose. My maid."

"Ah. Good. ... Captain Henry's *Charlotte* is one of the fastest merchantmen on the Atlantic. No ship can touch her under full sail. The Captain takes only a few passengers each voyage to round out his coffers."

"I have crossed the Channel before, but never the ocean. Katie and I are dubious about this voyage." Joanna paused and laid her letters aside. "Mr. Bushnell, may I be so bold as to ask a question that demands some trust? Let it suffice that we must keep a certain secrecy to this conversation. It is of a political nature."

"If I can answer, I will," Timothy said, abandoning the folds of his cravat, now that the subject of babes was ended.

"Am I to understand from hearth-side sparring matches between you and my father, good natured though they seemed, that you feel some sympathy with the failed effort of Charles Stuart to unseat King George?"

Timothy hesitated, looking to see where the gardeners were before he answered. "You must keep in absolute confidence what I am about to tell you, Mrs. Showcroft. This is a matter of extreme delicacy, for if it falls onto the wrong ears, it would mean the rack – or worse – for both of us."

"I understand delicacy, Mr. Bushnell."

"Then I will say that I am no King's man. I was born in Connecticut to Irish parents. I am a supporter of the ... of those who support the Jacobite cause."

"I am grateful for your confidence, Mr. Bushnell."

"Doubtless your question touches upon Mrs. Sherrie. You hinted that her circumstances are most awkward, but you have not elaborated. They will travel under the name Turnbull, which is unusual as, I recollect, they are not related to you. I have not had the pleasure of meeting the husband. Perhaps I should be privy to their story. I mislike deceiving Captain Henry."

"Mr. Sherrie was with Charles Edward Stuart's army and sustained serious injuries during the retreat to the border. Fortunately for him, Katie was out walking on her father's estate one day and discovered him in one of the hill caves. In great secrecy, she nursed him to health, risking much by doing so. She hid Allan at the hunting lodge and kept his presence a secret from her father. It would not do for an officer in the King's army to be embroiled in a scheme to keep a Jacobite hidden, would it?"

"My dear Mrs. Showcroft, I should imagine not!" Timothy said. "It would mean his head, and Katie's too!"

"After he recovered, Mr. Sherrie managed to make his way north to Arran, but, Mr. Bushnell, his fate was sealed. He loved Katie, and she loved him. He came south to see her again. When Katie's father discovered their *affaire*, he arranged a marriage to someone he deemed more suitable. She refused and eloped with Allan Sherrie. They were married at Gretna Green, and hid in London."

"And at the risk of great danger to her, and yourself, you arranged her sojourn here as Luke's nursemaid."

"Yes, and she would surely do the same for me. Poor Katie miscarried of a baby, a week or so before Luke was born, so I engaged her as his wet nurse. By doing so, I could hide both her and Mr. Sherrie, while we devised a scheme to spirit them both out of England."

"And where is that husband of hers, Mrs. Showcroft?"

"I should rather not disclose Mr. Sherrie's whereabouts, Sir. Such a secret may be dangerous to ..."

"You need not fear me," Timothy said. "I can see Allan Sherrie's need to leave fair England's shores quietly and quickly."

"Hetty never wanted to leave England with me, not without her husband, and Melrose could hardly be enticed to leave his position here. What better guise for Katie than traveling as baby's nursemaid and my lady's-maid, for the price of passage to America? Oh! Allan can travel as your manservant! You see, Mr. Bushnell, I assume their enemies will look for the name Sherrie on passenger lists. Once we reach the shores of America they may hope for freedom from this persecution. Until that moment, there is a price upon Mr. Sherrie's head."

"Ah, you are a brave woman, Mrs. Showcroft! That you would run your head into such danger for Mrs. Sherrie speaks of courage beyond measure."

"Sir, my loyalties lie with Katie and Mr. Sherrie. Father is a King's man, mind you, and he has no notion of their predicament. Well, 'tis prudent, of course, not to talk against the Whigs, or the King, if one is to prosper in business. Much as I love and respect him, I have no wish to explain Katie's presence to him, for fear he might think that the Sherries would be a prime dish to present to Prime Minister Pelham, and curry his favour."

"I daresay you are right," Timothy said.

"I am constantly in a flutter lest Katie and Allan will be found out, and that I shall be caught for harbouring them. I feel that I am walking the edge of a sharp sword which may tip and stab at any moment!"

"Then we must spirit them away quickly. If it be any consolation, your husband is not a supporter of King George either. Did he mention my name in your letter?"

"He did, but only in a salutatory way." Joanna took the letter from her pocket. "My husband says Riverview is furnished, but lacks certain comforts that I enjoy at Willowbank. He specifically refers to the need for good table linens, china and cutlery." Joanna gave Timothy the letter.

Timothy read quickly. "You can purchase most of these items in New Haven, but I recommend that you have Katie and Hetty pack any mementoes from Willowbank that you cannot bear to part with."

"Of course. I have directed them to pack fine soaps, several bolts of linen and cambric stuffs for dressmaking, Mother's silver tea service, and good Yorkshire cheeses. The cheeses are to be placed in my cabin on board the *Charlotte* with my travelling trunk. Would that I could tuck in Willowbank itself." Joanna, gazed fondly at the vine-covered mansion beyond the parterre. "I shall miss my home."

"I have said many times, Mrs. Showcroft, and I will be bold enough to say so again, it is not too late to change your mind," Timothy said. "Your husband would understand. He knows well that you are attached to your father and Willowbank. Perhaps 'twould be for the best if you chose to remain in England."

"I was persuaded to postpone my leaving once, Mr. Bushnell. That will not happen again. But, dear me, do I now hear you begging me to remain in England?"

Timothy turned from Joanna in embarrassment. "My apologies, Mrs. Showcroft. In honesty, I would not meddle so in your affairs. But pray consider: mayhap you will not like America? Virginia may not be civilized enough for you? And – I've no right to even speak of this, but – what if you have ... differences with Mr. Showcroft? You have only had the pleasure of his company on four occasions in the past four years."

"Mr. Bushnell! Sir! Pray credit me with the willingness to undertake this adventure. Understand, Sir, I am not a sugar cone to dissolve at the first sign of a storm. I am a little sturdier than these skirts."

"A gentle chide, Mrs. Showcroft. I fear that you might not understand the difficulties of living so far from home."

"Believe me, Sir, and let this be the last of the discussion, I have given very serious consideration to my decision."

"Then I shall leave you to get on with choosing what to have shipped to America. I shall arrange to have it taken to the dock."

Joanna watched Timothy's retreating back. She had grown to like the gentle, sensitive artist. He was quick-witted and amusing. But he could be exasperating, especially when he read her lectures about the discomforts and dangers to be met in the Colonies. And she was beginning to think that he was harbouring a serious case of lamb-love toward her.

The Nursery

"OH KATIE," Joanna said as she tried to snuggle a wiggling Luke. "My arms did ache so for a babe. Had Harrison Chambers and I married, we would by now have two or three children. My heart now cherishes this dear child. Yet, I fear he will suffer much on the voyage."

"Nay, if we do not fuss excessively over him, baby Luke will fare very well. He'll not know ship from shore. Very likely 'tis you and I who might suffer. As deeply indebted as my husband and I are to you, I must ask, my dear friend, are you sure that Virginia is where you truly desire to live? An ocean away from Willowbank?"

"True desire is swift and flies with swallow's wings, dear Katie. We have known each other for so long, I state without hesitation I am ripe for adventure. Katie, I am a woman in the full of my bloom, yet I have accomplished so little. And I must think of Luke. 'Tis only right that he be reared near his father."

"Hetty tells me that your husband protested mightily when you stated your intent."

"Since our marriage, my husband has given many reasons, until I am sick to death of them, why I must not join him in America."

"But a husband must have dominion over his wife —"

"Katie, I have seen my good husband for not more than two thousand hours during our marriage. Truthfully, I did keep careful count. 'Tis not even eighty days of wedded bliss I have known in the past four years."

"My dear," Katie said, suppressing a giggle. "You have always been quick with numbers, but this is taking arithmetic to monstrous extremes."

"Truly, out of all doubt, I must break the chains, gentle though they be, with which my father shackles me to Willowbank. Freedom will be sweet."

"But your father does place great trust in you, Joanna."

"I daresay that he does. But, truthfully, though he is my father, I fear he is not fully candid with me. There are certain informations in his business affairs that I swear I have not been privy to."

"He is ever 'my father' to you. Do you never not use endearments when speaking of him? 'Papa', or ..."

"I call him Father at the business table. I cannot trust myself to say 'Papa' at other times. It would never do to let endearments become too common in my speech."

"Upon my word, you have enjoyed an extraordinary life here, Joanna."

"Very true. Until my marriage, I could make visits to London – and to Paris before the King's ambitions took England into war with the French again. Now I have a huntsman to guard me. What company does visit comes to conduct business with Father. I spend my mornings with Father ciphering the accounts and rehearsing business affairs. I am kept like a prize hen in a cage – fed, watered, pampered – but never allowed freedom beyond that wire. Truthfully, America shall be my scratching yard."

"I daresay I shall miss London. What agreeable times we did have! My dear, you remember when we saw the King's paramour with the little black child traipsing behind?"

"Aye, but for a collar round his neck, the boy was like a pet dog. Your sleight of tongue was that the boy would at least be well fed."

"That is true," Katie said. "Surely he is better off than the children of our own poor."

"In his diet, perhaps. But when he grows, or she tires of him, what then, dear Katie? Will he be sold in the West Indies when he no longer pleases her? Every woman of society desires a bit of exotic at her heels now. What of them all when the fashion changes?"

"Joanna, my dear friend, in your zeal to change opinions and views – think of those on slavery – have you given thought to whom you might oppose – your husband? Your father?"

"Katie, dear, I am cursed with an overwhelming need to state my opinions, strong though they may be. I am utterly unable to understand why men of common sense do not see the barbarity of slavery."

"Perhaps they are common only and possess no sense? In truth, Joanna, I fear your husband will be less than pleased with your independent nature."

Joanna gently stroked Luke's chubby cheek. "Katie, I love my sweet babe, and you love him too."

"With all my heart," Katie said.

"May I be so bold as to ask if you feel the same affection for your husband? Is it possible to marry for more than convenience?"

"Such a question, Joanna! I should never marry but for love. I neither loved or respected the man my father chose. But ... I have such affection for my husband."

"I am envious, Katie. I respect my husband, but he did come with a bothersome marriage agreement which has recently given me pause for serious reflection. I ask you Katie, why must everything a woman owns become the property of her husband after marriage? Why can a woman not seek adventure like a man? Are men not mere mortals as we are?"

CHAPTER FOUR
THE CAROLINAS
Early April 1751

TALBOT reined his thoroughbred to a halt, dismounted and tethered the beast to the nearest tree. He tugged his kerchief out of his sleeve and, wiping the sweat from his brow, walked to the edge of the mountain clearing. Below, and to the east, lay fertile bottom lands. To his back, and west, mountain ridges folded to the horizon. At first glance, it appeared an inhospitable land, with no clearings, no habitations. But keen eyes could discern smoke curling skyward from hollows, and keen ears could hear the distant sound of axes against wood.

A late snow tinged the highest peaks. Ice still hung from cliffs in dark glens above fast-flowing streams and cascading falls. Talbot fully understood why the Highlanders chose the rugged mountains for their new homes in America. He was surrounded by land for the taking, water to run grist mills, abundant timber for the cutting. Free from oppression, the hardy Scots savoured freedom in their chosen land. By brute strength and determination they were carving a new life in the far mountain reaches of Carolina.

Glancing at the sun, Talbot reckoned he'd better ride. He had two hours in the saddle ahead of him. He reached into his saddle bag for some of the hard biscuits he had jammed into a pocket when he took his morning's leave of the inn. They would stave off hunger until he reached his destination. He knew there would be a good meal waiting at MacKinnon's.

Talbot mounted and rode west through a narrow defile toward the mountain's crest until he found the Trace. Turning south, he gave the horse its head on the treacherous mountain trail until they reached a level, forested valley where the sun's rays never fully penetrated the thick leaf cover.

The silence of the forest always gave Talbot a feeling of unease. He stopped once to drink from a cold mountain stream, throwing water over his face and hands as the horse drank beside him.

At first the trail was just wide enough for horse and rider. Then it became a cleared slash wide enough to accommodate a yoke of oxen. White stumps and wood chips showed that the trees had recently been cut. The horse shied once when a bear crossed the trail at the edge of sight in front of him. Talbot reined in and stroked the neck of the nervous animal. "Easy," he said. "We'll be there soon."

As the sun set across the valley, Talbot rode into a clearing. "Hello!" he shouted. "Hello, MacKinnons!"

The cabin, flanked by outbuildings, appeared in darkness against the trees. With a grown family, a daughter and two sons, Rory MacKinnon had built onto his cabin, making a large home for his station, though Talbot saw it as a rude shack. When he finally discerned there were people on the cabin's deep porch, Talbot dismounted to walk the rest of the way. "MacKinnon. 'Tis Talbot Showcroft, come to see you."

A young, red-haired woman, carrying a baby, separated herself from the family and walked toward Talbot.

"Mairi?" Talbot called, watching the woman approach. "Is it you?"

"Aye," Mairi replied. "'Tis I, carryin' your wee bairn. His name be Andre."

Talbot stopped walking. "My bairn?"

Mairi paused a couple of paces short of him and held the bundle that he might see the baby. Behind her stood her clansmen, her father, Rory, and her brothers, Roderick and Alex.

"Our bairnie, Tal ... born in December while ye were awa'."

Talbot was speechless. He looked from Mairi ... to the baby ... to Rory MacKinnon.

Rory stepped forward. "Come, Showcroft. I'd say tha' the babe's a bonny surprise. He gives us reason tae celebrate – a bairn for you, a grandson tae be mine, your safe return fra' England. Tell us aboot the trip. Did you manage tae get tae Scotia?"

MacKinnon put his arm around Talbot and led him toward the cabin. Several times Talbot glanced over his shoulder at the comely mother and the baby.

Mairi smiled, amused at how surprised Tal looked when presented with his son. But, of course, he wouldn't have known she was with child. He'd left the Carolinas for England before she'd had a chance to tell him.

"Take Tal's horse tae the byre," she said to one of her brothers. "'Tis food an' pipe you'll be wantin'," she said to Talbot when she reached the porch. "I'll hae brose an' tatties on the board afore you kin wash the trail off."

Later, Talbot sat smoking a pipe before the blazing fire in MacKinnon's common room, watching Mairi with the child. A fine kettle of fish, he thought. Two women, one wife – one mistress; two sons, one legitimate – one not. Mairi without a child, he could handle. What the hell was he to do now?

"Ere you pleased wi' the bonny bairn?" Mairi broke into his train of thought.

Rory, handing Talbot a hot toddy, said, "He'll be a braw wee lad ere long."

"I must say I am surprised." Talbot said looking at Mairi. "I did not know – "

"Course you wouldna'. Ye were awa'," Rory said. "Be there a kirkin' afore lang? We hae been waitin' your return."

"A wedding?"

"The kirkin' usually comes afore the birthin'." Rory laughed. "But in such a land, 'tis understood that bairns happen. 'Tis a heathen country, but we'll au' mak' it richt."

"We shall see about that," Talbot said. "Mairi? Why did you choose the name André? 'Tis not one that I know well."

"I heard it in Charles Town, in the marketplace. Andre is a guid name."

"Andrew," said Rory. "Andrew be a guid Scots name. Andrew Showcroft."

"Showcroft is a name that has nothing to do with Scotland," Talbot said.

"Wha' matters that now?" Rory said. "Tam, man, the bairn is tae be raised in the best conditions, truly. There be nae grubbin' in the dirt for him. He is the son of Talbot Showcroft, of Burnsall, England."

Damme, Talbot thought, settling further into his chair. What a confounded imbroglio to be in! And a worse one to get out of. These Highlanders possessed fierce tempers. No one could defile the only daughter of Rory MacKinnon and get away with it. He glanced around the room at MacKinnon's sons. They were large, strong men, ready to fight for a sister's reputation. If he confessed he was married and had a son, the chances of getting off MacKinnon's Trace alive would be slim.

"So Talbot, wha' aboot the kirkin', lad? Mairi be schooled; she's not thick-heided. She'll make a muckle guid wifie. She'll work hard an' bear many more bairns fer you. She'll make ye proud."

On The Mountain

MAIRI sat sidesaddle on the big bay, her arms around Talbot's waist. Eyes closed, she rested her a cheek against his linen shirt. She was thinking of Andre ... what a beautiful baby he was. She was thinking of Tal, how proud he must be of his child. Yet, for all that pride, the man hadn't held the boy since his arrival.

"Andre be a surprise fer ma mannie," she said, tightening her grip around Talbot's waist.

Talbot said nothing.

"Did ye no' get fither's letter in England?"

Talbot reined in so sharply the horse shied, and Mairi nearly lost her seat. "A letter went to England?"

"Aye," Mairi lifted her head. The horse pranced under the rein. "Look tae the horse or it'll hae us o'er the cliff."

"We'll stop here." Talbot dismounted and turned his back on Mairi.

Mairi slid gracefully to the ground. While Talbot tethered the bay, she walked to a large log, five feet from the edge of the cliff. It was a long ride up the mountain to the clearing but the view overlooking her father's trace was magnificent. Talbot stood near her, beside the log.

"You've changed, since last I saw ye'. I dinna think time would mak' such a difference in a man."

"It's not been so very long."

"Taken tae cuttin' fine hairs, you have," said Mairi, smiling. "'Tis the babe, is it not? You dinna expect tae see a bairn on your return."

Talbot rounded on Mairi. "Yes, 'tis the child. What an ignorant joke to play on me! Because of your stupidity, my life is considerably more complicated today than it was a week ago."

"My stupidity? Your life complicated?" Mairi gasped. "I couldna' find you tae tell ye. You canna' believe fither's fury when I showed wi' child in my belly. He mad' me come awa' frae Charles Town. It was a disgrace tae the MacKinnon name tae have a daughter expectin' and nae husband. I wrote the note fer fither. We wanted tae prepare ye for a kirkin'."

"No matter that I didn't receive a note," Talbot said, pacing to and fro.

"A' posted it myself. When we wed au' will be richt. You'll feel for the bairn. We'll make a life together."

His loud, cruel laugh echoed from cliff to valley. "You are expecting me to marry you? Marriage? Not with you." Talbot spat the words at Mairi.

"I dinnae ken you."

"Do you not? I don't understand you either. At no time did I give you the impression that our *affaire* would end in marriage. Why weren't you more careful, Mairi?"

"I be more careful? I tho' you said you loved me. I love you. I tho' tae please you wi' a bairn. I tho' we were tae kirk."

"Love me? Please me?" Talbot turned on Mairi. "When did we ever speak of love and – ye gods! Marriage?"

"We didna'." Mairi lowered her pretty hazel eyes. "But I took your advances tae be love."

"Well ... " Talbot hesitated. He did have a fondness for Mairi. But now he had to make sure that she would not interfere with his plans for Joanna and Luke.

"Well – what?"

"You are wrong, Mairi. I am a married man, with wife and child. You were a dalliance, a pretty, willing woman – nothing more."

"Ah, stupid I was! Willin', I was!" Mairi cried out. She took several steps towards Talbot. "You wined me, wooed me, bedded me ... but nary a word aboot havin' a wife. I chose tae believe you loved me, and when you saw Andre, you'd marry me."

"That was your bloody mistake," Talbot snarled at Mairi.

"My mistake?" Sensing his fury, Mairi turned away from Talbot and put some distance between them. "You truly be a married man? She be not just a lay-about?"

"Married and with a son. Both are on their way to Virginia as we speak. I might get away with having a mistress tucked away in the Carolinas. A son is out of the question."

Mairi whirled to face Talbot again, anger welling up. "You took me, knowin' you were kirked!"

"You didn't complain."

"Fither will kill you when he kens the truth. My brithers will kill you."

Talbot stood before Mairi, knowing what he had to do. If it wasn't for the marriage agreement ... but no bastard child must stand between himself and Turnbull's money. "Come now, my dear. In Scotland, you Highlanders breed like cats."

Mairi spat at Talbot and slapped his face.

Talbot grabbed Mairi's wrists. "He won't learn the truth, will he? You'll see to that."

"He kens the truth. You be the fither. As soon as your wife and bairn arrive in Virginia, it will nae take long for the word tae spread about them. Fither will ken ye took me wi' nae thought o' kirkin'."

"Andre's not my child, is he? With a French name he can't be."

"Andre be your bairn. I have known nae other man." Mairi looked Talbot squarely in the eye. "Let go my wrists, Tal."

"He is not." Talbot tightened his grip and pushed Mairi backward, dangerously close to the edge of the cliff.

"You be evil!" Mairi kicked at Talbot's legs and twisted in his grasp.

"It would be so easy to put you over the edge. An accident, I should say, the horse shied at a bear."

Mairi felt the wind from the cliff's updraft toying with the back of her skirt. She stopped struggling, realizing how close to the edge she was.

"Listen to me, damn you." Talbot hissed, his face close to hers. "Andre's not mine. You had an affair with another man in Charles Town. My friends will swear they saw you. You chose me as the father because you saw an opportunity to get off this hell-hole of a Trace."

"Nay," said Mairi. "Sae an untruth. I canna' lie for you."

"If it means your life, you can and will." Talbot forced Mairi to step backward. "Think of Andre without a mother. Who'd raise him? Your father? Your brothers?" Talbot's harsh laugh rang over the valley.

"Andre be your flesh an' blood, Talbot Showcroft. Laugh if you will, but the bairn be your son."

"Let's get the story right, Mairi girl." Twisting her wrists, Talbot forced her backward again. "He is not my son. In my generosity I might give you some money to raise him. I will tell your father I felt sorry for you, having to raise a child without a husband. But I will tell him I left Charles Town a month before the baby was conceived. And I will back that testimony up with witnesses."

"You are despicable. You are a daum, wretched man."

"That and more, yes, much more. Calling me vile names changes nothing. What will it be, Mairi? Death at the foot of the cliff or living to raise your child?"

"An' if I dinna die?"

"I will ensure you do."

In Charles Town, Mairi had often seen Talbot in a fit of temper. She knew he was capable of keeping his word. She lowered her head, closed her eyes and gave serious thought to her predicament.

Talbot tightened his grip. "I haven't all day, Mairi."

What would it be? Death at the hands of Talbot Showcroft? Life with Andre? But what was life without the man to whom she had surrendered her virginity? This was the man who was to be her salvation from a life of poverty and drudgery. He was to take her out of the backwoods and treat her like a lady.

"Mairi, I expect an answer now!"

Anger welled to the surface. How dare he threaten me! How dare he conceal a wife and child! How dare he choose them over Andre. Over me! Mairi thought. She needed time to seek revenge. She raised her head, eyes flashing. "Leave now. Go awa' and ne'er come again to MacKinnon's Trace. I'll tell fither I lied about Andre. I'll tell him you aren't the fither."

"I must go back to the cabin for my personal belongings," Talbot said, "my saddle bag, my blanket."

"Nay. My terms," Mairi said, choosing her words with care. "You promise ne'er tae return tae the Trace and I will tell fither the bairn is nae a Showcroft. But you will hae tae provide fer your child."

"There is ample coinage in the bag. Should I agree, how can I trust you to keep your word?"

She lifted her chin. "It is the word of Mairi MacKinnon. That word be as guid as the oath of Rory MacKinnon. Think well, Talbot Showcroft. If Fither chooses not tae believe my tale, you will be hunted down like a pole cat."

"You'll make your story convincing, I am sure." Talbot sneered. "If you don't – I have a long memory. Do not imagine you can leave this Trace to find me in Charles Town or Virginia."

"Let go o' me. Get on your horse an' leave. I ne'er want tae lay eyes on you again. If I do, beware! I'll kill you. If you come tae this valley ag'in, I'll kill you."

"You? Kill me?"

"Aye, and I will."

"I ought to throw you over the cliff now and save the bother of looking behind me all my life." Talbot's cruel laugh startled the horse.

"Aye, dou'tless, ye could kill me, and care no whit aboot me or your bairn," Mairi said. "But you won't. Because you like me, Talbot Showcroft, just a wee bit. And Fither may be scannin' from below. One of my kin might be on their way up-mountain now."

Talbot considered that. Someone down on MacKinnon's Trace might have their eagle-sharp eyes trained on the ridge. He released his grip, threw his hands in the air and stepped away from her. What Mairi said had the ring of truth to it. There was a strong chance one of the brothers was on his way up the trail. Hell, he could leave and if a future situation did arise with Mairi or the child he could take care of it, under better circumstances than he presently found himself. "Why should I trust you, Mairi? Why should I not believe that you will come looking for me in Charles Town?"

"'Tis the chance you'll hae to tak'," Mairi said. "'Tis that, or run the risk o' fither or brothers seeing you throw me o'er the edge. And I've nae dou't they be lookin' this wa'. Our voices carry on the wind. They've heard us a-branglin'."

"I trust no one," Talbot said. "Not women I bed, not my wife, not you. If it be any consolation, you are a pretty, young wench for whom I have more feelings than for my wife; but not enough to give up the benefits of marrying a Turnbull. I'll leave you now, but I warn you, never try to communicate with me, ever. Do you understand me?"

Mairi moved away from the cliff edge as Showcroft mounted the thoroughbred and rode off with nary a glance back at her. She watched until he rode out of sight then fell to the ground. Sobbing, she beat and tore at the earth with her fists. When all anger had been wrung from her body, she rose and trudged the long path to her father's home.

CHAPTER FIVE
AT SEA
Early April 1751

JOANNA lay in misery, Luke in her arms, dimly aware that the ship was lurching and rolling much more than usual. When, in her weakened state, she could not get up to investigate the increased activity on deck, she sent Katie to find Allan.

Not long after Katie left, Timothy entered the cabin, coughing to allow Joanna time to satisfy modesty, should it be necessary. "My apologies, Mrs. Showcroft, but Captain Henry has sent me to inform you of our circumstances."

Joanna struggled to sit up and, though fully clothed, pulled a blanket over herself. "I am presentable, Mr. Bushnell. Pray step forward."

"Captain Henry forbids cooking fires during a storm. The cook has been ordered to put a net in the copper and to stir up a batch of loblolly, enough to last a day or two, and then to douse the fire."

"'Tis very rough, and I smell rain in the air," Joanna said. "Mr. Bushnell, the truth. How severe is this storm?"

"Wind is up. Captain says we must prepare for a real blow." Timothy swayed back and forth with the motion of the ship. Joanna's insides heaved, if she but glanced his way.

"The glass is dropping fast and the sky to the northwest has looked threatening for hours. Henry has ordered the livestock tied down. Chicken crates are in the longboat, and it has been double-lashed. The crew is putting deadlights on all windows to keep the water out. 'Tis likely a vicious storm. Captain is ordering all to the great cabin, including you, Mrs. Showcroft, and Mrs. Sherrie."

"Indeed, that is a surprising request." Joanna shifted over, and Luke whimpered. She reached to comfort him. "This will not do. I cannot care for the poor babe. The ship is no sooner on the high seas than I am so ill I cannot lift my head without feeling I must retch. I am no milk-sop, Mr. Bushnell. 'Tis not in my nature to be a burden to anyone."

Timothy noticed that Joanna's hands shook as she tried to lift Luke. "The sea's a hard mistress, Mrs. Showcroft," he said. "The strong fall as quickly as the weak. We must hope to see this storm out with the help of God."

"Mr. Bushnell, I barely eat. Hard biscuit and fresh water stay down. I shall be a skeleton by the time the *Charlotte* reaches New Haven."

"I must assume 'tis loblolly made with sea water that has made you ill, Mrs. Showcroft. But there is, unfortunately for your circumstance, not enough casked water on board to allow for both consumption and cooking. Most persons can tolerate a certain amount of sea water when 'tis used for boiling up victuals."

"I am one of the few who cannot and must suffer the most disagreeable consequences, I fear." Joanna said. "I am not prone to hysteria, Mr. Bushnell, but 'tis difficult to remain calm under such circumstances as these. And the storm will frighten me so!"

"Mrs. Showcroft, I did make a promise to your father that, if 'tis at all in my power, I will allow nothing to happen to you," Timothy said. "Given that you are unwell, I will not stray far from you during the storm unless the captain requires an extra hand."

Joanna, in an attempt to make herself more comfortable, bumped Luke. Startled, he whimpered. "Hush, child. My dear, I have been so reliant on Katie that I am like a fish on land with this baby when she is away."

"I am confident that Mrs. Sherrie will be along soon," Timothy said. "I will admit hushing babes is not a man's job."

"Then would you not be better on deck?" Joanna asked, rubbing Luke's back to try to calm him. "Hush, wee child, hush."

"Indeed I should, Mrs. Showcroft, but I see the need to remain until Mrs. Sherrie returns."

"I will confide, Mr. Bushnell, I did not think that leaving Willowbank and Father would be so trying. Truth be known, I am extremely worried about Katie and Mr. Sherrie. I am also discouraged by the knowledge that I must spend at least a month on board this ship, with the probability of being ill for most of the passage." Joanna glanced round the small, crowded cabin. "Mr. Bushnell, I fear I shall never survive the journey!"

"Mrs. Showcroft, 'tis not in your nature to give up. Allan and Mrs. Sherrie are most capable of taking care of themselves, though I am glad I insisted on being truthful with Captain Henry. He would never have believed Allan Sherrie as an English Turnbull. And I recall that you were forewarned the voyage might be difficult. If this situation is intolerable, I must warn you now, that Virginia will present many trying circumstances."

"Virginia is furthest from my mind at this moment. Hush, hush, sweet child." Joanna tried rocking baby Luke by swaying to the boat's motion.

"'Tis my humble opinion that you would feel better if you took some air. The cure for sickness of the sea is to keep one's eyes on the horizon, to get one's sea legs under them. Mrs. Showcroft? Tell me immediately if I speak out of order, but might I ask where that fighting spirit is that I saw at Willowbank?"

"Mr. Bushnell, I must say that under the circumstances you are not speaking out of order, and I take your words seriously." The rocking did nothing to settle Luke. Joanna braced her back against the cabin's wall and held him close so he could hear the beating of her heart. If a few days at sea reduce me to this, she thought, I will be a blithering idiot in a month's time.

"I will make it my personal obligation to accompany you around the deck every day, after this storm," Timothy said.

"Mr. Bushnell, in all honesty, you have always shown me the utmost kindness and I have not acted nicely toward you at times, have I? I apologize for my bad behaviour and truly hope that in Virginia you will remain a friend?"

"Your apology is sincerely accepted, Mrs. Showcroft."

The sudden rolling lurch of the *Charlotte* to starboard brought an end to the conversation. Boots running across the deck demanded Timothy's immediate attention. Another roll to starboard and he was at the door. "I must see what is happening on deck, Mrs. Showcroft."

Timothy stepped into a hive of activity. Overhead, black clouds boiled in fury. Threatening dark skies swirled on the four horizons. Sails had been shortened. Wind blew through ripped back topsail. Crew was on the ratlines trying to reef the main gallant sail. Hi-men struggled to rig a storm jib. The *Charlotte* had been running with the sea, taking it on her prow. Now she'd slowed, turned and was rolling, taking the brunt of the wind on her port side. Captain Henry stood at the wheel shouting orders.

"How long before the full fury hits?" Timothy shouted, as he made his way toward Henry, working hard to stay on his feet.

"Wind's shiftin' fast. Thirty minutes ago it was howling from the east and we were close-hauled, tearing along right good enough. A blow east by nor'east spells trouble. Figured if we could put her in-stay we could ride the bugger out afore we lost sail. There's no figurin' what wind direction will be in an hour. Maybe two hours afore we're in the middle of it. It will blow a gale and travel fast, as destructive a beggar as ever there'll be."

"I talked with Mrs. Showcroft and must assume that Allan gave his wife the same message."

"Eh?" Captain Henry looked aloft. "Ye sons o' the devil, double reef that sail!" he shouted. "God damn it! Ere you deaf and insane? Double reef it!" He turned to Bushnell. "'Tis time to move the ladies to the great cabin 'til this un blows through. Find Sherrie, and the two o' you assist them. I've no man to spare. And Bushnell, be quick about it."

Allan and Timothy arrived at the ladies' cabin, clinging to the storm lines strung across the decks. Katie and Joanna huddled on the bunk. Katie, holding Luke, soothed him by keeping a finger in his mouth to suckle.

"What will ye need fer the babe an' yoursel's fer two or three days?" Allan asked.

"Cloths, blankets," Katie said.

"Gather quickly what you can," Timothy said. "All passengers must go to the great cabin *now*. We shall escort you."

Katie handed Luke to Joanna and opened the trunk. Allan held a blanket open for Katie to throw necessaries into it. "Katie, my girl, Mrs. Showcroft is too weak tae carry Luke and hersel' too. You'll tak' the babe wi you."

"Then you bring the rest of this trunk. I think we are ready, Allan. Tie Luke close to me with this shawl."

Timothy opened the door. "I think we should go now, Sherrie."

Allan led Katie out the door. "I'll come back tae help ye, Bushnell." With one arm around his wife and the babe, and the other on the storm line, he made for the great cabin.

"I will turn my back while you make yourself presentable, Mrs. Showcroft." Timothy fussed for several minutes by the trunk. "Prepared? Please excuse my boldness, but this must be done ..." He bent, and with effort, lifted Joanna from the bunk. "Have no fear. You are in no condition to walk and you are light as a feather to me. Pray believe I have no lewd intentions."

"I cannot but admire your confidence, Mr. Bushnell. Will my belongings survive? I think now of my cheeses."

"Mrs. Showcroft, rest assured that I will tie those cheeses down. Now, dear lady, pray this indiscretion does not get back to your husband," he said, daring to give Joanna the faintest smile. Stepping over the high sill Timothy staggered down the deck with his human cargo, praying all the while his legs would not give out.

Allan lurched along the storm line and put his arm around both Joanna and Timothy. "'Tis true that in strange circumstances, interesting occurrences do happen," he said. "When you tire o' the burden, hand her o'er Bushnell."

The great cabin, usually used as the men's dormitory, took on the look of a cheap inn. All loose items had been stacked and lashed together. Along with Joanna, Katie and Luke, five male passengers completed the roster. Feversham, Packer and Christie were London merchants. The fourth and fifth were Bushnell and Sherrie.

"Put Mrs. Showcroft here," Allan said, indicating the only bunk in the cabin. "'Tis more secure than a hammock. Katie, sit on the floor wi yer back against a wall an' hold tight to wee Luke. He's safer wi' you than with his mother. We'll cover you both wi' a blanket so you can feed the wee bairn."

With Joanna tucked in the narrow bunk, and Katie settled on the floor, Allan and Timothy made one last trip to the ladies cabin. They returned soaking wet and dishevelled with instructions from the Captain that no passengers were to leave the great cabin, unless at his command; that the lantern be extinguished and any person who insisted on staying in their hammocks must be tied in. He assured Joanna that her cheeses had been stowed in the empty trunk.

When the full furor of the storm struck the *Charlotte*, her passengers were still not prepared. Roaring gales broadsided the ship. She rolled dangerously to starboard then valiantly righted herself. When the second blast struck, she rolled again and hadn't righted herself completely before a third struck. Frightened beyond wits, Joanna screamed.

"Quit your screaming," Christie said. "It rattles the nerves, travels no any further than this cabin and does nothing to calm the storm. Better your breath be saved for prayers."

The *Charlotte* took another hard hit, rolled again and slowly righted herself. Forty-foot seas lifted her like a cork and danced her through the water. Thunder rolled and boomed – lightning cracked – wind howled like a banshee. Feversham and Packer, who had retched until there was no more in their stomachs to heave, sat in misery in a corner. Christie's murmured prayers implored any deity who would listen to spare the ship. Allan gathered Katie and Luke in his arms and, bracing himself against a wall, sang softly to them. Timothy wedged himself tighter against the wall and Joanna's bunk.

The *Charlotte* creaked and groaned as her timbers absorbed shock after shock of waves. Wind clawed her rigging, ravaged her decks and roared around the great cabin. Christie lost his balance and rolled around like a barrel. Joanna clung to the sides of the bunk and when, on sudden impulse, Timothy reached to touch one of her hands, she did not resist the gesture.

"For Christ sake!" Feversham shouted, "When's it going to let up?"

"When the guid Lord wants it tae," Allan said. "There's nae thing we can do."

Something careened wildly across the deck and bounced off the cabin's outer wall. Water breached the coaming and ran under the door.

Joanna was now quite unconsciously clutching Timothy's hand. "Can there be anything left on deck to be thrown about?"

No sooner had she spoken than there was an explosive crack of wood close by the cabin.

"The mast is down!" Christie yelled.

Timothy threw himself over Joanna just as part of the cabin's roof collapsed. Water poured through a gaping, jagged hole. The only sound above the wind and pelting rain was someone moaning in pain.

"Stay where ye be," commanded Allan. Calling each passenger's name, he received a response from everyone but Joanna and Timothy. "I am crawling tae the bunk. Christie, where are ye?"

Captain Henry banged on the cabin's door. Putting his shoulder against it, he heaved it open. Lantern in hand, he stepped over the coaming. "Top and gallant on the main fell over the cabin," he said, swinging the light around to survey the damage. Feversham and Packer were still huddled in their corner. Katie and baby were seated on the floor near the bunk. Christie was crawling across the floor toward Allan.

"Shine yer light on the bunk," Allan said.

The faint light revealed that Timothy lay across Joanna, blood flowing from a long deep gash on his forehead. Jagged edges of a heavy oak plank lay across his shoulders and pieces of another dangled precariously above him.

"Took a wee bit o' a blow, he did," Allan said.

"Right cracked his skull. Had he not been so brave Mrs. Showcroft would have that jagged plank right through her heart," Christie said.

While the Captain held the lantern, Christie lifted and steadied the plank while Allan gently slid Timothy off Joanna and onto the floor.

"Can ye hold it for a wee bit longer, Christie? I'd nae be trying tae move or sit up," Allan said to Joanna. "You'll kill yoursel' on tha' plank, Mrs. Showcroft. If Bushnell hadna' thrown himsel' o'er you, you'd be deid."

Joanna looked from the board to the blanket covering her, both red with Timothy's blood.

"Mrs. Showcroft, carefully slide out the bunk an' onto thc floor aside Katie," Allan said.

Joanna did as she was told, wiggling from bunk to floor and not a moment too soon as Christie, arms shaking with the effort of trying to hold the heavy plank, let go. The plank struck the bunk. Christie fell to the floor.

"You faring, Christie? Any o' you got a flask o' cawther?" Allan asked.

"Rum," Christie said, handing one across to Allan along with a linen handkerchief. "You will need this too."

"Guid man." Allan tipped the flask and poured rum Into Timothy's gash then covered the area with the handkerchief.

Timothy's eyelids fluttered.

"'Tis fortunate that plank missed his eyes," Captain Henry said. "Pour a little rum down his gullet."

With gentle hands, Allan rolled Timothy onto his back, covered him with a blanket and dribbled some of the liquor onto his lips. "Katie, can ya bind the man's heid wi' a cloth?"

Katie gave Luke over to Joanna and crawled toward her husband "We must thank God that Mr. Bushnell saved Mrs. Showcroft from death or a horrible disfiguration. But, what about his head? How badly is he hurt, Allan?"

"Bad enough he'll hae a muckle scar that'll tak' some talking aroun. It was a gallant act."

While Christie stayed by Timothy, alternately dribbling rum down both throats, Katie gently wiped the blood from Timothy's face and bound his head with one of Luke's clean clouts.

Captain Henry handed the lantern to Christie, saying, "You'll be needing this. Unless the storm's eye turns and the beggar comes back for a second try, we are clear. Damn well left word it came through. Stay clear of the planks. I'll haul everyone on deck soon enough. Sherrie, you are in charge here. Find somethin' to eat while there is still light."

"I have not tasted food for twelve hours," Christie said.

"I venture to say there was food brought from our cabin," Katie said, pointing toward a pile of wet blankets. "There should be hard biscuits and cold loblolly."

"Be our luck to have everything gone overboard," Feversham said. "How are we going to make do for the rest of the passage?"

"We're goin' tae carry on; that's what we're goin' tae do," Allan said. "From now on, everyone's going tae pull their stone, no exceptions."

Feeling completely helpless, Joanna held Luke close to her breast and hummed softly to him. The words, *Frailty, thy name is woman*, came to mind. She was the one feeling sorry for herself, wishing she had never undertaken the journey. She was the one who had not made any effort to help, who counted on Katie to provide her every need. She was the one who needed to do more.

After the Storm

"I'LL be da – I'll not be wastin' time tellin' what you can see for yourselves," Captain Henry said as he paced, hands behind his back, before a group of subdued crew and passengers. His efforts to keep his sea tongue in check before the ladies made Katie suppress a giggle. "We've shipped water, lost canvas, mast, jib and boom. Me best mate and the Jemmy Ducks is o'erboard, and Pete Hall's broke a leg. Cow's swimmin' with half the casked water. Rum's bobbin' on the sea, heading for Africa. We've rudder, steerin' and three chickens that didn't drown."

"Small consolation," muttered Christie.

"I've no choice but to make for Horta on Faial in the Azores, for repairs and supplies. With jury-riggin', best guessin', what sail can be raised and the condition of my ship, I reckon we are a week's sailin' away, luck be on our side. I've not a Mediterranean pass, but that damn tomfoolery'll not stop me, with my ship to refit. I've run up a red flag to discourage pirates. Pray we don't meet any. The flag's not likely to fool the heathen hordes."

Captain Henry stopped pacing in front of Allan. "You've proven your mettle, Sherrie. Might I prevail upon you to work the decks until we reach Horta?"

"Aye, Sir."

"Good, then. Bushnell." The captain addressed Timothy, who sat propped against a wall.

"Sir?"

"You keep to your bunk until a proper physician can be had in, to dress your wound. You and the mate'll share a cabin wi' the ladies, so you won't get wet if it rains again. Ladies – both of you," Captain Henry made a point of glancing in Joanna's direction. "Mr. Bushnell and the mate are in your care. Feversham, Packer and Christie, you go wherever, and do whatever I tell you. Getting my ship to Horta will take effort from all aboard."

"Is it hammocks on the deck, then?" Christie asked.

"Aye," Captain Henry said. "And I need not lecture you to conserve fresh water. We have only what was stored below. Gentlemen – Ladies? If you will?"

The men staggered to their feet and awaited orders.

"All right, ye scurvy sea dogs, hammocks up! To the ratlines! Break sail!" Captain Henry strode toward the wheel. "To Horta, and damn the consequences."

Christie and Packer helped Timothy to the ladies' cabin while Katie and Joanna, with Luke, followed behind.

"With the ship so damaged, we must be grateful we came through without greater harm," Joanna said. "My dear Katie, how shall we tend these men? I have never undertaken such a task before – and there are so few supplies."

"You forget, I nursed Allan to health. We shall need soft bindings, and diluted vinaigrette to keep the wounds clean. We shall, God willing, succeed," Katie said. "We must keep the mate's leg still to let it heal. We can bind it still with pieces of plank."

"I daresay we can tear our petticoats to make bindings," Joanna said. "The poor man is in such pain, he cannot bear to have his leg touched. I warrant you that he'll struggle when we try to bind it. But we can preach Christie's infamous comment – 'Quit your screaming. It won't go further than the cabin'. Mr. Bushnell will prove a much better patient."

"It was an exceedingly brave act for Timothy – to protect you with his body."

"Mr. Bushnell is ever the gentleman." Joanna smiled. "When he regained his senses, he was in a real pucker that he had been so forward as to throw himself over me. I assured him he was no less than a hero in my eyes."

"Ah, Joanna," Katie said, glancing at her friend, "'Tis so good to see you smile again. Are you feeling better, my dear?"

"Upon my word, I have always prided myself on not being a sop-eyed woman, but seasickness, and being homesick, wore me down. Let it suffice to say that I am finished feeling sorry for myself. There are those in worse shape than me on board. I will fulfill my share of responsibilities."

On the third day after the storm, while Katie and Joanna were spreading blankets on deck to dry, Allan shouted from the rigging, "Ship ahoy! Ship ahoy, starboard!"

Captain Henry scanned the vessel with his glass. A few tense moments ensued until he recognized the *Black Wing* out of Norfolk, usually under the command of Captain Anthony Makem. He ordered the red flag be taken down, and a distress flag run up to the yardarm. When the distance between the two ships narrowed, Captain Henry called across to the *Black Wing*.

"Ahoy, Makem, you ne'er-do-well. On your mother's grave, what are you doing in these waters?"

"Same as you, ye son of a sea cow," Makem's voice boomed across the water. "Appears I ran into the same storm as you. I'm limping into Horta."

"What are you carrying?" asked Captain Henry.

"But for trinkets, she's running empty," Makem said. "She was on her way out. I'll shadow you into port. What's your cargo?"

"'Tis not the moment to tell," Captain Henry said.

The two ships sailed side by side until they spotted a British man-of-war that drew up between them and escorted both into the outer harbour at Horta, before she turned and put to sea again heading for São Miguel.

CHAPTER SIX
HORTA
Late April 1751

THE *Charlotte* was made fast alongside the *Black Wing* for mooring, and several stout planks were placed between the two vessels. When Captain Henry announced he was sending a boat to shore and suggested Christie, Feversham and Packer should get their land legs under them again with a trip to the Monte de Guia, they climbed aboard. Henry advised Joanna and Katie stay on board, that he'd escort them personally to accommodation on shore after he'd spoken with Captain Makem. Within the half hour Makem boarded the *Charlotte* and went immediately to Captain Henry's cabin.

Joanna, carrying Luke who amused himself by tugging on his mother's hair, stood beside Katie at the portoise, enjoying the vibrant scene. Colourful bumboats circled the ship, their occupants hawking fresh fruit and vegetables. The aroma of flowers and spices wafted across the harbour. On the horizon, the Calderia's volcanic crater dominated a sky of high white clouds that floated through endless sapphire space. Among the sky, the hydrangea bushes, and the sea, Faial was a picture in blue.

"Captain Henry," the Bo'sun called. "British Attaché, a'starboard, comin' out to see ye."

Katie, using her hands to shade her eyes from the sun, watched the progress of a slender green boat that had pulled away from the dock, flying the British flag. "It cannot be," she muttered as she squinted at the boat. "By the Lord above, it is! Captain Henry! 'Tis he!"

She turned quickly from the railing and hurried to Captain Henry. "Sir, all is lost! That man in the boat – 'tis Major Straight – I refuse to call him a gentleman – the man I refused to marry!"

"Indeed that is the name of the Attaché at Horta. He will recognize you?" Captain Henry asked.

"Of course! He did spend days at our home in the country, while my father tried to persuade me to marry him."

"What's afoot, my friend?" Makem came up behind Henry.

"This is the lady we discussed ... the marriage that was not approved, the quick departure from England, the bounty on Allan Sherrie."

Makem acted at once. "I will hide you away, Madam. I've not much desire to see Major Straight meself."

"But, Captain ... "

"I will entertain no argument," Makem said making for the *Black Wing*. "Quickly now."

"Mrs. Showcroft," Captain Henry said. "Find Mr. Sherrie and tell him to find a bucket. He's to be on hands and knees, scrubbing th' deck and pay no heed to the Attaché or any of his men if they search the ship. They must not see his face. He must act deaf and dumb and do a bit o' prayin' while he's there."

Joanna, Luke snug in her arms, hurried to the great cabin, where Allan sat by Timothy's bunk.

"Beware of Christie, Feversham and Packer, Mrs. Showcroft," Timothy warned. "They're not to be trusted. I did hear Feversham asking Christie about Allan. I'd hazard one of them will inform Straight that Mrs. Sherrie's husband travels with her. You had best keep the babe with you. The situation may change to ugly."

"Wi' Katie on the *Black Wing*, Mrs. Showcroft'll hae little choice," Allan said. "Should Katie be found out, I will no' let her go wi'out a fight."

"Doubtless, Makem'll not let her be taken without a skirmish. We'd have no time to bargain for a child's safety. Under no circumstances must you be separated from Luke."

Joanna hurried along the deck with Luke now squirming in her arms, to pass Timothy's message on to Captain Henry.

"A stroke of luck that the beggars are on shore and haven't the opportunity to meet the Attaché," Captain Henry said. "We shall see how this drama plays out, Mrs. Showcroft, before I concern myself with the three malaperts."

"Permission to come aboard?"

"Granted," said Captain Henry striding to meet Major Straight as he boarded. "Welcome aboard the *Charlotte*."

Major James Straight pulled himself up the Jacob's ladder and stepped onto the deck. "Welcome to Horta." He favoured Captain Henry with a slight bow. "I am to understand that the island was not one of your ports of call?"

"I'd damn well rather be on the high sea makin' for New Haven," Captain Henry said.

"Aye, Sir; several other ships shared your fate. The storm did take its toll. 'Tis my understanding that three Portugese fishing vessels running together sank within sight of each other, one hundred miles out. Obviously they were caught in the same storm."

"If that be true, we are lucky to have come through with what damage we have," Captain Henry said.

"Captain Henry, 'tis my understanding that your plans were to sail well north of the Azores, and that you do not hold a Mediterranean pass, to allow safe passage through these seas. The Barbary pirates are under obligation by treaty between Portugal and England to respect that pass. I can arrange one for you, but your cargo must be inspected before it is given over."

"At your pleasure," Captain Henry said, "I carry little that would interest you or England."

Major Straight's eyes fell on Joanna, trying to comfort Luke, who was whimpering and pulling at her bodice. "You've been negligent, Captain. You've not introduced me to your passenger and her bawling little charge."

"Mrs. Talbot Showcroft, this is Major Straight."

The Major bowed. "My pleasure," he said. His eyes raked over Joanna's trim figure and rested on Luke. "Mrs. Showcroft, when I gaze upon a babe, I am reminded of the words of Jonathan Swift ..." Straight turned his attentions back to Captain Henry before Joanna could answer. "You are carrying other passengers?"

"A Mr. Bushnell is aboard. I will introduce you, if you will allow me ..."

As Captain Henry led the Major toward the great cabin, Luke's whimper changed to a bellow. Joanna tried rocking him ... singing to him ...

"That young rounder seems ready for his dinner." Captain Makem had come up behind Joanna.

"Unfortunately, Sir, you have his dinner plate stowed away on your vessel," Joanna said through gritted teeth as Luke clawed at her bodice.

"And I've returned to round up the husband," Makem said. "Look sharp! Major Straight has spied my superior figure."

"More likely he is disturbed by my son's tirade, Captain," Joanna said.

Major Straight had turned on his heel and was walking toward Makem. "Anthony Makem," Straight said. "I thought I heard your unpleasant voice. You are stretching your luck, anchoring here. The *Black Wing* is not welcome in my port. Neither is her captain."

"My good Major," Makem said. "'Tis not your port. This is Portuguese territory.

I've as much right as your men-of-war to be here. The *Black Wing* is running empty but I leave it to you, Sir, you are very welcome to inspect her. I venture to say that Caliganto would love to lay his ... eyes on you."

"I have, Captain, no intention of setting foot on that ship's deck," Major Straight said. "You have nothing on board that I desire."

"'Tis your choice," Makem said. "Some would give their empire for what I stow."

Major Straight turned his attention to Joanna and Luke and raised his voice to be heard over the bellowing. "Pray, Mrs Showcroft, why does a lady like you put up with a mewling, squalling babe? Do you not travel with a nursemaid?"

"I have a companion who assists me, Major Straight. She is ... not on board the *Charlotte* at this time."

"I venture that she seeks trouble on shore?"

"I've no doubt that trouble has found her," Joanna said.

Captain Henry interrupted the conversation. "Major Straight, if you could begin your inspection? I must be about giving attention to arrangements for repairs, Sir."

"I will suggest an inspection is not necessary at this time," Straight said. "Before you leave ..."

"Should that be the case, you are disembarking?" Captain Henry pointed toward the ladder.

"While repairs are underway, would the ladies and Mr. Bushnell care to make their home with me?" Straight looked at Henry but addressed the question to Joanna.

Makem answered quickly, "Mrs. Showcroft, her nursemaid and Mr. Bushnell have graciously accepted my offer to stay at Clifftop."

"Clifftop, that scurvy hellhole! Makem, I'll hazard Talbot Showcroft would mislike your dallying with his wife in that den of iniquity."

"Bollocks! Showcroft would damn well thank me for offering my protection to his wife while on Horta," Makem said. "I've no intention of dallying with the wife of a particular friend."

Major Straight bowed slightly toward Joanna. "I acquiesce. Pray remember, Mrs. Showcroft, my house is open and my hospitality is well known."

Before Joanna could respond to Straight, Makem said, "You were pleased to accept my invitation, were you not Mrs. Showcroft? You were quite persuaded that your good husband would want you to take advantage of my protection?"

"Oh ... verily ... yes. 'Tis a kind offer and accepted with gratitude," Joanna said, not daring to look at Captain Makem or Major Straight. Luke was still fussing mightily with her bodice, intent upon his dinner. Joanna pulled her shawl over him.

"So be it," Major Straight said. "Should you change your mind, Mrs. Showcroft, Captain Henry knows my house." With a wave of his hand, the Major stepped over gunwales of the *Charlotte* and climbed down the ladder into the waiting boat.

"That did not sit well with the Major," Captain Henry said. "How peculiar that he came aboard without a well-armed escort. More peculiar that he did not finish his search. I'm figurin' the bugger is lookin' for something – or some*one*. What think you, Makem?"

Makem watched the Major's boat retreat across the harbour. "I knew he wouldn't board the *Black Wing* without a half dozen men, when Caliganto's at hand. There's bad blood begs to be spilled between those two. Nay, the man would not have found Mrs. Sherrie. She is well hid. Best get a boat away and round up your three strays. Straight will be raging like a bull that he did not find what he sought. The son o' the devil will look to your passengers for answers. I'll be damned if he does not put a watch on the dock."

"I've sent a party to waylay the men on their way down the mountain. They've a boat ready at a fishing quay away from the main harbour to bring the three back to the *Charlotte* without attracting undue notice."

Makem turned to Joanna. "So, you are Showcroft's English wife. And this is your very hungry babe."

"I am indeed, Sir, daughter of Charles Turnbull, wife to Talbot Showcroft," said Joanna, "and this is Jonathan Luke."

"Captain Anthony Makem at your service." Makem made a leg with an elaborate flourish of his hat.

"Captain, I have forgot my manners. It was excessively kind of you to hide Mrs. Sherrie."

Makem smiled, showing excellent teeth. "'Tis my pleasure, Mrs. Showcroft. I revel in thwarting the law."

Allan rose from his knees on the deck, and, shifting the swabbing rag between his hands, approached them. Makem held out a friendly hand. "Mr. Sherrie, is it not? If 'tis not beneath your dignity, would ye dance this hungry infant across to your good wife. She is in my cabin with a brute of a fellow guarding the door. 'Tis understood both you and Mrs. Sherrie stay aboard the *Black Wing*, out of sight. Henry, a tryst is in order – in your cabin – after you've sorted out the three strays? Mrs. Showcroft, as you are embroiled with the Sherries, you will join us? Until then belike you could sit with Mr. Bushnell?"

Within the hour Makem came to fetch Joanna and assist a weak Timothy to the Captain's cabin. "To pick the bones," Makem said.

He placed himself by the door of the crowded cabin to ensure privacy. "Captain Henry and I mistrust Major Straight. This must be the plan until we leave harbour. With exception of Allan, we leave for Clifftop after dark. We do not believe that Major Straight will raid the inn. It is too far away, and hard to reach."

"What about Christie, Feversham and Packer?" Timothy asked.

"The *Doria* leaves on the tide tonight for Beaufort," Captain Henry said. "The captain can bunk three more people. I've ... *allowed* the beggars to continue their voyage on the packet as our lay-over at Horta could be a month or more. I was convincing enough they decided to ship out. Three extra passages will be paid by you, Mrs. Showcroft. I must recoup the funds."

"Yes, of course," Joanna said. "We must lie a month here?"

Makem laughed. "An exaggeration. We shall be eight or nine days under repair."

With little more palaver, the meeting dissolved, and Makem assisted Timothy back to his bunk.

Joanna lingered on deck, gazing out over the harbour. In the gloaming, Horta twinkled with lanterns and torches. Dolphins played around the boats in the harbour. Strains of some lively and exotic tune wafted across the water. Makem joined her there after settling Timothy.

"Mrs. Showcroft, I did meet with your husband just before I left America."

"Was he well?"

"In perfect health," Makem said. "He was busy about making arrangements for your arrival. The plantation he purchased on the James River is a fine one. As I recall, he did make mention of obligations in the Carolinas, but expected to be in New Haven in time to meet his wife."

"I believe my husband has many interests in the Carolinas."

"That he does ... Mrs. Showcroft, do I take an unwarranted liberty in saying that your protection of Mr. and Mrs. Sherrie is commendable?"

"I am cursed with a sentimental heart, Captain Makem. And I daresay the Sherries deserve to have some happiness. I will keep my promise made to see them safely to America."

Makem turned to look out over the harbour. "'Tis lovely, is it not Mrs. Showcroft?"

"Captain Makem, I doubt that a plantation in Virginia can equal this view. What a beautiful place it is!"

"'Tis easy to fall under the spell of the blue island. Like me, it has a reputation for seducing women with its charms."

"Such a brazen speech is unnecessary, Captain. Dare I ask why Major Straight does not wish to see you and the *Black Wing* in his port?"

"The Major – and I will not put 'good' and 'Major' in the same breath in this case – disapproves of my calling, particularly during war, when I will not take a side. Such a stand sits not well with a military man like Straight. 'That he's mad, 'tis true, 'tis true, 'tis pity.'"

"*Hamlet,*" Joanna said with a nod. "What, pray, is your cargo?"

"I captain a slaver," Makem said. "My cargo is Africans. Does that repel you?"

"Aye, it does!" Joanna said. "I am no friend to slavery. 'Tis an abhorrent practice. I have heard horrible stories about how some masters mistreat slaves. I believe slavery ought to be abolished."

"And you propose to live in Virginia?" Makem laughed heartily. "Opinion is the lowest form of argument, Mrs. Showcroft. Hearing is hear-say. Seeing is believing. You must live with slavery to fathom it."

"I intend to do so, Captain."

"Ah. Do I perceive the lady has a nose for adventure? Otherwise, methinks, she would not have married Talbot Showcroft."

"Captain Makem, I am not as fragile as some may think. My mother was given to saying that I was more like hearty Scottish heather than delicate English violets. I admit to speaking my mind and enjoying the occasional adventure."

Makem, charmed by Joanna's candour, said, "What you will most certainly enjoy, is the breathtaking view of Horta and Porto Pim from the top of Monte de Guia. It will be my pleasure to accompany you to the top, Mrs. Showcroft. I beg excuse. If we plan to leave for Clifftop by the appointed hour, I must talk with my crew and Allan Sherrie."

Good gracious, Joanna thought as she watched Captain Makem take his leave, the man might consort with the enemy – he trades people like furniture. He must have some redeeming qualities. He helped Katie in her predicament. He quotes Shakespeare. What did Mr. Bushnell say when he was told that the Captain was assisting the Sherries? "We must trust Makem. The man is the very salt of the earth. We are in good hands."

Clifftop, Horta
24 April 1751
My dearest Father:

Fate has played a hand in our voyage and placed us on the island of Faial, for repairs to the Charlotte. By any measure I do not find this a trying time.

I am lodged at Clifftop, a rather quaint inn built close by the headlands. I have fallen in love with the position of the inn – which is a two-storey affair made of peculiar black stone, stuccoed to give a clean look. It is quite remote with but one path to reach it. I may bore you with details Father, but the view from its vine-covered terrace, that is also the inn's cantina, is lovely. From three open sides I enjoy views of the harbour and town. The fourth wall has a huge fireplace built into the stone. A whole goat or sheep turns slowly on the spit, day and night. Everyone takes their meals here. A red tile roof shelters us from the hot sun. Oh, Father, if we had this climate at Willowbank, what couldn't be grown in our gardens!

I do find it exceedingly difficult to be around sailors. Not having been raised to hear it, I cannot bide their coarse language. If they are not cursing God and the devil, they are invoking the wrath of their mother by using her name in vain. At other times I fear they have nothing but the degradation of ladies on their minds. I have made it forcefully known that such verbiage will not be tolerated in my presence. To a man they did try to mend their tongues although the several captains find that hard to do.

I have been introduced to a most interesting personage, a free African by the name of Caliganto. He was schooled by his cohort, who carries a book – Shakespeare's Macbeth – to hearth-side of an evening. Caliganto speaks well when he is not giving voice to the language of the sea, and reads very well, indeed. This very circumstance is proof that schooling is of much benefit to slaves, just as I felt it would be.

You need not worry about baby Luke. He is in good health and thriving on the attentions of all who pass him by and find him charming. Although my first days at sea were trying in the extreme, with Mr. Bushnell's kind assistance, I managed to make a right good change in my sea disposition. My health, I must say is excellent, my appetite hearty. Like the flowers of these islands, the fruits are exotic but delicious, and I partake of many.

I took this opportunity to write because a ship leaves weekly for England – doubtless with dispatches from the island's British Attache. I do not pretend to know much about the political agreements – and disagreements – that our government has with various countries around the world. I will only say that the British Attache here cannot complain about his posting. His situation on this beautiful blue island can only enhance his disposition.

I will close now, Father, by saying that you must not worry about me. I send my sincerest and dearest love to you. As the full moon rises over Horta, I think of it rising over Willowbank.

Your loving daughter,
Joanna

CHAPTER SEVEN
CLIFFTOP

MAKEM'S plans for Clifftop included a rough-man guarding the gate at the head of the path that meandered down the steep cliff to the town, with the Captain having final word about who could enter or leave the inn. Makem also chose to keep Allan on the *Black Wing* so that husband and wife would not be seen together. "Walls have many eyes," he said in way of explaining his action.

"Captain, does having a guard not draw attention?" Joanna asked when told of the arrangement.

"'Tis common to post one when I am in this port, Mrs. Showcroft. I will insist that you all obey my order. 'Tis impossible to oversee repairs on the *Black Wing* and tend wandering ladies too."

"Do not let the gentleman mislead you, Mrs. Showcroft. Our good captain has enemies," Timothy said. Under Doctor Petrie's care, Timothy's wound had begun to heal, but he lay long hours in a cot to avoid headache. Without doubt he would be left with an impressive scar across his forehead.

Peter Hall, the other unfortunate storm casualty, lay in a painful state. Doctor Petrie examined the leg and made the decision not to amputate, as the limb was not severely crushed. Much time would be needed for healing, but the man owed much to Joanna and Katie that healing was even possible.

Early on the sixth day, Makem came upon Joanna as she sat by Peter's bed, composing a letter to the man's wife.

"How you faring Pete?" Makem gave the fellow a touch on the shoulder.

"Good woman's writin' me missus ta tell 'er all. She ain't schooled, so pastor'll jaw it to 'er. Capt'n arranged the necessaries, paid for me to go home soon's I heal proper."

Makem stood quietly observing Joanna until she finished the letter then motioned she should follow him into the passage.

"Mrs. Showcroft, in the strictest confidence, there is skulduggery about. Straight seems to know our plans before we make them. As we must take on supplies before departure, we have begun a strong rumour that both ships sail in forty-eight hours. When chickens and the cow are loaded last, the truth will be out about the time of our leaving. And beasties are difficult to disguise."

"Captain Henry appears excessively apprehensive, Captain Makem."

"As well he might." Makem cleared his throat. "Straight has promised an inspection before departure. Henry is thwarted in his desire to shift certain cargoes to a merchantman leaving for Beaufort. He does not wish to be caught shifting ... weaponry ... when his manifest lists none on board the *Charlotte*."

"Whom do you suspect of the tattling, Captain?"

"Would that I knew. To be truthful, Captain Henry and I believe that unlisted cargo is of secondary consequence to the Major. His first is Mrs. Sherrie. We believe he has knowledge that she is on Faial and will act to keep her here. And 'tis Allan Sherrie's life if Straight sniffs him out. His good wife will be forced to stay here under attention of the Major, on her father's orders, for 'tis he who put a price on Sherrie's head."

"The Major did not see her on board the *Black Wing* or the *Charlotte*."

"True. Pray attend now to what I say, Mrs. Showcroft. As Mr. and Mrs. Sherrie are of great interest to you, Captain Henry and I ask if we could impose upon your good graces to partake in a little skulduggery of our own kind."

"On my word, if it be of benefit to Katie, I will do whatever you ask," Joanna said.

"To put a fine point upon it, then, you must accept the invitation to visit the Major's compound. The gate-man has said one was delivered. We must ascertain what the beggar is about, what he knows and how the devil he hears of our plans."

"Aye, the invitation to a fête arrived this morning. I had intended to decline the Major's hospitality. I've no wish to sully my name by attending unescorted."

"Ah. Captain Henry and I have loosened that tangle. The Major would not welcome me at his fête uninvited, and I must ready the *Black Wing* for flight. Bushnell is not healed enough to leave his bed. Captain Henry is about his own business readying the *Charlotte* for early departure. Caliganto will see you to the gate and hand you in. He will revel in tickling the Major in his own territory."

"That leaves me to my own devices once inside the compound, Captain Makem."

"Dear lady, other ladies will attend. I do assure you Caliganto will stay near the gate. You need not fret, Mrs. Showcroft, I trust the man with my life. He will give no less for you, if need arises."

"'Tis a risky venture, Captain Makem, but methinks I must assist. I admit to never before undertaking such a bold adventure. The thought puts me in a flutter."

"In defense, 'tis prudent we pounce before Straight."

"There would be disagreeable consequences if gossip fell on Mr. Showcroft's ears before I arrived in Virginia."

"I understand there is a certain delicacy to this situation. Mrs. Showcroft, if I may be so bold as to give advice? Make yourself known to the ladies in attendance and intercourse with them. Never place yourself in a circumstance of compromise. Be sharp to all around you. Listen and observe with keen diligence."

"Indeed, Captain Makem, I cannot imagine the Major having villainous designs on me. It is Katie he desires."

"We know not what scruples the man possesses, Mrs. Showcroft."

"Believe me, Captain Makem, I will try to remain exceedingly calm when under fire, should the cannon be loaded."

"Is that why you shake like a leaf now?"

"Truthfully, Sir, my courage wanes."

"Here's to courage then." Makem bent his muscular frame and bussed Joanna lightly on the forehead. "I call that the first for courage," he whispered.

"Sir! I am not a pigeon for the plucking. You forget yourself!"

Quickly, Makem stepped away from Joanna. "Mrs. Showcroft, pray forgive my inexcusable behaviour. I forget my manners with a lady of quality. *Tempus fugit.* Make yourself pretty quickly."

The Fête

JOANNA, a vision in blue that matched the colour of her eyes, felt so exceedingly nervous that she hardly noticed the attention she drew as she entered the cantina. Timothy, beside the fire with Doctor Petrie, was at considerable trouble to take his eyes off the lady.

She paused by his chair. "'Tis good to see you off your cot and in the cantina, Mr. Bushnell."

Bushnell seemed capable only of a stuttered answer. "My ... the good d-doctor has decreed I must be on my feet ... Mrs. Showcroft. Indeed, the w-world does spin round."

"Bushnell, do refrain from covering the lady with your drool," Makem said. "Does Mrs. Showcroft need something to further strengthen her courage?"

In high blush and with a slight tremour in her voice, Joanna said, "The lady has received quite enough courage, good Lord of the Seas. She now desires a hand into the cart."

Caliganto delivered Joanna to Straight's compound at two o'clock, and handed her into the care of a maid. Positioning himself just inside the gate where he could see the gardens and most of the villa, he waited and watched.

Major Straight left off speaking with a group of gentlemen and hurried to greet

Joanna with an elaborate leg. "Mrs. Showcroft, I do not approve your choice of attendant, but my fête is graced by your presence. My guests are eager to meet you." With much flourishing, bowing and curtsying the gentlemen were introduced to the lady.

"My dear Major Straight," she said behind her fan as they moved on. "I shall never remember these exotic names, yet they come so easily off your tongue."

"A consequence of a posting in the Azores. Ah, Mrs. Showcroft, the ladies come swarming. I have business to discuss with Senhor Ferriera. The maid brings refreshment. Senhora de Gracie? May I have the pleasure of presenting Mrs. Talbot Showcroft. Here, Emelia! – Negus for the ladies?"

Senhora de Gracie, an enormously tall woman with jet-black hair over a wrinkled face, delighted in small talk: The basket market is grossly overpriced ... The best fish can be found at Ceccia's by the dock ... Major Straight does keep a proper English dining parlour with silver, damask, and a crystal épergne. "The man expected to bring a wife with him, after his most recent visit to England," she confided. "But today, I hear from one who knows that the lady spurned him – for a Highland Scot! My word upon it, he shall never live down the insult, my dear!"

Senhora de Gracie introduced to Joanna an effusive little man, Dutra Dornelles, who offered his arm and asked if the ladies had seen the views over the harbour. With a woman on each arm he strolled to an arbour at the highest point in the garden, where a perfect view of Horta's sheltered harbour, the docks, and rugged headlands, one of which held Clifftop, was to be had.

"Major Straight enjoys exceedingly beautiful views," Joanna said.

"With za telescopic, he can see every t'ing," Senhor Dornelles said, his hand cozy against Joanna's bodice.

"Senhor Dornelles. Unhand me or I shall call that monstrously huge African down by the gate to remove your unruly claw."

Senhora de Gracie had the good sense to step in. Madame and Monsieur Tourque joined them in the arbour. "Such a silly little man," Madame Tourque said. "He tries to handle every lady of consequence in Horta. You will recall, Mrs. Showcroft, we had a passing acquaintance in Paris at the Gallérie des Pères? You were then Miss Turnbull."

"Silly ninny that I am! I did not recognize you. Truthfully, I did not expect to see a French lady at the fête. The Major is so very ... English."

"I own a chandlery in Horta and Porta Delgardo on São Miguel," Monsieur Tourque explained. "The good Major purchases ship's supplies where the prices and quality are best. I conduct much business with him. I hear a man o' war is due on the tide after noon on the morrow, called hastily from outfitting in Porta Delgardo. Such a grand secret, indeed, that it is whispered in every corner of the garden."

"Then you must not tell it about, Monsieur."

"'Tis only a secret from those who will be caught like mice in treacle."

"Gracious! I shall ... Do trust me Monsieur, I shall only broach your confidences to the ... right people."

As the group made their way toward the lower garden, Senhora de Gracie said, "Mrs. Showcroft, have you made the acquaintance of Senhor Furtado and Senhora Ana Furtado de Mendoca and their charming daughter Maria – schooled in England, she is."

With much bowing and curtsying, introductions were accomplished, and Maria, a pretty, petite young flirt, took Joanna in hand. Joanna thought the young lady vaguely familiar to her. Maria seemed to enjoy an acquaintance with every gentleman in attendance, but paid particular attention to Sergeant O'Hearn, an Irish Guardsman who, in turn, appeared to pay assiduous attention to Major Straight.

"Sergeant O'Hearn is the Major's third ear," Maria said. "Whispers here – whispers there – whispers to the Major – always asks questions – always with money to give."

"My dear Miss de Mendoca, in your company, of course, I must meet this intriguing man."

Sergeant O'Hearn spent little time on introductory courtesies. "I observe that the younger lady residing at Clifftop does not accompany you." he said.

"Dear me, no, Sir. She is but a nursemaid to my son."

"A right charming lady, I hear."

"Sergeant O'Hearn, I venture to say the lady comes from a good military family. That bodes well, does it not? Would you and Miss de Mendoca be so kind as to show me the views from the arbour again? I was in the most disagreeable company of Senhor Dornelles on my previous visit, but was so distracted by his behaviour that I saw little."

"Mrs. Showcroft, it would indeed be my pleasure."

Once again, Joanna found herself in the arbour overlooking the harbour. "Why, 'tis fascinating. The volcano and headlands appear so far away. And the nesting birds on the cliffs cannot be seen at all. Yet with a telescope, I believe all could be viewed with perfect clarity."

"Major Straight's telescope is one o' the finest instruments on Faial. Of an evening he often partakes of a little peeping."

"By my faith, an intriguing pastime. Would you excuse me but a moment, Sergeant O'Hearn? I must speak with Miss de Mendoca upon a point of delicacy."

When O'Hearn moved out of hearing, Joanna asked Maria what a lady should do if her garters had to be tied again, and if she wished to adjust her toilette.

"A room has been made proper in the villa," Maria said. "A little medallion hangs from the latch."

Joanna took her leave of Miss Mendoca and Sergeant O'Hearn and strolled toward the villa, passing close by Caliganto on the way.

I did believe adventure might find me, Joanna thought, but by all that's merry, never did I think it would come so soon! Do not lose heart now, my girl; nothing can come of nothing. It cannot be so difficult to find a telescope.

Joanna stood for several minutes under the front portico, then entered Straight's lair. The villa was of simple design: a central hall with rooms to left and right; an intersecting corridor with rooms overlooking terrace and harbour.

Luck be on my side, no one in the hall ... no one in the dining parlour ... the salon. Joanna made her way to the intersecting corridor. Heart beating with the cadence of a drum, she noted four rooms – two to the left – two to the right. She chose left. The first room was obviously not used; no netting swathed the bed. The second chamber was evidently the one used by the Major. A large telescope stood in an open terrace door.

After checking that the corridor was clear, Joanna slipped in and hurried across to the scope. Looking through it, she exclaimed, "By the Gods! The man sees everything. Clifftop ... Katie sits now with my babe in the cantina." Joanna turned the scope toward the harbour. The *Black Wing*! Makem stands by the wheel. The *Charlotte*, surrounded by bumboats. Spying a small journal on a table, Joanna took a quick peek then tucked it in her reticule.

"Does the view please you?" Major Straight strode into the chamber from the terrace.

"By the devil, you did frighten me," Joanna said, stepping in front of the table so the Major would not detect the theft of the journal.

"Mrs. Showcroft, why do you present yourself in my bed chamber?"

"Suffice to say, Major, I wished to ... rearrange my bodice. Upon my word, I could not find your maid. It did take some time to find a proper *chambre pour les dames*."

"I put it to you that your reason for entering my private chamber has naught to do with furbishing your toilette."

"You shock me, Sir – "

"Do not treat me with contempt, Mrs. Showcroft. You are engaged in some other chicanery."

"Your comment does not warrant an answer. I shall take my leave now, Sir."

When Joanna turned to go, Straight extended an arm to stop her. As his hand brushed across her hair, a silver comb fell to the floor. "You shall tarry a little, Mrs. Showcroft." The hand fell onto a bare shoulder.

"Unhand me, Sir! You are no better than Senhor Dornelles."

"Does Mrs. Showcroft require my assistance?" Caliganto's form loomed in the terrace doorway.

"Caliganto! Major Straight has turned a quibble on the water into a full-blown storm. 'Tis best, methinks, to depart before scandal whispers that the ... gentleman ... did try to ... to bed me!"

"Ludicrous trumpery!" Straight said. "I did nothing of that sort."

"My dear Major. 'Tis your reputation against my word as a respectable lady, and I can be relentless in slander."

Joanna swept from the room, Caliganto close behind. They hurried to the donkey cart, Joanna expecting that at any moment that Straight would find that she had taken the journal and emerge in pursuit.

The Report

TIMOTHY Bushnell's room lay outside the prying scope's eye, and that is where Captains Henry and Makem, with Caliganto, Katie and Joanna, met to discuss the afternoon's skulking.

"By my faith, I was so excessively nervous!" Joanna said. "But I discovered that the Major knows very nearly everything. With his telescope he sees all that passes at Clifftop. He sees Katie. He may have sighted Mr. Sherrie, but he is not acquainted with him; he'd know only that Mr. Sherrie is a Highlander. Sergeant O'Hearn appears to be forever collecting informations as they come his way, and stoops to bribery if necessary. I recall seeing Miss de Mendoca at the gate, charming the guard. A man o' war is due in Horta with the tide on the morrow, and Monsieur Tourque tells me it will see action."

"By Jove," Makem said. "Captain Henry did doubt your capabilities, Mrs. Showcroft, and expressed as much this very day, but he need not have worried."

"Truly, I did doubt myself." Joanna said. "When I think of the consequences, had Caliganto not entered the room, I am all in a flutter."

"My eyes were on your doings and those of the Major." Caliganto said. "He afforded you ample time as he was charming other guests. My attentions were caught when you walked a second time to the arbour, and when you slipped in at the front entrance of the villa. I moved quickly when the Major followed you, after the Sergeant engaged him in conversation."

"I dare not dwell on the thought of being alone with that man."

"The Major's journals show us that he has had the telescope turned on us since we came into harbour." Henry said. "He knows repairs are very nearly finished, and we will soon be ready to leave. He will make his move to kidnap Miss Sherrie – this is the word he writes – as soon as the man o' war arrives from Porta Delgarda. The harbour will be blockaded and our ships searched."

"Winds favourable, and the tide with us, we leave on tonight's tide," Makem said. "We sail without the confounded chickens and the cow."

"I have ears too," Makem's first mate said. "I did hear that the Major has a ruckus to jury in Quebrada, mid-island. He travels overland later this day and plans to return on the morrow before noon. There'll be no scoping while he be away."

"We still have Sergeant O'Hearn to worry us," Timothy ventured.

"There is no woman cannot be disguised," Makem said, "nor no man cannot be bought. When the Major is well on his way, Bushnell does go down in the cart as himself. Katie shall be disguised as Pete, all trussed and wrapped. Young Luke is a large basket of fruit. Trunks shall be left at Clifftop. Belongings will be in sacks, in the donkey cart under straw."

"And I, Captain Makem?" Joanna said, a hint of mirth in her voice.

"You, Mrs. Showcroft, shall dress as a sailor, in Pete's clothes. Pete awaits his voyage home, which he will, no doubt, undertake wearing bits of Bushnell's fancy dress."

"And Allan?" Katie said.

"Your good husband shall sail with me on the *Black Wing* for Africa. There is no other way, Mrs. Sherrie. You'll be separated for some time, but by all that's good, I do promise I will bring him home."

"The gate-man will see all. If he tattles to Senhorita Maria, your plans are foiled," Timothy said.

"That rat-tattler will be given a few coins and it be suggested he find a nice Senhorita *pour faire l'amour*. By the time he climbs out of the hammock, the *Black Wing* will be well on her way to Africa – and the *Charlotte* to America."

CHAPTER EIGHT
THE SLAVE COAST, AFRICA
June 1751

FOR twelve days the captives walked through the jungle, coffled in single-file. Once a day the slave chain stopped for a meal of maize gruel. Although all knew they had been sold into the hands of a slave dealer, few knew where they were being taken and what their fate would be. When allowed to rest, they lay like cordwood and whispered in Kaio, Temne, Twi, Fula, Wolof.

"It was Kambu, the witch doctor who lured us to the watering hole with promises of a lion kill," Ndamma said. "He and Father fought over cattle and land. He was the one responsible for our capture."

"To kill us would have been kinder," Barika said, "and easy for one with his power."

"But our death would have brought him no wealth," Ndamma answered as their captors prodded them to their feet.

Women were treated no differently from men and boys. If ordered by the gang-boss, who was an ugly brute from one of the western tribes, Ndamma and Barika helped carry the children to keep the line moving steadily along.

On the morning of the twelfth day, the slave chain staggered out of the jungle onto a hot sand beach on the West African coast. There, a man called Ramki took charge.

"What is this big lake?" Barika asked.

Ndamma answered the question with trepidation. "This must be what Father described to me as the sea, over which boats travel to faraway lands. He said that it had the taste of an animal's lick and made one sick to drink it."

Ankles and wrists chained, Ndamma, Barika and the other boys and men were separated from the women and children and ordered to sit beneath a palm-thatched roof Ramki called a "slave castle". Weary, frightened and hungry, they stared across the endless expanse of water.

"Will we ever see our village again?" Barika asked his companion.

Ndamma shrugged. "Many people have been stolen away. None have returned."

"I am angry," said Barika. "You are the son of a Griot. From a child you were told our stories. You are the successor to a Griot. And now you are a prisoner."

"What does it matter now that I am keeper of the history? These men will never allow me to return to our tribe. Father will send warriors to look for us but Kambu will ensure they go in the wrong direction. It will be too late when Father realizes we have been sold."

"What is to happen now?"

"I do not know. Perhaps we are to be eaten."

"You must try to escape, Ndamma."

"There is no escape, Barika. I would be killed by the shooter before I found the path into the jungle. We must remember the wisdom of our people. To survive in a herd, an animal does not draw attention to itself. Neither should we."

"If we are separated, you must promise me to keep the history, wherever you are taken."

"You too must never forget your parentage, Barika."

On the fifth day at the slave castle, a strange smell came from the sea and then a ship appeared on the horizon, red sails contrasting with blue equatorial sky. The closer it came, the worse the smell. It stopped just outside the breakers, and, with a great clatter and splash, a long canoe was lowered to the water.

"On your feet! To the beach! Get along! Line up!" The gang boss marched back and forth shouting, snarling at the line, slashing the air with his whip. Men and boys were lined up one side of Ramki. Women and children were drawn up on the other.

When the canoe drew near the beach, several men jumped from it and pushed it further up the shore. Eight men alighted and walked toward the group.

"Look Ndamma!" Barika whispered. " How pale they are, and how smelly. They reek like a dung heap. There are two, men like us. The big one is dressed like them and carries a shooter and a long knife." When the gang boss cracked the whip close to the back of Barika's legs, he said no more for fear the next slash would land across his back.

A tall, muscular, red-bearded man approached Ramki. "Well, Ramki me-man. I see you have assembled a good lot this time."

"Hundred and twenty-nine, all young, healthy, strong, and the women of child-bearing age," Ramki said. "You have fine trade goods?"

The crew had already begun to unload the shore boat. Its cargo piled up around the tall man's feet.

"For you, cloth, beads, wine, axes, pots, china, blankets," Makem said.

"Your generosity is known, Captain Makem." Ramki moved toward the pile to have a look.

"No, no, Ramki. Not before the good doctor and I choose our cargo. No sad lobcocks this trip. I cannot bide running tight pack and having to score with quality what

I lose in numbers. Cargo's two hundred and three now, picked along the coast. Had a few drop of the flux so ordered anchor here to see what you blighters are offering."

"You avoiding Bance Island?"

"I curry no favour from the English or French. Took on a Krooman and ran the coast from one end to t'other ... a half-dozen here, twelve there. Spent time as a guest of Braffo, the Caboceiro of Annamaboe. This is my last stop before sailing west. I'd warrant, looking at the animal skins worn by some of these specimens, that they came from inland by at least fifteen day's walk. They've not had much contact with trade goods or Europeans."

"I buy good slaves. Some fast Quoja. Some strong Fula Jallon. Some spoils of war. Some sold for spite." Ramki bowed low then led Makem to the first captive in the line.

"Caliganto, lace the jacket of any jack-an-ape who tries to take payment without trade. Doctor Petrie? Time to cast eyes to the merchandise."

The sinewy, bald-headed man with a pronounced limp joined the Captain.

Makem and the doctor walked slowly down the line, followed by Ramki and a couple of roust-abouts. The doctor poked, prodded and checked teeth. "Been using the whip rather freely," he said, examining a deep gash across the back of one slave.

"A pack of animals," said Ramki.

"They can't escape," the doctor retorted. "Don't damage the goods."

Ndamma warily watched the proceedings. Those few chosen by the limp-man and the boss-man were freed of their chains but had their hands tied behind their backs and a rope put around their neck. The ropes were held fast by the boatmen. Those rejected by the white men were taken back to the slave castle.

Captain Makem stepped close to Ndamma and tapped his chest. "What tell the markings?"

"He is a Griot, keeps tribal stories in his head."

"Strapping young warrior," Makem said. "How old?"

Ramki fired the question at Ndamma.

"I am in this rainy season," Ndamma held up ten fingers, closed his fist then held up nine.

"And this one?" Makem stepped up to Barika.

Barika indicated in the same way that he was seventeen.

"They're healthy specimens. I'll claim both," Makem said. "They'll bring a goodly price in the Barbados."

While Ramki and Makem haggled over price, Caliganto, accompanied by a well-built, bare-chested white man, strolled down the line. When he came to Ndamma, he stopped to look closely at the young man's incised chest markings. "Your name?" Caliganto stood close and spoke quietly in Wolof.

Surprised to hear a language he understood, Ndamma answered, "I am Ndamma."

"And you?" Caliganto prodded Barika in the ribs.

"Barika, friend of Ndamma."

Caliganto turned his back to the boys. "Sherrie, shackle these two together. I claim them as privilege slaves."

Ndamma and Barika had their hands and necks tied, then were pushed toward the boat with others who were chosen. Packed into the long canoe, they were rowed to the *Black Wing*, boarded and shackled, twelve to a chain.

"Captain's losing money this run. We are not running full an' the buggers er dyin' o' the bloody runs," said a grimy, gap-toothed sailor giving Ndamma a hard prod in the ribs to get his message across. "Killick! Killick! Light along. Into the hold ye monkey eatin' bastards."

"Lubber," Sherrie shouted. "Bruise tha' boy an' yer filthy body waul feel-the-keel."

Below, a single lamp revealed rows and rows of Africans, lying on their sides, chained head to foot. The stench was overwhelming – human excrement – vomit – sweat. One-by-one the new slaves were laid on their side on hard wooden shelves. Ndamma couldn't talk with Barika. His feet touched his friend's head. He was wedged between others, his back to the chest of one, his chest to the back of another.

It was the unearthly moaning that sent shivers up Ndamma's spine and brought tears to his eyes. I will die before I live like this, he thought. Barika and I were raised together. We will die together.

Aboard the Black Wing

UNDER blue skies and full canvas the *Black Wing* sailed west, its slave cargo suffering from seasickness and melancholia. To ensure that the ship would not be bothered by pirates who plundered for more portable cargo, the red flag was run up, indicating slaves on board.

Once a day the captives, sixty at a time, were taken up on deck, given their meal and allowed one-half-hour of fresh air. Ndamma, who hadn't eaten for seven days, again refused the bowl of gruel. Barika, following his lead, turned the bowl away too. Weak and unsteady on their feet, they staggered along in chains until the other ten in their pack collectively decided to stand or sit. Their slave chain was always fed last, and given extra time on deck.

On the eighth day, while Ndamma and Barika leaned dizzily against the portoise, Caliganto came to speak with them. "Why do you not eat?" he asked.

"We have chosen to die. It is the honourable way for a warrior if he is captured."

"Honourable. But a worthless gesture. You see those fish?" Caliganto pointed at fins in the water alongside the ship. "Sharks, they be. Makem could make an example of both of you fast enough. Once the others see the flesh torn off your bones, none will be keen to starve themselves. I could order you whipped, then let you die from dirty wounds."

"Throw us over," Ndamma said, "but answer a question first. Why do you speak Wolof and Fula so well?"

"I'm Jesbau of your tribe, sold for debts by my father, twenty years ago."

"Jesbau, the famous lion killer of Fula Jallon?"

"The same fellow." Caliganto smiled.

"My father has spoken with reverence of you."

"He would need to," Caliganto said. "Now, is it food for the sharks or will you live like a warrior?"

"Undo us," Ndamma said, "so we can fight like warriors."

"That I cannot do," answered Caliganto.

"Undo all of us and we will conquer the ship and return to Bundu."

"Which way is Africa? What way is the village? Who can read a compass? Look around. Which way is north? Which is south? Which of you can sail this ship? Don't be a fool, Ndamma. You're better here than on shore with Ramki. It was good that Makem bought you. Believe me, bide your time. Freedom will come."

"You aren't free."

"I'm not a slave, Ndamma. Captain's company is my choice."

"Jesbau," Barika said. "We are treated worse than the pigs you have on deck."

"I can do nothing about that," Caliganto said. "You're two of three hundred. I can tell you how to prolong your lives."

"How?" asked Barika.

"Eat. We don't want a mutiny, so don't agitate the rest of the slaves. They see one, a Griot, and the other, the son of a chief, making trouble and think they can follow your example. I cannot treat you differently. Listen and learn the Sabir spoken aboard. If you know what's asked, and obey, you won't suffer at the hands of the whip-boy."

"I still wish to die," Ndamma said.

"You, of all people, should live," Caliganto answered. "That's why I speak with you. You are needed by Africans in America as keeper of their stories. Our people will recognize you by your markings. It will give some consolation to know a Griot is among them."

"Are there many from our tribe across this sea?"

"It's not only our tribe who will show respect. If you walk proudly and listen to them, all Africans will respect you."

"Will the one who buys me respect me, Jesbau?"

Caliganto laughed. "Young warrior, the world won't worship you. You will be a chattel to your master; something to be bought and sold, whipped when desired; fed if necessary. Are you man enough to face those hardships and yet lead your people? Or are you shark meat?"

Ndamma looked at the ocean where the sharks circled slowly. He then looked to all horizons, where only water and sky were visible.

"There is wisdom in your words, Jesbau. Is there ever freedom?"

"What is freedom? Do you not have to kill to eat, kill to own land, kill to survive?"

Caliganto said. "You can hold dreams in your heart, and freedom in your mind, until they become reality."

Ndamma considered Caliganto's questions. "If you were given your freedom," he asked, "why did you change your name? Why did you not return to Africa, to the village?"

"Makem changed my name to save my life after I killed a white man to save his," Caliganto answered. "By doing so he changed my country and my loyalty. I could never return to Africa after living away for so long. You cannot believe the riches America has to offer. But sometimes, in my heart I remember the songs, remember my village."

"If I choose to live, I may be like you and in time forget my people too."

Caliganto ran his fingers down the distinctive marks on Ndamma's chest. "You have the sign that reminds you who you are, and what you were meant to do, Ndamma. But it is in your heart whether you remember or forget. Tell me, is it the bowl of gruel ... or the sharks?"

"If we decide to live, we will eat tomorrow. Do you agree, Barika? If we don't eat, you may do as you wish with us."

"Fair enough," Caliganto said, turning away. He took several steps before turning back to Ndamma. "Does my father live? And my mother?"

"You have not forgot your family."

"I dream of them. You're as close to family as I have ever found on this slave ship."

"Your mother is dead. Your father is alive."

Caliganto smiled at Ndamma. "Tomorrow I'll ask about my brothers and sisters. Do my questions alone not give you reason to live?"

CHAPTER NINE
WILLIAMSBURG
June 1751

WITH less than a half-day's drive left before they reached Williamsburg, Timothy was eager to keep the coach on the road. "We are all knackered, but I should like to reach the capital before dark," he explained.

"Our journey is in your most capable hands, Mr. Bushnell, but I believe Katie and I ought to consider partaking of a meal soon."

"My sincere apologies, we should have broken bread at the last inn had it not been so crowded," Timothy said. He surveyed the surrounding land, then directed Ned the driver to stop by a stream. "I shall go to find suitable victuals while you compose yourselves for a rest."

Timothy went to the nearest farm to purchase bread, cheese and a small crock of milk. Ned spread a wide cloth for the use of his lady passengers, cooled and watered the horses and checked the harness.

Katie released Luke onto the blanket, then both she and Joanna made a dive for him as he scrambled for the stream. Finally, after a struggle that she could never win, Katie removed her stockings and his, and dangled him in the water. The babe stopped struggling to stare in fascination at this new sensation.

"'Tis so cool, Joanna. Come – you must paddle, too."

Joanna, who had been trying to remove road dust with a wet handkerchief, gave in to temptation, removed her stockings and waded into the ankle-deep stream. She dropped her skirts, wetting the hem, when a cart creaked by, the oxen prodded by a thin, poorly-dressed man who acknowledged the ladies by spitting in their direction. A milch cow bawled her indignation at being tied behind.

"Look, Mr. Bushnell returns – no, no, Luke, don't put that leaf in your mouth." Katie picked green from the baby's mouth and rinsed her hand in the stream. "You'll soon have tastier morsels."

Approaching, Timothy called, "I had luck! The lady of the house was glad of my coins." He set his purchases on the blanket, sat beside them and cut generous slices of bread. Cheese was divided the same way and handed around. "'Tis amusing that I buy this cheese when there are two rounds in boxes on the coach."

"I have said they are Yorkshire's best, Mr. Bushnell, and they must be kept for the Yule," Joanna said. "Even in America, I will not be without my Yorkshire cheese."

Ned produced a pewter mug from his pack, and warm milk was shared round.

"A pick-nick with friends," Katie said. "'Tis a rewarding meal, would you not agree, Mr. Bushnell?"

"Past doubt, it is," Timothy said. "This will be our last meal on the road. We should be Williamsburg by early evening, if all goes well. Riverview lies on the opposite side of the James River, not a half-day's journey directly from this point."

"I am utterly unable to understand why Mr. Showcroft could not meet us in New Haven!" Joanna said. "Should we perhaps have chosen New York as the meeting place?"

Timothy laughed. "'Tis for the best that we stayed north and west of the city of New York. It has not the veriest speck of majesty about it, though it boasts at least ten thousand citizens, and more than one hundred and fifty taverns where they quaff their ale. Perhaps your husband's business will take him there, then you, Mrs. Showcroft, may travel with him."

"It matters not which route we took," Katie said. "We have seen so much that is different to England. New Haven was ... colonial. But travel is wearying – so many miles between villages – so many days in the carriage!"

"Every view is pretty, and the country is so expansive compared with England," Joanna said. "I love to see such lush greenery, and the country simplicity of the buildings. But I must say the stench that marred several places I do not love. Whence comes this ... aroma?"

Timothy said, "Many of the streams drain swamps, and so they are ripe with decaying vegetation. That is what gives off a foul odour."

"'Tis not the stench that offends me, Mr. Bushnell," Katie said, "but having to share a bedchamber with bedbugs, mosquitoes and sometimes, other female travellers. Complete strangers to be sure," Katie said. "In England, we were not used to being so put upon."

"One cannot choose one's billet so carefully as perhaps one can in England," Timothy said.

"I beg pardon, Mrs. Showcroft," Ned said, "but we'd have been on-road longer if Mr. Bushnell hadn't the knowledge of handlin' a team-o'-four." The driver gave Timothy a slap on the shoulder. "I am not a young'un now. His takin' the reins did give my arms a rest."

"One of my many less obvious talents," Timothy said. "I do like upon occasion to keep my hand in by driving a team. And it does relieve the tedium of the road."

The conversation was interrupted by the approach of two men mounted on fine horses, one in front – the other behind – a group of seventeen slaves, coffled at wrists and ankles.

"Gentlemen, those situations I will be most diligent in attempting to abolish," Joanna said, nodding in their direction. "Where, pray tell, are those poor souls being taken?"

"To the Richmond slave auctions, I presume," Timothy said.

"So repulsive, Mr. Bushnell. How sad that humans must be tied together like cattle, auctioned like horses ... whipped like beasts."

"Turn a pig's eye to such, Mrs. Showcroft." Ned ventured to add his comments to the conversation. "'Tis the way of life hereabouts. Until my seven years passed, I was an indentured slave. I fell into bad circumstances in New Jersey and was sold to pay my debt."

"Pray, do you expect me to believe that?"

"Every word is true," Ned said.

"I am much obliged to you for being so honest. But my personal beliefs do not include slavery of black or white, yellow or brown colour. Knowledge and wealth does not give one race the right to abuse their power – to enslave another."

Timothy took up the challenge. "Riverview has slaves, Mrs. Showcroft. Is it your intention to set them free? Will you sweat in the cookhouse, work in the dairy, boil your own – and Riverview's – laundry? Are you fully instructed in Virginia's laws governing slaves? You must study realism, Mrs. Showcroft."

"I daresay I shall be obliged to confront the situation soon enough," Joanna said. "But, on my word, I'll not mistreat anyone. I'll not have them beaten or sold. I'll place them on the same plane as the staff are at Willowbank."

"I should hope there is some little difference, Joanna." Katie said quickly. "At Willowbank your staff live below stairs, in the attic, over the granary. They are paid a pittance and given food and clothing. I am to assume that here slaves live in quarters or lofts – are paid nothing, but receive food and are clothed at the master's expense."

"The difference," Joanna said, "is that we do not beat the staff at Willowbank. We do not call them slaves, and we do not buy and sell them."

"But, my dear Mrs. Showcroft, you do consider them inferior to your class, do you not? Willowbank may not have a caning closet, but many estates do," Timothy said. "I should think that, given time, your stance will soften toward slavery."

"I hope, Mr. Bushnell, that you might live long enough to digest your words!" Joanna rose from the log. "If we are in so great a hurry, should we not be on our way?"

Katie, not ready to give up the intercourse, gathered Luke in her arms and said, "And pray, where do I fit in? I live in genteel poverty. I tend to Luke as a slave might, but I am not a slave. I was reared in the most comfortable of circumstances but have not a coin to my name. Until Allan returns to my fold, I must rely on my best friend for food and shelter. I receive no payment for my services. Can my question be answered? Am I a slave or a free woman? Lady or servant?"

"Katie, never doubt that you are my companion and dear friend." Joanna placed her arm around Katie's shoulder. "You must know that you have a home at Riverview as long as you need one. We shall talk of financial settlements and your future ... but that circumstance is not to be discussed now."

"We must coach up and away," Timothy said. "Are the ladies in agreement that Mr. Showcroft not be told the entire saga of Mrs. Sherrie, Allan, Major Straight and our little coup at Horta?"

"Agreed, Mr. Bushnell," both women answered.

"Some adventures are best left untold," Timothy cautioned. "We do make mention that Horta was a stop for repairs to ship and body. Major Straight would be the only one to tell tales, and he will not be likely to do so."

"Ladies, gentleman," Ned said. "'Tis best to be on our way if you hope to make Williamsburg afore dark."

Timothy gave Joanna and Katie an assist into the coach then swung himself up beside Ned. Several hours later, as they approached Williamsburg, he hailed a gentleman on his steed, riding in the same direction, to ask if he'd be kind enough to bring Talbot Showcroft, staying at the Raleigh, word that his wife had arrived in Virginia.

On the outskirts of the town, Timothy climbed into the coach to act as guide, after instructing Ned to drive down Francis Street to Nassau Street, then up onto Duke of Gloucester Street and around Palace Green, so that Joanna and Katie could see the Governor's Palace before arriving at the inn. After days on the road, the jostling and noise of the busy capital would be a pleasant diversion.

Ned blew his horn to announce the coach's arrival as it approached the burned out shell of the Capital building on Francis Street. Chickens and children scattered. Barking dogs ran alongside in the dust churned up by the wheels. Groups of men turned around for a longer look as the conveyance passed.

"The Capital building served for more than forty years before it burned four years ago," Timothy explained as they passed the hulking ruin. "Chatter abounds that another will be built, but there is disagreement on how the structure should look."

Duke of Gloucester Street was busy. Well-dressed women picked their way around barrels, grain sacks and crates in front of prosperous looking shops to admire window displays. Children played hoops on the green. Wagons and carts lined the wide thoroughfare.

"The heart of Williamsburg must be the Governor's Palace. I daresay it presents itself in a much more pleasant aspect from the outside than inside. The interior is so poorly designed that large gatherings must be held in an open salon on the second floor." Timothy pointed to an impressive brick structure flanked by large outbuildings. "They raise the flag to show that the Lieutenant Governor is in residence. More than a few who would prefer that the British flag not fly over Williamsburg. England's far away and what is out of sight is not thought of kindly."

Joanna, her attention on the public green in front of the Palace said, "Do my eyes deceive? Do I see Mr. Jackson Shand?"

"Indeed! 'Tis Advocate Shand with his good wife," Timothy said.

"Could you afford a stop, Mr. Bushnell? He is an old acquaintance. I should like to give greeting to the gentleman."

Timothy bumped the top of the coach with the head of his cane to signal Ned to stop. Timothy stepped from the carriage and spoke with a balding, bespectacled man, who had a comely looking wife on his arm.

Jackson Shand came immediately to the coach, looked closely at Joanna and said, "By my faith! 'Tis Miss Turnbull!"

"Why, Mr. Shand, it is you! My eyes do not deceive me."

"You, dear lady, are the last person I should expect to put eyes upon in America," Jackson said, coming closer to the coach. "May I introduce my wife? Elizabeth, here is Miss Turnbull."

"I am delighted to meet you," Elizabeth said. "Your name seems familiar to me."

"Charles Turnbull's manor was my second home while I advanced my studies in England, Elizabeth. He is the spice merchant I told you about, with an absolute fascination for the number twelve. This charming lady was my constant tormentor while I was in residence at Willowbank. She used to spout all manner of cocklemania regarding how she'd like a turn at running the government, how by her own ideas, the world would be a better place."

"For shame, Jackson," Elizabeth said. "Why do you say such ridiculous things about such a lovely lady?"

"Nay, I do not ridicule. Miss Turnbull's arguments were most stimulating. Have you come to do that here, Miss Turnbull? To free all the slaves in the Colonies?"

"Perhaps. But, Mr. Shand, I am now Mrs. Talbot Showcroft. I believe we have a plantation near here."

"Dear me! You are Showcroft's wife?" Jackson said. "My word! I never gave thought ... speculation was rampant who the lady might be. Were you not to marry that pleasant young man ... Harrison Chambers, was it not ... Well! I'll be ... confounded!"

"Truly, Sir, I have much to impart. I am so pleased to be reacquainted ... and to meet Mrs. Shand."

"Would you be so kind as to take dinner with us on a Church Sunday?" Elizabeth said.

"It would delight me to do so. And I daresay Mr. Showcroft would be delighted with the invitation."

"Ah ... you do not mind children? There are five in our household."

"I find them fascinating. I am mother to one, sleeping peacefully at the moment."

"Will you introduce your companion to me?" Jackson said looking at Katie.

"My apologies, Mr. Shand. Mrs. Shand, this is my dear friend, Katie Tur ... Sherrie. Katie, Elizabeth's husband and my old friend, Mr. Jackson Shand, an advocate."

"Welcome to Williamsburg, Mrs. Sherrie." Jackson turned his attention again to Joanna. "Mrs. Showcroft, Mr. Bushnell knows our house. Over liquors, we have had many an animated discussion about the origin of etched rocks. You will remember then, Mrs. Showcroft, that you are expected to dine on the first Sunday when you attend Burton church. Until then, we shall take our leave."

As the Shands continued on their way, Joanna said, "Upon my word! Mr. Shand ... in Williamsburg. He did introduce me to ... a kind gentleman. He and my father were thick at the gentlemen's club in London because they were both interested in legal positions pertaining to importation of goods to and from the colonies and other parts of the world. I did not know where Mr. Shand settled after he left England. He did not keep up a correspondence."

Timothy banged on the roof with his cane and the coach continued along the street to the Raleigh. When the conveyance pulled up to the inn, he said. "I see Talbot has kept his word. There he stands waiting for you, Mrs. Showcroft."

Talbot stood ram-rod straight, hands behind his back. A well-proportioned black woman, coal-eyes sharp on the carriage, stood a pace behind him.

Excited, Joanna waved, expecting an acknowledgment. None was forthcoming. My husband appears more rugged, she thought, but if he is happy about my arrival, he certainly does not show it. She accepted Talbot's hand to alight the carriage. Yes, it was the same angular Talbot, impeccably dressed, a little taller than herself, brown hair tied severely behind the nape of his neck.

"Wife." Talbot bowed slightly.

When Katie, holding the sleeping babe, accepted the assistance of Timothy to alight the coach, Joanna made the introduction, "Katie, Talbot, you do remember – ?"

"I do not." Assuming his wife had the audacity to introduce a servant, Talbot turned his back on Katie. "Sukie," he ordered, "take the child."

"Yaus, Massa." The black woman moved to obey, her arms out to take the baby.

"I daresay that we can manage Luke," Joanna said.

"Sukie shall take the child," Talbot said again.

"Nay, but I insist that baby Luke stay with me and Mrs. Sherrie, until I have spoken with the woman you have chosen." Joanna stood her ground. "In truth, I will not hand my son to a stranger."

Talbot bowed stiffly then took Joanna roughly by the elbow. "By God, I'll not have you upbraid me in front of a slave. Sukie, show Mrs. Showcroft to her chamber, then take the nursemaid and child with you to the garden until arrangements can be made to accommodate her."

"Husband, you mistake. Mrs. Sherrie is no servant. She is my close friend and will need a room of her own, as befits a lady of quality."

Sukie nodded. "Massa, if de ladies follow me, dey can rest in de Missus' chamber."

Talbot waved his hand to dismiss Joanna. "I'll secure a chamber if another be empty. Bushnell, what does Henkle need to bring to Mrs. Showcroft's chamber?"

"Mr. Bushnell, please to be mindful of my cheeses," Joanna said.

"Indeed, Mrs. Showcroft, I will ensure that Henkle puts them in your room."

Sukie led the way to the inn's second floor, opened a door to a small bedchamber and stepped back to allow the women to enter.

Joanna glanced around the room. "Where are my husband's belongings?"

"Mr. Showcroft appears to have made other arrangements," Katie said, gently laying the sleeping babe on the bed.

"Missus?" Sukie said. "Child needs bein' cared for, while you be eatin'. Common room not be de place fo' tiny babe."

"I daresay you are right," Joanna said turning to the woman, tall like herself, older by perhaps fifteen years, clear bright eyes, broad shoulders. This woman fears no one, she thought – not me, not Talbot. "Your name is ... Sukie?"

"Yaus, Missus." Sukie squared her shoulders and returned Joanna's keen gaze.

"I will insist that you call me Ma'am as did my servants in England, Sukie. I will have it no other way."

"Yaus, I do dat ... Ma'am."

"You must understand that Katie and I have good reason for not giving my baby over to a person I do not know. But, I did detect the least speck of a smile when I was so bold as to disobey my husband's orders. I presume you are a Riverview slave and chosen because you have cared for children?"

"Yaus'am. Ah hab chillen, not so small as yo babe. De oder ... Ma'am ... must nurse de babe, but I can tend him. Massa say de child not in his presence when he be wif de ladies. Nothing will be a-happenin' to yo' babe in my care, Ma'am."

"Did Mr. Showcroft ... buy ... you for the plantation?"

"Aw, naw, Ma'am. Ah been at Riverview long time as cook-slave fo Massa MacGregor. Ah been bought by Massa Showcroft wif de plantation."

The honesty of Sukie's answers persuaded Joanna to change her mind. "I am all compliance now. Sukie, take Luke with you and return him to us after we have supped, unless he needs to be fed, or he misses his mother."

"Yaus'am. Ah not be far away," Sukie left with Luke snuggled in her arm, still asleep.

Boots scraping on the stairs and a knock at the door confirmed that trunks and cheeses had arrived. Joanna oversaw the placement of the trunks in the room, being particularly firm in ordering hers put on top of the sturdy wooden cheese boxes. Still thinking about Luke, she said, "I do hope I've not mistaken the matter in giving my sweet babe over. He will certainly scream when he wakes and sees his new nursemaid."

"I shouldn't worry," Katie said. "To be sure, at Willowbank, you played with baby Luke twice a day. You did not know to whom I entrusted him between visits. Luke will do perfectly well in that woman's capable hands. She does remind me of my beloved nanny. There is not a particle of difference but in her colour. Your husband very likely hoped to please you by bringing Sukie from the plantation as a nursemaid. Ah, Joanna, come look at this," Katie stood by an open window.

Below, Sukie was sharing a bench with a slender woman whose head was swathed in bright cotton cloth. Beside them two small children played with a kitten. The two women sang, Sukie in a deep, resonant voice. When a third slave appeared in a doorway, she added to the song in a beautiful contralto.

"'Tis lovely indeed," Joanna said. "See how tenderly she holds Luke."

"And you, my dear, were worried about her," Katie said. "Was your concern because of her colour?"

"It was not colour that gave me pause, Kate. I was – I am – exceedingly reluctant to trust Luke to a woman my husband chose ... I do worry about that sweet babe's safety."

Joanna and Katie, in their best English finery, went down to take dinner at the appointed hour, causing some commotion as they entered the common room. Talbot came to the door to lead them to a table near one of the windows overlooking the street.

"You have pleased me exceedingly with your dress," Talbot said. "'Tis important in Williamsburg to put on a good appearance."

The meal was constantly interrupted as men came forward on the pretense of paying their respects to Talbot and Timothy. In reality they fished for an introduction to the pretty women. When the subject of Timothy's ugly scar came up, true to his word, he did not elaborate on the time spent in Horta, but gave flippant answers which raised much hilarity among the men, and more than a few blushes among the women.

"Mr. Bushnell, your demeamor has changed," Joanna said by way of admonishment. "You have taken on the masque of a common vulgar seaman. 'Tis not pleasant to a lady's ears."

"Good Captain Henry confided, when we dropped anchor in New Haven, that he had been forced to run a tight Christian ship," Katie said. "Many of the sailors were tongue-bound in our presence."

In answer to a question Talbot asked, Joanna explained, without telling Allan Sherrie's whereabouts, that Katie would reside at Riverview until her husband arrived. "And, Husband, I must thank you for arranging a room for Mrs. Sherrie. We have stayed in so many inns not befitting to a lady."

"I did forfeit my room," Talbot said. "I stay at the Wetherburn for the night."

During their evening stroll Talbot and Timothy took pains to point out various homes and businesses, and made necessary introductions. Although Timothy took special pains to point out the Shand house, neither he nor Joanna alluded to the brief meeting.

"And do you approve the country, Wife?" Talbot asked.

"'Tis most interesting," Joanna said. "But, Husband, I shall reserve full judgement until I settle into Riverview and spend a few months in America. I observe that there is much unceremonious intercourse among the classes."

"Class means not a whit in the wilderness where 'tis every man for himself, and all the better for it," Talbot said. "When a savage attacks with a *tomahawk*, as their weapons are called, one does not pause to make a leg."

"Perhaps, Husband, the division by classes will have no place in this country. That would be pitisome, for it has taken centuries to form our traditions."

"'Tis still very common in settled areas. By the bye, you will receive many invitations to take tea. Those inviting you will expect to be invited to Riverview in return. Use your discretion, Wi ... Joanna. The plantation is a half-day's journey from here. As in England, hospitality is obligatory. No English lady or gentleman is turned away."

"But be prepared, the rabble may take tea and stay three months," Timothy said. "Virginia hospitality is legendary."

"If Mrs. Sherrie and Bushnell will excuse us – would you oblige me by tarrying awhile in Bruton Church cemetery?" Talbot asked Joanna.

When they were alone among the tombstones, Joanna impulsively bussed him on the cheek. "Ah, Talbot, 'tis good to be on terra firma and with you."

"Pray, do not demonstrate in such a public place, Joanna."

"But why do we hide in this graveyard if not for privacy's sake?" Joanna laughed. "There is none will rise to spy. No spectre will see and gossip." Suddenly craving intimacy, she put her hands up to touch Talbot's cheeks.

"I did require privacy to inform you that I have papers at the Raleigh that need your signature. Let us return to the inn," Talbot said, pulling her hands from his face.

"There is no hurry. We do have a long time together, God willing, and – "

"Let it suffice to say my time is short in Virginia. I leave for the West Indies two weeks on the morrow. I must oversee the harvest there, and will remain away from Riverview until after the Yule season."

"I have just arrived and you must leave?"

"You must resign yourself to the plantation way. 'Tis the custom in America for a man of means to be away much of a year."

"But I can travel with you – "

"Nay, Wife. You shall remain at Riverview." Talbot put Joanna's hand into the crook of his elbow to lead her from the cemetery. "I am persuaded that Katie Sherrie will make an suitable companion for you. Why is her husband not with her?"

"Mr. Sherrie was delayed and had to ... take another ship," Joanna said. "They lived in London and have ... business in America that must be attended to."

"What is the nature of his business?"

"I confess, I was so grateful that Katie agreed to accompany me and suckle Luke, I did not query too closely into her husband's affairs."

Better vague answers than the truth, Joanna reminded herself. The less he knows about Mr. and Mrs. Sherrie, the better for them. How my scruples have slipped, Joanna thought, that the untruths come so easily. Does my husband find it as easy to lie to me?

"Riverview has not been noted for its frolics in recent years. It may be lonely for you. You must encourage Mrs. Sherrie to stay, even after her husband arrives."

"I will make Riverview a beating heart. Fêtes and balls, hunts and horse races for you, Talbot."

"Pray, why for me?" Talbot stopped walking. "I do prefer privacy."

"I will plan them for myself then. Truthfully, Husband, I shall soon tire of roaming from room to room in a big house –"

"But dinners and fêtes suitable for the relief of boredom were held at Willowbank."

"You forget, Husband. My father did temper celebrations at Willowbank. To each there was, in the offing, a financial gain."

BACK at the inn, Joanna sat at a small table in a corner of the common room, and read a document spread before her by the light of several candles. When she finally glanced up at Talbot and Mr. Mithers, a bewigged, wiry little man who called himself a notary, she directed her remarks to both. "You display a shocking lack of honesty, and of sense, if you believe I might put my name to this." She had taken an instant dislike to Mithers, and her opinion of him did not change as she saw his face change when she made no move to take up the quill.

"Mrs. Showcroft, all is in perfect order," Mithers said, adjusting wire glasses perched on his thin, leathery nose.

"Nay, verily, nothing is in order," Joanna retorted, keeping her voice low so other patrons would not overhear. "I learned at my father's knee to read all documents carefully. This one has been drawn up according to instructions that are quite beside the mark. Here it states that I am to be sole owner of Riverview." Joanna pointed to a line just below the heading. "In fact, gentlemen, it is my father whose name must appear here. I am his agent only. And here ..." She pointed to another clause. "The document states that in the case of my demise, the property belongs to Mr. Showcroft."

"As so it should, Mrs. Showcroft, under law," Mithers said. "As your husband – "

"Father did particularly insist that as sole owner of the plantation, he has sole disposal of his land. It is to be inherited by Luke. If Luke is still a child, the estate is to be managed by such person as my father shall appoint in his last Will and Testament, until the child comes of age."

She turned to look at Talbot. "These facts were made perfectly clear to you by my father before you departed England," she said. "He and I know full well the Virginia law that gives a husband control over all that his wife owns. You are never to have ownership of, or control over, Riverview Plantation, Talbot. It belongs to Father, not to me, and not to you."

"To be honest, I do not recall any such conversation with your father," Talbot lied.

"Then 'tis to my credit that I do. I do also carry proof of that conversation." Joanna drew a letter from her reticule, an initialed copy of the one Charles Turnbull had handed Talbot the previous November. "Pray, Husband, why do we deal with this man, when a very capable advocate, and a good friend of the Turnbull family, Mr. Jackson Shand, lives here in Williamsburg? Let me tell you in no uncertain terms that I refuse to sign any document until all is put right, and Mr. Shand engaged to do the rewriting."

"That is damned codswallop!" sputtered Talbot. "Your name as owner is as good as that of your father. He'll not reside in the Colonies; you will. 'Tis preposterous that your father should interfere on this side of the Atlantic."

"Those, Sir, are his instructions, and my only terms for signing. I must also have four copies made. It shall be noted on the document that one is held by Advocate Shand – one by my father – one by me – and one by ..." Joanna paused then said, "Captain Anthony Makem."

"Makem! Makem of the *Black Wing*?" Talbot's outburst caused several men in the room to turn and glance at the trio. "How does Makem come into this scheme? How is it that you know him? What in Judas' name does this mean?"

Why did I involve Captain Makem? Joanna thought. How foolish of me! What possessed me to mention his name, especially in this situation? There is no retreat now. "I do trust him," Joanna said aloud. "Captain Makem and ... my father are acquainted."

"This must be utter stupidity!" Talbot paced before the table, drawing more attention from the inn's inquisitive patrons.

"Nay, a stroke of sanity," Joanna said. "I will stay in Williamsburg until the proper documents have been drawn up by Advocate Shand. I care not if he takes all night to do so. If the correct deeds are not forthcoming, mark my word, I will return to England immediately, and the payment with me. And Riverview will still belong to Mr. MacGregor."

Talbot stopped pacing, his face close to Joanna's. "You have the payment with you? I thought your father proposed a bill of credit in the Colonies. That was his last correspondence – that he was in the mire of setting up an account on this shore."

"I do have the payment. My father decided that a bill-of-credit could be abused. We shall handle any future financial decisions by request only." Joanna kept her voice low as her father had taught her to do in matters of dispute.

"Good God! This is foolish in the extreme!"

"This places an obstruction in the path of any low, devious person who might consider milking a Turnbull bill-of-credit," Joanna said. "It may mean that letters must be regular between Father and me, but 'tis in our best interests to proceed thus. It was Father's decision and I abide by it. For Heaven's sake, Husband, do not draw more attention by pacing about and raising your voice."

Talbot sat down, drew the document to him and gave a few minutes thought to his next step. He finally said, "I will have the changes made tonight."

"Gentlemen, I trust you will get word of this to Mr. Shand immediately. If by chance he wishes to see my letter, it shall be made available. I did speak briefly with the Shands when we arrived this afternoon. If you will excuse me – "

Talbot held his wife's arm, forcing her to stay seated. "The payment will be in coin? Where is it now?"

Joanna said firmly, "Unhand me, Sir. Believe me, it has been a long and tiresome day. I should retire to my bedchamber without delay."

When Showcroft made no effort to rise, Mithers said, "I will escort you from the room, Mrs. Showcroft." Taking Joanna's arm, he said to her as they walked through the knot of men who stood around the door, "Do I understand that you carry coinage on your person?"

"That, Sir, is not your concern." Leaving the despicable little fellow, Joanna made for her room. With pounding heart, she shut the door and, in a state of nervous agitation, paced to and fro as she thought about what had taken place in the Common Room.

How very silly of me to reveal that I carried payment for Mr. MacGregor with me. Talbot was so loud that anyone could have overheard the exchange. I must not sleep here alone. I will share Katie's room. But how if Talbot chances to look in before leaving the inn?

Hastily, Joanna arranged clothing and bed pillows to resemble a body, then pulled a blanket over her creation. *"That will do for a ruse should my husband open the door to peek in. But I am almost certain he has no intention of coming to my room tonight. He sleeps elsewhere."*

Joanna looked first to see if anyone was in the hall, then went quietly to Katie's bedchamber. She knocked softly, entered and closed the door carefully behind her

Katie, startled by the sight of a person in her room, gasped and looked to the cradle.

Joanna whispered, "'Tis I – Joanna. I must sleep the night here."

EARLY in the morning, before stirring began in earnest in the hall, Joanna slipped back to her chamber. She opened the door and looked in. Immediately, she closed it again and made her way back to Katie's room.

"Have our fears been justified? Have you been robbed?" Katie asked when Joanna stepped inside.

Joanna nodded. "Take Luke to Sukie, then please have the innkeeper wake Mr. Bushnell. If anyone should ask after me, you must say you have not spoken with me this morning. Wait for Mr. Bushnell, then bring him to my chamber."

Joanna returned to her room to wait for Timothy, and to give some serious thought to her predicament.

I thought that Father was in jest when he said that keeping one step ahead of Talbot would be my challenge. How did he state it? There's many a twist to the man's

game. Life in America was fast becoming a game – of wills – with possible deadly consequences if the results of an evening's dark side were considered.

A quarter-hour later a soft knock sounded at the door. Katie whispered, "Joanna, Mr. Bushnell is here."

Joanna opened the door just wide enough to admit the two, then closed it quickly behind them.

Timothy's hair was disheveled. He had dressed in haste, lacking boots in his desire to hurry. "What the thunder is this?" he gasped.

The contents of Joanna's trunk lay scattered around the room. A knife, which had been plunged into the dummy body, protruded from the bed covering.

"Joanna!" Katie exclaimed, "By my word, someone has attempted to kill you!"

"It does appear so." Joanna said giving Timothy a keen look.

"Why, pray, would any person make an attempt on your life, Mrs. Showcroft?" Timothy took a closer look at the knife. "Would robbery would be a motive?"

"'Tis possible." Joanna told of the events in the Common Room. "You are intimately acquainted with my husband, Mr. Bushnell. Do you perceive him as capable of murdering his wife?"

"My dear lady. Your question shocks me."

"It was meant to, Mr. Bushnell."

"Then I must answer honestly. I am at a loss to read your husband, but I do not believe that he would ... take such extreme measures ... Pray, I cannot conceive ..." All the while he was speaking, Timothy was fingering the handle of the knife.

"Mr. Bushnell, what do you truly believe was the reason?" Katie asked. "To rob or to kill Mrs. Showcroft?"

"The room was dark – there was no moon last night. I'd hazard the person rushed to stab first. He perhaps came in by the window and would not know immediately that a dummy was made in the bed. He entered, stabbed, discovered the deception – there is little similarity between pillow and a living being – then searched the trunk. In his haste, he left the knife. He was neither a professional assassin nor a thief. He was an opportunist, someone who needed money."

"I must ask, might he have heard the confrontation in the Common Room and thought to take advantage of a woman, and rob me," Joanna said. "Or, was he hired to murder me?"

"I must, in full honesty, say I do not know."

"Such a devious act cannot be dismissed, but what matters now is that I am alive and the coinage is accounted for."

"Where is it?" Timothy asked.

"With all respect, Mr. Bushnell, that is not your concern," Joanna said. "The question is what to do next?"

"Remove the knife," Timothy said. "Arrange the bed to make it appear that you slept in it. Come down for breakfast as though nothing untoward has happened – but first, allow me one hour with your husband in the common room. You must observe his expressions. Indeed, try to take notice of everyone's reaction to your entry. Many who were in the room last night stayed at the inn. If you, Mrs. Showcroft, watch your husband closely, Mrs. Sherrie and I will watch the others."

"Should we not inform the Watch?" asked Katie.

"No!" Timothy said. "Think of the scandal! You cannot wish to bring that upon yourself at the moment." Timothy reached for the knife.

"Pray leave the knife, Mr. Bushnell. I shall feel much safer with it in my possession."

"If you wish," Timothy said. "You must be careful, Mrs. Showcroft. 'Tis very sharp. If this becomes widely known, questions will be asked that have no possibility of being answered ... truthfully. Discretion is vital," Timothy said. "Until the common room?"

After the door closed, Katie wheeled to face Joanna, "My dear, do you truly think your husband has made an attempt on your life?"

"I do not like to think it, but I am not silly enough to believe he *could* not have aught to do with it. Certainly, this must not be made common knowledge. I am not very well acquainted with my husband, and certain ... circumstances of our marriage I do not discuss. I did say that I was concerned for Luke's safety. I did not say I fear that my own safety is of some concern too."

"We speak of death, Joanna. He could not possibly ... Your husband would not —"

"Aye, past doubt, there are two sides to every coin. It would behoove us to take breakfast. Heigh-ho! I will be most pleased when we have maids to help with our dressing! Until then, run and get what you need for your toilette, and we can assist each other in here, Katie."

"That I will. I dressed hastily to speak with the innkeeper. I'll return in a trice."

When Katie left, Joanna arranged the bed, chose what she would wear from the assortment thrown about, and then packed the trunk again, putting the knife in last.

Considering the situation, I am exceedingly calm, she thought as she sat on the bed waiting for Katie to return. What will the day bring that can compare to this strange occurrence?

If Talbot was responsible for the incident, he wore an unreadable mask. His face reflected no surprise when he saw Joanna enter the Common Room.

Katie, on the other hand, noted a rough-looking man hunched over a meal in a corner, who paid a great deal of attention to Joanna. "Who is that man?" she asked Timothy as soon as she had been placed at the table.

"That good-for-nothing is Flanagan, the overseer at Riverview. Deadly as a rattle-snake, rotten to the core," Timothy said.

"Was the chamber adequate for your needs?" Talbot asked as he held a chair for Joanna.

"I did sleep well, Husband. The air in Williamsburg is so agreeable that I stirred not. Forsooth, I slept so soundly a person could have danced a jig upon my body and I should not have noticed their presence." Joanna dared not look at Talbot's face for fear her eyes would give away the fact she was making a good joke of a parcel of untruths.

"As soon as Mithers and Shand have finished rewriting the document, and you have expressed satisfaction with it through your signature, we shall take our leave of Williamsburg. Pray, where is Jonathan Luke?"

Katie answered. "Sukie, sweet woman, is tending him this morning while we take advantage of a good meal."

"The woman is a slave," Talbot said. "She does what is required of her. That she does it well is a blessing, to be sure. Her name, however, is sufficient."

Katie gave Talbot a disagreeable look but ventured no response. Timothy had touched her arm very lightly under the table to signal that she must not rise to Talbot's bait.

Detestable person, she thought. Why had Joanna consented to marry the man?

"Pray allow me to remind you, Husband." Joanna said mildly, "Sukie is my property, and we shall call her sweet woman, or any other endearment that comes to mind, with no admonishment from you." And so the die is cast, she thought. This reunion appears to be one sparring match after another.

CHAPTER TEN
WILLIAMSBURG

Introductions

IN THAT way peculiar to tall men, Timothy lounged against a tree as he waited for Joanna and Katie to finish examining the goods in front of the Prentis Shop. He gave a slight bow to Sarah Binks, standing in the doorway of her husband's print shop, greeted several acquaintances, and wiled away his time with thoughts of the Virginia woods – with paints and canvas at hand. But before he could escape to such quietude, he had to consider an interesting proposal ...

Despite his protestations, Mrs. Showcroft had insisted he stay on at Riverview and keep her accounts. After breakfast she had again besought him to consent.

"But, Mrs. Showcroft, ciphering is not one of my finer accomplishments."

"You do not give yourself credit, Mr. Bushnell. I trust you have kept your own accounts, have you not? Of course you have, so why can you not do mine? To be sure, I have come to rely on your good advice and judgment."

"'Tis beyond my comprehension, Mrs. Showcroft. Why are you willing to trust me with the plantation's books? Have you not forgot 'twas your husband introduced us? Under the circumstances, I should hesitate to say that is a good recommendation."

"Your friendship with my husband does not signify, Mr. Bushnell."

"Truly, I have neglected my sketching and must soon give full attention to it."

"I have no hesitation in stating that you can keep my accounts and devote time to your own work as well. Did you not say that at one time you taught school?"

"That I did – but, Mrs. Showcroft – "

"Mr. Bushnell, I am at a loss to understand why you believe you are less than friend and confidant, especially after your heroic actions aboard the *Charlotte*. The truth be known, I do need your kind assistance. This morning you showed splendidly clear reasoning."

"You did show a commendable restraint, Mrs. Showcroft."

"I saw no point in making a scene."

"I confess I do not find town life to my liking."

"Nay, heed me for a moment. Riverview can be a base for your gathering, sketching and painting, and while you are there, you can cipher the plantation's acounts."

"I hardly envision myself being ... settled ... for want of a better word."

"Your freedom shall not be compromised. You could travel as – and where – you please."

"But, Mrs. Showcroft, what would your husband think if I were to accept the work, and reside at Riverview while he travels?"

"He is your friend, Mr. Bushnell. He must be pleased if you have an occupation. Your wage will be more than adequate."

Timothy had hesitated. Subscriptions for his book had fallen short in England. More to the point, while at Willowbank, he had developed a fervent admiration and respect for this lady. After Horta, he could not forget the vision of the lady-in-blue. A dark sliver of thought crossed his mind. Perhaps if certain circumstances played into his hands, he could do unto Talbot what ...

He was shaken from his reverie by the sound of voices. Joanna and Katie were strolling toward the tree with Henkle, a Riverview house slave, trailing behind laden with packages.

When Katie ventured into a millinery shop, Joanna instructed Henkle to wait by the shop's door. "Mr. Bushnell, good Sir, you frown as though the world has been lowered onto your shoulders. Has my proposal taxed your faculties?" Joanna said, accepting the offered seat on a bench under the tree.

"To confess, I have considered your offer." Timothy said, eyeing Sarah Binks, who stood on her front step, motioning that he should bring Joanna for an introduction.

"'Tis quite simple, Mr. Bushnell. To the point, Mrs. Sherrie and I place our trust in you. Pray, to whom did I turn after last night's disagreeable occurrence? My husband? Nay; not if I have the very least suspicion that he had a hand in the attempt on my life."

Timothy shuffled his feet. "Mrs. Showcroft, you cannot know your husband made any attempt on your life."

"That is very true. 'Tis certain some rounder did; and some rounder may make an attempt again. Mr. Bushnell, because of a marriage agreement – Sir, I do have reason to be frightened, and I have no one to whom I may turn, except you."

"I will do what I can," Timothy said.

Joanna's fan kept the flies at bay but did nothing to alleviate her nervous frustration. "I have great concern for Luke's safety. You, too, have concerns. I did overhear the instructions that you gave Sukie this morning to take babe away from the inn until we returned. In strong words, you do not trust my husband either, do you?"

"It was not ... I thought it best ... to be ... safe. Baby Luke is a helpless creature; he cannot defend himself."

"Precisely my *point d'appui*. Sir, pray give my proposal your consideration. If you accept, even for one year, I will be exceedingly grateful."

"I promise to give the request serious thought, Mrs. Showcroft. "I must tell you honestly there is one person in whom you can place complete trust in Williamsburg: Mrs. Sarah Binks. She is a Bray Associate and holds many of the opinions you do, including some of those you voice about slavery – education, for one instance. She can be taken into your confidence, and she has no liking for Mr. Showcroft. If Mrs. Binks perceives you are sincere, she will undoubtedly prove to be your best ally."

"Why does she hold my husband in disdain?"

Timothy ran a finger around his tight cravat. "I have divulged too much. And 'tis a trifling concern."

"Nay, but you have said too little, Mr. Bushnell. Even a trifling concern can grow. Why does she not like my husband?"

"She did approach your husband, seeking support for her school."

"And he refused."

"He did and stated quite publically that he thinks Mrs. Binks far too opinionated for a lady, and that her stand on educating slaves is outrageous. She rejoined with some choice verbiage."

"My dear!" Joanna said. "That would not sit well with Talbot!"

"The feud culminated in Mr. Binks' printing an unkind cut in his broadsheet about your husband. I must say that Mrs. Binks does share your nose for adventure!"

"Then, Sir, I should be delighted to meet Sarah Binks."

"And Mrs. Binks wishes to meet you. The print shop is but a step away."

"If the good lady is so eager to make my acquaintance, she might wish to speak with me alone. Rather than compromise yourself, Mr. Bushnell, perhaps you will introduce us then return to your lounging tree to await Mrs. Sherrie? When she has completed her expedition through the shops, could you accompany her to the Raleigh? Luke will doubtless be in full howl. He is a hungry wee lad. Would you instruct Henkle to take the packages back to the inn and be so kind as to come for me when Mr. Shand requires my signature?"

ADVOCATE Shand's quarters belied the man's very proper dress and decorum. Books spilled from bookcases onto chairs and floor. Sheafs of documents were piled high on mantel. Papers covered table top. A large floor clock ticked time as a caged canary burst into song at an open window.

Jackson Shand, his wig a little askew, cleared a chair of an assortment of leather-bound volumes and invited Joanna to sit. He then sent Lark, his manservant, for refreshment, and made himself comfortable at the table. "Now, we have some privacy, Mrs. Showcroft. You did say that you had a matter of some importance to tell me?"

"That I have, Mr. Shand. I am excessively pleased that you have agreed to act as my advocate in the Colonies; that you assisted with the agreement-of-purchase; and that you have consented to a few moments of private conversation after the signing. I vow, Mr. Mithers did appear just a mite piqued this day."

"Truly, I had not heard of the man," Jackson said, arranging papers so that he could place an elbow on the table. "He did not appear to be a man who knew his business. But all has been set aright. Riverview is in your father's name, as it should be. You are his agent in all plantation matters. Charles Turnbull is a wise man to trust his daughter with such a duty."

"Would that I should prove worthy of it," Joanna said. " We have known each other for a very long time, have we not, Mr. Shand?"

"Indeed, Mrs. Showcroft, my days at Willowbank are some of my fondest memories."

"Then, I must tell you that the purchase of Riverview is not, at the moment, on my mind." Joanna drew a paper from her reticule. "If you would read this, Sir?"

Jackson adjusted his glasses and gave full attention to the document. "My dear Ma'am! What would prompt such an odious agreement?"

"The very question I have asked of myself. My father's answer was ever that its intent was to protect my inheritance."

"Well, that could be," Jackson said. "But I have never seen such verbiage in any nuptial contract. He – or you – mistrusts Talbot Showcroft. And, if I may be so bold, it does appear that your father – or you – hopes to gain the man's property and money by most unusual means."

"The terms were agreed upon by my husband and Father. I was only made privy to details hours before the wedding. Father will say days, but my word upon it, it was hours."

"Such a twist to the life's play! I did believe when I left England that Harrison Chambers was your betrothed. Your father relished the man's company, as well."

Joanna heaved a sigh. "He was a great favourite with both of us, Mr. Shand. But Harrison wished to please Father and travelled to India, where he ... died." Joanna's voice broke. She found her linen square, then continued, "Sir, I did have a great affection for the man."

Jackson averted his eyes and played with papers on the table. "I thought him a decent young fellow, worthy of your attentions." He cleared his throat and said, "Then, after your mourning, you consulted cold good sense and married Talbot Showcroft."

"Would that I were in full possession of my senses at the time! I considered myself more spinster than comely young woman then. Talbot did present himself at a time when I was ... vulnerable, and Father did not dispute the match because he greatly desired a grandchild."

"Then, it was not an arranged marriage?" Jackson asked.

"Indeed not, Sir. I was a rebel at the time, angry at the circumstances which took Harrison away from me and prevented me from having a family ... children. Oh dear, I dare not say more but that it was my choice to marry Talbot. The man did court me in proper and charming fashion."

"He would, considering what he might win along with the lady," Jackson muttered as he swiped his hand across his mouth. Clearing his throat again, he said, "And the marriage has been satisfactory?"

"Mr. Shand. Even Kings must have a legal heir. And, with the occasional exception, rarely do they attain satisfaction through marriage."

Jackson pursed his lips and beat finger upon finger. "I will assume then that its course has had its boulders?"

"Fool I was to not see that circumstances made for a tangled, and perhaps dangerous, union. At the time, I saw none but what Talbot – and, methinks, Father – wished me to. There is naught for me, but to make the best of it. The world is all chances and I must take mine. I am not alone in this, Sir. Many women marry with naught but ... respect ... for their husbands."

"In your defense, I must say that you did appear to be following a father's inclinations. I also know your mother's influence was great, but she died some time ago, did she not?"

"She did, Sir, but she did warn me against the union. After she ... was gone, I had no reason to doubt Father's counsel. He told me the nuptial agreement answered all concerns about it."

Lark entered the room with a tea tray and waited politely. Advocate Shand hastily cleared a space on the table near the lady, and Lark set the tray down and backed out of the room.

"I assume this agreement has given you enough concern that you wished me to read it."

"It has, Sir. I believe it would be a great benefit, if baby Luke, or I were to di ... meet with an accident."

"My dear lady! Never say so!"

"'Tis my surmise. You are acquainted with my husband, Mr. Shand. You now know the terms of the agreement. I would suggest that you, as my advocate, keep both in mind, as I begin my life as Mrs. Talbot Showcroft in Virginia."

"Shall I keep this copy of the agreement, Mrs. Showcroft?"

Joanna smiled as she looked around the untidy room. "I will see to the task of copying the terms for you. You will be told where I have placed it at Riverview. Should the situation arise that you must question – or act – "

"Who is privy this information, Mrs. Showcroft?"

"I assume, only my husband, my father, you, and I are familiar with the terms."

"Then, should anything untoward happen, I shall be in constant communication with Mr. Turnbull. That I do promise. Now, shall we forget this sinister business and take tea before you rejoin your party at the Raleigh?"

Williamsburg
The Raleigh, 4 June 1751
My dearest Father:
I write in haste, as the carriage leaves for Riverview within the hour. You see that I have arrived safely in Virginia; the cheeses have also. The voyage had its frightening moments, and the ship needed to undergo repairs before continuing her voyage. I did not allude at that time to my adventures at Horta. They are best left untold until I see your face.

I have enclosed your copy of the agreement to purchase, duly signed and sealed. You will see that all is in order and that I have signed as your agent-in-charge. Please note that copies have been lodged with two trustworthy people: one is Jackson Shand, whom you will recall was a houseguest at Willowbank on diverse occasions.

I have seen some of the worst aspects of slavery and shudder at the cruelty that can occur, and, it appears, it does occur often. How one person can bully another so is beyond my understanding. My beliefs are stronger now, and I must do something about it.

Mr. Bushnell sends his regards. I do heed your advice and keep both my friends and my enemies close at hand.

With the attentions of three to spoil him now, Jonathan Luke fares well. He grows so fast that we are hard pressed to keep him in fitting clothing.

My husband was in fine fettle last night and gave me a short lesson of what I might expect in the future.

Please, Father dear, keep me in your mind and prayers as I begin this odyssey in America, and believe that I am,
as ever, your adoring daughter,
  Joanna

Introductions – Riverview

MIDMORNING, the first of the Showcroft entourage left the Raleigh for the James River ferry in a horse-cart, driven by Henkle. Sukie sat amid a jumble of trunks and packages, an eye on several riding horses tied behind. The rest of the party left directly after the noon meal. As Riverview's carriage passed the Binkses' house, Joanna spied Sarah in her garden. "Pray oblige me by stopping a moment. I have forgot to give the Binkses a firm date for their visit."

"If you must insist on associating with these people, send the woman a note," Talbot said.

"No, Husband, I do wish to speak with Sarah Binks now. Please ask the driver to stop."

"Come, Showcroft, 'tis a trifling matter that your wife wishes to speak with Mrs. Binks," Timothy said.

"If you must ... Stop the carriage," Talbot ordered.

Joanna heard the annoyance in Talbot's voice, but she was past caring. He had been in a boil for most of the morning. If the Binkses added salt to the pot ... "Mrs. Binks showed me the greatest courtesy this morning. You told me I must reciprocate with an invitation to Riverview. I shall be a moment only," she said. "Mr. Bushnell, if you would give me your hand?"

Sarah, a flower basket in hand, scurried to the gate Joanna approached. "A pleasant surprise! I did not expect to see you again this month."

Joanna positioned herself so that Talbot could not see her take several papers from her reticule. "I did see you in your garden, and your presence answered a prayer. I do beg your pardon for this haste, but I must ask a favour of you. Would you be so kind as to send these papers, in the strictest confidence, to my father at this address? They do pertain in small part to what we discussed this morning. This must reach England quickly."

"Your trust is most welcome, and heartily returned." Sarah extended her basket as though showing a flower, and Joanna dropped papers and coins into it. "I shall have them sent within this day."

"I forget my manners. Would you visit us at Riverview for a few days, three weeks from Sunday? My husband must travel to the Carolinas then. We shall have a capital time, and I shall explain this little matter to you in greater detail."

"I do accept your kind invitation, and I look forward to hearing your story. I have a little memoir which you might wish to read. It is that of the Royal African, the Prince of Annamaboe, who was sold into slavery, freed, then lionised in England."

"I have read about this African," Joanna said. "In London, his story was printed on broadsheets everywhere."

Sarah looked past Joanna's shoulder. "Your husband is out the carriage and walking this way. I would greet him with scant courtesy, and so shall take my leave." She turned her back and walked into the depths of the garden.

"If we are to arrive at Riverview before dusk, we must to be on our way," Talbot said, watching Sarah's retreating back. "You need not tarry here. You will not be bored by the drive, I assure you."

After the ferry ride across the James River, the road to Riverview lay west, beside vast plantations of tobacco fields, the slaves working in the hot sun. Humbler houses clustered by dusty crossroads. Inns were often surrounded by wagons and rough-looking men. Showcroft's carriage picked its way around ox-carts and farm conveyances whose occupants either tipped their hats to acknowledge the ladies, or ignored Talbot's entourage. Talbot's orders were to stop once to water the horses. Food for his passengers was a trifling affair he had not bothered to arrange. Joanna and Katie were less bored by the drive than starved of food and drink. Neither had eaten a proper mid-day meal. Poor Luke cried so lustily that Talbot finally ordered the coach stopped and some privacy afforded Katie so that she could tend his needs.

While he spoke with Timothy, Joanna took the opportunity to study her husband. Talbot's square-jawed face was uniquely handsome. Piercing blue eyes flashed, and his precisely groomed hair showed little grey. His frame fit comfortably into the carriage. Timothy, on the other hand, had fair hair which tended to untidy locks, sharp, Nordic features, slender artist's hands and the rangy build which forced him to sit at an angle on the inadequate seat and stretch his legs for comfort.

It was late afternoon when the carriage turned into a tree-lined avenue. One quarter of a mile up the lane, it rumbled over a stone bridge and through an oak grove. After the carriage rounded a bend at the edge of an orchard, Joanna was rewarded with a view of the plantation's "great house," an imposing four-storey red brick structure, dominated by a high, white portico. Lawns and carefully laid-out and trimmed flowerbeds bordered the circular drive. Wide steps swept up to intricately carved front doors which stood open to welcome the party. Joanna counted the upper-storey windows twice. There were nine. "'Tis the most beautiful house I have ever seen!" Joanna laughed in delight. Nine had no possibility of dividing or multiplying into twelve. "And such a beautiful setting! So like England's pastoral countryside. Is that our staff?"

The household slaves, including Sukie and Henkle, stood in a line up from the foot of the steps, each with the right hand touching the left shoulder. As the carriage drew up, they bowed low in unison. When the driver got down to hold the team, he too bowed.

"Are we to inspect a continental army?" Katie said with a light laugh as Timothy assisted her out of the carriage.

"I do hazard, 'tis MacGregor's demanded salute," Timothy said. "They are trying to please."

"I declare, they are well regimented and uniformed," Joanna said as she looked at the line. "Mr. MacGregor did dress his slaves in clan colours, methinks."

"The tartan has its purpose. 'Tis easy to spot, if a slave is abroad without permission. Once we dispense with these formalities we shall eat. We expect a meal within the hour." Talbot said to Sukie.

"Yaus, Massa," Sukie said as she reached to take a squirming, whimpering Luke from Katie.

"You have done well to arrange the staff to meet us," Joanna said. "I shall take the time on the morrow to talk with each. 'Tis beyond me at the moment to think past my dinner."

"Wife, have you lost your senses? We do not lower ourselves to useless chatter with the slaves," Talbot said, taking Joanna's arm. "Your mind is addled with hunger, mayhap. I did mean to reach Riverview before dark. Come along. I am puffed-proud to show you the grand stairway."

Riverview's main hall and staircase, one of the finest in Virginia, was impressive. "My home hides its true beauty where only the privileged may see it," she said. From a spacious mid-hall the stairs rose to a second floor landing with large windows that overlooked gardens, pasturage and the James River. They turned, then rose again to third-floor bed chambers. At the back of the entrance hall, doors opened to a wide, covered verandah with a view of flower gardens.

"You do agree that it is as handsome as Willowbank?"

"Indeed I do. 'Tis lovely."

"Then we take dinner shortly. Sukie, show the ladies to their bed chambers." Talbot brought his watch from his waistcoat pocket. "Shall we set the meal for twenty minutes from now?"

With Luke in lusty cry, Joanna said, "We must first find the nursery and satisfy your son's appetites. Perhaps dinner may be served in an hour if Sukie can have it ready. It appears the good woman is busy with cooking and caring for baby too."

Katie opened her arms to take Luke, smiling at Sukie as she did so. "I'll see to the needs of this young gentleman," she said. "You have much to do to ready the meal."

"Sukie will find a wet nurse for the child so that Mrs. Sherrie need not bother with that tedious work," Talbot said.

"To be sure, Mr. Showcroft, 'tis no bother," Katie said. "I love little Luke. May we see the nursery?"

Sukie led the way up the open stairway to second-floor bed chambers. She turned left, opened a door for Joanna, crossed the hall and opened another door for Katie. "De nursery is above yo chamber, up de back stair, Ma'am. Ah be a-sendin Kudie to de nursery to care fo de babe until yo can be a-comin' to feed him. Hot water's a-trottin' from the cook house soon's ah kin tell Cansu to bring it."

"Sukie, have the trunks been put in our rooms?"

"Yaus'am."

"And, are the cheese boxes in my room?"

"Yaus'am. Dey be der. If I may say so, Ma'am, de cheese do better if it be stored in de cellar."

"I daresay you're correct, Sukie, but for now they shall stay in my room."

"Yaus'am" Sukie eased the door shut as she left, and Joanna heard her hurrying steps down the back stairs.

How Joanna longed to lie upon the curtained bed! It looked so inviting and every bone in her body ached. With an effort, she resisted the urge. Her trunk had been unpacked. Combs and brushes, and all the articles for a lady's grooming needs were arranged conveniently on the dressing-table. Her lace-trimmed nightgown had been laid out on the bed. A timid knock at the door interrupted her survey of the room. "Yes, come in," Joanna called.

A girl, no more than thirteen years of age, carried a large jug of hot water into the room and placed the jug on the washstand. Another child, even younger, came behind with a plate of biscuits and a small jug of milk. Without saying a word, they both curtsied and backed out of the room.

Where to put the cheese boxes? The only place they could be accommodated was under the bed. They were heavy and awkward, but she managed to tuck them underneath, toward the headboard. She would be truly happy when Mr. MacGregor came for his payment. Where to put her important papers? Joanna's choice was the heavy drapery that covered the windows, and trailed to the floor. She examined the lining and hem, then searched her reticule for her sewing knife to slit one of the inner seams. After the documents were tucked into the opening, she rearranged the folds, and moved a chair in front of the drape. That would do until she could repair the seam.

TIMOTHY and Talbot stood at the foot of the grand stairway awaiting Joanna's and Katie's appearance.

It does not pay to separate a hungry man from his food, Joanna thought, looking at the impatient men. Odd that distinctive slope to my husband's left shoulder when he's lounging. 'Tis like the affliction Uncle Jonathan had, and not a common thing to see a man with it. Is it a Yorkshire trait, handed from the conquering races and passed through the generations? Mr. Bushnell has such a hangdog look about him.

Joanna said aloud, "We are princesses descending to court, Katie. And there are two exceptionally fine gentlemen waiting for our attention. What more to ask but a decent meal?"

Dinner was a quiet affair. Joanna was too tired to enjoy the well-prepared food. She tried to contribute intelligently, steering conversation toward Timothy's proposed book and differing opinions about the origins of etched rocks.

Wonder upon wonder, she thought. How can two men with such diverse interests be drawn together? Although her father's opinion was that the strong attract the weak, Joanna felt some other thing bound these two opposites together.

When she could no longer follow the small talk, and noticed Talbot fingering his watch – a sure sign that he wished to end the meal – Joanna met Katie's eye, and the ladies excused themselves from the table.

"Do you not wish to continue your inspection of the house tonight?" Talbot asked.

"I assume that you would prefer to share a pipe and port with Mr. Bushnell," Joanna said. "Perhaps we may take the grand tour on the morrow? I shall take proper pleasure in it when sleep does not beckon."

CHAPTER ELEVEN
RIVERVIEW

JOANNA put the final stitches in the drape's seam as a thin golden line appeared in the eastern sky, the beginnings of the sunrise of her first full day at Riverview. She opened the window to peer out at the morning. Smells of river, black earth and lye soap seeped in. As life stirred around the dependencies, smoke rose from chimneys and women's laughter rippled through the gardens.

Throwing a light cloak over her nightgown, Joanna gathered her silver-backed hair brush and a silver-bound ivory comb, and made her way down the back stairway to the stoop, her chestnut hair hanging unbridled to her waist. The heavy morning dew soaked through her soft leather slippers and wet the bottom of her cloak as she picked her way across the rough stone walkway toward the soap smell.

"Sukie?" she called as she passed through the gate in the high wall. "Sukie, I did see you here only a few moments ago."

Sukie's imposing figure suddenly filled the doorway of a low brick building. Behind her clouds of steam smelling of lye soap billowed out the door. Sukie wiped her hands on her apron. "Somepin's wrong, Ma'am?"

Joanna waved her brush. "By my life, I cannot stand this hair one moment longer. I refuse to wear wigs or hairpieces to hide the evidence that it has not seen soap or water in weeks. I vow 'tis no exaggeration to say my hair crawls with legged unmentionables. It shall be washed before breakfast."

Sukie stepped aside to let Joanna enter the hot, damp laundry, where huge kettles of water boiled on the open hearth and two young girls bent over wooden tubs, scrubbing clothes. "Beg yo pardon, Ma'am?" Sukie said. "Missus MacGregor neber had her head scrubbed."

"I daresay 'tis a simple request. Do you not wash your own?" Never in her life had Joanna been in a laundry. She struggled to breathe in the sweltering room. Outside, the soap smell had been intriguingly pleasant. Inside, it was an affront to delicate nostrils. She peered around, trying to make sense of the women's activities.

"Yaus'am," Sukie said, "In de riber is where ah be a-washin' my hair."

"Well, 'tis no great matter. I need assistance ... a seat. 'Tis rather close in this room."

Sukie motioned to a stool at a table near the door and pushed a pile of clothing out of the way.

"I can think of no better place to wash hair." Joanna said. "There is a ready supply of hot water ... soap ... cotton drying-cloths."

Sukie shrugged and told one of the girls to get a large pottery bowl from a shelf near the fire. The second was sent to the store's closet in the house for an old bed sheet. She grated a bit of lye soap from a large bar onto a crockery plate and made a paste of it with vinegar and water.

"People in dese parts don't be at a-washin' their hair," Sukie said. "Once I washed de daughter's hair ..."

Joanna sat quietly waiting for more information. Sukie provided none.

Sukie poured boiling water into the pottery bowl, tempered it with cold water from an oak cask, then took one of the brushes and ran it through Joanna's hair. "Yo be right, Ma'am. There's critters a-walkin' round." She threw Joanna's brush and comb into a pot of boiling water, stirred with a wooden stick, fished them out and set them on a window ledge to dry.

"You must rid me of them by any means," Joanna said. "At home, I insisted on having my hair combed clean then washed twice a week. I will have it the same way here."

"Today a-washin' then a-combin'" Sukie placed the bowl in the Missus' lap. "Critters don't take kindly to lye soap 'n' bindegar."

Joanna obediently held her head over the bowl while Sukie wet her hair, applied the soap paste, then vigorously rubbed and scrubbed her scalp. Sukie took a close look to check on her progress. Still seeing bugs and eggs, she applied more soap paste to the scalp and long hair hanging into the bowl, then scrubbed with a real vengeance.

The scrubbing hurt, but Joanna held her tongue. *The woman is doing as I asked, and I must not be ninny enough to whine.*

When Sukie was satisfied, she suggested the Missus hang her hair over the floor while she threw the soapy water out the door. The bowl was filled again, this time with cold water tipped with vinegar. "Two mo waters and de job be done."

Curiosity got the better of Joanna. Aromatic vinaigrettes she had used to revive someone from a faint, to clean a wound, but never had she been exposed to such a strong, sour smell. It certainly cleared the cobbles out of the head and opened the air tubes. "You do use casked vinegar muchly for the laundry."

"Makes de clothes soft, Ma'am," Sukie said as she swathed Joanna's head in a bed sheet. "If de Missus come dis way?" Sukie led the way out a side door, which faced away from the main house, and pointed toward a wooden bench. As Joanna sat still, Sukie set herself to untangling the hair with the comb, gently humming while she worked.

"Sukie, I am exceedingly pleased that you washed my hair."

"Bedding needs a-changin'. Other Missus' hair needs a-washin'. They ain't only one of dem critters. Your girl is Cansu. She can wash de hair. Cansu's good girl, works hard, knows her place."

"Then I will take it very kindly to have her take care of me."

"You trust me?" Sukie asked gently combing the wet hair.

"I have seen no reason why I should not. 'Tis to our benefit that we work together, Sukie. Mr. Showcroft arrived only recently did he not? Well, then, who took such good care of the house and gardens in his absence? How was this place run if there was no one in authority?"

"Overseer Flanagan," Sukie spat the name. "He gib de orders. Massa Showcroft did come once afer Massa MacGregor sold Riverview, left instructions what to do afore de Missus arrive. No one disobeys Flanagan wifout dey be punishment."

"Would you be so kind as to explain a few things for me, Sukie? My father says that I am cursed with a curiosity that demands answers, but I see it as a blessing. This question I should not have considered asking, but you, and Henkle, for that matter, speak fair English."

"I be Virginia born'd," Sukie said. "Henkle be Maryland born'd. Oder question, Ma'am?"

"As I remember, you said that you were the cook-slave, but you are this day overseeing the laundry. And by my word, the table was set well, the meal nicely done up, the chambers made ready for our arrival. Were you responsible for all these attentions?"

"Yaus'am, ah sho was. Missus MacGregor done took fo' slaves wif her, so ah be a-cookin' and a-washin' and a-sweepin' and a-cleanin' til ah's just 'bout all wore'd out."

"Then you must be my housekeeper-slave, Sukie, and supervise others to do much of this work. I do wish to be a good ... owner ... but I am not acquainted with the ... rules. At Willowbank, our housekeeper has been with my family for more than thirty years. I daresay the manor ran very well with little help from me beyond a few minutes a day with her. I must rely on you here."

"Yaus'am. But ah do dat an' yo must get de cook-slave."

"Let me tell you, Sukie, 'tis not my intention to purchase slaves. I do wish to see them freed!"

"Massa Showcroft done brung ten wif him from de auction at Richmond to work de fields."

"That was done without my permission," Joanna said.

"They was needed fo' de tobacco, Ma'am."

"Well, I do not wish to buy someone to do my cooking."

Sukie took her time to work a knot out of the Missus hair, then said. "Den who be doin' all de work?"

"It would be good if you could manage both until I can acquire a cook or a housekeeper without having to purchase one, Sukie. Oh, what a devilish trying circumstance to be in! 'But then, our remedies oft in ourselves do lie.'"

"Yaus'am. Ah do de work fo' you while yo be 'rangin' it."

"Mrs. MacGregor took the housekeeper with her?"

"No, Ma'am. Missus MacGregor was bein' her own housekeeper. She gib de orders! She was not de grand lady, like you be, Ma'am."

"Sukie, I wonder about so many things I find here. The first is difficult: why do African men and boys turn their eyes to the ground when they pass on the street? Upon my word, the men and boys look forever at their feet."

"Dat's de law, Ma'am. De law say dey not look white Missus in de face. Dey do ... dey rape ... if dey look at a white Missus."

"How absolutely silly," said Joanna. "To be sure, servants must show respect, but to examine one's feet all the day ... Another question is why, in villages and towns, do they scurry away when a white man approaches? This I did see in Williamsburg."

"Dat's de law, too, Ma'am. De law be written dat no more'n five slaves be in one place wifout Massa's permission or oberseer's orders."

"What other absurd rules are there, may I ask?"

Sukie combed steadily. "We mus' ask Massa's permission to leave de plantation to see our man. We must carry de paper on de road. An' Flannigan, he don't give de paper."

"If you break the rules, Sukie?"

"Wif Flanagan, de cat-o'-nine tails. Dey be a whippin', fo' sho'."

"How barbaric!"

"Flannigan be hard man, Ma'am."

"It makes no sense! Even if he is so cruel, why would anyone mark up a woman's back like that?"

"Sometimes he beat de house slaves wif a stick on de feet. Few have hand chop' off if dey be a-stealin' de chicken for dey' pot."

"Oh," cried Joanna, "Stop! I shall be ill!"

"It be de truf, Ma'am."

"Has it happened at Riverview?" When Sukie said nothing, Joanna continued. "Oh my dear, it has, hasn't it, under this Mr. Flanagan. I tell you it shall not happen again, not while I am here."

"I like to be a-believin', Ma'am."

"You may believe, Sukie. My father owns Riverview but I am the authority here. Oh! My word, what is the time, Sukie?"

Sukie shrugged, laughed heartily and squinted at the rising sun. "Dew's gold. Sky's pink. It be round 'bout half past de hour of five."

"A silly question, was it not? You've no watch. I must not tarry, Sukie. My husband and Mr. Bushnell will be looking for their breakfast."

"Den I scuttle," Sukie said. "I cook afore dey eat."

Joanna laughed. "My humblest thanks Sukie, for tending to my hair."

"Massa said not to t'ank de slaves."

"I believe it was mentioned," Joanna said. "But I do give thanks when, and to whom, I please."

"Please, Ma'am. If you sell slaves and dey be used to freedoms de Massas not usually gib, dey suffer by de new Massa. It be no favour to show kindness if you be a-sellin' us over soon."

"I assure you that I have no intention of selling anyone," Joanna said.

"De time be a-comin'," Sukie said. "De time be a-comin' ..."

"Your ma ... husband, what does he do at Riverview?" As soon as Joanna asked the question she remembered the thread of the previous conversation. "Tell me truly. You must have a paper to visit your husband. He does not reside at Riverview."

"Massa Showcroft sol' him to plantation twenty mile over. Twenty mile be de long walk, and nobody give permission for Juba to come to me. He leave widout de paper, he be whip'."

"Pray, why was he sold?"

"Flanagan tol' Massa Showcroft Juba stole wood to fix roofs at de gang quarters.

They be leakin' and oder field slaves do de same. Juba be de one Massa punish'. He be sold away from me."

"And your children, Sukie? You have not mentioned their names?"

"They be sold, long ago as young chillen, all gone way now ..." Tears welled up in Sukie's eyes then ran down her cheeks. "Ah be sorry Ma'am. I miss dem so."

Impulsively, Joanna reached to touch Sukie's arm. "I am sorry, Sukie."

"Ah loss all my chillen, and then I loss my man."

Joanna, her voice breaking, shook her head. "That is another thing that will change here. Where is your husband?"

"Sharmar," Sukie said. "South from here."

"And your children?"

"Ah don' know, Ma'am. Dey be so young when they be sold, and ah don' know where dey be now."

"Sukie, believe me," Joanna placed her hands on Sukie's shoulders. She would have embraced the black woman, but feared they would both break down completely. "I will do everything in my power to right this abhorrent circumstance."

CHAPTER TWELVE
RIVERVIEW

ALTHOUGH the mansion was much smaller than Willowbank, it was far more extensive inside than it appeared from the outside. The hallways ran east to west from the central stairway, making exploration of the plantation house easy. Joanna and Katie first looked through storage rooms – wine, fruit and vegetable cellars on the lowest level – with Sukie as guide.

"To be sure," Katie said. "Riverview will never lack victuals. 'Tis not yet harvest, yet your cellars are full."

"I confess I never did inspect the work rooms at Willowbank. I assumed all ran like a clock of its own accord. To see these makes me think all the better of the housekeepers and gardeners who kept us in good presence and shape."

The reception hall opened into a spacious dining parlour. Across the back corridor from the reception and dining parlour, windows in the ladies' day room opened onto rose arbours and formal gardens.

"Methinks with a few new appointments, this shall be our retreat from daily botherations," Joanna said.

To the left of the hall, a library opened onto the bed chamber that had been assigned to Timothy Bushnell. The library, to Joanna's standards, seemed sparse. It had not a tickling of the vast collection at Willowbank. "With a wee man to rear and his good schooling to think of, I will fill this room with books. Why, Katie, not one of Shakespeare's works is here!" she said. "And paintings. A library must have artistic works."

The smoking room, a richly smelling, mellow retreat, opened across the back corridor from the library. A small room at the end of the left hall had a second door opening to the outside, which caught Joanna's attention. "This is an office for Mr. Bushnell. See, the field workers can come and speak with him without tracking dirt through the hall."

In the corridors, two sets of back stairs served each floor, one to the left and one to the right of the central hall. Sukie showed them eight chambers on the second floor – four to left and four to right of the central stairway, and the same number on the third floor. "Ma'am, you like to see de attic and storerooms?"

"I believe we have taken too much of your time, Sukie. Could you show us the various outbuildings from the back stoop?" Joanna said. She turned to Cansu, who had been silently shadowing their steps. "Have Kudie bring Jonathan Luke to join us, that we may enjoy the sweet babe and the beauty of the garden."

Sukie, pointing as they emerged from the house onto the raised porch, told them, "Weavery and laundry be hid from de main house with hedges and slave gates. Massa MacGregor built dependencies fo' de house slaves; oder side, Kudie's weaving house, behind de high brick fence. Gang quarters, ober dere, back o' de woods. Carriage house, hen house, woodshed back o' de vege'ble gardens. Cookhouse right by de main house. And there be lofts ober de weavery and in de carriage house."

"I am very much obliged to you for your attentions, Sukie. ... Ah – " Joanna held out her arms as Kudie appeared with Luke riding her hip. He squealed and plunged for her arms.

Katie jumped to help, and Luke grabbed for her as well. Set down upon the path, Luke jumped and danced, grinning up at his mother, with Kudie holding one hand and Katie the other.

Joanna bent to touch his curls. "We shall give this active little man some air and walk in the gardens."

"Ma'am?" Sukie stood at the top of the wooden steps that led down to the garden.

"Yes, Sukie?" Joanna looked up, her attention only halfway drawn from Luke and his antics.

"Ma'am, dey be young woman called Willow, Massa bought wif slaves dis time for the ... fields. Yo' put her in de cook house and I be a-teachin' her to cook like me. She can be good cook-slave. Den I keep watch on her too ..."

"A prudent thought, Sukie," Joanna said. Sukie was indeed her ally. "Would you bring Willow to me?"

By the time Talbot found Joanna strolling through the vegetable gardens, Katie and Kudie had taken Luke back to the house for his afternoon rest. Talbot's manner was formal, as always, yet there was an endearing eagerness as he presented the virtues of this plantation he had bought for her with her father's money.

"Have you been exploring, Wife? I've been told that a dozen varieties of grapes grow on arbours next to the slave fence. Riverview has peach, pear and apple trees in the walled garden." He gestured expansively, sweeping his arm to encompass the view. "Toward the river, beyond the lawns and necessities, lies pasturage for sheep, milch cows and horses."

"'Tis beautiful, Husband. You chose well." She smiled up at him. "Shall we take a rest in the rose garden? I declare my feet are worn to my knees, I have walked so far today. Jonathan Luke did test us with his vigor. Katie tends him now."

My husband seems pleased today, Joanna thought as they made their way to a bench beneath the rose arbour.

"'Tis not on the regal scale of the manor at Willowbank; yet, does Riverview truly meet your expectations for a home in Virginia?" Talbot asked.

"Riverview appears comfortable. To be sure, the wait has been long and tedious until we could be together as a family. But I am here now – "

"Being together as 'a family' is important for you? My father and I were ... never close of company. My mother and I were very good friends."

"Truly, I loved both Mother and Father," Joanna said. "Mother's death, just before we wed, distressed me." She glanced at Talbot. "Mother was bitterly opposed to our marriage."

Talbot nodded. "And, Wife, did she voice particular concerns?"

"She did not. Mother's views and opinions often differed from Father's. Nay, I ought not have mentioned it. You seem so happy today 'tis unforgivable to introduce such talk." Joanna reached for a yellow rose. "But talk of fathers touches upon a circumstance that requires an explanation."

"What might that be?"

Joanna toyed with the rose. "I do wonder what beastly individual would send a father away from his family?"

"Send a – ? Whose father?"

"Sukie's husband."

Talbot grabbed for Joanna's arm. "Did the woman bother you with it? Did she?"

The rose fell to the ground as Joanna recoiled from his grasp. "I asked Sukie this morning while she was dressing my hair what work her husband did on the plantation. She said he did none here, that he had been sold to Sharmar. She did but answer my question."

Talbot stood and turned his back to Joanna. "By heaven, Joanna, you shall not meddle in the affairs of Riverview. Juba's sale does not concern you."

Joanna stood and stared at Talbot's back. "You mistake, Husband. Selling him *is* my concern. He belonged to my father, and so he was sold wrongfully."

Talbot swung around to confront Joanna. "You know nothing of slaves and their handling."

"I know that Sukie's husband was torn away with no thought of his family."

"Sukie's *husband?*" Talbot said with a short laugh. "Slaves do not marry. If she was tied up with him, so much the worse for her."

"Yet, the man was the property of my father, and I should have been consulted."

"Let us not split hairs, Wife. If you recall, you were on the high seas when he was sold. What matters it, Wife? Like cordwood, he can be sold."

"Sir, I demand that he be bought back. I care not what the circumstances. I care not what he did. He shall be returned to Riverview. You did separate a man from his wife, and that is cruel."

"I'll not tolerate your contradictions. He was insubordinate. He shall remain at Sharmar."

"And I, Sir, am ordering him returned immediately."

"The matter is easily settled. I need only sell the wife. The master at Sharmar will buy a good, strong woman for his fields."

"You cannot sell what is not yours. And you have no authority to punish Sukie for speaking to me. Do not scorn me, Sir." Joanna turned on her heel and made her exit, feeling his eyes on her retreating back. "Four and twenty hours, and we've had two confrontations," she muttered. "The devil take the man! He cannot be reasoned with."

In her bedchamber, Joanna paced the floor, fuming. "He shall beg my pardon. And return Sukie's husband. I'll have naught to do with him until he does." She slid the bolt on the door that linked their rooms. "I have lived without my husband's intimacy for months at a time; 'tis no bother to me now."

Suddenly, Joanna halted. "Silly girl," she scolded the image in her looking glass. "You have put yourself into such a dither that you forget 'tis for *you* to bargain the return of Sukie's husband."

CHAPTER THIRTEEN
THE BARBADOS

WITH a new moon and a myriad of stars overhead, there was no better place to be on a warm November night than in the bath house at Bush Hill. The gentle swish of the windmill's blades cutting through the air mingled with night-song from the savannah and the beat of drums from the slave quarters. Makem lay in the copper-lined bath soaking away the stench of the slave ship. It was the first bath he'd taken since the hot springs at Horta. "Five months is a long time to endure chiggers in the pants, Caliganto."

"And buggers in the belfry," Caliganto said, seated beside the tub, a sponge in one hand, his eyes on the book in the other.

"Had I a brimming glass, I'd toast Captain Croftan for once again allowing us the use of his bath house. Devil of it is, those Washington brothers bathe so often that we must move quick to get in here between their ablutions. Know you aught of them?"

Caliganto delivered a soft grunt and continued to read.

Unabashed, Makem scrubbed at one foot and then the other, reveling in the warm water and the leisure to gossip. "Young Lawrence, the one who coughs, looks not long for this life, but that George is a strapping man. He has a most inquisitive mind, does young George. They have rented Bush Hill, and take the baths daily." Makem sank further into the tub.

"That same young George did give me tolerable respect," Caliganto said, "after he learned I was no slave to leap to at his beck and call. Regardless his error, a hot bath is a privilege."

"A privilege and a luxury! The loquacious Miss Bayleys do need a word dropt in their ear. They smelled the least whiff of musty when I visited the plantation to settle accounts this morning. The scent of a lady is ripe indeed when water has not caressed her skin for many a day," Makem said.

"As is the scent of a man right off a slave ship," Caliganto murmured.

Makem glanced around the room. Other than wall pegs that held an assortment of clothing, the room, lit by a half dozen lanterns, was unadorned. Several chairs and a small table that held shaving accouterments, a ceramic bowl and pitcher stood near the open door. "Who needs the trappings of wealth? We have all any man can desire – fire, shelter, fish for our bellies, a warm tropical night for our ablutions, and a bare-breasted wench at beck and call if we're so inclined. What more could we ask, Caliganto?"

"The satisfaction of you tying your tongue and getting on with your over-long ablutions. Until you get out the bath, I am a pauper with a sponge. Ask me kindly, and promise to do the same for me, and I might be persuaded to scrub your back."

"Rare is the proper word for your present odoriferous condition, you blackguard."

"Better rare than raw."

Ndamma quietly entered the room, copper bucket in hand. Caliganto stuck his hand in to test the water and nodded. "Bend your head, Makem."

With a deft flip, Ndamma poured a stream of hot water over Makem's head.

"Delicious delirium," Makem said when Barika appeared behind Ndamma to repeat the cataract. "But, is it enough, Caliganto? You are not of the same rousing spirit since we departed Africa."

"You too have changed, my friend – since Horta. You question more, swear less."

"Aye, well ... I am disturbed by the plight of the Vision-in-Blue. We are both well acquainted with Talbot Showcroft. Methinks many factors play in the lady's life. I have some familiarity with Virginia's marriage laws. Charles Turnbull is a wealthy man, and his daughter is his only heir. Showcroft is not one to await nature to provide him with a dead man's shoes. Do you mind the information Bushnell confided to us? Think you the lady does truly know her husband's character? I fear her thirst for adventure has led her into troubled waters."

With a quick motion, Caliganto snatched a moth from the air as it fluttered over the tub. "Perhaps you misjudge Mrs. Showcroft's capabilities? She adventured the fête very handily."

"Aye, 'tis true. She is no green girl, but an exceptional lady – and beautiful. She appeals to me profoundly."

"As well she should, for you are no youth yourself, Makem. I see why you are stirred when you think long on the lady."

"It would be a betrayal of my manhood if I were not."

"Makem, you sea scoundrel, you are enamoured of Mrs. Showcroft!"

"To the depth of the cave, but I am not callow enough to believe she'd return that love."

"Why would any lady not give you the eye? You are devilish handsome, and William-and-Mary, *and* Baltimore educated, to boot. The side I see is not what you delight in presenting to the world."

"Ah, the paint that colours the world. What would my scurvy crew think if I addressed them thus:" Makem lifted his hand in a courtly flourish. "'Gentleman, pray would you raise the jib, if you please' – rather than with my usually handsome volley of compliments. And what, Caliganto, would they say if they knew you read Defoe?"

"'Twas you taught me how to read. You showed no hesitation when I asked to learn. Sailors would think no less of us, but they'd never obey orders if we did not round on them in the language of the sea."

"I am never coarse or vulgar but of necessity. Nevertheless, my eccentricities include a chivalrous bent. I have a concern for Mrs. Showcroft and her babe."

"Then, Makem, hear me out." Caliganto went to peer out the door. Ndamma and Barika were out of sight. Satisfied, he sat down. "Did I not take liberty of choosing privilege slaves this run?"

"You did."

"My first thought – order them fed, washed, shaved, oiled and sold. If my heart were not so large I should still sell them for a tidy sum. But conscience found me, for they are countrymen, Wangara, from the far mountains of the Fula Jallon. They were betrayed by one who felt slighted over some petty dispute. They were captured, sold to a Mandingo and marched to the coast where by hap-chance we bought them. Ndamma's markings gave me the clue. Both are healthy and learn quickly, as we have found out."

Makem laughed. "You do have a heart, Caliganto."

"If the occasion demands that it beat."

"Makem's Rant will be overrun with two-legged vermin, methinks."

"Nay, hear out my wandering tongue. I do not want them sold as whip-fodder for some ill-tempered master. My rare heartbeat also muses on Mrs. Showcroft. She was pleased that I could read, and surprised I could write. Of more importance, she gave me the respect of a free man, something that even after twelve years of freedom, does not occur often enough."

"Caliganto. You are as much a sap as I for that lady."

"I am more a sap for my countrymen."

"Human nature is the same in every country and amongst all complexions. All have pressing arguments for selling and buying their fellow men – hunger – war. The need for slaves to harvest sugar in the West Indies grows ever more urgent, and fuels greed on both sides of the Atlantic. And, I am not averse to filling a need when the spirit moves me. Neither are you. I believe some Africans are better off in America, even in less than ideal circumstances."

"But there must come a time, Makem, when conscience rather than money drives our decisions. One cannot drain a land of its people without draining oneself of humanity. We have both heard of John Newton, who claims to have seen the light, yet still he lends his talents to Manesty. He still captains a slaver, trades slaves, but says he now treats his cargo humanely. Is the man to be believed? Must he not leave the slave trade to make good his convictions?"

"Newton's opinions give pause for thoughtful reflection, nevertheless they are, for the time, mere opinions. Such people as Newton mean well, but until they break their own chain of abuse, their words are useless. I try to treat my cargo humanely, but have not reached the crossing where I find any of my actions abhorrent. Caliganto, you have been a slave, much whipped and abused. Why do you stay with me, my friend?"

"I do not judge you harshly and can think of no better place than by your side, my worthy friend. We share trust and loyalty, friendship and hearth-side. I desire no more – and no less than to be with you on the day you decide to become a lubber of the land, harvesting corn, rather than a tiller of the sea, harvesting slaves."

"I am indebted to you, Caliganto, for many things, including my life. I respect your judgement."

"No more indebted than I to you. Tell me. What are your thoughts about Ndamma and Barika? If a scoundrel like you can turn me from a piece of coal into a golden nugget, think what miracles can be wrought by Mrs. Showcroft upon Ndamma."

"Unless you wish them returned to their tribe, the young warriors would have no better situation," Makem said.

"Returned to Africa and given their freedom, they would undoubtedly be captured and sold again, into much worse circumstances. Freed here, they would meet the same fate. Fair find is fair game."

"Then what shall we do with them?" Makem asked.

"Take them to Virginia and give them to Mrs. Showcroft and Mrs. Sherrie. The ladies shall decide what should be done with Ndamma and Barika. If they must remain slaves, so be it. If freed, the return to Africa is at their choice, not ours. If good is to come of this, it will be that Ndamma and Barika will see what America holds for Africans if they are willing to wait and strive for it."

"Ndamma and Barika will be given over, Caliganto, but that does not abate my concern for Mrs. Showcroft and her babe."

"Ah," Caliganto said, "you bathe, and do not think beyond your bath-water. Ndamma and Barika can be much more than house servants. They can be your eyes and ears."

Riverview

8 November, 1751

Dearest Father:

I have not until today been able to find the time to write and I do Apologize. My last letter was the few unsatisfactory lines sent from Williamsburg in June. I shall now make up for my Lack of Attention. But where to begin?

Talbot left two weeks after I arrived for the Carolinas and did not return until the first of November, even though he said he would be back for the Harvest. No Explanation was given, and I chose not to question him about it. I'm learning to choose my Battles more carefully.

You no doubt are desirous of information about Jonathan Luke. My sweet baby has been through rather trying times recently. His Nurse, Katie Sherrie, sickened with a high Fever and took to her bed. Her Condition prevented her from nursing Luke, and he was without Milk. Fortunately, he had already learned to eat with a Spoon and silver Pusher. With the slave Kudie's assistance, I taught him how to drink from a Cup. Kudie is a clever woman; Weaving is one of her Talents. Now that Katie is better, Luke no longer requires her Ministrations. Oh, but we do enjoy his manly little Company!

I keep Luke close much of the time and lavish Attentions on him, doubly so to make up for his father's Absence. I must agree with you now that it was right he not be named after Talbot, but for his Great-Uncle Jonathan. That you and Talbot could agree to the combination of your brother's Name and your Middle Name amuses me.

I find that I am not much surprised by anything now. A Situation arose when one of your male slaves was sold, without my Permission. The slave, Juba, is husband to Sukie. Husband is perhaps not the correct word to use, as there is no blessing allowed in the Church. Another slave performs a broom-stick ceremony. As Sukie is invaluable to household operation, and, what is of more importance, no man should be separated from his Wife in such a cruel way, it was imperative that the man be Returned to resume his rightful place here.

Because Juba was sold to Sharmar, a large Plantation some miles away, I enlisted Mr. Bushnell's help to see that Juba was returned. A Letter was sent the plantation Owner, a Mr. Smart, explaining the Tangle. When he did not Reply, Mr. Bushnell rode down to meet with the man. Of course, the fellow refused to Listen, did not sell Juba back to Riverview. I then spoke with Advocate Shand who wrote a Letter, explaining that the sale was Invalid, because Talbot had no Authority to act on your Behalf.

Mr. Shand rode to Sharmar to deliver the letter By Hand and found that Juba was no longer there. He had been sent to Another Plantation, owned by the same man. Verily, we had to threaten an Action in Court before Smart agreed to sell Juba back to you, that is, to me, for the same Price he had paid. It was three weeks before Mr. Bushnell collected Juba.

It was apparent from his wounds that Sharmar's Overseer and Owner, took their Frustrations out on the poor man. Why? Why must some people treat others like dogs? Is there an Answer?

At Riverview, we were busy this Autumn putting-by produce and Fruit for the Winter Months. With so many mouths to feed, Sukie gathered every available person to assist with Pickling, Salting and Drying. I was never Party to such activity at Willowbank, as all was in the hands of Housekeeper, Cook and Gardeners. Our new Cook, Willow, still has much to learn, but Sukie is a capable Teacher and will soon have her making Gâteau Noir and Boeuf avec les Épices.

I do miss your special blends of Tea, Father and wonder if you could have a Six Month's supply shipped to Riverview. If you could include a selection of fresh Spices, Cinnamon being one that is in short supply at the moment, we would all be Grateful.

In Closing I send my fondest Love and I shall give Luke a kiss for you. Mr. Bushnell asks to be Remembered as well.

Yours affectionately,
Joanna.

CHAPTER FOURTEEN
MAKEM'S RETURN
Riverview, December 2, 1751

A VOLLEY of gunfire brought everyone to the front steps. An odd mounted procession came into view at the bend in the carriage road, led by none other than Captain Anthony Makem. He was followed by Caliganto and Allan. Behind them one African rode a mule and another drove a wagon loaded with boxes, trunks and packs.

"Makem, me man!" Talbot called. "Have you no respect for the Sabbath?"

"The Sabbath, is it?" Makem shouted back. "Then God be praised, I'm here."

Henkle and several small boys scurried out to hold bridles. Allan leapt from the saddle and ran for Katie who was dashing for him. He caught her up and swung her off her feet, whirling round and round in a circle of joy. He didn't let her down until they had shared a long and passionate kiss. Whatever endearments he whispered into her ear made his wife blush and giggle like a schoolgirl.

Makem dismounted and watched with a grin as he walked toward the group now assembled at the bottom of the steps. "Restraint my dear fellow!" Makem laughed. "'Tis the Sabbath, ye heathen, when entreaties are made to God, not to a wife." The bearded giant swaggered toward Joanna. When he stood head and shoulders above her, Makem swept an exaggerated leg, ceremoniously taking Joanna's hand to kiss. "Mrs. Showcroft, a pleasure once again."

"You have been too long among Frenchmen," Talbot said, "that you slobber over my wife's hand."

"*Mais oui*, Showcroft, you jealous beggar. I have taken the liberty of bringing a shipment that was languishing in a warehouse on the docks at New Haven. Bushnell, not such a dastardly scar after all, I see." Makem slapped Timothy on the back then shook Talbot's hand. "Begorrah, I did trot these lads all the way from Africa for you, Showcroft."

"And a healthy pair they appear," Talbot said. "How much?"

Makem held up his hand. "But coming up your carriage way, we decided not to sell them to you." He motioned to Caliganto to bring Ndamma and Barika forward. "Ladies." Makem winked and clapped his hands to gain their attention.

Joanna could not help but smile. Captain Makem was certainly playing the act to its fullest.

"I am in a generous mood today, it being the Sabbath and all that," Makem said. "Therefore, to you, Mrs. Showcroft, I give Ndamma, Griot of his tribe."

Ndamma, pushed by Caliganto toward Joanna, fell on his knees at her feet.

"Griot is a title given? A position like a Prince?" Joanna asked.

"My good lady, a Griot, is a tribal history keeper. To be such, he must have a good memory. A tradition in his homeland is to keep history through story telling. I hazard that his abilities will serve him well, and you. And for Mrs. Sherrie, I present Barika, son of the Chief of the same tribe."

Barika mimicked Ndamma, throwing himself at Katie's feet.

"Captain, please tell them to rise," said Joanna. "Welcome to Riverview," she managed before her husband interrupted.

"Becoming rather friendly with your cargo, Makem?" Talbot's eyebrows arched in surprise. "When has it become *de rigueur* to name your merchandise? Are you not the gentleman who has said, 'If you give them a name, you give them a face'?"

"My good man, 'tis a special occasion," Makem said. "These two have carried names since Caliganto introduced them as tribesmen and kept them as privilege slaves."

"Doth a kind heart perhaps beat in that chest, after all, Captain Makem?" Joanna asked.

"Name a slave and command a higher price for him," Talbot said. "You are not handing this pair off. How much must come out of my purse, Makem? I should hazard that these are each worth of at least thirty pounds."

"And I insist, no price. Ndamma is our gift to Mrs. Showcroft. Barika is our gift to Mrs. Sherrie."

"Why?" Talbot's eyes narrowed.

"Why?" said Makem. "It being very near the festive season and as 'tis the end of an eventful trip, we are in a generous mood."

"Henkle," Talbot ordered. "Take these slaves to the quarters."

"I think not," said Makem. "'Tis for Mrs. Showcroft and Mrs. Sherrie to decide whether they labour in the house or fields. A Griot should not be sent to the fields. Neither should the son of a chief."

Joanna took her cue from Makem's assertion. "If Katie is in agreement, Henkle may take these two young men to the cookhouse where Sukie can find suitable clothing and a meal. It will be decided later where they will billet."

"Wife!" Talbot exclaimed. "Upon my word, leave well enough alone."

"As Captain Makem said, this one ... Ndamma? ... is his gift to me. The other ... Barika ... was presented to Katie. I am quite certain that she will agree with my decision."

"Oh, yes." Katie, clinging to Allan, nodded agreement.

After Caliganto spoke quietly to Ndamma and Barika, they stood and, eyes to the ground, backed away from the ladies.

"Then, gentlemen, shall we think of unloading this wagon?" Makem spoke to Talbot but kept his eyes on Joanna. "Caliganto, would you see to it, and then join Ndamma and Barika in the cookhouse while I induce the Lord and Lady of the manor, and their friends, to give me a good, long drink of something much stronger than water."

"Caliganto, if you please," Joanna said. "Henkle does know where the cargo must go until it can be sorted properly."

Talbot pulled her roughly up the steps by her arm. "Thunderation, do not talk to slaves as though they were gentlemen of the first order."

"Ah, to be sure, Showcroft," Makem said. "When one talks to slaves, one must shout and swear because one considers them stupid, must one not? In truth, Caliganto is a free man. He could be seated among us at your groaning board if an invitation were extended – and if he chose to do so."

"By the Lord," Talbot said. "You have been too long at sea, Makem. Have you forgotten your manners? This is Mr. Sherrie, I presume."

Makem slapped his forehead. "Sherrie, my friend!" he called across the step. "Tarry not with your wife. M' Lord desires an introduction. By your leave, this is the manor-house man I have been jawing about. Showcroft, here is Allan Sherrie, a young fellow I met ... just off ship ... looking for his good wife at Riverview."

"Welcome to Riverview," Talbot said. "Joanna, this is – "

Joanna offered her hand. "'Tis a pleasure to meet you again, Mr. Sherrie."

"I assumed you had not met Mr. Sherrie."

"How silly of me, that I did not mention we ... met ... briefly."

Makem broke into the awkward conversation. "A drink, if you please, Lord of the Manor. It has been a thirsty ride. My friend Sherrie will attest to that honest fact. Mrs. Showcroft, I do not see your child. He'll be a sturdy fellow now."

"Luke is cutting teeth, Captain Makem. He runs a fever. Kudie has his care at the moment."

As the group entered the great hall, Joanna excused herself, saying she had to speak with Sukie about the meal. She found Caliganto, Ndamma and Barika at the cookhouse table devouring cornbread and molasses. The two young men leapt to their feet and went down on their knees again when they saw their mistress.

"Please, Caliganto, you must tell them not to grovel. Sukie, where can these young men be billeted?"

"Dey kin sleep in de loft ober de carriage house, Ma'am."

"Would you be so kind as to see that they have bedding?"

"Yaus'am. You want Massa Caliganto in de carriage house too?"

Joanna hesitated. Where does one lodge a free black man? Perhaps Makem would expect Caliganto to share his room.

"By your leave, Mrs. Showcroft," Caliganto said. "The carriage house would be best. Ndamma and Barika will need settling in."

Joanna nodded, grateful this African gentleman had the grace to rescue her from the dilemma. "Thank you, Caliganto. Then Sukie, can you serve dinner in one hour? I must assume that Captain Makem has not broken bread for some hours."

"Yaus'am, I kin do dat."

Dinner was an interesting affair. Allan and Katie seemed to have difficulty giving attention to the conversation.

Joanna envied their intimacy. "It has been such a stretch since the Sherries have been together and they do have such an affection for each other."

"The love-sick calf missed her like a sane man misses smoke and drink," Makem said.

Talbot said to Joanna. "Makem tells me the slave he gave you is clever and should be given consideration for the child's servant. I do maintain a healthy male slave must learn a trade or work the tobacco. But that decision is beyond my making. He is yours."

Ndamma and Barika don't need to feel Flanagan's lash or Talbot's tongue, Joanna thought. Taking her cue from Makem's previous counsel, she said, "Ndamma will be trained for house duty. After a period of time – when he is better known by myself – I will consider the decision to have him attend Luke."

When Makem took an opportunity to wink boldly at her down the table, Joanna blushed mightily and gave a quick glance at Talbot, who was busy cutting cheese and missed the flirtatious, risky act. "May I be so bold as to ask, what your plans are, Captain Makem?"

"With your kind permission, Mrs. Showcroft, I wish to spend the Yule season at Riverview. I will put to sea again in late February at the earliest."

"Of course, you must be our guest," Joanna said. "We are planning a hunt and Grand Ball that I am sure you will enjoy, Captain Makem."

"It makes no matter whether you give permission or not," said Talbot. "Makem does as he pleases. He will sponge our hospitality for as long as he sees fit." Talbot helped himself to apple cake. "You do appear to be acquainted with my wife, Makem? Strange that you did not see fit to mention her in our frequent conversations. I do recall a meeting in February, in Williamsburg, where you expressed surprise I was married."

"We did meet briefly in Horta when the *Black Wing* and the *Charlotte* lay over for repairs in May. That is where I met your good wife and your heir."

"I was under the impression you knew Joanna's father," Talbot said. "Did you not say so, Joanna?"

"Ah. Well ..." Makem raised his eyebrows at Joanna. "Being introduced to the daughter of the manor, and meeting a married lady – with a name, as you say – is a very different thing."

Although Talbot seemed satisfied, Makem had not finished with him. "Verily, I am not the only cheat in this room. In all our meetings over the past four years, you did not tell me you had married a Joanna Turnbull."

"Enough." Talbot filled his wine glass. "Mayhap I erred in not naming my wife." He raised the glass in toast. "To Joanna!"

"Joanna!" Makem raised his glass high, drained it, and held it out for Henkle to fill it again.

Joanna acknowledged the toast. Then, knowing the men were ready for their port, cigars and privacy, she sought Katie's eye and found that Katie had been seeking hers. "By your leave, gentlemen? You must have much to say."

As soon as the ladies reached the drawing room, they were joined by Allan, who had had little trouble excusing himself from the cigars and port. Joanna sent Katie and Allan on their way, their hands finding each other, and Katie's head resting upon Allan's shoulder.

In a few minutes, she glanced out the window, and spied Allan and Katie strolling toward the back stoop, arms entwined. Allan, muscular from his months at sea, kept his gaze fixed upon Katie's pretty face. The look of glowing adoration on Katie's face gave Joanna an ache in her heart.

The course of love does smoothly run for the Sherries. I have never gazed at my husband with such adulation, Joanna thought, as she made her way to her bedchamber. She reached into the drapery's hem and retrieved Anthony's copy of the purchase document. Oh dear, she wondered. When did I begun to think of the Captain in the intimacy of his Christian name?

Joanna next checked the bedchamber that had been assigned the Captain. Talbot never spoke of his marriage until February of this year, she thought as she straightened a pillow. Did it mean so little to him? Had Talbot ever glanced adoringly at her as Allan did toward Katie? Put his arm around her of a tender moment? She placed the copy of the document on a table beside the bed. Why was she happier to see the Captain ride up the carriageway than Talbot when he had arrived from the south?

CALIGANTO, Ndamma and Barika were standing by the hearth when she entered the cookhouse again. The fire's light dancing off his tall frame outlined the raised markings on Ndamma's chest. Barika, equally tall, had no distinctive marks. Though the young men did not go down on their knees they did avert their eyes.

"Henkle got de clothing, Ma'am," Sukie stood by the table sorting clothes.

"'Twould be best if the men tend the flower and vegetable gardens while learning the work of the house." Joanna turned to Caliganto. "I assume these young men are here due in part to your entreaty with the Captain?"

"By your leave, Mrs. Showcroft, they are from my tribe. I could not bide them sold to a harsh master."

"Would you please explain to Ndamma and ... Barika that they will be clothed, fed, taught. If I find Ndamma trustworthy, he shall be made responsible for Jonathan Luke. If they obey, no harm will come to them at my hands. If not, of course ..."

"They will punished," Caliganto said.

"Be kind enough to tell them that Sukie will give them orders as well as I, and that I do respect Ndamma's position as a history keeper. That must be important for him."

"Captain Makem says he is a library on feet," Caliganto said. He turned to Ndamma and Barika and began an animated conversation in Fula.

"Caliganto, your ability to speak many languages is impressive," Joanna said.

Caliganto thanked her with a short bow. "By your leave, Ma'am, Ndamma wishes you to bring him a pebble. It is important that it be small, one you like and that you give it into his hand. By handing him a stone, you add your story to his bag of stones. 'Tis an honour to be included."

"His bag of stones?"

"It is the Griot's way of remembering people."

"'Tis an unusual request," Joanna said. She remembered an accretion of colourful pebbles by the spring house. With Henkle holding a lantern, she searched the pile, discarded some of the heavier ones and finally picked up a white quartz stone tipped with yellow. Returning to the cookhouse, she handed it to Ndamma who turned it over several times before nodding approval.

Sukie followed Joanna from the cookhouse. "Ma'am, Flanagan will be a-beatin' Ndamma and Barika."

Joanna stopped walking. "Why?"

"So they know'd who's boss'am," she said. "He come and get them at night ... jus' some night, he come wif henchmen."

Joanna gave her words some thought. "Then we shall make it look as though Ndamma and Barika are billeted in the carriage house, but we shall bunk them elsewhere ... in the attic of the main house. Let them in after dark each night. Impress upon them that they must be perfectly quiet so no one will suspect where they are sleeping. Choose a storeroom on Captain Makem's side of the house. Intruders would have to pass by his door to get to the attic."

"Ma'am, most want dem taught fear of de lash."

"Sukie, is there an answer for those that are like Flanagan and ... my husband, who only seek to bully and maltreat slaves?"

Sukie shook her head. "No, Ma'am. They always be people like Flanagan. Missus

MacGregor had me beat for underdone goose. She had me struck for overdone chicken. You is de different one, Ma'am."

"I am not known for walking the same path as most people. However, I shall consider having you beaten, too, if word of where we have tucked Ndamma and Barika is whispered – even to the other household slaves. Not one word, Sukie ... to anyone – 'tis just you, me, Caliganto, and the Captain."

"Yaus,am. Ma'am, thank you for a-bringin' Juba home."

"'Twas a taxing situation, Sukie. But all came right in the end. You must believe that I am exceedingly sorry that I have not yet located your children. I will do my best not to fail in that endeavour."

"De kindness is a-bein' carried here." Sukie placed a hand on her chest near her heart.

Sukie's heartfelt thanks buoyed Joanna's step as she made her way to the nursery. When her knock on the door raised no answer, she tried the latch. The door swung open to reveal Kudie sleeping in a rocking chair by the fire. Kudie's eyes opened at the sound of the latch.

"Kudie!" Joanna snapped. "You must stay alert. Do not make the mistake of leaving the hook off the door again." Joanna crossed to Luke's cot and felt his cheek. Cooler now, she thought, and he sleeps better. When she bent to kiss her babe, the room seemed to spin round. How very weary she was! From early morning until that moment, she had not a moment's rest.

Reminding Kudie about the hook, Joanna descended the back stairway to her bedchamber. By the light of a candle, she held the banister and counted the steps – seventeen to the second floor. As Joanna rounded the newel post, she heard her name whispered: "Mrs. Showcroft! Mrs. Showcroft!"

The candle's light played over the features of Anthony Makem, lurking in the shadowy area behind the stairway.

"On my word, you frightened me, Captain Makem. Why do you hide in dark corners like a rat?"

Makem snuffed the candle's flame with his fingers. "Mr. Bushnell told me of the attempted murder in Williamsburg. I must talk with you." He took her arm and drew her into his hideaway.

"Captain Makem, unhand me this instant. My husband ..."

"Your husband sleeps off the effects of strong liquor under Bushnell's watchful eye. I wished to speak with you before you retired. I do ... fear for your safety, and for that of your child. Pray trust me, Mrs. Showcroft. If you do, we must talk."

"I have trusted you before, Captain Makem. But we must not converse here. Kudie sleeps above. The Sherrie's room is on this floor."

"The arbour in the rose garden? I will meet you there. You must believe that 'though this be madness, yet there is method n't.'"

Joanna stepped away from Makem to make her way to her bed chamber for a shawl. Below her, she heard him descend the stairs to the first floor.

MAKEM was waiting, carrying his long dark cloak, which he threw over her shoulders. "It would not do for a slave to spot your pale gown in the moonlight, Mrs. Showcroft. I shall keep a sharp eye on the back door. Now, you must tell me what happened at the Raleigh."

Joanna described the events of the night in careful detail.

"If I had more than a suspicion your husband was responsible, I should spit him on the point of my sword now," Makem said.

"Mrs. Sherrie did notice that Mr. Flanagan took a great interest in me. But Captain Makem, I do not believe the attempt was made by my husband, and I cannot prove Mr. Flanagan knew of the plot. If Mr. Bushnell is correct, it was a bumbling clown who saw the opportunity to strike gold."

"Pray what is the true reason you chose to live in Virginia, Mrs. Showcroft? In his drunken maunderings, your husband did vaguely allude to a marriage agreement."

"I will say nothing of the agreement but that I feel 'tis ... part of my present dilemma. I did wish to try to make this marriage a happy one, for Jonathan Luke as well as for myself. As my husband would not reside in England, I determined to live in America."

"Dare to look at me, Mrs. Showcroft." Makem placed his hand under Joanna's chin and forced her to look him in the face.

Pushing his hand away, Joanna said, "Shame, Captain Makem, do not take advantage of me."

"Nay, do not run from me. Listen carefully to what I say. I will not allow anything untoward to happen to you. I promise that, if it be in my power, I will defend you to the death. A kiss to seal the promise." Makem's long passionate kiss left Joanna breathless. "That is your second lot of courage." He slipped his right hand around Joanna's waist to emphasize his amorous ambitions.

"Please, Captain Makem, cease this scurrilous behaviour. Do not ... play with my feelings."

"Feelings, Mrs. Showcroft? Do you fully comprehend the intricacies of high feelings?"

"I ... I try to. Oh, Captain Makem, do not complicate my life."

"And you, Mrs. Showcroft ... Joanna. Dear Joanna ... Joanna?"

Joanna twisted from Makem's grasp, threw the cloak to the ground and ran from the arbour.

Riverview
7 December 1751
My Dearest Father;

I am sure that by now, barring shipwreck, you are in receipt of my last letter. You will not regret putting your money into a plantation along the James River in Virginia. From MacGregor's account books, it is evident that the crops give a healthy profit. The fields have been most productive this year and the river setting is magnificent, even in winter.

The burden of holding Mr. MacGregor's payment in escrow is over, as he came north to collect, and was most agreeable to payment in pieces of eight. I found him a pleasant man, and advanced in his thinking. Although he is a strong advocate for slavery, he did give considerable attention to the billeting of household slaves by having small dwellings, called dependencies, built at Riverview. They are thus close by at all times, but behind a high fence. Household slaves do usually sleep on blankets and cots close to where they do their daily chores. They are much more comfortably housed at Riverview than most, and even given some privacy – though I suspect MacGregor merely did not want them under foot.

While counting the coins, I found extra, and thank you for your generosity. Some monies will be put into a few refinements. One which I intend to institute quickly is new livery. Although I like colours, I have no further desire to see my household slaves wear MacGregor's tartan. I find it interesting that it is allowable to flaunt and wear the tartan in Virginia when that practise is banned at home.

If you would send some examples of our old livery, I should be grateful. Ask Mrs. Blackstone to choose some for both male and female. I am sure the pieces can be copied here. Would you be so kind as to ask Hetttie Melrose to choose eight of my best summer gowns, at least two of damask, and a dozen of my best contouche. These should be carefully wrapped in linen and packed into the crate. The social season is far more extensive than I was led to believe, and I find myself without gowns for next summer's soirées, and no time to have new ones made.

An interesting and unusual thing occurred recently. I have been given many gifts – books, flowers, sweets – but never a human being. Captain Makem, whom I met under most interesting circumstances, presented me with an African slave, a young man nearly twenty years of age. Markings were incised on his chest to show that he would inherit the job of tribal story teller from his father. To disfigure a human being in such a way is disgusting and beyond my comprehension.

Baby Luke did finally cut his large teeth. He is the darling of the household. When he cannot capture attention with his smile, he does so with a lusty cry. The only person not charmed is his father.

Although Talbot and I have had a number of trifling arguments, we seem to have come to the conclusion that we must put on the appearance, at least, of civility between us. My time is now taken up with preparations for the Yule. We shall host twenty-nine guests for three days of hunting. Sixty invitations did go out to attend our Grand Ball. I have ordered a sheep butchered for my slaves' celebration in the gang quarters, much to their delight.

A favour, Father: Could you send, by fast packet, several rounds of hard cheese? Escorting two cheese boxes of coinage – and I did always refer to them as cheeses – has given me a great desire and appetite for good Yorkshire cheese.

In closing Father, I beg you to write soon.

Your loving daughter,

Joanna

CHAPTER FIFTEEN
THE CARD GAME
December 1751

MAKEM and Talbot faced each other over the gaming table in the smoking room, their features lit by candle and hearth fire. Rain lashed the windows, driven by a wind that swooped across barren winter fields and howled around buildings. The hall clock struck two hours past midnight.

"'Tis good the rain stayed away until all your guests departed this afternoon." Makem settled more comfortably into his chair. "Yours was a fête to remember, Showcroft. Your wife knows well the art of entertainment." Makem placed his cards on the table, and awaited Talbot's reaction.

Talbot spread his cards. "Your shuffle," he said, pushing the deck toward his adversary, who gathered them, shuffled and dealt.

Picking up his cards, Makem frowned, drew a coin from his pile, and threw to the middle of Talbot's hoard. "For one who professes to be a recluse, you did enjoy the last few days. You could not have been a better host. Have you had a change of heart, Showcroft?" Makem fanned his cards, contemplating his next play. "Are you capable of becoming a family man?"

Talbot drew on his pipe, blew smoke rings toward the ceiling and said, "I'm no fool. I can take pleasure in good company if I choose to do so. My wife took great pains to provide a pleasant evening. Why should I not have a good time? And you, Makem my friend? You seemed to enjoy yourself immensely at my expense. You sniffed after my wife all evening, like a hound after a rabbit."

"I paid every lady in the room equal attention." Makem waited for Talbot to exchange a card. "As for the dance, begorra, I'm Irish enough to have a jolly time. Dancing round the scurvy beggars on the *Black Wing* affords no pleasure, and 'tis not often the opportunity arises to be in such excellent company."

"You find my wife attractive?"

"She is a delightful and clever lady." Makem exchanged cards. "But I need not list your wife's charms in any great detail. You did wed her."

"It was for more than beauty and cleverness that I married Joanna Turnbull." Talbot placed his cards on the table.

Makem laid his down, reached across and helped himself to a coin. "Ah, yes. How silly of me to forget, the marriage laws." He stretched his long legs under the table. "Under those laws, everything your wife owns is yours. Turnbull's fortunes are within your reach. But I know that a man like Charles Turnbull, dead or alive, would not make it particularly easy for you to lay your hands on his considerable wealth."

Talbot frowned and held the cards unshuffled. He drew pensively on his pipe, frowning at Makem. "My wife gains nothing until her father dies. But our marriage agreement states that if she has an affair with another man I get half of everything Charles Turnbull owns, immediately. Any children get the other half when they come of age. If there is a bastard child results from that liaison, I do possess everything. Of course, as his only child, my wife inherits all when her father dies – so the Turnbull fortunes are all but mine now, according to Virginia marriage laws. If Joanna should die before her father, Luke is the heir. But until he comes of age, the maintenance of his inheritance will be my duty. And if Luke perchance dies before he comes of age ... Need I say more?"

"What is the other side of the agreement?" Makem asked.

"There is no other side."

Makem shook his head and laughed. "Nay, Turnbull's not a stupid man."

Talbot checked his pipe. "The same rules apply. If I have an *affaire* with another woman, my wife immediately becomes mistress of half of my wealth. If a bastard Showcroft arises from any indiscretion of mine, I lose all. When I die, she acquires two thirds of the estate and all children of Showcroft blood share one third when they come of age. Turnbull has also sworn that he will not marry; thus, Joanna is heir apparent, rather than a mere heir presumptive."

"You signed such an agreement?"

"'Twas signed, and witnessed, at the marriage ceremony. You have no idea of the extent of the Turnbull holdings, nor what I will do to relieve Charles Turnbull of them."

"I begin to see how devious and greedy you really are." Makem got up, poked at the fire and leaned against the mantel. "Why such venom, Showcroft? You are a wealthy man already."

"Charles Turnbull ruined my father's business, which in turn ruined my chances of inheriting it."

"I gather that you have no intention of divulging any little indiscretions to your wife?"

"What are you jawing about?" Talbot glowered at Makem.

"You know damn well what I am 'jawing about': your liaison with Mairi MacKinnon in Charles Town, as well as any number of slave-children running around the gang quarters in the Carolinas."

"My connection with Mairi MacKinnon was short-lived and of no consequence to the agreement. And it was understood privately between Turnbull and me that indiscretions with slave women are irrelevant."

"So if you were to confess all ...?"

"Hell and damnation! What, and ruin my chance to procure Turnbull's fortune? Do you think me an idiot?"

"As I have only heard rumours of this liaison, it is not my affair, for the present," Makem said. "Your wife shall hear nothing from me. The confession, if one is to be made, must come from you. But, Showcroft, take heed ... I have said, *for the present*."

"Nay, but you mistake, Makem. It could be your affair. You are evidently attracted to my wife. How much would it take to cross the line?"

"Hold your tongue, Sir!" snapped Makem. "I'll not be party to your little game."

"Nay, 'twas but a thought," said Talbot. "Shall we play cards, or will you chew at me all night?"

Makem stayed by the fire. "Our friend, Timothy Bushnell. Where does he fit into your scheme?"

"*L'homme galante*," Talbot said. "He remains under my thumb. I threw him at my wife in England. Alas, he knows not how to handle a lady. 'Tis my wife invited him to take residence here. She has some insane notion he can be a bookkeeper." Talbot laughed. "His presence amounts to nothing. There's no fire in him. He prefers the company of rocks and flowers to women. Why would anyone bother with him? Do you know where he is now? Up country, in Quinnehtukqut to celebrate the Yule with his mother, sketching whatever crosses his path, completely besotted by a scattering of bloody rocks."

"Your wife places trust in Mr. Bushnell. He saved her life on the *Charlotte*. You trust him because you've bought his loyalty and thus tied his tongue."

"You're wrong Makem. I trust no one. Not even you," Talbot said. "I was mightily surprised to hear the man had the pluck to place himself between my wife and the planks."

"You are a ruthless cad, Showcroft. I wonder sometimes why I tolerate you."

"'Tis obvious, I should have thought. A roof over your head, a groaning board for your stomach, a market for your slaves, and a lady for your vanity."

"Aye," said Makem. "I do agree the room, the board, and the market all draw me, but your wife appeals to my brain, not my vanity. I am intrigued that she would marry you."

"Are you?" Talbot ruffled the cards. "I can be quite charming, I assure you – if the stakes are high enough."

Makem snorted. "*Quality folk* look down on me because I'm a slaver. I ship every run with better men than you."

Talbot laughed. "You've ever a sharp tongue in your head, Makem. I too am intrigued. What happened between you and my wife that she would entrust you with her important papers? Your previous explanation did not impress me."

"Nor will this one. I've no intention of telling you. 'Tis not your affair."

"Perhaps an indiscretion has already been committed, and I need only prove it?"

Makem drew himself up to full height and gave Talbot a scathing look. "To suggest such is to toss me your gauntlet. How dare you, Sir! Do you wish to name your friends and step outside? Swords? Pistols? The choice be yours."

"No, no ... no great haste," Talbot said. "Can you not take a proper ribbing from an old friend?"

"Not at the expense of your good wife." Makem resumed his seat and began to gather his coins. "Let me tell you this," he said in a soft voice that made Talbot more uneasy than thunderous bellows. "If I return from sea to find your wife or baby harmed; or if I find Mrs. Showcroft distressed in any way; or if I find either one of 'em dead under odd circumstances, I will hold you fully responsible, Showcroft. I will hunt you down if I must. Your life will not be worth a turnip. You'll not live to spend Turnbull's money."

Talbot smiled. "Aha, so there is more to the relationship than meets the eye."

"Aye, there is. Its name is chivalry," retorted Makem. "A cheat like you would not know the word." He tucked his winnings in a pocket and turned for the door.

"You'll be sailing soon?" Talbot called after him.

"On my own bloody, sweet time," Makem shot back. "By the bye, Talbot my cunning friend, Miss MacKinnon just might be trying to find you. Talk around the dock in Charles Town is that a Scottish lady was seeking you, wanted to speak with you – badly enough she left word at a few inns you have been known to frequent."

CHAPTER SIXTEEN
FLANAGAN'S FOLLY
January 1752

JOANNA watched the moonlit yard from a window in Katie's darkened second floor bed chamber, the two women clinging to each other in excited anticipation. If Sukie had the information accurately, Flanagan would strike tonight.

The wait was not long. Three men lurked in the shadows near the woodshed, then crept along the side of the carriage house. One after the other, they entered the building through a lower door, left conveniently ajar for their benefit.

Joanna waited, a tiny smile curving her lips. Within moments the three erupted from the building, shouting hideous oaths. Makem and Caliganto followed, wielding clubs. Caliganto landed a vicious blow to the shoulder of one of the men. Makem chased Flanagan down, tripped him, and then kicked until the overseer scrambled up and vanished howling into the night.

While Makem chased Flanagan, Caliganto ducked into the cookhouse, where Juba and Sukie would swear he had been all evening. Joanna and Katie watched until Makem re-appeared, and moments later heard his soft tread on the stairs as he made his way to his bed chamber.

In the morning, summoned by Talbot, Flanagan limped carefully into the main house nursing an ugly, seeping wound on his cheek. "Thrown from a horse. Hit a fence post," he explained.

Makem clattered down the grand staircase, timing his descent to coincide with Flanagan's arrival. "Ah, Flanagan, me boyo! And how do you do this fine morning?"

Flanagan spat at the Captain's boots. "If I'd had my pistol, you'd be deader than a leg o' mutton," he muttered. "And that black monkey of yours would be swingin' from a tree."

"What! Devil got yer tongue? Speak up, mouse. I can't hear you," Makem said. "You say you've a mind to shoot someone?"

Ignoring the exchange, Talbot waved Flanagan into the plantation office to give him the orders for the day, and sent him out by the office door. Returning to the hall, he found Makem, who appeared to be waiting for him.

Talbot rounded on Makem. "You're damn well stretching your luck by interfering with the running of this plantation. I'm telling you to keep to your own affairs."

"Are you not stretching yours a bit by *running* the plantation?" Makem retorted. "Does it not belong to Charlie Turnbull? And should not your wife be making the decisions and giving Flanagan his orders?"

"Leave be," Talbot said. "You stop interfering in my affairs, Makem. Leave while you can use your own legs."

"Never think to threaten me, laddie. I know too much."

Talbot spun on his heel as Joanna hearing the raised voices, came downstairs to reconcile the two friends.

CHAPTER SEVENTEEN
FLIGHT
Early February 1752

ENGLAND had its share of miserable days, but none compared to Virginia's unpredictable winter. Although Henkle stoked the fire, drew the heavy winter curtains across the windows, and rolled sandcats against the outer doors of the day room to repel drafts, the room's occupants could not keep warm. Joanna, with a shawl wrapped around her shoulders and blanket covering her legs, stayed close to the fire, keeping her hands supple with needlework. Katie, suffering a cold, snuggled under a counterpane. Allan, seated on the floor beside Katie, worked a small knife with a whetstone. Makem, seated opposite Joanna, gave his attention to *King Lear*. Luke, under Kudie's care, played in the cookhouse where it was warmer than the day room or the nursery.

When Henkle slipped into the room to tell the Missus that Mrs. Binks had arrived and waited to see her, Joanna set her needlework aside. "How pleasant, to be sure! Bring her here, to the fire."

Sarah came through the door, licks of cold air sneaking in with her. "'Tis snowing now," Sarah said. "Verily, I rode through a thundershower but a quarter-hour back on the road. I am almost sorry I allowed Henkle to relieve me of my husband's great-coat!"

"Why are you out in such a terrible storm, Mrs. Binks?" Makem jumped up to lead her to the hearth.

Joanna rose and, chafing one of Sarah's cold hands, assisted her to the high-backed arm-chair. "We all share this hearth today. 'Tis the only room out of the biting east wind. Henkle, put another log on the fire. Ask Willow to bring tea. My dear, you do not usually ride horses! This visit must be of enormous importance!"

"Nay, upon my word, I cannot stop for tea," Sarah said. She drew a letter from her reticule. "This I did abscond with before my husband saw it. He would be under obligation to print the news. 'Tis addressed to his broadsheet. Do you recognize the seal?"

"Why, 'tis Major Straight's," Joanna said, turning the envelope in her hand. "'Tis the same seal as that on the invitation to the Major's fête."

The name brought Allan to his feet. "Damn!" he said coming to stand beside Makem.

"What a time for Straight to surface!" Katie exclaimed. "'Tis devastating news!"

"Indeed, 'tis the Major," said Sarah. "I do recall your story about his pretensions to your hand, Katie, and his determination to capture you, Allan. I considered the letter important. Though 'tis against my principles to do such a thing, I took the liberty of pilfering and reading it. I deemed it important to deliver it by hand and with haste; hence the ride through the snow on a charger."

"I am sure the good Lord will look kindly upon your skullduggery," Joanna said. She opened the letter, scanned it, and then read its contents aloud.

"Be noted tha' the bounty has been raised," Allan said. "'Tis worthwhile fer someone tae secure my curly locks. We canna' stay in Virginee."

Sarah nodded. "I am sorry for your plight. Far too many people in Virginia would try for that bounty. 'Twould set many a joint of beef on a family's table. Mr. Flanagan, is one. 'Tis my view that you and Katie must be allowed to choose the course of your lives."

"I have been cursed with the attentions of a man whom I perceived long ago to be quite mad," Katie said. "I am excessively grateful to you for bringing us the letter, Sarah."

"Your honesty and friendship are my justification." Sarah said. "By my word, rough times are ahead. My thoughts will be with you. I must take my leave if I am to reach home before dark. Would you come to the door with me, Joanna?"

"Indeed I will," Joanna said.

Makem trailed the ladies through the hall, where the ever-watchful Henkle put the dried and warmed great-coat onto Sarah Binks.

"By the bye," Sarah said. "A letter has arrived from a young New Jersey man, John Woolman, who does hold many of our views. He will be in Williamsburg on business, in April, and has accepted our invitation to stay with us. You must come also, to speak with him. He has asked that my husband consider arranging for him to address members of the Bray Associates."

"Why, Sarah, how kind! I have heard of John Woolman from a tinkerman who traveled near his home. I do believe Mr. Woolman told the fellow his work was honest and honourable as he did not own a slave."

"On my word, you do converse with the oddest people, some quite below your class. Nay, pray do not come outside. 'Tis devilish cold and you must not get the ague."

"Many thanks, Sarah. Ride well."

"I must see Mrs. Binks properly mounted," Makem said.

Joanna watched at a library window until Sarah had disappeared around the bend in the lane, then met Makem in the hall.

"'Tis fortunate Bushnell and Flanagan accompany your husband in Williamsburg, Mrs. Showcroft. Now comes the dodging. We must hide the Sherries—quickly. 'Tis Flanagan we must fear. Straight has declared his intention of handing both Allan and Katie to the King's men for hanging. He is beyond wanting Katie for his own pleasure. Damn, the man knows how to hold a grudge! Shall we join the Sherries?"

The mood in the day room was as volatile as the weather by the time Allan, Katie, Makem and Joanna had finished reading the letter a second time.

Makem stood with his back to the fire. "The devil's in it that he has probably sent a letter only to Williamsburg because he knows that Mrs. Showcroft resides near the Capital, and that you, Katie, were last in her company."

"Ah, but where to go, where to hide?" Katie said.

"I've family in the Carolinas," Allan said. "But I dinna think you should make the journey in your delicate condition, Katie."

"I will fare well, Allan. I am not yet certain I am with child."

Makem pursed his lips and rocked on his heels. "Can these relatives be trusted?"

"They be clansmen ... kinfolk."

"What clan?"

"MacKinnon."

Makem stopped rocking. He glanced at Joanna then said, "Where are they located, in the Carolinas?"

"Last word tae reach me was they lived tae the north and west, i' the mountains o'er the Trace Cut."

"Their names?" demanded Makem.

"Rory, fither of Roderick, Alex, and a daughter, Mairi."

Makem smiled. Well damme! he thought. "So, you are one of the MacKinnon clan that roams the mountains down Carolina way. A good hiding place for you, Sherrie! You'll be safe enough. We must put you on the road as soon as may be arranged."

"I will provide funds for the journey, of course," Joanna said.

Makem was smiling. "You should use the name MacKinnon. Caliganto will guide you a way. Trust him on what you must bring and the best route. Barika must go with you, as well. Be canny about whom you talk to on the way. And –" Makem looked toward Joanna. "They must leave before Showcroft and Bushnell return. The fewer who know the plans, the better."

"My husband will surely query their sudden leaving," Joanna said.

"Nay, he'll not know 'twas sudden. I'll invite them to join me on an excursion. By the time we reappear, Caliganto will have returned, and the Sherries will be well on their road to the Carolinas. My story will be that while with me, Sherrie met a man from Baltimore who did offer a good position with a merchant. And, Sherrie decided to act quickly lest it be taken up by another."

Allan spoke up. "We've a long way to travel, Mrs. Showcroft. We'll need good horses."

"Of course. Choose what you like from the stable."

"Let us see to the horses," Makem said, putting his arm around Allan's shoulder. "The ladies have much to say to each other. Mrs. Showcroft, may we send word to your husband that I ride to Richmond to take in the slave auction? Say that Showcroft and Bushnell must stay at the Wetherburn to await my arrival tonight. On the morrow, we shall travel the north road, skirting Riverview. Doubtless, Flanagan will return to Riverview before your husband and Mr. Bushnell."

As soon as the men left, Joanna knelt by Katie's chair. "Oh my dear, I shall miss you so." She held her arms out to her friend. "On my word, I shall worry sore about you. In your delicate condition, how will you make such a long journey by horseback?"

Breaking into sobs, Katie leaned forward and threw her arms around Joanna's neck. "I must trust Allan to keep me safe. 'Tis so unfair, Joanna. I did naught but refuse Major Straight's arrangement."

"Aye, I know ... I know. A man's passion can be a terrible thing. 'Tis a crazed man who would be capable of such a dire purpose. Surely, 'tis he who influences your father." Joanna kissed Katie's forehead then gently stoked tears from her companion's cheeks with her fingers. "Hush, now. Hush, Katie. Pray do not weep."

"Oh, Joanna, does my father not see how dangerous the man is? In his insistent stupidity, why did he offer a bounty and place us in this predicament? How can I leave you ... leave Riverview! We have been so very happy here."

"Do not blame your father. As an officer, he could not but support the King. He had only your best in his heart," Joanna said taking hold of Katie's hands. "We knew this might happen one day. We knew Major Straight or the King's men could find you."

"But now that the time has come, we shall be so far apart," Katie cried. "I shall make a point of writing when we are settled."

"If Captain Makem is right, then my husband and Mr. Bushnell must not see your letters," Joanna said.

Katie found her linen square and dabbed at her eyes. "I shall use a nom de plume – MacKinnon ... and send the letters to the care of Sarah Binks."

"Aye, Sarah would be a good agent. But you must write immediately to your father to beg him to remove this bounty. Tell him that you have found happiness in America; that it holds great promise for you. His forgiveness is so precious to you. Beg him to respond under cover to me, at Riverview, to keep the appearance that you still live here. I shall see that you receive his correspondence."

"Shall we see each other again?" There was desperation in Katie's question, the pain of parting in her eyes.

"We must believe so, Katie dearest," Joanna said. She did not fuss with her kerchief, but allowed her tears to spill out of her eyes and down her cheeks. "My dear, dear friend. What shall I do without your companionship? Come, my dear –"

Joanna stood and helped Katie up, and the two clung to each other, afraid to part for fear it was the last time they would embrace as friends – as sisters. "Come, we must choose what to pack."

Several hours later, with Allan and Katie safely on their way under the care of Caliganto, Joanna once again sat opposite Makem by the day room's hearth. With the pain of separation still heavy on her heart, she watched the man savour a hot toddy, a smile on his face.

As though reading her mind, Makem said. "Ah, Mrs. Showcroft, once again we find ourselves in the middle of a web of deceit and lies. I've my own reasons for finding this imbroglio rather amusing. And, in pleasant company to boot. To the Sherries!" He raised his glass. "Pray why was I not made party to Mrs. Sherrie's good news?"

"'Twas was only this past fortnight that she thought her malady might be the result of being in the motherly way. Until there was surety, no person but Mr. Sherrie and I were privy to the information. Do explain, Captain Makem, why I must not tell Mr. Bushnell the truth of their departure? The gentleman has been a tower of strength in Katie's troubles."

"But where is the man now? Riding with your husband and Flanagan. He is often, and long, with both. This gives me cause to think, and it should you also. 'Tis like to pairing a mouse with a snake and your husband is not the mouse."

"Perhaps Mr. Bushnell's company with my husband has to do with personal debt. I suspect the gentleman owes Talbot money."

"Then, what remnant of sanity persuaded you to make him your bookkeeper? Did you mean to give a thief the keys to your strong box? Damnation, Mrs. Showcroft. Mr. Bushnell is ... unpredictable."

Joanna stretched her feet toward the hearth. "How so, Captain Makem?"

"When the man is with pigs, he roots with the best of them. When he is with sheep, he follows the flock. And, on occasion, he does behave like a thoroughbred. Today, I do think he roots with the pigs."

Joanna laughed. "Captain Makem! You refer to my husband as a pig!"

"Well, the man is not in the same pen with me."

"Pray what are you – my friend?"

"Bull o' the herd." Makem smiled. "Pray be serious, Mrs. Showcroft. Do you trust Bushnell? In truth?"

"I do indeed trust Mr. Bushnell," Joanna said without hesitation.

Makem looked keenly at Joanna over his drink and thought, my girl, you most beautiful of women, I am privy to such information as you know little about." He took a swig. "You must gain Mr. Bushnell's loyalty so that when your husband is here, Bushnell prefers your company to his. Do not play the coquette, however. Mr. Bushnell courted a damsel once, was hard-smitten. He has not recovered from the blow."

"He has not mentioned her."

"Indeed he will not, nor must you ask."

"I do not interfere in anyone's private affairs," Joanna said. "You are in a mood to read me lectures this day."

"That I am and I will, Mrs. Showcroft. I see that you have taken meagre steps toward managing the plantation. Why have you not dismissed Flanagan?"

"Truthfully, Captain Makem, I have not the slightest notion of how a plantation must be managed."

"But I believe you said that you did assist your father with his business interests."

"Indeed, I was privy to his business arrangements, but only to the least smattering of detailed practical information. I ordered ships to travel to Ceylon for tea, but cannot tell how that crop is harvested. I do know how to arrange for storage and sale of sugar from the West Indies, but have no idea how the crop is raised and made into sugar."

"Am I to understand that you have no comprehension of how Riverview's crops are grown – the planting, tending, harvesting?"

"None, Captain Makem. To maintain my father's Virginia business interests, I did ... compromise my ideals and allow Flanagan to stay as overseer. And I do regret that mightily, Sir."

"Then, Mrs. Showcroft, you must gain the courage to honour your principles."

"Mr. Bushnell is no better informed. He relies heavily on the advice of Mr. Flanagan, and I rely heavily on my bookkeeper."

"Flanagan obeys your husband. Thus, your husband is still very much the master here. You do yourself no credit, Mrs. Showcroft. Flanagan is a brutish man. You must know that."

"I know that he uses force, Captain Makem, but Mr. Bushnell sees no need to interfere, which left me with no one to confide my concerns to, except Katie. And now that dear Katie is gone, I will be very much left to my own devices. Believe me, I have discussed Mr. Flanagan with Mr. Bushnell. But he says the man should not be dismissed until the tobacco crop is planted."

"I can understand your plight, Mrs. Showcroft, but you must take full control."

"'Tis best not to pull the lion's tail if one wants a peaceable kingdom. Truly, Captain Makem, I am very much afraid of Mr. Flanagan, and I believe Mr. Bushnell is, too. I dare not let my husband know my ... weakness ... inadequacy, so the man stays on, not with my blessing."

"Look not beyond the borders of the plantation for an answer. Caliganto speaks highly of Juba —"

Joanna raised her hands to protest. "I am not well enough acquainted with Juba, or his abilities, to consider him for the task. But you are a fine one to give advice. Do you not make your living buying and selling slaves? Do you treat them any better than Flanagan would?"

"You speak the truth, but for the moment you must forget what I do — and heed my counsel."

"Upon my word, Captain Makem, I am but a weak and feeble woman —"

"Only a woman!" Makem's hearty laugh filled the room. "Do not, dear lady, give me that speechifying. I say you've more nerve in your little finger than most men have in their entire lives. It might behoove you to try 'I am but a weak and feeble woman' on Mr. Bushnell, but such excuses do not work with me."

"My father says that I am born to business, not to ladylike pursuits. But I do have ... I am ... to misquote: 'a wise woman who knows herself a fool.' I do not always accomplish what I wish to, Sir."

"Never say so, Mrs. Showcroft. You can do whatever you set your mind to." Makem finished his drink and his lecture, feeling better for having delivered himself of his rant. "Did your husband mention he leaves for the south within the week?"

"That he did."

"I must be off to spend the intervening days with him. I will see that he does not tarry in the wrong places while in my company. He is a married man with no need for life in the back alleys of Richmond."

"And you, Captain Makem? Does the bull condescend to root with the pigs in Richmond? And if my husband did ... tarry, would you be kind enough to tell me, Sir?"

"I should think ... not, Mrs. Showcroft. 'Tis ... a man's business. And 'tis that man must confess his own ... indiscretions. I sail for England as soon as I take my leave of your husband in Richmond, then Africa in four weeks, so I shall not see you again before I leave."

"You must sharpen your tongue before you sail, Captain Makem. You must become a sea captain with bawdy language and coarse way to frighten men into mice."

"No life is without caprice, Mrs. Showcroft. I must take my leave to be party to an excursion where we shall be as lively as grigs for several days."

"Would that I could depart for several days to be as lively as a grig, or as happy as a purring cat. However, with Mr. Bushnell gone with my husband — "

"Will your husband see nothing wrong with Mr. Bushnell staying here now that Mrs. Sherrie has left? That situation is ripe for malicious whisperings."

"I daresay he does know Mr. Bushnell is no flirt, and will think naught of the situation."

"Then he will not give ear to the rumours that will spread about our *tête-à-tête* this afternoon. I do believe that Henkle has been outside the door throughout our discourse."

"Really! I will talk with Sukie about that. She will take him in hand."

"You do place great trust in Sukie."

"I must."

Joanna watched Makem depart from windows filled with views of rain-laden clouds and grey sinister day. Even the river looked black and angry. The news that Anthony must sail again was the last thing she wanted to hear ... and there, she thought, I have compromised again! I think of the Captain, 'tis his given name, Anthony, comes to mind.

With the Sherries gone, and the men staying in Richmond, the manor seemed a foreboding, lonely place. It would be empty all evening, but for herself on the second floor, Luke and Kudie above her on the third floor, Ndamma in the attic. The day room suddenly became oppressive with its heavy winter drapery and dark wood floor. What she needed most was to snuggle Luke and the company of another female. Joanna drew a shawl about her shoulders and went to the cookhouse.

If Sukie thought the presence of the mistress in her domain unusual, she had the good sense not to mention it. A seat was drawn close to the fire and the Missus made comfortable. She was included, respectfully, in the talk. She sat in a comfortable chair to rock Luke into his afternoon rest. The pungent odour of herbs surrounded her – leg o' mutton roasting on the spit, a large cauldron of soup bubbling on the hook, a bowl of warm spicy applesauce on the table. Willow hummed as she churned butter. Ndamma carried water from the well, and wood from the pile, and then settled down in a corner with pieces of paper on which the Missus had drawn pictures. Beneath each was written a word – cup, plate, knife, book ...

A home-longing for her own ingle at Willowbank settled so heavily over Joanna that she struggled to blink back tears. Luke, now almost sixteen months old, finally settled down, sighed and snuggled against her chest. Joanna rubbed his back and gently curled his locks around her fingers. My boy, you are so tiny, so vulnerable. Ndamma is being instructed as to your care and attention. Soon, you will have a proper protector.

Joanna's eyes wandered to Ndamma, labouring quietly over the words, repeating each softly. Ndamma and Barika – like brothers, she thought. Oh my word, I have forgot that they had been inseparable since they arrived, and now Barika is gone. Ndamma must feel as I do with Katie gone. He too will be lonely this night and for many more to come.

"Sukie, I must speak with Ndamma. Can you help me?"

"Yaus-am. He be a-speakin' mo' de English now, Ma'am. And ah be a-speakin de Wolof."

"Then ask if he would leave the attic and sleep on the second floor tonight, outside my chamber's door. I will be quite alone until my husband and Mr. Bushnell return. I mislike the quiet. 'Tis lonely for four in such a big house, methinks. If Luke's cot is brought to my chamber, Ndamma can keep watch over both his mistress and the babe. He must miss his friend. He will be as lonely as I."

"He be dat. Ma'am, you must *tell* him what you be a-wantin', not *ask* nice-like."

"Nay, Sukie. If I am to trust him, it must be Ndamma's choice, not my command."

Sukie called Ndamma from his corner and conveyed her the Missus' message. Without hesitation Ndamma agreed.

"Kudie will be in de room wif yo, Ma'am. Ndamma will sleep across de door."

"Thank you," Joanna said. She gazed around at the faces of those she was coming to trust more than her own family.

CHAPTER EIGHTEEN
GUARDIAN
Early March, 1752

WHEN Ndamma gave his signal at the nursery door, Kudie opened it, and stepped aside with a coquettish smile to let him in. Ndamma returned her greeting with a broad grin. He held the door open until the comely woman reached the back stairway. She looked back once to see if he was watching as, of course, he was.

Ndamma checked to see that no one lurked in the dim recesses of the hall, then closed the door and slid the bolt quietly home. He approached the child's cot and placed the back of his hand close to Luke's nostrils. The child was breathing as he should.

The man watched the boy sleeping for a moment, then leaned out the window and looked in all directions. His sharp eyes caught the movement of a cat down by the cook house. Kudie was on the pathway to the dependencies.

Ndamma undressed before the window. Folding each article of clothing, he placed it on the sill to air. Tight clothing was foreign to him. He hated wearing it, but people did not walk naturally in this land. Shoes were particularly obnoxious to him. Whoever heard of encumbering one's feet with heavy coverings?

Kudie had stopped and was looking back toward the nursery. My body pleases her, he thought, as he turned slowly around. To his satisfaction she stood still and watched his display.

Ndamma reached for a sheaf of papers on the mantel, then sat on the floor, his back to the cot, to look at them. Once he had five pages; now he had fifty, and he knew how to count them in English. The number twelve held his interest – twelve eggs, twelve apples. He liked the way it sounded, the way it looked, printed on the page. When he finished his memorization, he checked Luke's breathing again and took a blanket from the bed the Missus had provided. Reaching under the straw mattress, Ndamma retrieved his bag of stones, but left the knife. Caliganto had warned that it must be kept in the room to protect the child and it must never be shown, for a slave caught with a weapon would be whipped by Flanagan. The Missus knew of the weapon and trusted him to have it. He spread the blanket on the floor in front of the door then put his bag beside it.

Ndamma lay on his back, alert to every sound and movement. Caliganto told him the woman and child must be protected, and he took his responsibilities seriously. The Missus had saved him from Flanagan's ire. As a warrior, he owed her his life. If anyone dared enter the child's room, he would kill them if he did not know their step. He knew the sound of the Missus' step, and those of Sukie, Mr. Bushnell and Kudie. Master Showcroft never visited his baby. If the Master tried, Caliganto said he was to be let in, but watched carefully.

Ndamma reached into the bag and felt for Barika's sharp stone. He rubbed it, then held it to his cheek and grieved for the friend who had been taken from him. Barika's memory was always with him. Ndamma took time to think about things, especially when he sat in Sukie's cookhouse. Kind Sukie understood the ache in his heart for family and homeland.

CHAPTER NINETEEN
CONFRONTATION
Late March 1752

SPRING came quickly to Riverview, bringing an awakening of Ndamma's traditional responsibilities with it. Trees and flowers bloomed in great profusion in his new country as they did in Africa when the earth awakened. In his home village the new season was celebrated with a Ngongo, at which the Griot spoke and gathered stories. Ndamma reasoned that the Missus' people would want him to learn their stories as well. Therefore, they needed to hold a Jama, a celebration of feasting, singing, story telling and history gathering by the Griot. He spoke with Sukie, who approached the Missus.

"As a prince is a prince regardless, whether his royal birth be African or English; a Griot is a Griot and must be treated with respect. You have my permission. Have extra chickens prepared for the meal," Joanna said. "Will the ... slaves know what Ndamma hopes to do?"

"Yaus'am. Ah been a-speakin' to dem who be far from Africa," Sukie said. "They respeck de Griot."

Joanna was not invited and was of many minds about the assembly. Did the invitation not come because she could not be welcome at a slave celebration? Did they assume she would come because she owned them? Should she have asked permission? When the chosen day dawned, Joanna's curiosity got the best of her, and despite Timothy's warnings that she would be intruding, she made up her mind to attend.

Timothy had very good reasons for advising her not to intrude. He had heard Flanagan was recruiting henchmen. Timothy had his suspicions; Flanagan had a reputation for carrying a gun when he was out for revenge.

"Oblige me for a moment, Mrs. Showcroft," Timothy said. "We have not been invited; so we have no place at this private gathering. Consider this: your slaves are present at your fêtes only to serve your guests. There will be much palaver that you need not be privy to. We do not know what might happen during the evening."

"Nay, Mr. Bushnell, I insist on attending, even if you will not accompany me. But, I daresay it would not do for the mistress of the plantation to be in the slave quarters alone. Come, Mr. Bushnell. We would do nothing to interfere with the ceremony."

"I've no wish to, but if you insist I must accompany you. But we do not interfere with the ceremony, and if possible, we keep hidden. I will also carry a pistol."

Joanna gave a surprised crow of laughter. "Pray, where would you get a pistol? Why must you arm yourself?"

"I must be ready for anything," Timothy said. "Makem gave me a pistol before he left. I am not ignorant of the use of weaponry, Mrs. Showcroft. I have taken to practice shooting to understand the action of this double-barreled gun."

With a full moon overhead, Timothy and Joanna, wearing dark cloaks to be unobtrusive, walked to the gang quarters and stood in the shadows beside one of the cabins to watch. Dogs sniffed them out and announced their arrival, but nobody took notice of them.

Excited children ran around adults who squatted on the ground or on logs.

Ndamma sat on a bench before the fire. Sukie had outlined the distinctive marks on his chest with ochre and wrapped his waist with a strip of red cloth that fell to his ankles.

Soon Ndamma, with great dignity and presence of moment, asked that all who wished to address him make themselves known.

Holding the hand of young boy, Cansu came forward and spoke. As Ndamma questioned, her answers were whispered throughout the assembly.

"My word," Joanna whispered. "I did not know Cansu had a sibling!"

Timothy listened intently. "I believe the mother was taken away by Mrs. MacGregor, and she is left to care for the child. She says that she has no father and that Sukie has become their mother."

"How dreadful! I did not know. I must bring that child into the household immediately."

At the end of Cansu's story, she gave a small pebble to Ndamma. He turned it slowly in his right hand, rubbed it with his fingers, then placed it before him on a red cloth.

The next several slaves who presented stones spoke a language that Timothy did not understand.

"The young man standing now appears to be weeping," Joanna said. "I do wish that I was a scholar in African languages like Caliganto, to understand what weighs on his mind."

"I believe he is one of the slaves your husband bought for the plantation before you arrived. 'Tis probable he is newly arrived in Virginia and misses his home."

When a tall, stoop-shouldered elder limped toward Ndamma to speak, Joanna said, "I do not recognize that man. Why have I not seen him before?"

"He is Ol' Jobe," Timothy said. "He belongs to the Wakeville Plantation. He must have sneaked away to hear Ndamma."

"Will he be punished for coming?"

"If he is found out – doubtless. At least nine of the slaves here I do not recognize. They do not belong to you."

"Such is the draw of a Griot?"

"Such is the curiosity of a slave," Timothy said. "Shh. I believe Ndamma is finished."

The gathering broke into rhythmic chanting and dancing accompanied by log drums, beaded gourds and hand-clapping.

Ndamma called for silence again. The people obeyed immediately. This Griot was a tangible link to their ancestral homeland, though he had been separated from his African history stones when he was sold from his village. Ndamma could, if he wished, tell stories that he had heard at his father's knee – homeland history passed through generations. He took a soft leather pouch from his waist and tipped its contents onto the cloth. He had been collecting stories about the Missus and Massa Bushnell, Sukie and Caliganto, and might tell them this evening.

Ndamma chose a stone, held it for all to see, then wove its story. Silence fell over the circle and the occasional head turned to the hiding place.

"What is Ndamma saying? His English is so broken," Joanna asked. "They have become so quiet and look to us."

"I believe he has chosen your stone. He tells tales about the Mistress."

"Dear me!" Joanna said. "Am I to be angry at his imprudence or curious at his words?"

"You are expected to be pleased at the respect shown in the choosing of your stone."

"Indeed he does speak in a reverent tone. What does he say?"

Timothy strained to hear. "He is telling the story of how you saved him from the whip – and fed him well – and now teaches him English, and how to count."

"That he tries to speak in English must mean that he wishes me to hear. Might this be his way of expressing gratitude?"

"Indeed, it is."

"How excessively kind of the young man!"

Ndamma finished speaking and gave the stone to Sukie, who put it back into the pouch. Ndamma then chose another and made to speak.

The spell cast by Ndamma's voice was broken by horses galloping into the clearing. Flanagan and three cohorts reined their mounts at the edge of the firelight. Frightened slaves leapt to their feet, caught up their children, and melted into the shadows. Only Ndamma and Sukie remained seated, backs to Flanagan. Ndamma gathered the stones on the cloth, handing them to Sukie who secreted them away.

"Meeting unlawfully?" Flanagan snapped his whip. The rawhide licked past Sukie's face as it landed across Ndamma's back. Blood spurted, then ran, soaking the red cloth at his waist.

Ndamma gasped in pain but held his ground. Sukie put her hand out to steady him.

Joanna lifted her skirts, the better to run. Timothy caught her arm. "Don't interfere. The man is out for blood and revenge. He will be drunk and not care whose back he shreds."

"Not interfere?" Joanna broke free of Timothy's grip. "Mr. Bushnell, whose side do you take – humanity or inhumanity – Flanagan's or mine?"

Hearing the whip strike bare flesh again, Joanna ran into the clearing and put herself between Ndamma and Flanagan. "Stop!" she commanded. "Put your whips away, all of you."

"If it ain't the little lady herself," Flanagan slowly coiled his whip for another blow.

Behind Joanna, Ndamma still crouched, blood dripping from his wounds. He turned, muscles taut, ready to protect the Missus.

"Step aside. I'm gonna whip this boy for meeting without my permission," Flanagan said.

"*Your* permission?" Joanna said. "I have given *my* slaves *my* permission to gather here. That is all they need."

Flanagan threw back his head and showing a mouth of yellow teeth, snarled "Get out my way, woman."

Joanna stood her ground, as her temper rose. A parcel of sea language was on the tip of her tongue, and she had to remind herself she was a decent lady. "You mistake, Mr. Flanagan. You are dismissed. I no longer require your services. Leave my plantation, you and your friends."

"Dismissed? Did you hear that boys? Dismissed, the lady says," Flanagan said in a high attempt at mimicking Joanna's voice. "Move!" He yanked his reins, causing the horse to rear.

Joanna held her ground, eyes blazing, hands on hips.

"Come on, Flanagan," one of the men said. "Ye didn't say we were gonna' tangle with the lady."

"Shut up. Step away from your mistress' skirts," Flanagan ordered Ndamma.

"Stay where you are, Ndamma." Joanna commanded. "Hell and damnation! Leave now, or I will see you arrested, Flanagan." She was so angry now that her legs shook and she cared not what foul verbiage crossed her tongue.

Flanagan spat on the ground. "What's he to you, a black lover?"

"How dare you! Go or I shall have you physically removed. You are trespassing on my land. Leave now."

Flanagan roared. "High words from a low lady. Who's to remove me? Slaves won't dare touch me. Punishment for fightin' with a white man, even under orders, is death, an' they know it. Are you, little lady, gonna to throw me off? Come and try! Step away from the boy so I can finish with him."

Joanna took a step toward Flanagan. "Nay, villain, you will have to strike me senseless before you touch Ndamma again."

"If that's the way you want it," said Flanagan.

"Leave off, Flanagan," one of the men shouted. "I don't want nothin' to do with strikin' a lady."

Flanagan sneered and spat again. He raised the whip. Before he could bring it down, a shot rang out. Blood spurted from Flanagan's shoulder. Howling, he dropped the whip. When he reached with his bridle hand for the pistol in his belt, he wrenched at the horse's bit. The animal reared again, and his hoof grazed Joanna. She staggered, but regained her footing.

"Do not try it, Sir." Timothy stepped from the shadows, a gun pointed directly at Flanagan's chest. "Or my next shot will pierce your heart. Back away. All of you, or I will shoot him."

Flanagan's henchmen backed away.

"Flanagan, I will shoot you dead if you so much as spit. Hand Mrs. Showcroft your gun, handle first."

"You're a fool, Bushnell. You cain't shoot."

"I just did. If I shoot again, you shall die. Look well, Flanagan." Timothy stepped toward Flanagan and aimed his pistol directly at the man's chest. "I'll not miss."

A moment's hesitation, and Flanagan handed his gun over. "Another time, another place, Bushnell."

When Joanna took the pistol and gave it to Timothy, he turned it on Flanagan. "Two guns. Two balls. Far more effective than one," he said. "You!" Timothy addressed one of the men at the back. "You live in the cottage by the ferry. I had the privilege of sharing a room with you in Williamsburg in June, did I not? You spoke of a wife and a half-dozen children. You don't want to be entangled in this. If you hang for attempted murder, who will keep them?"

The man backed his horse a step or two away from Flanagan.

"Ride to the village," Timothy ordered him. "Wake the watch. Send them to Riverview, then go home and stay there. 'Tis your only chance to save yourself and your family. Do you hear me, Sir?"

The man nodded – "Aye," – turned his horse and rode off.

"You other scurvy scoundrels, hand your weapons to Mrs. Showcroft and disappear, and that hastily."

One man turned his horse and left. The other rode to Joanna, handed over his whip, and mumbled an apology before he rode away.

"Dismount, Flanagan," Timothy said, his pistol still steady on Flanagan's chest. "Juba, I see you by the fire. Oblige us by using the horse's reins to tie this man's hands behind his back."

The horse stomped nervously when Juba approached to tie Flanagan's wrists.

"Tether the horse, for Christ's sake," Flanagan said. "He'll drag me if he's spooked."

"Oh, sure, you would cut a fine figure running beside a horse! And you'd look better dragging behind," Timothy said. "You've visited that gruesome punishment on any number of slaves, Flanagan. Henkle, hold the horse. I want to see this man in the public gaol in Williamsburg."

Henkle stepped forward, afraid to obey, but afraid not to. Never before had he been asked to act against a white man.

"Henkle, der no be a-whuppin' dis time round fo' de job done," Juba said. "You hol' de horse fo' de Massa Bushnell."

Timothy's Decision

JOANNA remembered bending to examine Ndamma and seeing raw, broken flesh and blood. She woke up in her bed chamber, Sukie bathing her face.

"You is a brave lady, for sho'." Sukie's movements were gentle, her voice soothing. "You sho' was full up wif fine snuff las' night, Ma'am!"

"I fainted, didn't I?"

"You fa' dead away." Sukie smiled.

"Flanagan?"

"He be a-locked in de icehouse so's he cain't run 'way."

"Mr. Bushnell?"

"In his office. He don't be a-eatin', don't be a-speakin'."

"Ndamma?"

"Ah did dress his back. He restin', best as he can."

"If you would tell Cansu to come, I must dress and speak with Mr. Bushnell."

Sukie wrung out the napkin she had been using, and gathered up the bowl and spare cloths. As soon as Sukie left the room, Joanna retrieved the knife she'd kept from the incident at the Raleigh ten months before, and made her way to Timothy's office.

Walking in without knocking, she sat opposite her bookkeeper. He played absently with a stick of sealing wax. When Joanna placed the knife on the desk he glanced at it, then looked at her with dull eyes. "I will pack and leave immediately."

"By my life, you shall not."

"'Tis evident I can no longer enjoy your hospitality."

"I do not force you to go."

Timothy's eyes were red from lack of sleep. "How did you know it was my knife?"

"At the pick-nick on the way to Williamsburg, you used it to slice the bread and cheese. It has a most distinctive handle."

"Believe me, I did not try to kill you, Mrs. Showcroft."

"I became inquisitive after the incident," said Joanna. "When Katie told me that Mr. Flanagan had paid particular attention to my presence in the dining room, I spoke with the innkeeper. Hear me out, Mr. Bushnell. Did you not sleep in a room with three other men?"

"I did."

"And Flanagan was not one of them?"

"He was not."

"So he did not enter my room. But, I believe that one of the men you shared the room with did take your knife, did he not?

"Please believe me, the men who shared the room were complete strangers. I did not know my knife was stolen until I saw it stuck in the pillow-dummy. I had shared a room with a murderer!"

When Timothy said nothing, Joanna continued, "Really, Mr. Bushnell! Your good name and reputation were used in a dastardly crime. Had the man succeeded in murdering me, your knife, with that carved bone handle, would have been found, and you would have been arrested for murder. He would have disappeared, perhaps with the coinage. Mr. Timothy Bushnell would have hanged for a murder he did not commit. My husband would not have bothered to save you from hanging I'm certain, as if I were dead, he would be very much closer to inheriting Father's fortune."

"Mrs. Showcroft, do you truly suspect your husband?"

"I do not want to think it of him. But I believe Mr. Flanagan was party to the attempt and he does cozy up to Talbot." Joanna reached across the desk to touch Timothy's hand. "Pray do not leave, Mr. Bushnell. You are important at Riverview and shall be for a long time. We have discussed this. I know nothing of overseeing the field work."

Timothy let her fingers linger on his hand for a moment before he pulled it away. "You put your trust in the wrong man, Mrs. Showcroft."

"'Tis not a trifling matter to save the same lady's life twice, Mr. Bushnell. Your very actions demand that you stay."

Timothy's eyes searched Joanna's face. "How can you trust me now?"

"I have always trusted you, Mr. Bushnell. If I did not think you worthy of my confidence, I should have given the knife over to the authorities in Williamsburg – or would do so now."

Sukie knocked at the door then slipped in with a tray. "Law be here again, to speak wif you, Ma'am."

"Please give them something to eat and assure them I need a few moments to dress. Have Cansu attend me. Pray, what did you tell them, Mr. Bushnell?"

"The truth. That you, as agent for the plantation's owner – your father – had the right to give your slaves permission to meet; that Flanagan attacked you and did try to strike you with his whip; that as your father's factor, you had the right to dismiss him; that I shot at him to save your life."

"Do you believe that you will be charged? Attempted murder upon Mr. Flanagan?"

"I do not think so."

"The other men that were dismissed from the incident? Was mention made of them?"

"I left that for your decision. I assure you, Mrs. Showcroft, the authorities do not care a spit why the gathering was held. What a Griot does is of no consequence to them."

"But you do foresee trouble?"

"I do. You must speak very cautiously, Mrs. Showcroft. Your husband has friends in most unusual places. 'Tis difficult to ascertain how these people think. Should they not believe you have the authority to run Riverview, they will side with Flanagan."

"But Mr. Flanagan would have struck me!"

"Indeed, he is that vile. He will argue that he was only threatening you and had no intention of letting loose with the whip."

"Nay, I do not believe that."

"If you recall, he did not know you were there. Indeed, you did not dismiss him until after he struck Ndamma, and you made your presence known. He can say that as overseer he thought the slaves were meeting illegally, and so had the right to punish, and that punishment was administered in his own cruel way. He will state that he was following your husband's orders. As 'tis possible he was."

"I was amazingly stupid to think I could let the Flanagan question lie fallow. I thought to counsel with Advocate Shand about him."

"Your husband departed two months ago. While you have overseen the operations of the house, Flanagan has been overseeing the field operations in his usual brutish way, without so much as one ill word from you or me, because we are both frightened of the man. Indeed, he deals with me, thinking that I was in consultation with your husband before he left."

"Did you consult with my husband?"

"To a degree. Let me continue. Flanagan has now been dismissed, and unless you hope to take a hand in planting, harvesting and all else that it takes to run this plantation, an overseer must be hired quickly."

"What will happen immediately?"

"Flanagan will not be kept in the public gaol. I must assume he will leave Virginia, possibly go down country to Talbot's rice plantations."

"I am all reason now. I will use my wiles on the gentlemen awaiting my presence to assure you are not charged. To prove I am the person capable of sanctioning a gathering, I will show them the confirmation of my authority to run Riverview. I will state that there was a misunderstanding between myself and Mr. Flanagan, that he intimidated me, so much I wished to shoot him myself, had I a gun in my hand."

"No, do not! I should not advance further than "that he intimidated me.""

"Of course, they would think less of me as a lady. 'Tis not the proper thing to state my mind as I might wish.""

"I must be perfectly candid. You have lived in America long enough to learn that high opinions and ideals, however virtuous they appear to be, do not mix well with realities. Most circumstances and situations need rational thinking and reasonable answers.""

Joanna smiled. "Now. Mr. Bushnell, you have touched on the reason why I wish you to stay. I admit to some shocking faults. One of them is that I am cursed with optimism and high expectations. I see that some of my lofty ideals are not in keeping with situations at hand. Perhaps you would ... verily, I was hoping you would consider another responsibility ... overseer −"

"Not in God's lifetime! Bookkeeping I may do, and an adequate job is done of it, too. But your overseer? Never!"

"Then I must speak with Mr. Shand. This plantation cannot run itself."

"We should both speak with Juba, who knows what must be done. Give him the authority and he will handle it capably."

"Ah, yes! Captain Makem did once mention Juba. I have paid particular attention to him of late. Yes, we should ask Juba to assist until I can speak with Mr. Shand."

"Mrs. Showcroft, I am sorry ... about the Raleigh ... about −"

Joanna put her hand up to silence Timothy. "Nay, had you explained the circumstances, right after the incident at the inn, it would have been accepted as an apology then. There's no need now. 'Tis months too late."

"I thought greatly about it, but could not bring myself to tell you," Timothy said. "May I ask for one more month, Mrs. Showcroft? Let me take to the woods with my paints. I must contemplate alone. Frankly, your presence does complicate my ... situation."

"You will return, Mr. Bushnell?"

"I do swear that at months' end I will return with an answer. If it be yes, then I am at Riverview for as long as your need for me lasts."

"Mr. Bushnell, you have the hands of an artist and the heart of a lion."

"Now you flatter me."

"Captain Makem would not have given you the pistol but that he considers the words 'loyalty' and 'trust' in the same thought as your name."

"Before he departed, Makem told me that should anything untoward happen to you, or Luke, I will find myself at the bottom of the sea, talking with the fish."

"Captain Makem does speak his mind."

"You must know by now that I need no Makems to bully me into protecting you."

"After all the adventures we have shared, I do know. but − may I say what is forthright but what you may not wish to hear?"

"I will not stop you."

"You have displayed a shocking puppetry around my husband. He pulls a string and you dance. I do believe he has lent you money and you have no means to pay it back.""

"That is true."

"Then, you must find the courage to turn from him. Talbot cannot steal your considerable talent. If you are honest and straightforward, many people will respect you. Should you return to Riverview, I will pay you handsomely for your counsel, enough to allow you to repay your debt.

"I've a difficult decision to make."

"One month. Now, I must meet the authorities. Will you accompany me during their questioning, Mr. Bushnell?"

"That is neither necessary, nor the best course, Mrs. Showcroft. You are most ... appealing in that soft blue contouche with your hair ... curling over your shoulders. Questions cannot be too severe if you appear to them as you look this very moment. Well. I have spoken very much out of turn."

Joanna blushed and stuttered, "I do ... thank you, Mr. Bushnell, for your ... kind words."

"It was a compliment, sincerely meant."

"And sincerely taken," said Joanna.

CHAPTER TWENTY
WILLIAMSBURG
April, 1752

THE Shand family's salon was a happy, comfortable place. Joanna, with Elizabeth's youngest on her knee, watched Luke playing on the floor with several of the older children. Elizabeth, heavily with child, was semi-reclined on a sofa. Laughter drifted through the open windows from the cookhouse where the household slaves were having their afternoon meal.

After dinner, Joanna had asked Jackson if she might speak of business, although it was a Sunday. Jackson listened attentively as Joanna explained her dismissal of Flanagan; that Timothy had left for a month; that Talbot was not expected from Planter's Hall for months, and that the tobacco fields, according to Juba, needed attention. With Flanagan gone, there was no one to oversee the workers.

"Ah yes, Mrs. Showcroft, interesting news does travel quickly. Your troubles are the talk of Williamsburg, thanks, of course, to Flanagan." Jackson said. "My first remark is that this is not the most advantageous time to dismiss your overseer. You say he threatened to whip you?"

Joanna detailed the incidents that led to Flanagan's attack. "I daresay I should have dismissed him shortly after my arrival at Riverview. But, truthfully, thoughts of the plantation's losses should the fields not be tended properly kept me from doing so. Now, I do not need a lecture on money ruling head, and head ruling heart, Mr.

Jackson. I do need a good overseer. Do you know anyone could fill the position well?"

"The fellow must have the respect of the slaves, even if he gains it by cruel means. Flanagan, for all his posturings and penchant for violence, did get work done."

"I will not have my slaves beaten into submission, Mr. Shand."

"Not beaten? Dear Mrs. Showcroft, Flanagan did not stroke your slaves with a feather! I am completely at a loss to understand, given your beliefs, why for the past months, you have turned a blind eye, and tolerated his cruelty, for the excuse that you did not wish to lose money. You have perhaps lost enthusiasm for some of your more strongly held beliefs?"

"Mr. Shand, you are being unfair. I do not adhere to Flanagan's brutish ways, but I feared his temper would be turned on Mr. Bushnell and me if we interfered. He has now been dismissed, and I request your help to find another overseer, one who does not use brutality to get work done."

Jackson sighed. "Always the crusader, Mrs. Showcroft. I beg you to explain how one gains the respect of slaves if not through cruel means on occasion?"

"With kindness and respect."

"Kindness is often an open invitation to steal, and slacken off work. Give slaves one concession, and they take ten."

"I cannot bring myself to believe that, Mr. Shand."

"'Tis true, my dear," Elizabeth interjected. "It does happen among my household slaves. Give one an old garment and they all desire one. They'll steal a bed sheet to sew one, if they can. If I give one loaf, I must resign myself to losing twelve loaves shortly thereafter."

"Mrs. Shand! You can well afford to hand away a few loaves of bread and bits of clothing."

"Doubtless, but that is my choice, not their right, Mrs. Showcroft!"

"Ladies, 'tis the Sabbath and I will allow no cat-clawing in this house. I notice, Mrs. Showcroft, that you say 'my slaves' – why not 'my freed people'?" Jackson said "Have you freed any of them? I venture that you have found your firebrand ideals diluted by life's realities."

"In my defense, I have been in America only a few months," Joanna said.

"Admit, Mrs. Showcroft, that to run a large plantation one must own slaves, must one not? And those slaves must have children to please the mistress and keep the wheels of commerce running smoothly from generation to generation without undue expense. Why, dear lady, you can sell those children and bring in money for your father, if they are not required at Riverview."

"How can you propose such a thing! 'Tis impossible for my ... *slaves* to have true freedom. If I should free them today, and send them on their way, they would be quite simply be caught up by some scurrilous scoundrel and enslaved again."

"Ah, you have examined the possibility of freeing slaves and found it more difficult than you had at first thought."

"I have. And I have found that most slaves have their intellect crushed into hopeless despondency. Some know not the value of time or material things or the prudent use of money. They must be taught these things."

"You conjure trouble, Mrs. Showcroft —"

"Mr. Shand, have I not lodged a letter with you giving direction that if my father should lose Riverview or I become incapable, Riverview's slaves are to be given over into your custody until such time as they may be given their freedom with monies to assist them find a new life, either under your direction or that of Mr. Bushnell?"

"That you have, Mrs. Showcroft, and it speaks well of you that you did so."

"Pray then do not bait me with absurdities, Mr. Shand. I will not debate you today. I must find an overseer!"

"With your views, you would not wish to hire the few that come to mind at the moment. There are always men seeking work, but most are rude, crude and far worse than Flanagan."

"What about Irish O'Brien?" Elizabeth said.

"Carter hired him last week. He would have been a good man."

"I heard about a Mr. Glaston," Joanna volunteered.

"By all that is right, do not hire that man!" Jackson said. "He is a nincompoop, been in the stocks more than once for petty crime. There is never an abundance of good overseers, and those who rule with kindness are nonexistent. Flanagan's sort prevails. Pray who has been doing the overseeing since Flanagan left? Bushnell?"

"Juba. He is a very good fellow; he works hard and knows how the work must be done, when and by whom. I can say with full confidence that my husband will be furious when he comes home to find Juba in charge."

"To the Devil with Showcroft! And I do beg the Lord of the Sabbath to excuse my language. 'Tis you who runs the plantation, is it not? You say truly that Riverview must show profit. If Juba provides the work to that end, methinks he is your best choice. Advocate Shand sighed and rose from his chair. "I will take a stroll, ladies. I shall travel through the streets of our Capital, and ask a few questions over back fences. Whyte's slaves or Dinwiddie's may know what Juba did that prompted his sale, for we never did hear the truth. I shall return in due course."

As soon as Jackson left, Elizabeth said, "I do beg your pardon for my outburst, Joanna. You will do me the pleasure of staying the night, won't you?"

"I beg your pardon, as well. And I shall accept your kind offer. I am not expected at Riverview until Wednesday. While I am here, I hope to meet John Woolman, who is a guest of Sarah Binks. I am all aflutter to hear his views on slavery. He has come to the Capital on other business, but he is to give his time to expound his own discourse. I am told he makes some interesting commentary."

"I should not place much credence in radical views, and especially those that plead for the abolition of slavery," Elizabeth said. "Nothing will come of it. A few people, such as the Binkses, and Quakers, of course, advocate for freedom of

Africans. Why, who would do our work, Joanna? Who would plant the tobacco, care for our children?"

"Without a doubt, you should invite Mr. Woolman for tea!"

"With many a doubt I should entertain that idea! By the bye, Constance Blaikley will call upon me tomorrow to confirm arrangements for my travail. You will have the pleasure of meeting her if this Mr. Woolman does not claim your ear for too long."

Joanna leaned back in her chair, looked at the tow-headed child in her arms, and the happy family at her feet. "You are most fortunate that Mr. Shand loves children. My husband declares we must have no more. He rarely pays attention to his son, and, to say truth, even more rarely to me, when he is at home."

"You must impart your secret, Joanna."

"Gillenia Trifoliatta ... Cohosh ... Tansy – a concoction brewed up by Sukie. And, of course, Talbot is mostly away –"

"Verily, I have tried every concoction suggested." Elizabeth sighed. "Shall we call the nursemaids and take a rest before my husband returns?"

"Father sent a copy of Shakespeare's *Julius Caesar*, which demands my attention. I will avail myself of a bench in your rose garden. Luke will require tending, methinks."

As Joanna crossed to the window to call Ndamma, Elizabeth said, "Do be honest, is there nothing better that magnificent African can do than act as nurse to a child?"

"Nay, as I explained before, Ndamma is Luke's guardian," Joanna said. "And indeed he is becoming a clever young man."

Ndamma and several young slave girls arrived to claim their charges. He gathered Luke into his arms, talking softly to him. The child smiled, winding his arms around the African's neck.

"Truly," Elizabeth said. "I see with mine own eyes how close the two have become. If we are speaking of clever, did my husband tell you who that Mithers fellow is, the man that came to the Raleigh with the papers for signing? It seems he is no notary. 'Tis without a doubt a mystery, but when Jackson was in Baltimore he saw the man, clerking in a shipyard owned by –"

"My husband," Joanna finished. "His name figured in one of the account books at Riverview. Does your husband discuss everything with you?"

"Never fret, my dear. He does not. What I do hear does not filter through the locks."

Jackson returned for tea and told of his findings. "You are acquainted with MacGregor, Mrs. Showcroft?"

"We met when he rode north for his money."

"Well, here's comedy. MacGregor's eldest daughter would not leave the male slaves to their own devices. From the time she turned into a comely lass, she was, in the simplest terms, a flirt. MacGregor built quarters for his house slaves away from the manor, so that choice temptation would not be billeted on pallets in corners of the house near their work – and near his daughter!"

"That explains the dependencies that my house slaves do enjoy, the high fence and slave gates. I had surmised that he was advanced in his views. In reality he was attempting to separate his daughter from her ... victims, for want of a better word."

"That does partially explain the arrangement," Jackson said. "But hear me out. The daughter did turn her full attention to Juba. She became infatuated with him. No matter what the man did, where he went, she dogged him. MacGregor blamed Juba for leading her along and had him punished. When Sukie told Mrs. MacGregor that her daughter was chasing not only Juba but every male slave on the plantation, she was punished too – a terrible whipping, I do hear, but on her feet to avoid marking her for sale."

Jackson went on to explain that the daughter was hastily married off to a fellow from Norfolk, newly arrived from Scotland, when it became apparent Sukie's defense of Juba was truthful. The joke is that Sukie took revenge for the beatings by washing the girl's blond hair on her wedding day with a little indigo dye added to the rinse water. The girl went to her new husband with green hair!"

Joanna broke into unsuppressed giggles. "And I trusted Sukie to wash my hair, the first day at Riverview! 'Twas my husband who sold Juba. Yet, 'twas Mr. MacGregor who had fair reason for selling Sukie, but did not. Such tangled webs."

"My opinion is that Juba should continue as your overseer," Jackson said. "He appears a capable fellow. If your good husband gives you trouble, tell him that Juba was retained on my counsel. Consider, Mrs. Showcroft, that if punishment must be meted out, 'tis Juba giving it to a fellow African. Having been at the end of a stinging cat, he might use less violent means –"

"Mr. Shand! Do not speak such nonsense."

"'Tis truth. If your husband complains overmuch about Juba, send the beggar to see me. I do have several skeletons to rattle before him.

"My husband does not debate issues very well," Joanna said. "He never could last through an evening with my father."

"I daresay you give him greater trouble," Jackson said. Turning to Elizabeth, he continued. "Regardless of who was invited to Willowbank, this lady could chew with the best of them."

"Those debates were where I really began to institute strong opinions about certain questions. Although 'tis discouraged among ladies of quality, I insist on questioning everything, and then form my own judgements."

"Strong opinions! My dear, Mrs. Showcroft? Most were directly opposite general opinion."

"Some good did come of the debates, Mr. Shand. On several occasions you did bring members of the Bray Associates to Willowbank. I began to sympathise with some of their more enlightened beliefs. One of them was that every child, black or white, is entitled to schooling, although I do think religion should not be attached to it."

"I daresay it must have been an interesting time," Elizabeth said.

CHAPTER TWENTY-ONE
MacKINNON'S TRACE
April 1752

FOG blanketed the ridge, obscuring the view of the wooded valley that cradled MacKinnon's Trace. Allan cautioned Barika, who was leading Katie's horse, to follow directly behind him, and stay close to the cliff face as he made his way down the narrow trail. Allan heard the sound of axes chopping wood and realized he'd best let it be known there were strangers on the mountain.

"Ailpein!" Allan called, then listened intently for a reply. "Ailpein" he called louder now, splitting the thick fog with his deep-voiced MacKinnon cry. "Ailpein" rang down the trail at regular intervals until the chopping stopped.

"Cuinhnich Bas Ailpein," a voice came finally through the mist. "Who be ye?"

"Allan Sherrie."

"Stay whar ye are. We'll come tae ye."

Two figures soon appeared out of the fog. Allan helped Katie to dismount, and all three stood together to meet them.

"MacKinnon clansmen?" Allan asked.

"Aye," came the answer.

"You're a guid sicht. We've ridden o'er the whole of the western Carolinas tae look for ye. An o'er-mountain innkeeper did finally direct us up the Trace Cut. We hae been several months on the trail."

"Who be your mither?" queried one of the men, looking closely at Allan.

"Elizabeth, sister of John the Red, cousin of Rory MacKinnon."

"And who be he?" The questioner singled out Barika.

"A friend. Barika, helpin' us oot."

The men nodded. "Come awa' then. I'm Roderick, the younger. This is Alex, my brither."

"We be kin," said Alex.

Allan extended his hands to both men. "'Tis my Katie beside me."

"The two of ye, walk wi' me. Ale'll lead yer frien' and the horses. Stay tae the left. Ye're close tae the edge."

A short way down the path the party walked out of the fog and into sunlight.

"'Tis the way o' it," Roderick said. "A fog rolls o'er the top and nae reaches the boddin. Or a fog comes o'er the boddin and ne'er reaches the top. Whaur'd you travel fra?"

"Virginee."

"Lang way fer a Clansman's welcome."

The MacKinnon clearing was bounded by stout fence, which didn't keep the pigs from rooting around the main cabin, and sheep from grazing the foot paths. Chickens scattered when the group approached, clucking their indignation.

"Fither," Roderick called. "Kinfolk's here."

Rory stepped off the porch, an imposing figure with his long white hair and beard. He gave his hand to Allan. "A Sherrie tae be sure, " he remarked. "Ere ye one saw action in '45?"

"Aye, one o' many."

"An' who be the lassie?"

Allan introduced Katie.

"Bonnie indeed," Rory said. "And bonnie horseflesh, as well. Where'd you git the animals?"

"They were a gift, Sir," Katie said.

"Sich a benefactor I've yet tae see!" laughed Rory. "A hielan' welcome, lad and lassie. 'Tis our ingle ken'lt." He led the way into his spacious log cabin while Barika went with Roderick and Alex to tend the horses. Rory motioned to a chair by the hearth. "Sit, Katie Sherrie. Ye look tired. Andre, let the lady hae the guid chair."

A small child toddled from the rocking chair to the older man who picked him up and held him close.

"My gran' bairnie," Rory said. "Ye be hungry? There's tolerable chicken stew and biscuits. Yer man eat with ye?"

"He does," Allan said. "He is a free man."

"Dinna matter anywa'; slave or free, he is welcome at my board," Rory set the child down and busied himself setting wooden bowls and spoons on a table. For the men he set burled wooden drinking vessels, for Katie a delicate flowered china cup. The child wandered over to Katie who lifted him onto her lap. The little urchin needed a good wash, his hair combed and his tattered clothing mended, she thought, hugging him close.

When Rory went to the door and shouted to his sons to bring Barika in for the evening meal, they washed on the porch, noisily entered and sat at the table, Barika between Alex and Roderick.

"'Tis expecket you waul fill yer wyme at my groanin' board," Rory said. He lifted a heavy iron stew pot from the hearth crane and placed it in the centre of the table. Putting a handful of dried herbs in a pitcher, he added hot water then stacked corn biscuits on the wooden trestle. "Herb tea," he explained to Katie as he poured her a cup.

A second pitcher, which contained home brew, was put on the table for the men.

"Andre can sit with me," Katie said as she sat the child beside her on the bench.

"Wheest!" Rory bent his head for a silent grace then the men fell greedily on the food. Allan filled Katie's bowl and she in turn tended to Andre's. When the biscuits disappeared, Rory replenished the supply from a crock by the hearth. Barely a word was spoken during the meal. When it finished, the men took pipes from the wall rack and went to sit on the porch.

Katie stacked the bowls, cleaned the table and joined them. Rocking Andre to sleep on her knee, she looked out across the clearing to the mountains and steep ridge they had earlier descended. Lush green forest surrounded MacKinnon's Trace.

The sun gave a brilliant display of red and gold in a deep blue sky as it slowly set behind grey silhouetted western mountains. Its rays bathed the ridge, now devoid of fog, in a golden light that showed just how dangerous a trail they had traversed. Cattle lowed in their byre. Horses and oxen slept under a tree in the south pasture while a sheep dog lay nearby, alert to the sounds in the surrounding forest.

As no woman shared the dwelling with the MacKinnon men, Katie wondered about Andre's presence in the gathering. "Which of your sons is Andre's father, Mr. MacKinnon?"

"He be my daughter's bairn," Rory answered. "Why did you come lookin' fer yer kin?" He spoke to Allan.

Allan drew on his pipe before answering. "I am a hunted man wi' a price on my heid. I came lookin' for safety among my ain folk."

"An your crime, 'sides that o' fightin' fer Bonnie Prince Charlie?"

"I stole a lassie's heart awa' fra a British Officer." Allan truthfully related Major Straight's involvement with Katie and the letter that made them fugitives.

"Where'd you hide in Virginee?"

"Riverview, outside Williamsburg."

"Who be your protectors?"

"Joanna Showcroft."

Rory stopped rocking. Roderick and Alex stopped whittling.

"You lived under the same roof as Talbot Showcroft?" Rory said.

"Fer a short time." Allan glanced at Katie. "'Twas more under the protection o' Mrs. Showcroft."

"Ye better do yer best tae explain." Rory looked from Katie to Allan. "You may be foe rither than kin."

"Why so?" Katie asked.

"'Tis a long tale, Katie Sherrie. Perhaps you'd like tae begin with yourn."

Between them, Allan and Katie told Rory everything ... England ... Horta ... Captain Makem ... Major Straight ... Africa ... Virginia ... their flight to the Carolinas. "We lay low fer a month o'er-mountain when Katie lost her baby. 'Tis the second we lost."

"An' Showcroft knew not who ye were kin tae, or that ye were comin' here?"

"Nothing, Sir," said Katie. "Joanna would never tell. Captain Makem insisted on secrecy."

"A guid man is this Makem-man," Roderick said.

"You are Katie tae us an' thar's no cause tae dibble the Sir," Rory said. "We are simple folk aroun' the Trace. When did this kirkin' between Showcroft an' a Turnbull tak' place?"

"In 1746," Katie said.

"An' the child was born?"

"In October of 1750."

"Stupid git!" Rory slammed his fist into the side of the chair. "Dirty blackguard!"

Katie held Andre to her and shrank from Rory, who'd stood up and come to her chair.

Allan immediately stepped to his wife's side, ready to protect her. Barika stood too, prepared to fight.

"That bairn," Rory whispered hoarsely, "is the son o' Talbot Showcroft but I canna' prove it."

"Explain yourself," said Allan, standing his ground, watching Rory closely. "Don't frighten Katie or the child."

Rory turned from Allan to look over the mountain. "Ye see the ridge? Mairi threw hersel' off that ridge not two months ago, after she weaned the bairn. Tae her dying day, she claimed he was the son o' some gaberlunzie in Charles Town. I knew, and my sons knew, he belonged tae Showcroft. He was here when the babe was in arms. He left wi' nae words."

"How do you know it was his?" Katie asked.

"Mairi said the child was his. Then she changed the story, said she'd lied an' wanted tae trick Showcroft intae believin' he be the fither. Said she did this because she wanted a better life fer hersel' and the bairn. She wanted tae be a lady. This was nae good enough fer her."

"Why would he come out here?"

"Tae look fer Mairi. She was nae in Charles Town when he returned fra England. He was here in April, 1751. Only he dinna' expect tae see Mairi wi' his bairn." Rory closed his eyes. "I can see my daughter. Her face ne'er leaves ma heid. The man's a murderer and an' adulterer. But I canna prove ilka true."

"Showcroft would not wish you to prove it either," said Katie. "I should be sure he left no trace that he had a liaison with your daughter."

"Swore aw doot I'd kill him," Rory looked at his sons. "They be for huntin' him doun, but I want the sweet pleasure. I hae tae be sure. There may hae been ... but why did she jump fra the ridge?"

"She jumped? Was there no message left?" Katie looked at the jagged ridge which the low angle of the setting sun had now turned blood red. "Could it have been an accident?"

"'Twas nae accident. It was in daylight wi' nae fog. She left clothin' fer the bairn."

"You must believe us, Mr. MacKinnon. We did not come as Mr. Showcroft's agents. We came seeking a home, a safe haven, away from Major Straight's far-reaching hand. Mrs. Showcroft is a kind and considerate lady who knows nothing of her husband's infidelity. Indeed, she put herself at great risk to save Allan and me at Horta."

"My grudge be nowt wi' the lady," Rory said. "Ye're safe here as lang as no one blithers. We'll fight fer ye. We're awa' on the western side o' the hielands. We ken the neighbours. They be Prince Charlie Hielanders an' will protect ye. There's work fer ye. Andre needs a mother's care."

"You are very kind," said Katie.

"Wheest," Rory raised his hand for silence. "For this you'll promise ne'er tae speak o' Virginee. You'll cut yer ties wi' the Showcrofts."

" But, I did promise to write, under cover to a mutual acquaintance," said Katie. "Mrs. ... Joanna is a sister to me."

"The line is drawn," Rory said. "Nae contact or nae protection. Yer herts er in Virginee nae doot. Yer loyalty be wi' MacKinnons."

Allan squeezed Katie's free hand. "On Ailpein, we promise," he said.

"The word o' MacKinnon," said Rory. "Do I ken the same fra yer wifie?"

"I do promise," Katie said, a catch in her voice.

"Ye've witnessed that?" Rory addressed his sons and Barika. "When I can avenge Mairi's death, the ban will be taken awa', Goads wull," Rory looked kindly toward Katie. "'Tis fer yer ain protection, lassie."

"But Joanna was so kind to us," Katie whispered.

Roderick spoke up. "I can tak' one o' the horses o'er-mountain tae clansmen in Charles Town. They can put word oot among kin up an' doun coast tha' we are lookin' fer Captain Makem. When his ship comes in tae dock, kinfolk can deliver the horse tae Makem whare'er he be an he'll know tha' they be safe."

Rory ran his hands through his long beard and pursed his lips in thought. "I'll agree tae that. Go tae Charles Town. Let the word be oot that we are lookin' fer Makem's ship. If all be agreeable, Katie an' Allan will live wi' us. Thar's room fer you until yer family grows. An' grow it will in the Carolina air." Rory smiled at Katie. "An' ilka couthie thing tae hae some help raisin' Andre. There's plenty land fer that streak too." Rory pointed at Barika.

"Thank ye'. I'd licht tae stay awheel," Barika said smiling at his joke. "I hae been aroun' Scots fer far too lang."

"Ach, you'll make a guid clansman." Rory laughed. "– 'wi that Scottish brogue you've picked up fra yer frien' Allan."

Katie caressed the sleeping child. "He will be one of my own."

"When the time be richt, the laddie waul claim the Showcroft name," Rory said. "He is entitled tae it. An' I'll prove it tae be his if 'tis the last thing I do afore meetin' my creator."

CHAPTER TWENTY-TWO
RIVERVIEW
May 1752

TALBOT was in a blind fury. His coat and hat were thrown on the floor by the door. Muddy boots left a trail on the hearth rugs as he paced the library, slashing the table with his riding crop. When he heard Joanna enter the room, he angrily spat toward the hearth then spun around to confront her.

"Husband. You have arrived. When did you ride in?" Joanna rushed toward him, but stopped when she saw the look on his face.

"You fired Flanagan," he hissed. "Without my permission, you fired my overseer."

"That I did." Joanna circled the table, Talbot following her.

"Stupid cow, you ought never to have interfered."

"I had the right to dismiss him. He did threaten me with a whip."

"Right?" Talbot sneered. "Do you not understand you have no rights here? Damme, I've put up with this talk of your rights quite long enough."

When he slashed the crop against a chair to emphasize his point, Joanna moved quickly to stay out of range.

"I've been exceedingly patient, played your game, did not object when you hired Bushnell. I tolerated that African in the house. But no more, Wife. Flanagan will come back. The damned African goes to the fields. And you obey me."

Joanna had allowed herself to be backed against the fireplace. Like a caged animal, she had nowhere to go. She fought back. "'Tis a fine husband you are," she said pointing an accusing finger at Talbot. "You return home from a long absence, do not ask after my health nor after your son. You do not mention that the fields, despite Flanagan's absence, look very good. No, you instantly harp about a man who deserved to be dismissed; a man who attempted to murder me. Indeed, I think it would not be a bother for you, Husband, if I were murdered – would it?"

Talbot did not back away from her, he stepped closer. "In your ignorance you have jeopardized the operation of this plantation. You have now a lying, no-good slave in charge –"

Joanna interrupted. "Juba is a good man. Look around you, Husband. The crops are planted. The plantation is producing well. I should hazard that there is not much of concern, nothing to worry over."

"Nothing to worry over?" Talbot spat the words. "When Flanagan's back as overseer, then I'll not worry."

"You mistake, Sir. Flanagan shall not come back," Joanna said. "He dare not step foot on my land again. I will not have him here. I will have him arrested."

"You won't have him! You! Stupid sow, 'tis I who make that decision."

"Nay, Husband. What trumpery! As you do not own Riverview – you've naught to do with its management. How Riverview fares is my concern, and I take it on fully." Joanna's fingers brushed the top of the fire poker and closed around the handle. A shadowy figure moved at the door to the hall.

"The devil you say! 'Tis all my concern," shouted Talbot. "And you shall learn that lesson by the hard route, Wife." He raised the crop.

Joanna was quicker and faced him up with the sharp poker.

The crop stopped in midair. At the same moment he saw the poker, he remembered Makem's threat. "Put the poker down, Wife."

"Nay. Nay, strike me," Joanna said getting a firmer grip. "Have you not wanted to for a very long time? Strike me, and it shall be the first and last time, Talbot Showcroft. I will carry a big knife, and you do sleep soundly."

Talbot seized Joanna's wrist. "Drop the poker."

Joanna twisted away. The poker's weight continued the arc, brought the sharp end up hard and caught Talbot's elbow. He howled.

"Do not touch me again," Joanna warned through clenched teeth, the poker poised to smash her husband's head.

The figure slipped from one side of the door to the other, closer to Talbot's back.

"An arrogant hag, are you not, when you wield a heavy stick?" Talbot dropped his crop to nurse his elbow.

Joanna kept the poker poised to strike again. "I am practical, husband," said Joanna, "but stupid."

Talbot sneered. "You admit to a fault?"

"Excessively stupid. I refused to see properly the man I married. Stupider still, that I never considered the marriage agreement carefully. Ah, Husband, you were indeed charming, eligible, and wealthy. And I did believe that you had an affection for me."

"You mistook me."

"Mother did not. She saw your faults keenly. She told me you were shallow, devious and dangerous. But I was foolish enough to think she may have been misguided, perhaps by a dislike for your mother. You did play your part well, for what little I saw of you."

"My thanks for the compliment."

"It was strange and bothersome that you changed after the news that I was carrying your child. Methinks now that I could easily be dismissed, forgotten. I could languish in England until I tired of your short visits. If I came to America, an accident could be arranged; nay, a murder. That was tried in Williamsburg. But a child did present you with complications."

"Considerably."

"Father did inform me of the business between your father and him. He said emphatically that he had been cheated by a Showcroft. We are cut from the same bolt, my father and I. My word upon it, but I will not disappoint him if in any way he has been wronged."

"He, wronged?" exploded Talbot. "That cheat! Truth is in the reverse. Charles Turnbull brought my father to his knees, and ruined my family's fortunes. Showcrofts were the ones that lost most of their investment."

"No matter who wronged whom," said Joanna, "'tis I now must bear the consequences, and I find it very disagreeable indeed. I did come to America to try to make a decent life for Luke – to protect Father's wealth – to face you directly. With a remnant of sanity, I felt you had some decency in your person, some little hint of kindness. 'Oft expectation fails.' I was much mistaken. You have proven time after time there is not a shred of kindness, decency, fairness in your constitution. I have not the least speck of respect left for you at this moment."

"You have come off the mountain and must finally acknowledge life as it is," Talbot said. "'Tis hardly pretty, is it?"

"Nay, Husband, there is no need for life to be ugly," Joanna replied. "But you make it so and you have no intention of changing your ways."

"You are not without faults, Wife." Talbot stepped back. "Disarm yourself. I will not attack you."

Joanna lowered the poker, but didn't drop it.

"Not now, nor ever, Sir," she said. "You are excessively stupid also, Husband. Harm Luke and you shall live to regret it. You cannot look behind you for the rest of your life. Indeed, if I am found dead under unusual circumstances, you will be the first suspect of the crime."

"But nothing would be done," Talbot retorted. "A woman's life is not worth much here."

"Advocate Shand and Father would never allow my death to go fallow. Nor would Captain Makem, nor Mr. Bushnell. Indeed, it would be madness for you to harm an innocent child who is your flesh and blood – or your wife."

"Bah! There was never a need to plot against the child. He is no threat. Some illness will seize him soon enough; children fall sick and die every day."

Joanna moved away from the fireplace, never turning her back to Talbot, nor letting go the poker. "By your very words, you are a disagreeable, despicable creature – a horrid man."

"Aye, I swear I did not attain the position I enjoy by being pleasant or honest."

Joanna lifted her skirts to back toward the door. "What will it be in this house, Husband – full war or an uneasy peace? Whatever you choose, I am in charge here, and damn the Virginia law or any other that treats a lady as a chattel. You are in my father's house, the home of the man you call your enemy. Choose."

"I can live as easily with war as with peace." Talbot leaned on the table. "Should I choose war? Perhaps. But to what purpose? Time shall be my friend. It will extract a toll. Like a play, life will stage its course. I can wait the turn of the page. My choice – an uneasy peace."

"And the less I see of you, the better I shall like it," Joanna said. "You are no father to your son, nor husband to your wife."

"Stupid witch, I had no intention of being either when I wed you."

"Someone should strike you dead," Joanna said.

"You did have the opportunity to try." Talbot rubbed his sore elbow. "There is one stipulation I must request to this truce. We do keep appearances, of course. Idle gossip bandied about us, especially in Williamsburg where I do business with men of considerable influence, would not be proper, or tolerated."

"You have a great talent for distorting the truth, Husband. And for demanding that others do so too."

"There is one more thing," Talbot said. "Break the nuptial agreement, Wife, and

I'll show no mercy." Talbot walked toward Joanna. "I will seize everything you and your father own if you dare misbehave."

"Aye, and the same applies to you, Husband. I gain all you own if I can prove you have broken the agreement."

"By the Gods, I can wait you out," retorted Talbot. "Your father is an old man and miles away from here. He could be dead now, for all the news you receive."

"Have you finished berating your wife?" Joanna said. She took her time to stand aside so that Talbot could pass through the door to the hall.

With trembling hands, Joanna placed the poker in its stand on the hearth, leaned against the mantel to steady herself, and fought the urge to weep. He had denied nothing, she thought. It was he who conspired to have me murdered. I had the faintest hope my suspicions would not prove true.

At the sound of footsteps, Joanna's eyes opened, and her hands sought the poker again.

Timothy stood by the door to his bedchamber, pistol in hand. "He would not have struck you, Mrs. Showcroft. The gun was pointed directly at him."

"Then you were not the person at the door?"

"That was Ndamma. He was in a real pucker that your husband would harm you."

"Mr. Bushnell, I am sorry that you had to hear this quarrel." Joanna lowered her eyes. "I did not know you were in your office."

"Ndamma fetched me from the garden. I hastened to my office, while he went to the hall door. Pray do not agitate yourself. I heard nothing that I have not already surmised. Accept my apologies for eavesdropping, but it could not be avoided. When I thought you might come to harm, I took pistol to hand."

"Why, Timothy! You would have shot my husband if he had struck me?"

"Yes, but be assured, Mrs. Showcroft, I should not have aimed for a vital part," said Timothy. "I do not relish the thought of hanging for murder. And I am sure, dear lady, that Ndamma would have attacked him, too."

"Let me tell you, Sir, I am glad you are back at Riverview. There were times when I felt I was one against the world. Perhaps, Mr. Bushnell, you had better put the gun away. If my husband returns, he would see your purpose and that would not bode well for you."

"Nay, I have decided to stand my ground," Timothy said. "Talbot Showcroft has taken too much of my life and turned it to his gain."

"Ah, you have found your feet, as my father would say. I congratulate you." Joanna turned to leave and turned back. "Dear me, my manners! My heartfelt thanks, Sir. Once again you come to my rescue."

"Ndamma and I should have defended you, Mrs. Showcroft, whatever the cost to either of us."

"Mr. Bushnell, would you please find the young man and ask him to come to my day room? I must thank him for his actions, and his concern."

Riverview
22 May, 1752
My dear Father,
Your last is at hand, and I thank you for the long and detailed correspondence. Your News brings me into life at Willowbank with great clarity. I have not had much time to miss my old Home, but I think of you often, especially at night when my mind is quiet.

There is little time for frivolous matters at the moment. The past few months have not been without significant Milestones. I exert all my energy in Riverview, and without Talbot's interference.

Mr. Bushnell and I witnessed one African celebration, but it was not without Consequences, one of them resulting in my dismissing Flanagan, the overseer. A nastier, more vile creature would be hard to find. Oh, There was a terrible scene when my Husband did take me to task for the man's Dismissal. The other Consequence, and may it be positive, is that my Slaves now understand I will keep my Word and will stand up for them. If I am loyal to them, they will give back in kind.

One thing rankles me, Father. Talbot labours under the impression you ruined his Father through bad business dealings. I was led to believe that you were the one wronged by George Showcroft. As I do not believe I saw the Ledgers that held these Accounts, at your earliest, please to advise me, which of us is right.

Now that I have relieved my Conscience of that Burden, on to other news …

When I arrived in Virginia, I had firm ideas about how I should reckon with Slavery. I had Dreams of lining my slaves up and stating, 'as of this hour, Freedom is yours'. But that will not come to pass. Indeed, some have known no other place but Riverview as their Home. Others have lived half their lives here. I justify owning them by reasoning that as long as they are here, and I am in charge, they shall not be beaten, branded or sold. They shall be fed, housed, clothed and allowed to speak their mind. They will be given pin-money – not a great amount, just enough to show my appreciation for their loyalty.

In the above Regard, I feel I am living on an island surrounded by two-legged sharks whose voracious Appetites demand slaves be owned and dominated. Not even Jackson Shand shares my Views. As idealistic as he was in England, he did not carry through in Virginia when he was faced with Slavery. He advises me that giving pin money is a dangerous thing to do. I cannot think how, unless he fears they will save the money to eventually buy their Freedom. By the bye, I have heard arguments that Slaves can be Indentured, and by serving Seven Years could be Freed. But I have been made to understand that being Free does not mean true Freedom, if one is Black.

I do have nagging concerns regards persons – and I have one Gentleman in mind as I pen this – who show what they truly are – or believe – one instance, and than Turn-coat in another. I think now of his views on Slavery. Peculiar? Nay, intriguing. Enough of this meandering Mind.

Luke resembles you more every day. Did I mention that he has that peculiar Turnbull Birthmark on his shoulder, like Uncle Jonathan's? Because he was so swaddled as a babe, you would not have known of it on those occasions you held him. He is learning to walk and keeps us in constant Motion. He smiles and babbles when I sing to him, which I do often.

I have mentioned Mr. Bushnell previously. He is an adequate Bookkeeper but possesses other qualities that make him a valuable Friend and Accomplice in conspiracy. My best friend, Katie, and her husband have left Riverview to make a life for themselves elsewhere.

A request before I quit this letter. Could you choose a score of Books from Willowbank's Library that would be suitable for a person who has little Knowledge of the Civilized World as we know it? I recall that you own tomes that would be à propos. Pray do not part with any that are valuable, as I doubt they will be returned. Could you, dear Father, include a copy of Shakespeare's The Tempest?"

As always, I remain, your busy Daughter
Joanna

CHAPTER TWENTY-THREE
RIVERVIEW
1752-1753

NDAMMA learned English so quickly Joanna decided to take his education further by opening a school for her young slaves. As Talbot now rarely came to Riverview, she had little need to consider his opinions. She received objections from a quarter she had not expected.

"Mrs. Showcroft, 'tis commendable to have compassion," Timothy said, "but quite another to give slaves an education."

"To be sure, everyone should learn to read and write," Joanna said. "The land of their birth and their colour matters not."

"Dear lady, not everyone is liberal in their views like yourself."

"Do I care about disapproval, when there are minds to fill with knowledge?" Joanna said. "I'll hazard that there are others who feel as I do: Sarah Binks who, with the Bray Associates, wishes to open a school in Williamsburg for young slave children."

"Yet they have not succeeded in their desire, have they?"

"Williamsburg does have an open attitude. Eventually, I believe, the Binkses will succeed. Ndamma is nearing twenty-one years of age – he is clever and needs to be schooled. If 'tis within my power, I will have him taught."

"Others will not look kindly on your attempts; those who believe slaves must earn their keep by the sweat of their brow."

"And, by all that I have seen, a pitiful keep it is, Mr. Bushnell. It would be against my beliefs not to educate my ... slaves, here and now. I am burning with desire for a school; aye, and I shall do more. It will be a community school, if enough children can be found to attend."

"Some fear educating slaves is the first step toward freedom. I do believe there should be some schooling done. But I fear you will suffer greatly at the hands of those people who have no intention of letting their slaves attain the instruments of freedom."

"True, Sir. And there are some who believe that educating women will lead to insanity! Even Captain Makem did see the need to tutor Caliganto. Those who will not allow schooling are as much captives as their slaves. Their prison is fear of the future."

"Fear of the future does enslave man to mediocrity."

"Well spoken, Mr. Bushnell! Father's fortune can fund a school. But we must be careful to choose the right teacher."

"We must find one who agrees with your noble ideas," Timothy said.

"There, Sir, you use the word 'we'. If you are committed to my school, I shall charge that you be the instructor," Joanna said. "Did you not once say that you taught for a year in a private situation in Charles Town?"

In the end Joanna and Timothy agreed that a school would be suitable, if kept small and held at Riverview. It would convene for an hour each day in a converted storehouse. Joanna coaxed Timothy into teaching duties while she searched for an instructor who could meet her standards.

NDAMMA was told that he would be properly schooled by Mr. Bushnell. He expressed pleasure, but went to Sukie to receive her wise advice on questions he could not ask the Missus.

"If I fill my head with too much of their learning, will I not forget my homeland?" Ndamma asked. "Will I become so different from my people that I cease to be one of them?"

"You be a-learnin' from the Missus' papers wif de pictures."

"I am," Ndamma said. "But the Missus wishes me to learn sums, write words, read a book."

"Take all de schoolin' you can," Sukie counselled. "If Missus not be at Riverview, you'd be sold fas'nough and not a-learnin' to bide anyt'ing but de sting of de whip."

"But I will be different from Juba, from Kudie, from you. My head will be full of things that matter not to you."

"Matter not to me? Do you not understand what you can do wif deir language an' deir numbers? You can use dem to speak fo' us in ways dat dey understand. You can stand up fo' us and fo' every slave, if you know'd how dey think and what is printed in deir books."

"But Sukie, I'll not be free. If I speak and am not free, I will suffer at the hands of those who believe we should not be schooled. I'll be no good if I die under the lash."

"Think beyond de whip, Ndamma. Your mind be de one thing dat can fly beyond de chains. Some day Missus will see dat you use what you learn."

"Missus says I can write what is in my head."

"Dis be true, Ndamma. The Missus'people open a book to read deir history while you must be a-openin' de pouch of stones to do de same thing. If you die," Sukie said, "will anyone be a-takin' yo place? You need to learn how to write, to put what is in yo head on de paper. Then yo people can read it."

"Not if they do not learn to read and write, Sukie."

Sukie took Ndamma's hands in hers. "Perhaps, de day will come when our people will know how to do dem both. You must lead them. Make dese hands work fo' you, by a-holdin' a pen, not by a-hoein' a field. Yo be doin' fine. Yo already be a-talkin' like dem, Ndamma, very good talk."

By the time the school began, Ndamma had made up his mind to learn as much as possible, but he wished to take a Christian name. He also asked if he could, at some time, purchase his freedom.

His questions caught Joanna by surprise. "Am I not treating you well," she asked, "that you want your freedom?"

"It is in the heart of every slave to be free, even if well treated."

"You cannot buy your freedom from me. When the proper time arrives, it will be given to you. And why do you want to assume a new name?"

"To live in your world, one must have a white man's name."

"Ndamma's a noble name."

"It is to be used among my people. Among your people I must adopt a proper Christian name."

"You have considered this seriously, Ndamma? Will one of our names suit a young man of your stature?"

"My stature is only as an African. Others do not respect the marks of a Griot."

"You are to a manor born, just as I. The difference is that we were born to different manors in two separate hemispheres. In England, you would be a Prince in the right circumstances."

"Here I am a slave. I am a body to work. I can be sold, traded, beaten. At one time, I was a gift, to be given away. I was fortunate as Makem and Caliganto chose a good home for Barika and me." Ndamma hung his head to hide his pain. "Barika is ever in my thoughts."

"I wish I could tell you something about Barika." Joanna touched Ndamma lightly on a sleeve. "If you're determined to take another name, choose wisely. Let me know your decision and I will arrange to have you baptized at Bruton Church, to have everything legally presented."

Even though Joanna found out quickly enough that no plantation owners around Riverview had any desire to have their young slaves taught, that did not stop her from opening her school.

"'Tis the mind that makes the body rich.' Shakespeare penned the truth, Mr. Bushnell. Mr. Glenn from the crossroads does understand his children must have some schooling," Joanna said when the blacksmith approached her and requested that the older two children in his family might attend.

Timothy's tutelage soon turned the scholars from skepticism to boundless enthusiasm for learning. Through gentle persuasion, Timothy managed to make schooling interesting for both himself and his students.

All his charges were quick to learn English and sums, but Ndamma's ability to absorb new information intrigued Timothy. The young man was possessed of a quest for knowledge that was insatiable. More and more Timothy and Joanna encouraged him to speak, question and argue.

One day Timothy asked Ndamma to stay after lessons. "You asked me a question several weeks ago," he said. "I am now prepared to answer it."

"Which name do you choose?" Ndamma asked.

"I have given it great thought," Timothy said. "Both are excellent choices. Adrian is Latin for black; David means Lion Killer. I should choose David. A name ought to tell a story, which in your case is true."

"You chose wisely. David's the name I prefer."

"David Showcroft."

"No!" Ndamma said. "Not Showcroft. Never!"

"A slave usually takes the name of the master."

"I will never use the name Showcroft. I will be known as David Bridge."

"Why Bridge?"

"I am a bridge between Africa and America, between differing peoples and civilizations."

"Most interesting," Timothy said. "Think of this. Pont is French for Bridge. David du Pont ... David of the Bridge."

"Yes," Ndamma said. "I prefer that. I will from now on be known as David duPont."

"May I be honest?" When Ndamma nodded, Timothy continued, "You do understand that knowledge does not turn aside whips, nor does it stop a noose from tightening around a neck. Knowledge can sometimes lead to trouble. Are we headed for trouble with your learning so much so quickly? Where will you take this knowledge?"

Ndamma touched the leather pouch at his side. "These people must not be forgotten. Perhaps I cannot stop the whip but I can strengthen my ring of stones. One day these stones will be cast to the ground or become pebbles in a stream. There will be a time when no one will remember or understand their importance."

"I did not understand the true significance of your pebbles," Timothy said.

Ndamma opened the pouch and removed several small stones. "This is Rukan of the Jungle who was put on a ship at ten rains and sold three times. He's the manservant of Advocate Shand. This is Sukie, of Riverview, her mother was from the village of Iudam in my country. Sukie is the mother of seven and woman of Juba of the lower coast."

"By schooling, you will soon be able to record their stories, preserve their history through the written word."

"I may write their story down," Ndamma said, rubbing a stone between his fingers and closing his eyes, "but I can never put on paper the life I feel with my hands, and in my heart, by holding a chosen pebble. My father, unto my father's father, twelve times removed, knew that to be a history keeper, one must feel the life in the stone. How do I write that?"

"I cannot pretend to know everything," Timothy said. "But I can say that you have given each stone a life by memorizing its shape and texture while remembering the history of the person who handed it to you. 'Tis clever, but not a way I should choose to record history."

"It is our way and not yours," Ndamma said. "With a Christian name and freedom, I can travel, talk to Africans, hear their stories, write them down. Will you choose a stone for my pouch, you of little belief?"

Timothy adjusted his glasses and said, "Only if you know me as the educator who once argued vehemently that Africans should not be taught. How wrong I was!"

"You have changed your mind, Teacher Bushnell?"

"Yes, David du Pont. I freely admit that I was wrong. And I apologize."

Riverview Plantation
19, October 1753
Dear Father,
You must think I have left the Power to write, but not so. I do often think of putting Pen to Paper, but running a plantation occupies so much of my time that little interval is left for such pleasures as letter Writing. This one I shall make long enough to appease your Anger and satiate your Curiosity.

About my Husband, I can only say that since he capitulated and allowed me run Riverview, I have seen little of him, so cannot comment on his Wealth and Humour, good or foul. Even though I am now Privy to the true details of the business failure between George Showcroft and yourself, my Heart has so hardened toward Talbot, my love of Fair Play has faded. It matters not now who lost what and how. I am, however, very disappointed, and troubled that you have been less than honest with me.

Luke is a good little boy, with his Grandmother's eyes and your Raucous Laugh. He learns new words every day and likes to be with Kudie in the Weaving house when he is not with Ndamma or Sukie. He now has his own Pony and does spend much time with it. My special time with my handsome little Man is in the Evening before he is given over to Ndamma for care and Protection.

I do believe I mentioned in my last letter that Katie and her Husband left Riverview. I have not received word since their Departure so cannot tell you much about them. Katie was the Sister I never had, and I miss her very much.

I know I wrote about Mr. Flanagan. He has left the region, but Mr. Bushnell says he's heard the man is the Overseer at Talbot's plantation in the Carolinas. Poor slaves, should that be true.

Ndamma has shown so much Interest in learning to do Sums, to read and write that I've begun to operate a modest School. At present there are nine Riverview slaves and Ndamma who have chosen to get an education. I also have two young Girls, Ettie and Louise Glen who walk two miles to attend. I will not force anyone to take schooling if they do not see the blessings of Learning. Ndamma is attempting to read your books. I thank you for them. He is also writing very well. Every day his Speech improves to the point where I fear he will lose his African tongue. He speaks none of the lazy English that my slaves use on the Plantation. I do read Shakespeare to him and he listens with Attention and asks good Questions. Kudie sat for one Reading then said – laus, Ma'am, ah sho don't know'd a word yo was a-speakin'.

Mr. Bushnell is their Teacher ... one hour a day for the general attendees. He spends much more time with Ndamma during the evening hours if both have time. A year ago he did turn his Attention once again to painting with oils and is bothering over a Portrait of me in a Blue Gown which I wore at Horta. He has also painted me standing in a field of Virginia Bluebells but says that he cannot seem to get the colours right. I see nothing wrong with the work.

When I speak of Colour, I must think of Virginia. It is difficult not to be captivated by the beauty of the Colony. Father, you would not believe the Skies. Words cannot adequately describe the depth of the Colour, seventeen shades of Blue, Captain Makem states. He tells me that Virginia's mountains fold to the western horizon in soft blues and greens. He says that in the autumn the Mountains on the western frontier are turned into a palette of gold and red, purple and yellow. I imagine the scene, but my world is so small I can only attest to the brilliant show of Colour around the Plantation, the James River and Williamsburg. Oh, Father, the springtime with the pinks and whites of spring Beauty, Red bud, Mountain laurel and Dogwood, Apple and Peach blossoms! England's spring pales in comparison to Virginia's.

Of the Happenings in Williamsburg, the Burgesses are looking forward to meeting in their new Capitol building that is so near completion it will be occupied before Yuletide. When I attend Bruton Parish Church, I stay for several Days either with The Shands, or with the Binks family, when the Shand household is overwhelmed with other company. Captain Makem did make me *laugh when he stated that Mr. Shand is a good Advocate, but he is not clever enough to hand a letter of Cease and Desist to the Stork.*

Captain Anthony Makem is the ship's captain who, after the Storm, assisted Katie and me in the Azores. When he comes, he stays for two or three weeks and visits with Mr. Bushnell. You need not worry, Father. I should not break the terms of the Nuptial Agreement. Captain Makem is a good friend, and only that. He is, to be sure, a Puzzle who can turn two faces to the sun in the crack of the tongue.

Regards that Document, one of the reasons why I am in America, I fulfill my side of the bargain, but cannot prove that Talbot has not broken his. I know not what he does when he is away from Virginia, and he is a man. Need I say more? This fact bothers me, but I have no means of Spying on him. I can only hope my Kindness and Attentions to certain Friends of his, will result in tales being Told, should they need to be. Enough said about a husband in Name only.

There is a great Difference between a Manor house in England and a manor House in Virginia. At Willowbank the Housekeepers did have responsibility for overseeing smooth Operation, meeting with me once a week. The Gardener ruled over his domain. The Knowledge that I must be more involved in such a Practical way in Virginia did not enter my mind. At Riverview, I do spend much time worrying over the performance of the house slaves. Truthfully, Sukie is most capable, but I must am constantly in motion as someone requires my opinion, my presence, my response. But if I did not watch them, they would Skulk in corners listening to my every Word with Mr. Bushnell. On occasion, when Henkle is not in Attendance, I have stooped to throwing a log on the fire myself to keep warm. That would be an unheard task for a proper lady in England or even in Williamsburg. Does not Mrs. Glenn of the rossroads make her own fire, I ask? I am built of the same Flesh and blood, doubtless have the same Yearnings and dreams. I do it and feel good for having served myself.

I hope this letter finds your Gout improved. Take care, dear Father. I promise to write again soon.
Ever Your loving Daughter,
Joanna

CHAPTER TWENTY-FOUR
WILLOWBANK
6 June 1754

MAKEM stood in the main hall at Willowbank, a man out of place in the surroundings, waiting to meet Charles Turnbull. Resplendent in riding gear befitting a country gentleman, his hair was held by a bow at his nape, and his beard had been neatly trimmed. His boots mirrored the oak floor. Feeling naked without his sword which he surrendered, reluctantly, to a hulking butler, along with his hat, Makem took careful note of his surroundings.

Heavy drapery hung at the multi-paned windows. Light sparkled off gilded wood. Portraits of prominent Turnbulls and Bells lined walls, interspersed with bold and colourfully executed canvases of battle scenes and pastoral landscapes. As he glanced from portrait to portrait, he saw that Joanna had inherited her striking Celtic features from her mother's side of the family.

A door opened at the far end of the gallery and the butler reappeared, bowed and said, "Come this way please, Captain Makem. We'll take the stairs."

Makem was led up the wide staircase lined with Italian tapestries, to a second-floor salon. At a heavy door, the butler knocked, then ushered Makem into the room. Instinctively, Makem's hand fell to where his sword had hung. It took a few moments after he stepped into Turnbull's sitting room, panelled in deep mahogany, for his eyes to grow accustomed to the darkness. The only bright spot was a fire that burned cheerily on the hearth.

"Ah, James, you have brought Captain Makem. I should stand to greet you properly, Sir," a voice said, "but my foot has put me at a disadvantage. I sit here, by the fire. James, would you open the curtains, please."

The heavy drapery was pulled to allow some natural light to penetrate the room. James took a spile from the fire and lit several candles. Makem peered through the dimness to find a paunchy man whose thinning grey hair lay sparse on his head.

"That's better," he said. "Pray sit down, Captain Makem. You've nothing to fear from me."

Makem lowered himself into a comfortable leather chair opposite Charles Turnbull.

"James," Turnbull said. "Please bring a tray of refreshment. The gentleman must be famished. And some rum, too, if you please. Sir, you have caught me at an inconvenient time. I suffer occasionally from a dreary head and must sit in a darkened room to quiet it down. The gout too does keep me chair-bound on occasion."

"The curtains need not be open," Makem said.

"I prefer to see my guests in proper light." Deep-set brown eyes searched Makem's face. Fingers tapped restlessly on the arm of the chair. "Your name is familiar, Sir."

"We've not had the pleasure of meeting," Makem said. "I have a passing acquaintance of your daughter and am a friend of her husband."

Charles smiled. "I'll hazard 'tis burdensome to be a friend to both at the same time."

"It does present its difficulties," Makem said.

"To what do I owe the pleasure of your visit?"

"I promised Mrs. Showcroft that if I were in England I should visit you. As I find myself on your fair shores, I have kept that promise."

"She has mentioned you in her letters, infrequent though they may be."

"In a kindly way, I hope, Sir," Makem said.

When James entered the room with a tray heaped with buttered bread, sliced mutton, condiments and fruit, Charles said, "Leave us to this, James. The Captain appears quite capable of serving himself. Pour a glass before you go." Charles settled back in his chair, right foot on the gout stool, to enjoy his rum. "Forbidden fruit," he said. "It does aggravate the gout, but as a libation it cannot be surpassed. Captain Anthony Makem, what ship do you command?"

"The *Black Wing* out of Norfolk, Virginia."

"Your cargo?"

"Africans." Makem helped himself to bread and meat and glanced at his host. "You show no surprise at my *mode du travail*. Many, and your daughter is a fine example, find it distasteful and offensive."

Charles sipped his rum. "She would, but someone must do it, to feed the appetite of the West Indies and colonies for labour." He savoured his drink. "I do like an honest man. But you brought no slaves to our fair shores. We have the Irish who work for such a pittance it may as well be nothing."

Makem smiled. "I did not run empty. The *Black Wing* is docked at Liverpool. My mate, Caliganto, oversees the unloading of a shipment of sundries from the West Indies, sugar the important cargo. As soon as she's unloaded and I've concluded my business, we sail for Africa. I want to make Norfolk before the new year."

Turnbull grimaced as he moved the elevated foot. "Too much hearty living, Sir, and I now occasionally pay the price. How fares my daughter?"

"She was well, six months past. She has succeeded handsomely in taking responsibility at Riverview, with the capable assistance of Mr. Bushnell and a man named Juba, who is one of your slaves."

"And Jonathan Luke?"

"A strapping, inquisitive lad. He resembles you in some features. To be sure, he is devoted to his mother."

"Truly, I do miss my daughter," Charles said. "Would you be kind enough to replenish my glass? I'll not have servants lurking in corners listening to every word. I suppose I should next be asking after the health of Showcroft, but truthfully I do not care to know."

Makem laughed. "You speak in a straightforward manner, Mr. Turnbull."

Charles leaned forward in his chair, toying with his glass. "You've not traveled to Willowbank to bring greetings from my daughter. I assume you want information."

"That is the exact truth. I do hope for answers," Makem said helping himself to another slice of bread.

"What is your interest in this family?"

"My association with Showcroft is both business and personal. We have had an acquaintance since he arrived in the Colonies and bought his first rice plantation."

"And Joanna?"

"I first met your daughter at Horta when we shared a bit of skullduggery that concerned a fellow by the name of Major Straight. Does that name mean anything to you, Sir?"

"It does not." Charles said.

"Mrs. Showcroft and I met again when I was a guest at Riverview over the Yule season in '51. At that time, she revealed that I was embroiled in her affairs. My name is on the document that pertains to the Plantation."

"Ah, that document," Charles said."My first thought was that you were witness to the signing, but in interesting fact, she did trust you with a copy of the paper. Pray go on."

"I do try to reacquaint myself with the Showcrofts when in Virginia." Makem raised his hands. "But, I assure you, Turnbull, matters between your daughter and me are no more than what they ought to be."

"I certainly hope so. If it were anything else –"

"I'd scuttle your neatly contrived plans to best Talbot Showcroft," Makem finished.

"Aha!" Charles said. "Now we do come to the root of this visit, why you are not dallying with my daughter."

"Framing it crudely, Sir. Showcroft advised me of the terms in the marriage document. What is truly behind such an agreement between him and your daughter?"

"That is no concern of yours," Charles said.

Makem slipped from his chair to poke at the fire, giving Charles time to reconsider. When he sat down again, he said, "It could prove beneficial for you to confide in me."

"You have information on Showcroft?"

"If I knew the reasons behind the document, I might provide assistance, Turnbull. I must make mention of the names Joseph Manesty and Richard Oswald –"

"You dangle Manesty and Oswald like a piece of juicy meat."

"I do indeed," Makem said, "and you know why."

Charles lay back in his chair, rubbing his hands together like a miser about to count his money. "If you are here at the request of Joanna, then I believe she knows you very well, trusts you, and wishes me to meet you personally."

"I assure you there is nothing –"

Charles put his hands up for silence. "My daughter deems you trustworthy, Captain. I tell you in the strictest confidence. Talbot ... may be the product of an *affaire du coeur* between my brother, Jonathan, and Mrs. Jane Showcroft. Jonathan was to have wed another. But, when the promise of hand did not result in marriage, he found solace and companionship close by – with a married lady."

"Not an uncommon thing, methinks, if I am to believe the gossip in London," Makem said.

"Only four people knew of the *affaire* – my brother, Talbot's mother, my wife, and I. I had no reason to doubt the story, for I saw them together on any number of occasions."

"I must assume that Mrs. Showcroft's husband was not privy to his wife's indiscretion. If indeed the babe is your brother's child, Showcroft assumed it was his flesh and blood."

"You read me aright, Captain. At the time, Willowbank, sailing ships, British manufactories, land holdings in India and Ceylon, all financial investments, belonged equally to my brother and me. When he died – Talbot was fourteen years of age at the time Jonathan's holdings came into my hands. I in turn have willed everything to Joanna."

"No provision was made by your brother for Talbot Showcroft? Does that not seem strange, if indeed he did sire him?"

"No. My brother was a miserly man, Captain Makem. He would not give freely of his wealth to a love-child. The waters were further muddied because I conducted business dealings with Jane's husband, George Showcroft, that did not work out to his satisfaction. They resulted in the gentleman sustaining considerable losses."

"If you be willing to gamble, you be willing to lose," Makem said.

"Precisely," Charles said. "But he was very sore about the loss and thought I had somehow cheated him. Of course, his venom, aimed at any Turnbull, passed to his wife. After Showcroft died, his widow demanded that her son receive 'his share' of Turnbull wealth."

"You were not inclined to accede to this demand on behalf of her son."

"Indeed not. Talbot was already making his mark in the Colonies – a rice plantation, holdings in Charles Town, and in the Barbados. I did not deny that he ... may be my brother's child, nor did I say he was. I did wonder what proof-of-parentage she might possess. What could she have that would hold up in court but a signed document from Jonathan?"

"I do believe that you were not obliged to give over anything, if George Showcroft never repudiated Talbot, and unless documentary proofs of his paternity were put in evidence," Makem said.

"And those documents believed by the courts. If they decided to take the action a step further and go to court ... Well, even if they did not have a strong case to put forward, a court could favour him. Historically, our courts lean toward men when property and financial settlements are concerned. I stood to lose at least half Turnbull fortunes to a man who might not deserve them."

"If he could be your brother's son, it might have been a rightful decision."

"Ah, but what proof was in their hands? When I pressed to see their documentation, Showcroft played another card and began to woo Joanna. So effective were his advances that she was smitten with the man. He was relentless."

"And you said nothing, knowing the sort of man Showcroft was."

"On the contrary, I did try to talk to Joanna. Her mother, too, did attempt to sway her, but nothing would break her determination to believe that Showcroft was a decent man who truly wished to wed her. He was not often in England, and she was not privy to men's club gossip to know the true nature of the man. Joanna was at the time ... headstrong. To be sure, I did not myself perceive the depth of the man's villainy."

"The marriage agreement, Mr. Turnbull?"

"It was my wife who first proposed a marriage agreement. She fretted constantly over the fix Joanna was putting herself into. Ah, Lillian, she was always one to play a game!"

"And your thoughts, Sir?"

"To say truth, the more Lillian talked of an agreement, the more I began to realize how ... beneficial it might prove to be ... in certain circumstances. Even though my wife died – quite suddenly while riding, a peculiar accident, not two months before the wedding – I did have the contract drawn up – on my own terms."

"Showcroft did not pother over the agreement?"

"He did not. He was most agreeable. I surmise he saw it as a way to acquire the Turnbull fortune, because indeed he did not hold credible evidence of his parentage. Do you know, Captain, he is keenly well-informed of my wealth, down to the last vessel on the sea, but I have little information on his."

"The man does have substantial holdings in America; he is wealthy in his own right. Were you not chancing your daughter would spurn an agreement?"

"But remember, Joanna did truly believe Talbot was besotted with her. She thought his advances sincere. He can be very charming and persuasive if he chooses. She wished to marry him regardless the circumstances. Such a stubborn daughter she was!"

"Showcroft's charming side, I have not seen."

"When it became apparent they would wed, though Willowbank was in mourning for Lillian, I did discuss the document with my daughter."

"Precisely, Sir, when did you speak to her?"

"After all arrangements for the wedding were made, I told Joanna that her mother had wanted her to sign the document. She was, shall I say, surprised by its terms."

"I should think so," Makem said. "Putting a daughter into such a position is unimaginable."

"I had my reasons for leaving the revelation to the last minute. I did not wish the pair to run off to Gretna Green. Had that happened, what card would Showcroft play next – I daresay a neatly contrived accident might carry me off, perhaps before my Will could be altered? 'Twas a difficult position –"

"I must assume your daughter was not told the true reason for the nuptial agreement – the liaison – a possible court action –"

"Joanna was told that business dealings had gone sour between me and George Showcroft, that is all. I told her that it was George Showcroft who lost my money, not I who lost his. Captain, marriage agreements are not uncommon in England. Many are archaic in nature. Joanna's is ... unusual in its terms."

"And if your daughter had refused to sign? Refused to – play the game, for want of a better phrase?"

"You must understand, Makem, that Joanna is an uncommon lady, as you no doubt have perceived."

"Had she been told the truth –"

Charles interrupted. "The truth, Makem, is that Showcroft blames me for putting his father into poverty, and believes himself entitled to half the Turnbull interests – my hard-come-by wealth, which is Joanna's to inherit."

"Why did you not merely offer Talbot recompense for what George Showcroft lost through the bad investments? Your generous offer might have appeased him."

"If you truly believe that, Makem, you do not know Talbot Showcroft. Nay, whatever I might offer, he would eventually demand more. 'Tis bred in his bones to grasp continuously."

"Greed and madness make easy bedfellows," Makem said. "Please continue with the tale."

"I did manage to persuade my daughter that the agreement was a logical – nay interesting – way to settle any dispute over my fortune. I told her that Showcroft gave no trouble over the document. I played to her love of the game. I played to her sense of family, to her love for her mother."

"You played to her fragility, Sir. This was not a game!"

"Perhaps it was, Captain Makem."

"Sir, to allow her to wed Talbot Showcroft!"

"There was more to the tale. Joanna was astute enough to take seriously her obligation to produce an heir. At her ... advanced age, if she did not marry soon, there would be no children – no Turnbull heirs. She would be the last of the line. Our family has been involved in the East Indian and African spice trade for nearly two centuries, Captain Makem. There is one more important fact Joanna did consider. If the marriage did prove strong, the alliance of Showcroft and Turnbull business interests would make a powerful force."

"I doubt, Sir, she realized how vicious, unworthy and calculating a man Showcroft is."

"Undoubtedly, she underestimated him, as did I. However the wheel turns, 'tis indeed now a case of tenacity triumphant, the most virtuous winning. My belief is Talbot cannot keep his animal nature in check and will break the terms of the agreement with some bit of white flesh he has lollied after."

"And you do not see dark-skinned offspring as relevant? As heirs?"

"Piffle, Sir."

Makem sat for a long time, staring into the fire. When he finally spoke, he could not conceal his contempt. "Your daughter thought that she was being courted for love. Talbot knew he was courting for revenge. And in the end, it all comes down to who is unfaithful first, or who dies first – continence and longevity will win out. You do understand that Showcroft only signed the agreement because he knew that he could dispose of his wife, if necessary. Now, your daughter's life is at great risk as is, mayhap, that of your grandson."

"I did speak with her before she sailed. She knows of the danger by now, I am sure."

"And she has no idea she may have wed her first cousin?"

"Of course not. That was left out of any discussion – by me, and by her mother. Captain, you know first cousins marry regularly. It may be frowned upon on some circles, but rarely is it forbidden."

Makem left his chair and stood by a window, his back to Charles. "Does Talbot not have an unfair advantage in this ... game? He could use the information, be it correct – or not – to appeal to your daughter's sense of integrity."

"That is his card to play if he chooses, but he must provide her proof, and I do believe that he has none. George Showcroft never repudiated him; my brother never acknowledged him; his own mother never took formal action – indeed, she would be mad to attempt any such thing, if she wished to be received in decent society. Talbot Showcroft has little but noise to back him."

"The question is 'Have you proof?'"

Charles hesitated before answering. "Perhaps. But that matters not now. You must understand that although both have much to lose, both have advantages in this game," Charles said. "My daughter's advantage is that she is a determiined and virtuous lady, headstrong though she may be at times. I should hope that her love for Willowbank, and her father, will not allow her to do anything to imperil its future. She knows the full extent of Turnbull wealth, and what it would mean to ... lose."

Makem watched gardeners trimming the formal maze. That's what life must be like for Joanna, he thought. She must find her way through a maze. How could a mother and father play such games with their daughter?

"What information do you have that would interest me?" Charles asked.

"At present, nothing that would aid your cause." Makem turned from the window. "However, your daughter's is not the only life in danger. Talbot Showcroft is a powerful enemy. He must rid himself of you before your daughter inherits."

"I am familiar with the Showcroft venom. His slimy tendrils reach from Virginia and Carolina to England and beyond. I never venture from Willowbank without a well-armed attendant. I do surround myself with loyal people, and I ensured that Joanna was guarded when she resided here." Charles smiled. "Is there anything more, Captain Makem?"

"Do you know a Colonel William Barker, near Sheffield? His daughter Katie was Luke's wet-nurse and your daughter's companion. I must visit the gentleman before I leave England."

"I have heard of him, but not of late. Won't you partake my hospitality for several days? 'Tis lonely without Joanna."

"The invitation is gratifying, but I must be to horse and away. The *Black Wing* sails in a fortnight. Have you a message you wish me to give your daughter?"

"Please tell her that her father thinks of her often. May I venture an old man's advice? I admit to some shocking faults, Makem, but I do love my daughter. If I had no love for her, I should not have reared her in my image and likeness. I have groomed Joanna from an early age to assume responsibility for my business interests."

"A dutiful daughter indeed she is."

"And I do trust our talk will go no further than this room?"

"You have my word."

"Is that good enough? Why should I trust you?"

"Sir, you already have. And I do carry a stick that could offend unless you place some trust in me. Why is it that your daughter knows nothing of your heavy financial involvement with slavery? Why is it that she, who has been groomed to carry on your business interests, has never met Joseph Manesty and Richard Oswald, that they were never extended an invitation to visit Willowbank while your daughter lived here?"

Charles put up a hand to interrupt, but Makem forged on."Pray allow me, Sir. I have taken the liberty of speaking with Manesty and Oswald at your London club. They assure me that you are a good friend, and business partner. They impart the information, as I have long suspected, that you sail your own slave fleet. Where are those ships buried under in your books? Spice ships perhaps? I should venture to guess that there is no visible financial record of Turnbull dealings with slavery that your daughter has seen. You have been careful to keep all slave-dealings hidden from her eyes."

"There are ways to conceal business endeavours, my dear fellow. Joanna has not been made party to the details. She sees only what I wish her to see, Captain Makem. All business pertaining to slavery is taken care of in London, and in the Barbados where I assume that you first sniffed me out, by agents. You must admit, my good fellow, knowing Joanna's high ideals concerning slavery, it would hardly sit well with her that part of this pampered life was paid for by trade in slaves. And, bear in mind, it would not be in her best interests, or mine, to have the information imparted by you."

"I have stated that you can trust me ... for the present."

"Then I must. I did not send Joanna to Virginia, you know. I did not demand she go. The decision was hers. And you must understand 'tis in her nature to try to make good the sham of the marriage. She cherishes a strong loyalty to what the Turnbulls have achieved. She does wish to prove that her strong beliefs have weight, and I believe she feels there might be something lacking in life as she knew it at Willowbank – and I, in part, quote her, Captain."

"I cannot imagine what that might be," Makem said, "unless it is to find a simpler life with someone whom she can truly love, who will truly love her. Perhaps she is trying to be less a copy of her father and more a person of her own principles. She deserves better than a life fraught with miserable people, fanatical worship of money, and no love at all."

"Mind your tongue, Makem. Whatever she is seeking – or lacking – Joanna must find by her own devices."

Makem stood and extended his hand to Charles Turnbull.

"Please do not say it was a pleasure meeting me," Charles said, touching the offered hand. "I feel the disdain you have for me at this moment."

"I am unable to fathom how a father could manipulate his daughter in such scurrilous manner."

"Ah, there is the mistake, Captain, the one quality that you fail to see in my daughter. Like her mother, Joanna has always taken life as theatre, and she becomes a willing participant in its acts. Characters enter and exit. Incidents present themselves. Life's plot takes unexpected turns."

"An actor does know the script."

"Joanna's acts are never scripted. She has always reveled in managing the unexpected twists as they come. Please, Captain Makem, do not let your love for my daughter ruin the game. Remember that Joanna has it in her power to return your love if she chooses to play her marks so. She can throw everything to the winds for true love. And, you must believe me, Sir, I will bide her final decision."

"One plays a game best if one knows the rules."

"Safe voyage, Captain Makem. I shall ring for James to show you out. Ah – Could I impose on your generosity?" Charles asked. "If a portrait of Joanna's mother were brought to the *Black Wing*, would you deliver it to Riverview when you are next in the area of Williamsburg?"

"It will be months at sea, but I'll guard it as if I were guarding your daughter's life."

"Then the delivery shall be arranged. One more thing, before you go," Charles said. "Did you not feel you were being played like a chess piece, today, Captain? For all her kindness and concern, my daughter learned from a master how to use people to advantage. Do be careful, Makem, that you don't become one of her pawns. Alternately, the right man may ... I will say no more."

"Then I'll take my leave."

"Ah, just one more question – why is it you speak like a learned man and act the gentleman when your occupation dictates a different posture? Not that I hold inferior views of sea captains. especially those that command slavers. You are quite simply not what I expected, Captain Makem."

"'Tis nothing to concern yourself with," Makem said, as he left the room. James, who hovered just outside the door, conducted him down the grand stairway.

"A moment, please, James." Makem paused in the hall, eyes again drawn to the portrait of Charles Turnbull's wife. Joanna inherited her beauty from her mother, he thought, but she received her tenacity from her father. Duty and allegiances to him strengthened her resolve to outwit the man she married. Was there something about Joanna that he had not yet perceived? Did a streak of madness run through the Turnbull family? Did her father really love her enough that he would bide her wishes if she did choose to throw his fortunes over for true love?

James handed over Makem's sword and hat at the door. "Safe passage, Captain Makem."

"Good diligence on your part." Makem mounted his horse and put many miles between Willowbank and himself before dark.

Riverview Plantation
7 July 1755
Dear Father:

Never did I miss Willowbank so much as on the 6th of June when I woke in a Melancholia and remained that way for the day. I put off writing until now for fear its Ancestral Walls would call me home.

I vowed I should leave the curse of number 12 behind and have managed to avoid the confounded eccentricity until recently. Ndamma, who now wishes to be called David duPont, came to me with a request. He asked if he could celebrate his Birthday according to our Calendar. As he had no idea on which day he had been born in Africa, he chose December 12th. If he was born in our year 1731 that would make him in your eyes, a perfect twelve. When I asked why he chose such a date, he said, without encouragement, that he liked the number 12. He is, dear Father, a man after your own heart.

Summer Sunsets are so beautiful in Virginia. They take one's breath away. To dispel my gloom, I sat by the River to watch it. With the glorious display of turquoise melding into bird's egg blue then deep navy, and pink clouds tinged with the deepest of purple, my mood lifted and remained high on a soft wind that blew from the south.

I thought, What difference between life at Willowbank and life at Riverview! You spend your days fitting Moneymaking Schemes into your overwhelming desire to worship the number 12, and any of its Compatibilities. Mr. Bushnell spends his days bent over the plantation's Books or at an Easel with Brush in hand. To make matters worse, he now will not let me see the Portrait, and locks it in his bedchamber when I enter the office.

Why is it that humans must be Dominated by someone or something? In your case, 'tis your silly fixation with the Number 12. In mine 'tis Talbot who still dominates me to a certain extent. And I, in turn, dominate my slaves. I am ashamed to say that I have still not reached the point where I can set them Free. I find that I cannot find enough free men to work for me and therefore I must run this plantation with slaves. 'Tis my Opinion that there are too many Opportunities in this country for ambitious Men that don't include Field Work. No white man, unless he is indentured, will bend his back for anyone but himself and his betterment.

Five years ago I was determined to change the world. The world, that is Riverview, is beginning to change me. Making money for you, and trying to best my husband, has compromised my ideals.

My one bright spot is Ndamma – David – who is ever the sponge for knowledge. If there is a shining example of what Education can do, he is it. But, I fear, he is caught between two worlds, two cultures, just as I am caught between two countries, two ideals. Breaking free will be more difficult for David.

Luke is well, a handsome boy with a shock of brown hair but no Penchant for Mathematics. Unfortunately, the demands of managing a plantation are such that I don't spend as much time with him as I should. But he is an understanding little Gentleman and finds his way around the plantation more like a little native than a proper English child. When Ndamma is not in the classroom, he is kept in motion attempting to keep up with the boy. Sukie says that he is a-messin' and a-guamin.

Captain Makem graciously delivered mother's Portrait, stayed for a few days over the Yule season, then left for Baltimore. I do thank you for the painting. It hangs above the fireplace in the library. Could I prevail upon your generosity once again? Would you please acquire a copy of Samuel Johnson's <u>Dictionary of the English Language</u> *which I have been informed has been published? I want that tome to be part of Riverview's library.*

As for Talbot, I have no idea where he is at the moment, nor do I much care. He will be home for the festive season, no doubt.

At Willowbank I had household staff and your business associates who came regularly. At Riverview, I have my household slaves and the occasional business associate who visits. Have you ever noticed, Father, that you can be surrounded by people yet feel that you are the loneliest person in the world.
As ever, your daughter,
Joanna

CHAPTER TWENTY-FIVE
MACKINNON'S TRACE
Late Autumn 1755

FROM beneath the oak tree in the upper meadow, Katie surveyed her kingdom. A new wooden bridge crossed spring-fed Elder Creek which rose on the ridge before meandering through rich bottomland. Ancient mountains wore autumn's brilliant mantle on their slopes. Billowing clouds rose over the western rim and, driven by a freshening wind, curled across the sky, painting fast-moving patterns across fields of golden corn. Mairi's Overlook was free of fog, sharp of detail.

Barika and Alex harvested corn on one side of the creek. Allan and Roderick worked oxen in a field on the other. A milch cow, Rory's present to Katie for birthing Thomas, her first live baby, was pastured with the horses near the open-sided byre. The pigsty, surrounded by a newly built stone fence, was well away from the house, but not too near the deep woodlands where bear roamed freely.

A log fence, interwoven with twigs and vine, kept the hens out of Katie's kitchen garden. Allan had diverted the spring's water so that it flowed through a spring house and into a wooden drinking trough before running by the chicken yard and into a small pond in a hollow that the geese claimed as home. The cabin, anchored to the trace by two massive stone chimneys on north and south sides, was sheltered by old hickory and oak trees. In a quiet corner of the clearing, near a gnarled ancient maple tree, a simple stone marked Mairi's grave.

Pumpkins were stacked high at the end of the cabin's west porch. Some Katie would peel and cut into strips for drying. Others would be stored in the lean-to for animal feed. The winter's supply of wood was stacked against outside walls.

Rory appeared on the porch and waved a white cloth. That was her signal that Thomas was awake. He called to Andre, who was helping to put apples in barrels, and pointed in Katie's direction. Little Andre left his work and started up the valley toward the oak, his sturdy legs churning through the meadow's stubble.

Rory MacKinnon had suggested Katie be left alone for a while. The day before, Barika and Alex had returned from Wilmington with supplies. One of the items used to protect a crockery jug for its journey over-mountain was a ten-month-old British broadsheet. On it, Katie read of her father's death. Until the end of his life, her father had not forgiven her.

His demise, the paper stated came ... *after an evening at the British Officers Club. While in the company of a gentleman of the British Army he appeared to fall, hitting his head on the cobblestone street. He died within a short time of a broken head. It is believed he left no heirs.*

As she watched Allan work alongside Roderick, Katie did not for one moment regret her decision to marry him and immigrate to the Colonies. She had, in Rory's terms, rekindled her hearth in the highlands. Katie stood and placed her hand to the small of her back. Although only four months along in her pregnancy, she already felt the strain of carrying this babe. She walked carefully through the meadow, watching Andre run to her. Under the influence of the men, Barika in particular, Andre was going to be a man's man, as Rory put it.

To survive in the highlands of the Carolinas, Rory had explained to Allan and Barika shortly after they arrived, a man had to be cunning and alert. Most people took a man for his abilities, not for his background or colour. In the MacKinnon household, Barika was treated as an equal. He quickly learned the ways of the mountains, as he had in his youth learned the ways of the jungle. When the chores for the day were finished, Andre attached himself to the strong, gentle African who treated him as a baby brother. Katie tempered the male influence by giving the boy a mother's love.

Katie laughed aloud as she recalled the men's reaction to her news about the latest pregnancy. Allan was overjoyed. Rory was excited. Roderick and Alex were less than enthusiastic, as their living quarters shrank with each addition to the family.

"We'll add tae the cabin," Rory said. "We'll cut the north slope this winter an' hew the timber. We'll build another section, just like this one an' link the two with an ell.

Then you an' Allan can hae yer ain hame."

"'Tis sorry we are to put you out," Katie said.

"The tract o' land in the cove o'er Booker's Hill be ours. There be room fer everyone when the time comes tae move. I am payin' Allan and Barika in land, nae money, Katie. An' now, four miles awa' be the Webster family."

"With their four daughters," said Roderick grinning.

"Life can only get better," laughed Allan. "It always does when women be aroun'."

Andre met Katie in the middle of the slope and took her hand. "Gran'pa says not to fall."

"It would not be good for me to tumble down-meadow," admitted Katie. "How many apples did you pick?"

"Sacks o' 'em."

"Goodness. I will never get everything preserved this year. Look at these hands, Andre." She held up rough, red hands. "My mother would never have permitted her daughter to have hands like this. They are not the hands of a lady, you see. But these are something to be proud of. They are the trademark of a hard-working mountain woman."

"A lady," Andre said.

Katie ruffled the little moudiewart's hair. He was going to be a tall, handsome, intelligent lad. A brief thought of Luke Showcroft crossed her mind. Was he as tall as Andre? As strapping a lad? "Do you want to learn sums tonight? Or shall I read to you?"

"Barika an' Alex are takin' me coon huntin'. Gran'pa says I can go."

"Sums are important," Katie said making a mental note to talk with Barika about taking such a young boy hunting.

"Not near as excitin' as coon huntin'. Alex says sums don't put tatties on the table."

"I can't argue with that."

"'Sides, four coon skins gets him a tin plate an' cup. That's sums, isn't it? Four is two?"

Katie sighed. "I do suppose in mountain terms it is."

Andre pointed to a granite rock, half-buried mid-field. "Don't trip, maw. D'ye miss yer paw? I donna' miss my mither cause I didna' know her."

Katie looked at the wise, talkative little man. She had poured all the love she had for her father, Luke and Joanna into raising Andre. She had emptied her heart out to him as she rocked him to sleep, talked to him, read to him, told him stories, sang the old songs. He was quick to learn and responded with equal love and attention. The mountains raise men quickly, she thought. He's so young, yet hardly a child anymore.

"At first I missed him, and I felt the loss of my ancestral home. It was a beautiful place with rose gardens, ivy covered walls. And there were miles and miles of moor. But I love Allan, just as you love the mountains." Katie stopped to catch her breath. "Oh, I loved my father, too. I did try to forgive him and to forget my old home once I came across the sea."

"Why did you come o'er?"

"I could settle for Father and a man I did not love, or Allan, whom I love dearly. I chose Allan and all that came with him. But death is so final, and I never said a proper farewell, or told Father that I did love him. Now, I will never have the opportunity."

Katie heard Thomas' lusty cry. "We had better walk faster. Sounds as though Grandpa has his hands full."

"He canna' but watch the babe. Soon as he can walk proper again, he'll be stumpin' in the fields."

"You be careful, Andre. You could twist your ankle in a sinkhole just as Grandpa did. Then you'll have to stay inside and do sums all day."

CHAPTER TWENTY-SIX
WILLIAMSBURG
November 10, 1755

The Lieutenant Governor's Rout

THE King's Birth-Night celebrations were much anticipated in Williamsburg. Festivities continued for a week, with the final day given over to a fair on the Palace Green, and the Lieutenant Governor's Rout in the evening. The town's population swelled for the occasion. Inns were packed. Private homes hosted friends and relatives. Even without an invitation to the ball, folks came to town just for the show, knowing the best of colonial society would make an appearance.

On Birth-Night they gathered on the Green for the display of pomp and ceremony that accompanied a Rout and fireworks. The palace tower made a brilliant artificial moon with lanthorns in its windows. Torches lined the drive to the imposing red brick mansion. Wrought iron gates were thrown open to welcome invited guests. Liveried servants waited at open doors to take cloaks. The interior of the palace was bathed in the light from scores of candles in wall sconces, chandeliers, on mantels, tables and sideboards. Over-door decorations were thick with greenery and entwined with colourful ribbon. Footmen served claret cup, wines and pasties.

With jewels shimmering in the light, lavishly costumed ladies curtsied and flirted their way through the public rooms, wisely staying clear of fires on the hearth and candle-stands. Skirts too close to open flames could ignite and bring the evening to a disastrous close. In the palace's entrance hall, men in elaborate satins and velvets competed for attention with the display of weaponry on walls and ceiling and the polished silver. Outdoors, on the side lawn, a few gentlemen kept an eye on a second floor bed chamber window. When a white handkerchief was waved, the Lieutenant Governor was ready to receive his guests. The gentlemen moved to entrances to claim their wives for the reception line.

Joanna watched Talbot stop several times to acknowledge greetings from friends before he reached her. They made a striking couple, she in a deep green silk gown *à l'anglais* with low neckline, and Talbot resplendent in claret-coloured silk and silver brocade waistcoat, with lace jabot and cuffs, gold buttons and silver buckles.

"I understand the Lieutenant Governor has an important guest assisting tonight." Talbot gave Joanna his arm as they joined the line at the foot of the stairway. The receiving line began in a large open salon at the head of the stairs.

"Does anyone know who the person might be? I do hope that 'tis the Emperor of the Cherokee Nation with his good wife. I did enjoy their company three years ago this month at the King's Birthday Ball."

"Rumour has it that 'tis Colonel Washington, come from Winchester to try for a seat in the House of Burgesses. The governor has been closeted at the Palace since the fellow arrived this afternoon. None knows the name, not even Makem."

"Captain Makem is in attendance?"

"He arrived before the noon-day gun. Did you not know he had returned?"

Joanna lifted her full skirt to ascend the stairs gracefully. "How, or why, would I know, Husband? I assumed he was yet on the high seas."

"He spoke of naught but you when he was in Charles Town."

"If he had taken pen to paper, you would have been told," Joanna said. "But, Sir, you neglected to mention your visit to Charles Town. Truly, I am never privy to your travel plans."

"Do you look for a quarrel?" Talbot said.

"That would hardly be proper at the moment." Joanna fanned herself, glancing around. Makem stood in the lower hall, by the front entrance. "Such a display of weaponry in the entry," she said.

"English pomposity," Talbot said. "On my word, Makem is here, below us."

When Makem favoured them with a graceful leg, Joanna tipped her fan toward her bosom to acknowledge his greeting. He bowed again and made a signal with his hand. Joanna frowned. Was he attempting to tell her to go to the bottom of the stairs? In this press? She shrugged and shook her head slightly.

Talbot took Makem's signal as being for him. "I believe the man does wish to speak with me. I will seek him out after we have been received," he said. "The place is in shockingly poor taste. A reception salon on the second floor where the bedchambers are located is an unaccountable breach of design for a public building. And that Dinwiddie would not use the new ballroom to receive this night ..."

Joanna had to agree. Those already through the line who were descending to the public rooms shared the same space as those ascending. Women, in their large skirts, inched past each other, leaving no room for the gestures of formal greeting. Five steps and Joanna would be at the head of the stairs. She could now see the wigged heads of the official party. My dear! No! She gasped and fanned vigorously.

Major James Straight stood beside Lieutenant Governor Dinwiddie.

Talbot took firm grip on her arm. "We have almost reached Dinwiddie. 'Tis warm, but do not faint now and make a scene."

Joanna held the open fan before her face. "I fare well," she managed to say. "'Tis a little musty with perfume and powder." She tried to compose herself in the few minutes left before confronting Straight.

So that is what the Captain was trying to indicate, she thought. He knew Straight was with the Lieutenant Governor.

"We are very near now," Talbot said. "An introduction and curtsy then we will take some air."

"I am quite beyond a faint," Joanna said. Be still my heart! she thought. There is no retreat. I must meet Straight head on.

Joanna looked behind her for Makem. He was not visible on the grand stairway. As she moved toward Dinwiddie, Straight's eyes never left her face. Joanna curtsied low before the Lieutenant Governor and his lady then moved on to stand before the Major.

"My wife," Talbot made the introductions.

"We need no introduction," said the Major. "We have a passing acquaintance."

Joanna lowered her eyes and curtsied. "We have met," she said. "It was at Horta, was it not? I accepted your invitation to an afternoon fête." She summoned the courage to look directly at the Major.

Straight's eyes blazed but his voice betrayed nothing. "I shall demand a dance later," he said. "Call it payment for a debt not collected." With a flourish of his hand, he dismissed Joanna.

"Another secret?" Talbot asked as they made their way back down the stairs. "I had no notion you knew the Major."

"He was Attaché at Horta when the *Charlotte* lay over for repairs." Joanna tried to dismiss the meeting as being inconsequential. "To be sure, the gentleman did not impress me at that time. An invitation was extended for me to stay at his compound while repairs were made to the ship. I declined the offer as Captain ... Henry had made other arrangements."

"You seem to have made an impression on him, Wife. His eyes ate you."

Makem, waiting at the foot of the stairs, looked keenly at Joanna. "You look a bit piqued, my lady. Perhaps a stroll through the formal gardens?"

"Truthfully, I could take some air," Joanna said.

With Makem on one side and Talbot on the other, the trio made their way to a bench in the formal garden. "Courage, my lady. Our worst fears may have been realized," Makem whispered as Joanna sat down. "The Major's out for blood."

While the men engaged in a serious discussion some distance away, Joanna tried to collect her thoughts. Why would James Straight appear more than four years after his first futile attempt to kidnap Katie? Was he in Virginia to sniff out her trail? Had he been posted to Williamsburg? It was obvious from the punch-pleased look on Straight's face that he knew Joanna would be in attendance at the Rout.

After the meeting, Makem left the garden without speaking to Joanna, while Talbot offered his arm and walked her toward the palace.

"How do you know Major Straight?" Joanna asked Talbot.

"Our paths cross infrequently. He interferes with my business interests. He is military and English. Makem and I do break rules on occasion. What is your association with him?"

"As I told you, I attended an afternoon fête at his compound. I sensed that he was a dangerous man, and kept up my guard with him."

Talbot laughed. "Are you so conceited? Do you think he wanted to seduce you? He could have had any native woman he desired."

"That is disgusting, Husband."

"'Tis truth. If I remember correctly, Straight was spurned by an English lady, and never forgot the insult. I met with the Major in London three years ago, on my last voyage. He still talked of it. I find it strange he would not have mentioned that he met you at Horta? What is this debt you owe him?"

"I've no notion," Joanna lied. "Perhaps 'twas a remark made for effect." She played with her fan. "No matter. That fête was years ago. Listen, the violins. Shall we to-foot?"

The couple were immediately drawn into a minuet. Joanna mechanically performed the steps, smiling at her various partners and answering their small talk, but she covertly surveyed the room for either Makem or Straight. In the second dance, Joanna found herself in a set with Jackson Shand. "Have you seen Captain Makem? My husband has been looking for him."

"No," Jackson said as he turned her, then bowed to her deep curtsy. "Major Straight was asking after you not long ago."

Joanna begged off the next set and retreated to the entrance hall. Captain Makem was not among the cluster of men talking near the door. She climbed the stairs to the second floor powdering room, with an eye out for Straight. When she finished her toilette, Joanna stepped out to cross the reception salon.

James Straight moved from the shadows and stood in front of her. "Well, my pretty bird. Any tricks up those delicate sleeves tonight?"

Joanna tried to step aside.

"Not so quick. I have something that is yours. Do you prefer I give it to you now, or later – downstairs?" Straight held the comb that had fallen from Joanna's hair in his bedchamber. "Would not your husband like to hear the story of this little object? Could I not smear a lady's reputation with a tale about this comb?"

"Blackmail does not suit me," Joanna said. "I shall say you pressed yourself upon me after I, by honest mistake, stepped into your chamber to adjust my bodice."

"And I shall say that you begged me to seduce you." Straight seized Joanna's arm and twisted. "We must talk. I demand to know the whereabouts of Katie Sherrie."

"Are you mad, Sir?"

"You know where she is." Straight tightened his grasp.

"Unhand me, Major! I shall scream."

"You are too much a lady to make a scene here. Shall we walk in the garden? Damme! Someone on the stairs!" Straight released his grip.

"Why, Mistress Hartwell! And Mistress Randolph, is it?" Joanna said, walking toward the head of the stairs. "Such a lovely night, is it not?"

Straight shrank into the shadows so that the ladies could see only Joanna as they passed. As soon as the ladies entered the powdering room, he seized Joanna again and pulled her toward the door of his bed chamber. "We shall converse, now!"

"Have you taken leave of all your senses, Major Straight? Are you utterly mad?"

Straight tightened his grip. "A kiss – and then a walk." He bent to Joanna and forced his lips upon hers. Joanna pushed at his chest, struggling, and broke away from him. When he pulled at her again, she screamed and fell gracefully to the floor, limp in a supposed faint.

The Mistresses Hartwell and Randolph rushed from the powdering room. Joanna lay limp on the floor, as a shadowy figure skulked in the back hall. Mistress Randolph screamed and ran toward the stairs.

Straight bent over Joanna, and chafed her hands. "I had but emerged from my bed chamber –"

The figure in the back hall turned and vanished down the servants' stairs. Talbot pushed through the crowd that had gathered, and knelt beside Joanna. Lieutenant Governor Dinwiddie was steps behind him.

"Place her in my chamber," Straight said. "This way."

"These marks on her arms," Talbot said. "How, by the love of God, did my wife acquire such bruises?"

"That rogue Makem, was in the hallway not a quarter-hour ago," the Major said.

"Captain Makem volunteered to undertake an important errand for me. I believe he has been gone this half-hour," Dinwiddie said.

Joanna stirred – moaned – shook her head and blinked, to make her entrance as convincing as her exit.

Talbot reached to assist her to her feet.

"How – how monstrous silly of me. I dropped my comb." She looked from Talbot to the Lieutenant Governor. "I did not see the Major emerge from his room ... he reached to retrieve it, and I – I was startled." She turned appealing eyes on Dinwiddie and several of the men. "After those tales tonight of native women and the Azores ... I took fright and fainted."

Mrs. Hartwell tried without success to hide a giggle behind her lacy fan. Several men laughed heartily. The Major's lips were a thin, angry line, his eyes cold, ugly, haunting.

"A lady can never be certain with a man as handsome and ... manly as Major Straight," Joanna sighed.

Straight flourished a low bow to Joanna. "A pretty compliment," he whispered hoarsely, "from a – *lady* – who leaves her combs in strangers' bed chambers."

"That is slander." Talbot stood ramrod straight. "and certainly cause for a quarrel. Name your friends, Sir, and choose your weapon."

Straight sneered. "And a widow maker I am, Showcroft."

"Gentlemen!" Jackson Shand stepped between the two. "Straight's comment is no cause to spill blood. I was in the hallway ... back there ... examining some weaponry. Mrs. Showcroft had come upstairs and mistook the Major's chamber for the powdering room. She retreated quickly enough when she saw her error. I am sure the lady was just as startled to find the Major in the doorway as he was to see her attempting to enter it."

"Ah. A misunderstanding," said Dinwiddie. "Come, gentlemen. A lady is rarely cause for a duel, far less to die for." He gave his arm to Joanna. "May I escort you down the stairs? Pray accept my apologies for that last remark."

Joanna accepted the arm and turned her back on both Talbot and James Straight.

"Put the comb away quickly, my dear." Dinwiddie whispered into her ear. "It does not match those in your hair. May I suggest you and your husband quit my house immediately? I've no wish for bloodshed at my celebration. If Straight must challenge your husband, he shall do so elsewhere. He has already challenged Makem, who would dearly love to put his hands around the man's scrawny neck."

"Your Excellency, what has passed is not what it appears ... I did not ..." Joanna said. "Believe me, Sir, Major Straight has no grounds for his slurs."

"No matter," said the Governor. "'Tis likely the Major will follow you to Riverview. Be warned, he will not leave without the information he wants."

Joanna had expected an angry exchange with Talbot when she asked him to take her home, pleading Dinwiddie's advice. But Talbot calmly declared that they should return to Jackson Shand's home, where they were staying for the celebration.

"Pray desist from these silly games, Joanna. You know why we were asked to leave." Talbot lifted her cloak to reveal the bruises on her arms. "Straight inflicted these. Fear not; I shan't rush back to confront him. I am not that chivalrous."

"But you did challenge him." Joanna twitched her cloak from his hand.

"A moment of insanity, nothing more. I demand the truth, Wife, and nothing less."

Joanna smoothed the folds of her cloak, giving herself time to think. "Husband, I do believe that Major Straight is a madman who will leave no one in peace until he gets whatever he seeks. The English lady who spurned him was Katie Sherrie ... my friend Katie."

"Of course! She was with you at Horta."

"Fate and circumstances placed her and the Major on Faial. Soon after we arrived for repairs, Captain Henry saw that the Major had designs, not only on Katie, but also on the *Charlotte*'s cargo. We devised a scheme, using a modicum of deception and deceit on the Major. I played a leading role in thwarting his attempts to spy upon ships, cargo and Katie Sherrie. Of course, Captain Makem assisted. Mr. Sherrie sailed with him for Africa to avoid detection."

"Straight accosted you in the hall and demanded to know where Katie is?"

"He did."

"And where is she, Wife?"

"Alas, I do not know. After word came that the price on Mr. Sherrie's head had been increased, three years ago, they left Riverview. I've not seen or heard of them since."

"Not one word?"

"Nay, not one. Talbot, I have no need to lie to you. 'Tis as though the earth has swallowed them up. Truly it would be to their advantage to correspond with me. I did give them money when they left, and promised to back a business venture when they settled. And yet I have heard nothing."

"That agrees with Makem's information. It appears that Straight received a letter from Baltimore, reporting that the man he was looking for had at one time sailed on the *Black Wing*. It would make sense Straight would travel to Norfolk to find Makem, then come after you, surmising that the Sherries were here."

"Straight is not rational; quite mad. He is intent upon Katie and believes he can make her accept him. He means to kill her husband and spirit her away."

"I see why the woman refused to wed him. Damme. You must make Major Straight understand you do not know Mrs. Sherrie's whereabouts."

"I shall agree to meet him," Joanna said. "But I will do this alone, in Williamsburg. I request that only Lieutenant Governor Dinwiddie accompany me."

"An absurdity, Joanna. I demand to attend."

"'Tis not my habit to ask your assistance when the imbroglio is of my making," Joanna said. "There'll be blood spilled if you and Straight are in the same room. We do have our differences, but your life shall not be endangered because of Katie and Allan Sherrie."

"It would serve your purpose well to have me thrown into a duel with the Major, would it not? Should I not be present to keep up appearances?"

"I do not play my games by your rules, Husband. Believe me, my intentions do not include having you killed for your wealth."

Retribution

A STORM passed over Williamsburg during the night. It settled the dust, left pools of water everywhere, and shrouded the early dawn in a muggy fog. Joanna, hearing loud voices on the green, slipped from beneath damp bedding to glance out the window. Talbot stood in the middle of a large group of armed men. Hurrying from her room, Joanna met Elizabeth at the foot of the stairs.

"Come into the library, Joanna."

"'Tis barely daybreak. Why are those men armed?"

"Major Straight's body was found on the post road one hour ago."

Joanna stared open-mouthed at Elizabeth. "The Major dead? An accident?"

"'Twas no accident. He appears to have struggled with someone. His horse was found in a field a half a mile from the scene. Nothing of his had been taken."

"Could he have fallen from his horse?"

"Nay, Joanna, he was strangled. Someone killed him with their bare hands. The marks are on his neck."

"What a dreadful way to die, even for the Major!"

"But who has the strength to overpower Straight and strangulate him bare-handed? Straight was a strong man. The conclusion is not pleasant. Joanna, whom do you know that has such strength – and the motive for killing the man?"

Joanna thought for a moment. "Oh, Devil take it! No!" she cried out. "I can only think of Caliganto or Captain Makem."

"The same conclusion has been reached by that unruly mob. They are ready to go seek both men. Your husband is trying to talk some sense to them."

Joanna leapt to her feet. "But 'tis only conjecture that Caliganto or Captain Makem killed the man. There must be others with the same strength and capability."

"To what purpose? Those near the Palace last night heard the Captain and Major Straight in a violent argument."

"Upon my word, we must tell them –"

"Tell them what?" Elizabeth interrupted her. "You do not have an excuse for Captain Makem and Caliganto, unless they slept at your feet last night. You are showing a shocking lack of good sense."

Joanna paced back and forth before the library windows, eyes on the mob. "They will not give a fair trial to anyone, certainly not to Caliganto."

"Joanna, do allow your husband to manage them. By the bye, he insists you return to Riverview and has ordered your carriage to be ready for half after seven o'clock."

"I refuse to leave," Joanna said.

"Your husband made a great point of sending you back to Riverview immediately. On my word, there's nothing you can do here, Joanna."

"Where is Captain Makem?"

Elizabeth put her hand on Joanna's arm to stop her pacing. "He has not been seen since the Rout."

"I must find him. He must be warned."

"Joanna Showcroft! Are you putting the Captain's life over that of your husband?"

"Elizabeth! How can you ask such a question?"

"Your husband is not above suspicion. He challenged the Major at the Palace. If he did not have the strength to kill the man with his bare hands, he knew some who would be only too happy to do the deed."

"But he is now in the centre of the mob."

"People saw him leave the rout with you. He has stated that he was with you all night. Was he indeed? I think not, if my servants' whisperings are true."

"My husband ... would never kill the Major on my behalf," said Joanna.

"Perhaps he has his own reasons for wishing the Major dead. You must return to Riverview, Joanna. If your husband wants you there, he must have his reasons."

The ride to the plantation never seemed longer. Her mind in a turmoil, Joanna went over all the previous evening's circumstances. Questions boiled to the surface. Where was the Major going on the post road? The road led south to Norfolk. Riverview lay west and across the James River. Talbot had not slept in her room. She heard him slip out of his chamber shortly after the house quieted down for the night. Where had he gone? Where had Makem gone?

As the carriage crossed the bridge and the orchard came into view, Joanna took note of three new horses grazing among the trees. She ordered the driver to stop and stood to have a better look at the animals. One was, beyond any doubt, the horse that Makem liked to ride. The second was Caliganto's black steed. The other ... ? Puzzled, she asked for a hand out of the carriage to have a closer look at the animal.

Timothy met her at the front entrance. "You have company, Mrs. Showcroft," he said, "Makem and Caliganto are in the cookhouse."

They made their way quickly to the building where Makem and Caliganto were seated at Sukie's bake table, devouring cornmeal bread and honey. "Captain, I was done up with fright thinking that you or Caliganto had been injured."

"By whom, dear lady?" Makem asked.

"The Devil's in it that Major Straight has been murdered by strangulation, on the Norfolk Post Road. Indeed the word is that the marks left by the murderer's hands are still on his neck. The Williamsburg mob believes the only person capable of doing the deed is you or Caliganto."

Makem and Caliganto exchanged glances. "An absurd assumption for anyone to reach. We came directly to Riverview after I left the Rout."

Timothy spoke up. "Makem and I have been together since he arrived. Many months have passed since his last visit and we had much to talk about."

"That does give Captain Makem an excuse but, Sir, there is Caliganto must be considered."

Sukie spoke from behind a wooden clothes rack. "Ma'am, Caliganto gib de hand cause Cansu and Kudie be in de weaving room."

"My word! And who will believe that one sat and chattered all night while the other did spend hours in the cookhouse. Not I, for one!"

"Mrs. Showcroft is all reason and rationality," Timothy said. "The man was a Major in the King's Army. His death will not go unpunished. We must have affidavits drawn up, and witnessed, that you were here, gentlemen."

"Advocate Shand! They shall be drawn up then delivered to Mr. Shand," Joanna said. "Henkle can ride them to Williamsburg. We must have writing materials ... in the house." She suddenly noticed that Anthony and Caliganto were underclothed. "Why do you sit in underpinnings, Captain Makem? Caliganto?"

"Begorra, if a heavy rain did not catch us on the road last night." Makem. said, looking again at Caliganto. "Sukie is drying a few trifles by the fire."

"We did have a fast shower in Williamsburg last night," Joanna admitted.

"Rained here, Ma'am," Sukie said. "It done gif me a baf when ah was a-comin' to de cookhouse."

"When you gentlemen are presentable, please oblige me by coming to the day room where we shall tend to those affidavits."

Joanna left the cookhouse and walked through the flower garden to the back entry. Stooping to smell a winter rose, she frowned, snapped the blossom off, shook it, looked round the garden then back toward the cookhouse.

When Anthony appeared, Joanna was ready for him. "A monstrous lie. No shower passed over Riverview last night," she said. "There appears no great quantity of water in the gardens. Roads this side of the river were not muddy this morning."

"Devilish lies all of us have been telling, milady included." Makem. said.

"Do tell, why is your clothing wet?"

"Mrs. Showcroft, Do not inquire too closely into this."

"The Major's body was found on a muddy road. Sukie is washing some pieces of clothing that obviously belong to both of you. Captain Makem, are you or Caliganto responsible for the Major's death? Did my husband share your plans for his demise?"

Makem's eyes narrowed. "I should be beholden to you if you did not delve into the affair." Makem put his hand on Joanna's arm. "You fare no better than the mob with your conjecturing. Speak no more about the matter. Why do you not ask me instead about the Sherries?"

"Then, that horse in the orchard is one of those I gave to Mr. Sherrie!"

"The fellow who handed the horse over in Charles Town was of few words, but I took it as a sign that they did arrive safely to Allan's kinfolk. Until but lately, I had heard nothing of them."

"Because your advice was to say and do nothing, I did not attempt to find Katie," Joanna said.

"And good counsel that was. Charles Town was, and verily still is, crawling with British soldiers. The bounty remains on Sherrie's head."

Timothy arrived with a pen, inkwell, paper, wax and seal in hand. "Am I to be included in this conversation?" he said, setting his load on a table.

"I am exceedingly happy to say that the Captain has word from Katie," Joanna said.

"'Tis not word from Mrs. Sherrie herself," Makem said. "But, by a little bribery and the taking of much libation with the man of few words, I did find that she birthed a little baby and that they are still in the mountains."

"I daresay that with Major Straight's death, the bounty will be lifted. Can we now find Katie?" Joanna asked. "MacKinnons are in the Carolinas. You have travelled the Carolinas, Mr. Bushnell. You did tell me that you had been there gathering stones and sketching."

"'Tis a big country," Timothy said, giving Makem a furtive glance. "I may have heard of the family. They are Highland Scots, keep pretty well to themselves."

"Until the news about Straight's death is generally known in America and Britain, and the bounty removed, Allan is still a hunted man. He must stay in hiding for a wee while," Makem said.

"Talbot travels in the Carolinas," Joanna looked from Makem to Timothy. "Perhaps he has knowledge of the family?"

"Let us leave your husband out of this," Makem said quickly.

"Why must he be kept ignorant? He now knows of their plight." Joanna said.

"Why place trust in your husband? Hell and the Devil confound it, he has not changed colours during the past three years. The truth is that he is a bigger sapskull!" Makem rose from his chair and came to Joanna. He knelt on one knee before her and took both her hands in his. "You must trust me, as you have never trusted a person before. On my life, do not speak of the MacKinnons in your husband's hearing. 'Tis a matter of life or death."

Joanna could not bear to pull her hands away from Makem's gentle touch. "Whose life? Whose death, Captain Makem?" Her voice betrayed her emotion.

"Yours, my dear. Believe me, speak to him of MacKinnons and your life may be at great risk – and I should not be here to protect you." If he could get Joanna to look at him, Makem knew that she would agree to his demands. "Mrs. Showcroft, look into my eyes and swear on your mother's grave you will not speak to your husband. Look at me!"

Joanna refused to look, though his voice was so compelling, so sincere, so commanding.

"Mrs. Showcroft! Look at me!"

Joanna could do nothing else but look at Anthony Makem. Her love for the man mirrored in his eyes. His desire for her was palpable. She had to quickly avert her eyes for fear she would lean over and kiss him – passionately.

"Mrs. Showcroft ... Joanna –" Anthony's entreaty was interrupted by Timothy's coughing. Damme! He had forgotten that Bushnell was in the room.

"I ... I understand there is a certain ... delicacy to this circumstance," Timothy stammered. Perhaps if I make arrangements for your trip, Makem?" Timothy cleared his throat, backed toward the door.

"Yes, do that, Bushnell." Makem had not let go of Joanna's hands. "Joanna," he said softly, "A man's life has been taken that others might live in peace. Your silence must be guaranteed for the same reason. I was in the back hall at the palace. I saw him attack you. I could have throttled him then."

"'Tis a crime committed, Captain." Joanna managed to regain some of her composure.

"'Tis justice meted. Straight decreed Sherrie's fate, death on capture. He was no man to sit in judgement of others. He was demented, his brain was rotted by the men's disease. He was no longer capable of thinking as a sane person."

Joanna bowed her head. "'Tis a life taken, Captain Makem. God forgive us all for our deceptions, lies and deceits." She reluctantly removed her hands from Anthony's.

"Listen to me. Your husband is here for the festive season, but I am away. Please, do take care. Place your trust in Ndamma ... David. He knows what must be done if —"

"David is all hero in my eyes. He is my constant shadow when I lack company. It seems, but for Mr. Bushnell and David, the men of my circle are rarely near me. Talbot arrives to quarrel, and then he is gone. You no sooner arrive than you are off. Where does the wind take you now?"

"The *Black Wing* is docked near Norfolk. My crew are to take her down-river, and we shall board her off the headland. I shall stay away from Virginia until our names have been cleared. You've enough on your plate without me to complicate your life."

"Please. Please, say no more."

"Bushnell knows where to find me when I am ashore if there is anything you need, want ... desire."

Joanna could hardly bear the passionate desires she harboured when Anthony tenderly kissed her on the cheek, then the hand. Abruptly, he left the room, with no look back, no words of endearment.

Oh my heart! Joanna thought. You will never know how much you have complicated my life, Anthony Makem. Will you ever experience the beautiful, heartbreaking, enduring love I now harbour for you?

CHAPTER TWENTY-SEVEN
RICHMOND
Late Spring 1756

BUYING slaves was not something Timothy liked to do. He hated the crowds, the smells and the rowdiness. But it was not a job for Joanna, and that was why he and David were at Wilson's Black Auction in Richmond, Dealer in Grains and Slaves, as the sign over the front door of the dingy shop read.

It was David's presence that disturbed him most. Timothy could not imagine what it must be like for him to see his countrymen treated like animals, sold like cattle. Yet, David must have had a reason for wanting to see Richmond, because he had asked to serve as Timothy's translator.

After Juba said that more help was needed to work the fields, Timothy consulted with Joanna, giving reasons for the purchase of more slaves. To his surprise, she offered little resistance. She agreed, but refused to attend the auction, saying that as it was a man's job; he would have to do it.

The rub was that he did not like buying humans beings as though they were hogs. Although he had been raised in a house that depended on slave labour, he had never taken a firm stand on slavery. But during his time at Riverview with David, he had been forced to give more thought to the argument.

Most of the slaves that were for sale were penned in at the side of the building, a board fence separating men and boys from the women and children. The newly arrived Africans were herded like cattle into one pen. Those Timothy looked over first, concentrating on a dozen or so men that might be suitable. But, due to the nature of the work at the plantation, he decided it would be best to choose slaves that already had some instruction and knew hard work. Those slaves that were being sold by their masters were imprisoned in another enclosure. They were packed so close together that he could not correctly ascertain their physical condition. Each would have to go on the block before he made a decision.

Timothy had attended enough slave auctions to be an astute buyer. He had an artist's eye for anatomy and could judge a well-proportioned body, regardless of the quantity of oil used make a slave look better. He justified the purchases he had to make this time by thinking they would fare better on Joanna's plantation than elsewhere. Juba demanded hard work and, knowing Miz Showcroft's revulsion against punishment, got it without resorting to much violence.

Timothy stood with David just behind him, waiting the start of the auction. David stood with eyes to the ground, the obedient slave, rather than the active student Timothy had become accustomed to.

A hand came to rest on Timothy's right shoulder. "Hello, Bushnell!"

Surprised by a familiar voice, Timothy turned. An old classmate stood beside him. "George Brockie! How long has it been? Five years?"

"Liverpool, I believe."

"Indeed. I was there waiting to sail with Mrs. Showcroft. You were to bargain the price of some weaponry with Charles Turnbull, were you not?"

"That is right. And that hard-nosed beggar charged me a goodly sum above what the guns were worth. If you are selling your manservant, there is no need to put him on the block, I will buy him now. How much?"

Timothy looked puzzled, then laughed. "David? He is not my slave and definitely not for sale. He belongs to Mrs. Showcroft. He assists me on this expedition."

"How fares Mrs. Showcroft? When we last spoke, you thought she would have some difficulty with certain customs in the Colonies."

"Mrs. Showcroft is well and has adapted to Virginia and plantation life. I have been hired by her. I did hold wrong opinions about the lady. She was thrust upon me, and my views were shaped by her husband's views of his fair bride."

"Showcroft could trust you with his property, methinks you said. I hear the lady has some of her father's traits – hard, opinionated and a little eccentric."

"I do not pass judgement," Timothy said. "She is also kind, considerate and fair in her dealings."

"Come now, Bushnell. You work for her?"

"As her bookkeeper. I manage the plantation accounts."

"Dear fellow, have you given up your artistic endeavours, your book?"

"That I accomplish, too."

George laughed. "What did the lady offer to change you from a wandering scallywag artist into a keeper of accounts?"

"A steady wage, a roof over my head, friendship and respect."

"And Showcroft must be overwhelmed to have you underfoot."

"He spends little time at the plantation," Timothy said. "When he is there, he tolerates my position in the household. Fortunately, 'tis not me he rails against in his fits of temper."

"I pity the poor devils he owns. He has a rice plantation down south, does he not?"

"Several rice plantations, among other ventures, including an experiment with indigo. If you travel this way, come see me at Riverview."

"Riverview," George muttered. "That name has a familiar ring about it." Frowning, he ran a hand through his beard. "Ah, now I do remember," he said. "While in London a year and a half ago, over Mistletide, I spent a week in the same lodging as a Major Straight, a most disagreeable fellow. He swung between bouts of dark depression and senseless drunkenness. You look startled, Bushnell."

"I knew the man. He was murdered near Williamsburg last November."

"By the Devil, I had not heard. 'Tis no shock, however. He made enemies easily."

"Go on," Timothy urged. "You've not connected him with Riverview."

"In his drunken tirades he vowed he would find *her* at Riverview. No one knew what he was blathering about. He had only one visitor, a distinguished old army officer – had a big estate on the moors – who tried to persuade him to forget her. Poor fellow died in a fall one night while in the company of Straight, who left London within a week afterward. At the lodging, we all thought the old man's death was suspicious, but no enquiry was made by the authorities."

"You must come to Riverview, Brockie!" Timothy said. "Mrs. Showcroft will want to hear what you have just told me."

"Sir ... Teacher Bushnell," David interrupted. Both men looked at the African.

"Look!" David raised his eyes to the block where a tall, thin boy stood, his eyes glazed with fatigue. Although he had been cleaned up and oiled, the boy's back was so scarred it obviously had felt the whip more than once.

"Looks like he doesn't obey orders." George said.

"The marks," David said. "Look at the marks on his chest."

Timothy looked again at the boy, whose ribs stuck out on his naked body. He could faintly see markings on the laboring chest. "What of them, David?"

"He is a Griot, like me." David said. "He must be from the Fula Jallon. He has suffered much at the hands of cruel masters. Look at his back, his buttocks. He has been beaten, mutilated." David lowered his eyes and moved automatically toward the block, heading for his countryman.

Timothy threw an arm across David's chest. "No! Do not interfere. It will do the boy no good and you will suffer too!"

"You'd best act soon if you want him. Someone sees he has promise," George said. "He's already bid at twenty and going."

"Twenty-one," shouted Timothy. "Twenty-four," he answered a challenge from the auctioneer and looked around for those bidding against him. "Are you sure that he is from your tribal land, David?"

"Yes. On my history stones. The markings. He must be from another tribe in the Fula Jallon where they mark at an early age, like me."

"He will be a healthy specimen when some meat has been put on his bones," George said.

"Sir," David pleaded. "He is whipped because he has spirit to fight back. He will not change. He does not understand humility; he will ever fight back."

"Twenty-eight," Timothy bid. "If we buy him, you can give him direction, David."

David, feeling he must give directions immediately, again made for the platform, shouting in Wolof. He was stopped again by Timothy's arm across his chest.

The bedraggled boy looked up, strained against his shackles and began to shout. That action brought a quick yank at the chain around his neck.

"For God's sake, David. You are drawing attention to us." Timothy grasped David's arm. "Thirty-three!" Timothy raised the bid. "Quiet or I will cease bidding. We'll move closer. Say something to him to settle him down. He will be choked to death if he does not stop struggling against his shackles. Do not leap toward him or you will get the same treatment. Stay calm."

The crowd, interested in the two bidders, opened a path for Bushnell's party as they approached the block. They got close enough that David could speak softly to the boy.

"Thirty-four! Thirty-four over here." The auctioneer pointed a finger at Timothy's rival.

"Thirty-five," Timothy answered.

Another challenge came from the opposite side of the block.

"Thirty-eight," Timothy called.

His rival, a plantation owner from the Virginia neck, glowered at him and shouted, "Forty."

"Forty-five," said Timothy, facing his competition.

The crowd gasped. Few would pay forty-five pounds for such a puny, disobedient slave.

"Forty-six." The Virginian sneered.

"Forty-eight," Timothy roared.

"Forty-eight! Forty-eight!" the auctioneer repeated. "Do I hear forty-nine, Mr. Barlow?"

Barlow looked at the African then at Timothy. "The git's not worth it."

"Forty-eight ... forty-eight. Sold to Mr. Bushnell for forty-eight pounds. Claim your prize, Sir."

The crowd laughed and jeered.

"Brockie, come with us. David, control yourself until we leave the square. Tell the lad to follow us."

The young African's neck and arms were unshackled. "You will be keeping the leg shackles on this-un. He runs away and spits on authority every chance comes his way," the roust-about slave-guard said. "You bought yourself a bad-um, Sir. You'll be bringing him back here to sell again, quick enough."

David spoke quietly to the boy, and he stopped struggling and began to shake.

"Unshackle his legs," said Timothy. "He hasn't enough strength to run from us? Brockie, be kind enough to take my letter of credit from Riverview and bid for me! I need four more strong, young males for field labour. Hire a wagon from the livery and bring them directly to Riverview. I will meet you there and clear any further expenses you might have incurred. I must march these two away from the crowd."

"Fortunately for you, I'm not otherwise obligated, and my curiousity about the daughter of Charles Turnbull makes the prospect entertaining," George said. "The directions to the plantation?"

"East of here on the south bank of the James River. Ask anyone. They all know Mrs. Showcroft. Do not use excessive violence on the slaves. Mrs. Showcroft abhors physical punishment. No marks, you hear? And, feed them well along the way. That will be the first question the good lady will ask."

David placed his arm around his countryman's body and the three walked away. None of the curious followed. They were all immersed in the bidding for a comely young woman with a babe in her arms.

Timothy led his charges to a narrow passageway between two buildings and stood blocking the view as the two embraced. David wept for his kin; the boy for freedom. Timothy found himself weeping for both, and in that moment knew he could no longer stomach slavery. After some time, he said over his shoulder, "David, we must get the horses and be off. Once we have left Richmond, you can both wash in a stream. I'll purchase clothing so that the lad will be presentable to Mrs. Showcroft."

"His name is Jento," David said walking from the alley, his arm around the boy.

"Good. Jento. Come along, then."

"He has refused to eat for four days."

Timothy looked at the bag of bones called Jento. "The last thing Joanna needs is another house slave, and a skeleton in skin at that."

"Jento is now indebted to you, Teacher Bushnell."

"We ought really be speaking of this at Riverview." Timothy said. "Let us make haste. Can you carry him?"

"'Tis no hardship. I will carry my brother," David said, scooping Jento into his arms. He walked obediently behind Timothy, the scrawny lad weeping against his chest. David did not speak until they reached Timothy's lodgings. "Teacher Bushnell, you could purchase Jento from the Missus? He could buy his freedom from you, or work the debt off in your service?"

Timothy sighed. Life at Riverview was ever more complicated. "Take him to the stable and ready the horses. I shall have the cook pack bread and cheese and settle the account. He – Jento, is it? – can share your horse as he is sharing your arms." Timothy looked again at the scarred back of the young boy. "Curse the slave traders for their business! Curse cruel masters for their work. No human should look like that."

"You curse your friends. Have you forgotten Captain Makem?"

"The whole business is intolerable," said Timothy. "Makem begins to show enough compassion that he must harbour second thoughts about slavery. You see to the boy and pack your things. I shall bring clothing along shortly."

CHAPTER TWENTY-EIGHT
MacKINNON'S TRACE
June 1756

The Discovery

DURING one of the hottest days in June, Katie sat with Nellie Webster on the porch watching the men work in the fields. The younger woman had eyes for none but Roderick. It was clear that Roderick hounded after her. As the men bent their backs to the hard labour, he wandered to the spring more than once to have a drink and sly peek at his girl.

"Look how Alex does chide his brother for not heeding his work," Nellie said. "I believe Alex does not like me, Mrs. Sherrie."

"'Tis understandable, Nellie. They have been their own company on the Trace for a long time until the pretty Webster girls came! I daresay that Alex is a little piqued with the attentions that you give Roderick. They did both court you, my dear."

"But I chose Roderick," Nellie said, "and we'll wed after harvest."

"If you treat Alex with good humour, he will become reconciled. You must bring your sister Rebecca to visit more often. I do believe that Alex had a spark for her when she assisted at the lying-in this spring. We shall play a game of match-making, Nellie."

"I did come to tell Roderick that I'll not see him for a fortnight. Another lying-in needs my time. Roderick does insist that we live on the Trace after we wed. That is why he worked so hard to ready your cabin, Mrs. Sherrie."

"And I take pride in his work." Indeed, Katie did like her own cabin. The menfolk did a fine job on the new addition, giving Allan and her much needed privacy. The ell, linking the old cabin with the new, served as common and keeping rooms. Alex, Roderick, Barika and Rory had moved out of their cramped sleeping room and commandeered the main floor of the older building, with its garret under the sloping roof. "I must now prepare a place for you, Nellie, in the MacKinnon home."

"Shall I help you clean the garret, Mrs. Sherrie?"

"No, Nellie. 'Tis dark and hot mid-day. I've no liking for going up there myself. I wait to do the deed on a cooler day. If I need assistance, I will ask Rebecca to come, if your mother does not need her."

Accordingly, on a cool afternoon, Katie gathered her strength and abandoned her chair. With both children asleep and the menfolk in the fields, she took a broom and a lantern, and climbed the ladder. After the wedding, Roderick and Nellie could use the garret as a bedchamber until a home was finished. If dormers were built into the sloping roof, there would be plenty of light and fresh air. But the space must be cleaned before it was used.

Rory had laid a wood floor in the garret to hold the weight of trunks and wooden crates. The garret, which had been Mairi's sleeping room, was now little used and smelled of dust, dried fruits and herbs, soot and old wood. Bags of dried apples, pumpkin rings and strings of herbs hung from nails. Mice scurried away as Katie swept her way across the floor. She placed the lantern on a small box by the chimney, where she was able to stand upright to survey the space.

When the hole was broken through to the ell, and a stairway built, it would be easier to get to the new chamber. Nellie was hooking a rug for the floor. Katie herself was stitching a counterpane. During the winter Allan would build some shelving.

By the dim light, Katie took down the strings of herbs and bags of dried fruit. She began at one end and swept the dirt in front of her to the other, sneezing and coughing as dust swirled round her. She could not move the heavy large trunks, so she swept around them. Once, she put her broom down, went to check the children, and brought a second lantern for more light.

Katie was hot and tired by the time she reached the chimney end of the garret. When she sat down to rest, she noticed intricate brass fittings on the corners of a large, leather-bound chest. Intrigued, she removed years of dust and cobwebs from the lid, opened it and peeked inside. A Bible lay on top of a carefully folded paisley shawl. Katie lifted the edge of the shawl and saw a white lace-trimmed shift. On top of it lay a delicate crystal perfume bottle.

Katie shivered. "My dear God! I feel as though I have opened Mairi's grave!"

Her first instinct was to drop the lid and forget what she saw. But like a magnet, lantern-light glinting on glass drew her to lift the bottle from its resting-place.

Katie held the phial to the light. This was costly perfume, the sort bought in France. Where would Mairi get such an item? Katie looked under the shawl again. The lace-trimmed shift was lavish. Further searching revealed several pretty gowns, a jeweled brooch and an ivory comb.

Katie tugged the chest away from the chimney face then took the broom to strike down the cobwebs behind it. The lantern's light played across the buckles of a leather saddle bag, which had been pushed into an aumbry toward the back of the chimney. A large stone near the bottom of the chimney had been removed to make a recess for the cache. The hole was so well concealed no one would know, without close inspection, that anything could be hidden inside.

Katie pulled at the heavy bag to dislodge it, and several gold coins spilled from a side pouch. "My Lord!" she exclaimed, holding one in her hand. "What have I uncovered?" Her hands shook as she undid the buckles. "A man's shirt," she said pulling it out, "shaving strop and razor, another shirt, breeches, tobacco ..." In a side pouch she counted another ten gold coins.

In the bottom of the bag, Katie's hand closed around a bundle of papers. She removed them, sat on the floor, pulled the lantern close, and read. One had instructions from Charles Turnbull, outlining the terms for purchase of property; a second was a letter from Mairi addressed to Talbot Showcroft at Planter's Hall, outside Charles Town. An account book and some receipts were bundled with the letter.

"The proof Rory needs to show Talbot Showcroft was here," Katie said aloud. "Mairi hid this well from her father and brothers." Katie read the letter again. Why no mention of Andre? She looked closely at the date: 14 November, 1751, written almost one year after Andre's birth. Why is the letter here? Did she not send it? Was it returned? Did Mairi record the birth?

Katie bit her lower lip and deep in thought, drummed her fingers against the chest. What would I do given the circumstances? "Mairi's Bible!" Births, marriages and deaths are recorded in a holy book. There was one entry. Andre, born December 1, 1750, *the son of Talbot Showcroft*.

Katie climbed down the ladder and rushed to the cabin door, with what speed she could muster. "Rory! Allan!" She called until she saw Allan drop the reins of the oxen and run toward the cabin, followed by the other men. All will come to rights now, she thought, clutching the Bible. Wiping tears from her eyes with a corner of her apron, Katie sat on the steps to wait for Rory.

With the contents of the bag spread on the keeping room table, Allan read the letters and Bible entry aloud.

"'Tis the proof I need," Rory said. "Katie, I canna' thank ye enough."

"There are questions," said Allan. "Why did Mairi keep the bag? Why did she hide it? Why did she write tae Showcroft a year after Andre's birth askin' tae see him?"

"I canna' answer any o' them," Rory said.

"'Tis likely she hid the bag tae cover her dealings wi' Showcroft," Allan said. "Maybe the money was left fer Andre's upbringing."

"Tainted money," Alex said. "She wouldna' hae a thing tae do wi' it and she knew we wouldna' either."

"Mairi knew tha' we wouldna' touch her fal-da-rals if she took her ain life. We dinna' want tae disturb the theurgy, ye ken."

"Without a lantern the aumbry is impossible to see. You would never have found the saddlebag," Katie said.

"Everything should be burned," Roderick said.

"No!" Katie said. "What is in the trunk are all Andre has that belonged to his mother. Do you not see? That is why Mairi did not destroy them. Let Andre decide, when he is older, what he wishes done with them."

"Now you hae proof, Rory, what'll ye do?" Allan said.

"Face him up," said Rory. "When the crops are in an' I can travel, I'm gaen tae pay Virginee a wee veesit."

"You do know the consequences of such a trip," Katie said. "Showcroft is a vindictive man. He'll not take kindly to the news."

"I will bide my time," Rory said, "but I am gaen tae avenge Mairi's death."

"What happened? Tell me the story again," Katie said.

Allan tamped his pipe and relit it while the menfolk made themselves comfortable by the fire. Rory coughed. "Bring a jug, Alex. 'Tis difficult fer me tae tell. Mairi had been ailin' the days afore she jumped. She wasna' hersel'. She was frettie. Roderick hear'd her leave the cabin late, the nicht. He tho' she'd gaun tae sleep on the porch where it was cool. In the mornin' she not be here to break the fast, and we couldna' find her on the cleared land. We searched an' called all the day. Rory took a drink. Alex refilled everyone's cup.

"Roderick was ridin' up the ridge after the nicht meal tae bring the neighbours and search.. We tho' she wandered intae the forest in a fever. He saw her body at the foot o' the cliff on the wa' up."

"How do you know she jumped? She could have fallen over, especially if she was sick with a fever."

"She had tae open an' close the gate so the sheep wouldna' escape. She was dressed in her best as if she were preparin' fer a layin'-away. A person in a fever does na' do that sort o' thing." Roderick said.

Rory raised his glass. "To Mairi."

"Mairi!" Everyone drank.

Later, in Allan's arms, Katie said, "What if Mairi was dressed to meet Talbot? The letter was dated November 1751. She died in early March 1752, just before we arrived. She asked to meet him in the letter. Alex said that he took letters to kin and brought several back. Maybe someone was helping her in Charles Town. Perhaps, she was headed up-mountain to meet him, away from the Trace."

Allan kissed Katie's forehead. "What might you be thinkin', Katie girl?"

"She could have been pushed over the edge," Katie said. "How would she get to Charles Town alone? By any circumstance, Talbot would never meet her in Charles Town. He might have arranged to meet her here – some place where he would not so readily be seen. He could have sent her letter back with one of his own, asking to meet her. Perhaps she thought he might renew their love. Maybe he arranged for someone else to meet her – to kill her. If you recall, he was to leave Riverview for the south shortly after we did."

"By the gods, Katie, ye're saying she might have been murdered!"

"Aye, murdered," Katie whispered. "Maybe she wanted to blackmail him. Maybe Flanagan came over-mountain –"

"Hush, Katie." Allan tightened his arms around his wife. "We had best leave well enough alone. If Rory gets it in his heid Mairi was murdered by Showcroft or Flanagan, he would kill them both and then hang for it, sure as I'm a' lyin' here wi' you."

Katie shivered. "Mayhap she had a letter from Showcroft. She would not walk over-mountain in her finery in the dark. She would wait for someone to bring a horse. And she was leaving Andre on the Trace. They found no letter, but that need not mean there was none."

"I dinna' tell Rory," Allan said, "but Showcroft is doun the southern coastal way in the autumn. It may be Rory willna' get tae see him."

"I wish that I could write to Joanna. 'Tis not right that she does not know where we are, has no notion about her husband's dalliance."

"'Tis no' for us tae tell, Katie. 'Tis no affair of ours. 'Tis fer Rory tae tell. Appears tae me Mrs. Showcroft is a vera lonely lady," Allan said, drawing Katie closer to him, "a lady who is ever tae doin' frae duty, not frae love."

CHAPTER TWENTY-NINE
RIVERVIEW
August, 1756

The Wedding

NDAMMA and Jento sat by the fire in the gang quarters waiting for the celebration to begin. Good food had put meat on the skeletal frame that Timothy bought from Joanna and made his attendant. Both men were muscular, but Jento was a head shorter than Ndamma and six years younger.

Jento looked on Ndamma with admiration as the two shared a bench; and Ndamma showed respect for his young companion. Ndamma's glance around the clearing took in buildings, trees, fire pit. He closed his eyes and, listening to familiar sounds, tried to believe he was sitting by a fire in his home village. Children's laughter filled the air. Axe struck wood. Several women sang as they turned the huge spit that held the meat.

A union, in Virginia and in the homeland, was cause for celebration, Ndamma thought. Mistress Showcroft was kindly obliging, and gave permission for Henkle and Lily to join according to tribal custom. She also left orders for a sheep to be slaughtered for the feast, and had another cabin built for Lily and Henkle in the gang quarters. Like every other, it held one room with a hearth and a loft. Her generous gift of a cot, two blankets, a cooking pot, six laying hens and a bolt of coloured cloth was accepted with silent approval. Mistress Showcroft would be welcome at the ceremony, but she, Teacher Bushnell, and Luke were engaged to visit the Binkses in Williamsburg and attend a service of thanksgiving at Bruton Church.

The two Griots rose. The singing stopped as Sukie walked into the clearing followed by Henkle and Lily. After them came a young male child, carrying a corn broom. When Sukie stepped up to Ndamma and asked permission for the wedding ceremony to begin, Ndamma nodded then held out his hand. Henkle and Lily, their hands working together, gave Ndamma one carefully chosen stone. Ndamma accepted the offering with his right hand. He turned the couple's stone slowly and, satisfied with the choice, placed it in his pouch. He returned to each their individual stones with his left hand. In giving back their individual stones, he sanctioned the union, showing that he saw them now as one.

After the child had solemnly laid the broom on the ground before Ndamma, the assembly moved closer. Henkle seized Lily's hand and both leapt over the broomstick. Henkle turned, retrieved the stick, held it over his head and tossed it in the fire. As flames consumed the corn, Henkle lifted Lily into his arms and carried her into their hut, stepping through a doorway hung heavy with fruit and vegetables.

The women returned to the spit while young and old danced round the clearing, beating drums and shaking gourds. Hot coals were heaped over sweet potatoes that had been placed beside the pit. Grease from the roasting meat flared and sputtered as it fell into the flames.

"Your family grows," Sukie said, touching the pouch as she sat beside Ndamma.

Ndamma laughed, slipping easily into Wolof. "I should have asked for a union stone a long time ago."

"There will be a new slave for Miz Showcroft in three months," Sukie confirmed.

"A lucky child," Ndamma said, "to have Henkle as a father."

"No slave child is born with luck," Sukie said. "Not even one born to our Mistress."

Ndamma gazed into the fire. "You speak against her?"

"I do speak not against her. I speak against slavery. And Miz Showcroft still owns slaves."

"You would not hurt her?"

Sukie looked steadily at Ndamma "I will not hurt her, no. Nor will I willingly allow anyone else do so."

Searching his pouch for Sukie's stone, Ndamma's fingers closed around its familiar form. He held it out to her. "Take this and tell me you will never cause her harm, nor cause Luke to come to harm. Throw it in the fire and leave my side if you cannot swear on your stone."

Sukie took the stone. "Why are you so suspicious, Ndamma? Have I done anything wrong?"

"I have an uneasy feeling in my heart. I sense change on the wind."

"Trouble will not come from me," Sukie said. She held the stone to her heart. "What else does the wind tell you?"

Ndamma glanced up, through the tops of the old oaks to the starlit sky. Ever since he had found Jento at the slave auction, he had been uneasy, restless, questioning. "I believe that sadness will fall with the autumn leaves."

"Many things pull Miz Showcroft one way – then another," Sukie said. "Perhaps she soon must choose whether she wants to live in this world or the other across the sea. Then she must decide what happens to us. A great loneliness surrounds our Mistress now."

"It is in her heart to do what is right," Ndamma said. "There must come a time when all questions are answered and all things corrected."

"Ndamma, I will die a slave. Leaves will have to fall from many trees, for many years, before every thing will be corrected and every question answered. Why you were brought here, Ndamma, and why the Missus came? And why your lives joined? Do your whispering winds answer?"

"Teacher Bushnell says there is a reason – an answer – an action and a consequence for everything. My father would say that one can not amend life, for it was meant to be; regardless of what occurs, what one does or says, it is correct. If this be so, my capture and enslavement were meant to be. It did take a long time for me to accept that."

"You are a fool, Ndamma. Schooling has made you eloquent but stupid. No one was born to be a slave." Sukie looked around the gang quarters. Miz Showcroft's slaves were ready for the feast. They were dressed in their finery, gave what they had for the meal – a few maize cakes, some fruit, a chicken. "Ndamma, do you truly think these people want to be here? How do you explain Jento?"

"Perhaps it is all they know. Perhaps they would be afraid to leave, because they fear what they do not know." Ndamma looked affectionately at Jento. "Jento will be the history keeper when I am gone. He is here for that reason, just as I was at the slave auction on the day he was sold."

"Do you have scales on your eyes and flaps on your ears?" Sukie asked. "Have you not seen and heard whispers for freedom? Are you planning your escape?"

"I will not escape, but I will leave," said Ndamma. "My destiny is not at Riverview, or in Virginia. I knew that the day I carried Jento in my arms at Richmond."

"So it will come to pass then?" Sukie asked. "If you believe, you can make it happen?"

"If you believe that you will be free one day, you will make that happen too," Ndamma said. "Or Mistress Showcroft will make it happen for you."

"The more clever one gets, the more nonsense one speaks." The smell of roasted potatoes and hot mutton reminded Sukie the meal was ready. "If I can rouse Henkle and Lily, we can have the celebration feast."

Sukie made for the door of the cabin, the crowd behind her. Banging on the wood, she demanded, "Def Jam. Oo dem you long to? De cot or de Jama? De moments am a-flyin'. De feast am a-waitin'."

When Henkle and Lily opened the door, they were scooped up and carried to the fireside where they shared the place of honour with Ndamma and Jento.

Far into the night, while the shadows of dancing figures played on the huts, Ndamma sat by the fire, trying to understand the dreams that had plagued him since Jento's arrival – dreams of Barika, the sea, a big house, and the number twelve.

CHAPTER THIRTY
RIVERVIEW
September 1756

RIDING was one of Joanna's few diversions to relieve the tedium of living so far from Williamsburg. She loved to be in the saddle. At least once a month, she, Timothy, Juba, and Luke on his pony, rode the plantation's boundaries. At other times, when Timothy was free, Joanna accompanied him further afield, in a bid for bold independence. She was done up with false rumours and whisperings, and determined she would set her own rules of decorum.

Joanna sat her saddle well, riding with her hair netted and her waist free of constricting stays. For each outing, Sukie packed a lunch, and the two rode until a good subject was found for sketching – a boat on the river, a flock of sheep under an soaring elm, a stone dyke.

Along a quiet byway one September day, the riders passed two local women who had deliberately paused to look at them. "I wonder what scandalous whisperings they are concocting?" Joanna said, touching the crop to her horse to move up beside Timothy.

"Why would they conjure anything?"

"Come now, Mr. Bushnell. You have heard the talk. My husband is away for months. Your attendance at Riverview has not gone without notice. Silly tongues must wag to be happy."

Timothy laughed. "As a lady, you must know how they think."

"Aha, then there is talk!" Joanna said.

"I am never privy to the ladies' side," Timothy admitted. "I hear only what the men have to say, and even then in limited rations."

"And what have the men to say?"

"They do question why you do not go to the Carolinas with your husband."

"I once did think of doing so – going to Planter's Hall. Thinking with reason, my father does expect me to manage Riverview. And, if I made the journey, I fear that my life would hang in precarious balance. I place no trust in my husband and would not subject Luke to such danger."

"Most men grudgingly admit you do manage the plantation well. And I believe they see little to wonder about, in my position as your bookkeeper. They did lay heavy bets against Juba's competence. Almost to a man they think your stand on slavery absurd."

"I am not in the habit of easy intercourse with other plantation owners, but I have felt no disagreeable consequences. They do give me the upmost respect on those occasions when we meet. Their wives talk little of business. But, Mr. Bushnell, for everyone to embrace my opinions would be beyond belief."

"They do take great satisfaction, in that, regardless of what you say, you have not freed your slaves; that you now understand a plantation cannot be run without them."

"Do they not think kindness has its benefits? Indeed, my people break rules – but they are well fed, paid a little, and they are content enough with their lot."

"Mrs. Showcroft, you have just said *my people*, as though you were their leader, their chief."

When Joanna did not answer, Timothy knew he had struck a sore point. He spurred his horse to a trot, to give Joanna time to think of her answer.

The two rode in silence until they reached a spring bubbling by the side of the road where they stopped to allow the horses to drink.

"If I speak of my slaves as my people, and see myself as their chief, what does it matter? But, I do try to abide my principles about slavery, do I not, Sir? You must admit that my ... slaves enjoy a number of freedoms that others do not have."

"Freedoms given, limited though they may be, challenge your slaves, Mrs. Showcroft. Have you thought of what is accomplished by educating David and allowing him so much freedom, without being free?"

"You know well, Mr. Bushnell, he is being given the opportunity to better himself."

"If by bettering himself he does lose his African culture, Mrs. Showcroft, what then? And you have not yet afforded him the opportunity to enjoy life as a free man in our society."

"But he *chose* to be educated."

"True. But he needs to be free, free to go home to Africa or to stay in America." Timothy pointed to a large moss-covered oak near the spring. "Let us stop here."

"Nay, you must believe me, Mr. Bushnell. Freedom will come."

Timothy assisted Joanna to dismount. "And what, I ask, is David to do with his education? He is a strapping young man who commands respect among his people, but very little anywhere else."

"What he does is his choice," Joanna said. "At the right time, his preference will be put to use in freedom. That time has not arrived, and – America might not be the place. I do wonder what Captain Makem and Caliganto were thinking when they gave David to me."

"I never question Makem's actions. He is a man unto himself."

Joanna retrieved the food hamper and blanket. While Timothy tethered the horses, she busied herself about setting out the meal.

"What do you know about the Captain?" Joanna asked when Timothy joined her.

Timothy laughed. "As much as he allows me to know."

"Where is he now? They have been cleared of the Straight affair, but Captain Makem has vanished."

"Perhaps the man has not vanished. Possibly he has. The sea can be a harsh mistress, Mrs. Showcroft. It is a fact of life," said Timothy quietly, "that he may not come back. You must accept that, if you are a ... friend of Makem's."

"I do try not to think of the possible consequences of being a seaman," Joanna said. "When the Captain is not at sea, where does he stay?"

"He and Caliganto run bachelor's hall at Makem's Rant, a cottage overlooking the ocean, south of Norfolk, close by the island light."

"Has he ever been wed?" Joanna asked, handing over a large piece of fried chicken. Keep a man plied with food and he will chatter, she thought as she watched Timothy take a bite of succulent thigh.

"I've not been told he has," Timothy said licking his lips. "I do not believe he is the marrying sort."

"How did Makem and my husband meet?"

"'Tis a good story. Makem was literally thrown up at your husband's door. When his ship, the *Angel*, was dismasted in a storm off the Carolina coast, Makem ran her right up on the beach on your husband's place in Carolina. Opposites do attract; and both are shrewd men of business. Your husband has a need for slaves. Makem supplies that need."

"Captain Makem knows my thoughts on his trade in human cargo, especially with my husband. I have told him – many times."

"Makem was not always a slave trader, Mrs. Showcroft." Timothy reached for a thick piece of buttered corn bread and a chunk of hard cheese. "He was a privateer when the *Angel* foundered. He reveled in plundering Spanish vessels out of South America."

"Ah. That confirms some of my suspicions about the man," Joanna said.

"It put him in the same patch as Caliganto, who was a prisoner on a Spanish ship. Caliganto did kill some important Spaniard and was being taken to Spain for execution. Makem pirated the ship and boarded it, looking for treasure. He found Caliganto, in chains, more dead than alive, and freed him. I should say Caliganto is a fighter. Even in his weakened condition he cracked a few Spaniards' skulls in the fight. He has saved Makem's life, more than once – and Makem has saved his life in return. Makem does see the worth in a good man."

"Then, how can Makem sell people like china or furniture? How can he justify such action?"

"Perhaps the Captain has asked himself the same question. The last news of the *Black Wing* was that it was plying the Caribbean route. That tells me Makem did not sail the full triangle – his course leaves out England and Africa."

"I am at a loss to understand why he has not communicated with you, Mr. Bushnell."

"That I have no answer for."

While Joanna packed the remnants of lunch, Timothy set out sketching materials. "We will spend an hour or so here, Mrs. Showcroft. I should prefer not to return to Riverview for the moment. Bookkeeping can be suffocating work."

Although Joanna had enjoyed the Timothy Bushnell's company for nearly six

years, rarely did she touch on his private life. She ventured now to gain more information. "Sketching has never been agreeable to me. It did rank with needlework as
something to learn because a lady is expected to. The artist who executed my mother's
portrait – the painting that Captain Makem delivered from Willowbank – did attempt
to teach me, but failed miserably. I've a mind more to numerals than fancy-work."

"George Barker is an excellent portraitist. The colouring of the face is right. The
hands holding the Bible are exceedingly well done; every detail is perfection."

"I am sadly ignorant of the subtleties of the painting. Juba and Henkle unwrapped
and hung the picture. I do confess that I did not look closely at it. You are the man for
detail, Mr. Bushnell. If there is one hair out of place, you take notice."

"An artist's eye is a practiced eye, Mrs. Showcroft." Timothy gave Joanna paper and
pencil. "Concentrate now on that dyke." Leaning closer to her, he pointed toward a
stone fence covered with tangled grapevines. "Try to catch the shadowing on the stones."

Instead of drawing the hedgerow, Timothy drew Joanna's fingers clutching the
pencil. As near as he was to the lady, he could not bear to look at her face.

Worthless man that I am, he thought, I am content to sit by this lady and watch her
sketch. Makem would have seduced her by now! You're a fool, Timothy Bushnell!
You've not been able to enjoy a closeness with a lady. Not since –

"My dear Sir, I never knew you were so skilled at sketching the human form. The
detail of the fingers is magnificent! But you have not sketched a proper lady's fingers.
Those appear to be a working woman's hands." Joanna lifted her hands to the light.
"Gracious, I do have a working woman's knobbly hands!"

"To be honest, I had not concentrated on close detailing in human hands, or feet.
I have been so enamored with rocks and flowers that I never gave much time to
drawing the human figure – not until I began to paint your portrait, Mrs. Showcroft."

"Mr. Bushnell? May I be so bold as to ask a question of some delicate nature?
Please do not feel you must answer it." When Timothy nodded, Joanna continued,
"Have you ever considered marriage?"

Timothy stammered, "I ... did cherish a great affection for a lady once. It seems to
be a long time ago."

"Did she die?"

"Die? No, she did not. I could not provide what she wanted – a comfortable life.
The lady deserted me for one who could."

"Poor Mr. Bushnell!"

"'Twas I introduced them, put one with the other. The whole adventure did put
me off courting and marriage forever. Mrs. Showcroft, a man should probably not
profess such feelings but – I did truly love her." Timothy thought of the spring day in
Charles Town when he introduced Mairi MacKinnon to Talbot Showcroft, and his
hand worked furiously at his sketch. The one thing that swept away painful thoughts
from his mind was to put pencil or paint to paper, rather than knife into flesh –
Showcroft's flesh.

Wisely, Joanna did not pursue the question. She did pity the man who had become her close friend ... almost like a brother if the truth be known. But, as she turned to her drawing, her thoughts wandered to another man – another place – another time.

Riverview Plantation
4 October 1756
Dear Father,
You will think that a second Letter within a Month is most unusual. Believe me, Father, this Tirade is important and necessary.

I have heard recently, and not from my good husband, that he will not be home until December. I shall miss the November festivities in Williamsburg. I have not seen Talbot in nine months. What is the use of Marrying? And, I ask, what is the use of the Agreement? I know not what he does. He knows not what I am about.

I am becoming a Shrew, something I promised myself I would never be. I am turning my anger at Talbot toward my slaves. I found myself so angry after I heard the news that I almost struck Kudie. I had my hand raised to strike before I saw the Horror in her eyes. For one brief moment, I thought I must carry through with the blow. She would not obey me in the Future if I did not. Then, horrified, I put my hand down, apologized and began to weep. You always blame your acts of Poor Judgement and Failure on the absence of the Number Twelve. I have no such Excuse, dear Father.

I do not imagine that you are surprised that Riverview still owns slaves. I am not the Joanna of high Principle who left England. This land of extraordinary Beauty and Promise has compromised my Ideals to the point where I now willingly accept things that are neither good nor right.

Now, I understand that in order to justify those compromises, I have put my energies and hopes on David. He is Proof that my theories could hold true. And, Father, he has responded. Oh yes, beyond my wildest dreams, so I do have Vindication. There is more hope for slaves in Education than in Freedom. David will have Freedom soon. There is a sinister side to David's story. I know that I am making him a Perfect Copy of myself which means that he will be a close Copy of you.

In all the tears and self-examination, it occurred to me that I am no different from you. You rarely got angry, rarely raised your hand or voice. The only time I saw you angry enough to strike was when Mother spoke with you about my marriage to Talbot. You did not stop yourself, however. You struck her, Father, and she fell against a newel post and cut her cheek. Did you not think I saw?

You asked about Mr. Bushnell as though you worry he is becoming more than a bookkeeper to me. The poor dear man puts all his Feelings onto canvas. I do not encourage him because I do believe that I love another. I shall not divulge his name until I am sure that he will have me.

Does this News upset you, Father? I know what I am about to give up. I intend to let my feelings be known and 'may the winds blow as they list'. If those winds do shake your Empire, so be it. I have no Choice but Freedom – from living in your wake, from trying to be like you. I will not lose your fortunes so much as gain my Life. And life is what I desire now, Father, Life that might hold the veriest speck of Affection, perhaps Happiness. You do know that I came to America for many reasons, but one of them not apparent to me. You did promise that if it did become clear, whatever it might be, you would give your full Blessing and Support. I will hold you to that Promise.

I leave for Williamsburg within the hour with this letter to ensure that it will be sent with no Tampering of Seal. Wish me good fortune, Father. You can do no more now. You are Helpless to interfere. Miles of ocean between us do have their Virtues.

Joanna

CHAPTER THIRTY-ONE
RIVERVIEW
October 1756

Rory's Revenge

RORY and Barika reined their horses in at the bend in the carriage way to take in the view. The glow of the autumn sun, low on the horizon, bathed the stately manor in burnished gold. A half-dozen fine-looking riding horses grazed in a field to the right of the road; a herd of milch cows grazed the orchard on the left. Several gardeners worked in the formal beds that flanked the upper drive, preparing them for winter.

"How many years hae it been?" Rory asked.

"More than four," Barika said.

"An' I hae not seen Talbot Showcroft in almost six. He wouldna' wish tae see me now."

"I am fortunate that Katie made me a free man. I often wonder about Ndamma's fate."

"Aye, Katie is a wise, compassionate woman." Rory wiped his face on a sleeve, ran a hand through his hair and brushed dust from his clothing. Checking one more time to assure himself the saddlebag was still behind him, he said, "We hae been on the road a lang time. I canna' remember when my hair was last cut. But we changed bootie this mornin'. We dinna' want tae look the Gadhel, do we?"

Barika paused in beating dust from his hat to point toward the house. "I told you it was as pretty as any we have seen on the way north. Let's hope our reception is as pleasant."

"Weel, let's make ourselves known." The pair stopped before the front steps and a groom ran to take the reins. "We will manage the horses, laddie. We're here tae see the master o' the hoose."

"He be not home, Massa."

"Is he tae be expecket soon?"

"No, Massa."

Rory turned in his saddle. "Daum, Barika.!" He turned again to the groom. "Can we ride tae meet him?"

"Can I be of assistance, Sir?" Joanna hurried down the steps, Henkle behind her. "I did see you at the bend in the carriageway. Indeed, you appear to have ridden many miles today. May I offer Riverview's hospitality?" She stepped closer to the mounted men and looked closely at Barika. "Alas, Mr. Showcroft's not here and is not expected until December. Is this your manservant?" Joanna kept her eyes steady on Barika's face.

"He is my kizzen," Rory said, smiling. His horse danced a little when Joanna brushed by it.

Joanna stepped closer to Barika. "Upon my word, 'tis Barika! You are Ndamma's ... David's friend Barika."

"That I am, Ma'am."

"Henkle. Quickly! Find David! I believe that he is in the classroom ... or the library. Pray, gentleman ... Come inside!" Joanna addressed Rory. "Whom do I have the pleasure of welcoming to Riverview?"

Rory dismounted and gave the reins to the groom. "I am Rory MacKinnon." He bowed slightly, extending his hand.

"Mr. MacKinnon! This is indeed a pleasure." Joanna touched Rory's hand. "Have you brought news of Katie and Allan Sherrie? Dear me, my joy has caused me to forget my manners. You are tired and hungry. Your horses will be seen to, and your gear taken into the house, and ..."

"No!" Rory exclaimed, putting a hand in the air to stop the groom from taking his horse. "Haud yer havers. If you'll not be minding, we'll be awa'."

"Why, I'll not hear of your leaving," said Joanna. "My company is not disagreeable. 'Tis as good, if not better, than my husband's."

"Barika! Is it my brother?" David's cry interrupted her as he ran down the steps. Barika met him halfway. The two embraced, slapped each other's backs, stood away, took a good look, and embraced again.

Joanna placed a hand on Rory's arm. "Sir, how can you think to separate those two after such a reunion? I insist you stay, and am eager to hear your news. I must hear your news of Katie!"

With David and Barika were still locked in an embrace, Rory relented. "We'll be acceptin' your hospitality," he said. "But we canna' stay lang. A moment here, fellow!" Rory intercepted the groom as he was collecting the reins, and heaved the saddlebag from his horse.

"Henkle will carry that," Joanna said.

"I am not used tae bein' waited," Rory said. "I'll carry it mysel'."

"David. Barika can billet with you. Be sure he has all he needs, and see that he is comfortable and well fed." Joanna spoke directly to Barika. "Again, welcome to Riverview, Barika. David has fretted over your fate for years. Oh, but I am so pleased to see you!"

"As pleased as I am to be here," Barika said.

Joanna accepted Rory's arm to climb the steps. "I have waited so long to hear from Katie. You must tell all and without delay."

Rory laughed shortly. Telling all was exactly what he intended to do – but not to Showcroft's English lady. "An' you dinna expect Mr. Showcroft tae be hame until the Yule?"

"I have been told he went to the West Indies. He spends little time here, Mr. MacKinnon."

"Yer fields hae a man's hand on them."

"Thank you. I accept that as a compliment. 'Tis Juba, the overseer, who manages the fields."

When Sukie met them in the hall Joanna said, "I will show Mr. MacKinnon to a room. Please send food and drink to the library. I believe that our guest prefers libations a bit stronger than tea. And could you instruct Kudie to bring hot water to the green bed chamber?"

Rory laughed again. "You are a wise lassie."

"It requires no wisdom to see that you and Barika do look road weary."

"That we are," Rory said, running dirty fingers through dirtier hair. "Barika be wi' me 'cause Katie said I am too daum old tae traipse roun' America by m'self."

"Your visit must be important, that you make the effort."

"Aye, 'tis that."

Joanna lifted her skirt to clear the steps as she and Rory climbed slowly. "Truly, I do not wish to hurry you, Mr. MacKinnon, but I am all aflutter to hear about Katie. Is she well?"

"Aye," Rory said. "I'll feel guid an' mair inclined tae gabnash after I rinse the dust."

"Let us not delay the process, then, Mr. MacKinnon."

"Rory," the Scotsman said. "Ye hae permission tae call me Rory."

Later, in the library, Rory, comfortable in a chair, legs on a gout stool, a glass of whiskey in hand, looked around the assembly. Timothy had joined Joanna in the welcoming committee and stood by the hearth, smoking a pipe. Joanna sat opposite Rory, a class of negus in her hand. Henkle hovered near, ready to replenish food and drink.

"Katie will be a good mother," Joanna said. "She was wonderful with Luke."

"Aye, she be a guid wifie and mither," Rory said. "She is guid tae my boys too, vera' guid tae Alex, after Roderick took tae kirkin'."

"We had such a close friendship, I cannot understand why there was no correspondence," Joanna said.

"She had her ain reasons," Rory said. "I am here tae tell the tale."

"By the bye, I do have news for her," Joanna said. "Major Straight came to Williamsburg looking for her. She'll not have heard that he was very likely responsible for her father's death, and was himself murdered last year. You see, Captain Makem did visit her father in an attempt to sort out the tangle. During his visit, Katie's father promised to journey to London to speak with Major Straight of his determination to remove the bounty. He was in Straight's company when he died."

"She doesna' know," Rory said.

"I will put pen to paper and write all – but she must answer me," Joanna said.

Rory settled further into his chair and held his glass out for a refill. When Timothy obliged, Rory gave him a close look. The man was vaguely familiar. Or was it his name that rang in his mind? When their eyes met, Rory quickly turned his attention to the painting over the fireplace. "A bonny lassie," he said, nodding toward the portrait.

"'Tis my mother, a very good likeness."

"Aye, and your fither? Is he keepin'?"

"In his last letter he said he was well. Letters do take so long to come. England's news is ancient by the time 'tis delivered here. And to be answered, Mr. MacKinnon ... 'tis perhaps three months if both crossings are made with no difficulty."

"Aye. Hae ye tho' o' returnin' to England?"

"Oh, yes," said Joanna. "I do miss Willowbank. Perhaps I only imagine it, but the air is different there."

"Aye, I ken wha' you're sayin'," Rory said. "I canna forget the scent o' the heather, and the peat burnin' on the hearth. I can see the mist o'er loch an' glen."

"Will you go back?"

"Nay," said Rory. "I've nae hame tae go to. My croft was burnt behind me. I had a price on my heid. My sheep were slaughtered. My wifie died afore we boarded ship. O'er hame I'd be hanged if I chopped a tree or kil't a hind. All I had was my bairns and all we carried on our backs when we arrived in America. I hae a guid life in the Carolinas. There's wood fer burning an' game fer huntin'. But, if I could smell the peat fire one mair time –"

"Or ride over the moors ..." Joanna said.

"Ye'll go hame ... if only fer a veesit."

"'Tis something I might choose to do someday," Joanna said. "But I do believe that once I am there, I shall miss Virginia. 'Tis –" Joanna's train of thought was broken when Luke burst into the room. "Why, Luke! Mr. MacKinnon, this is my son, Jonathan Luke Showcroft. Mr. MacKinnon is a friend, Luke. Make a leg please."

Luke stood before Rory and instead of making the requested leg, gave his hand. "I was looking for tea cakes," the little man said. "Mama always serves tea cakes to her guests."

"I do apologize for this childish want of conduct. Luke, have you forgotten how to greet a gentleman? A hand is not proper. 'Tis a leg you should present."

"A hand is good, akin to gold in the mountains, Mrs. Showcroft. 'Tis a pleasure to take yer hand, laddie. I hae a grandson that be close tae yer age," Rory said.

So this is Andre's rival, the legal son, he thought. He's a tall boy, has the stature of Showcroft, the eyes of his mother.

"Does he have to do lessons?" Luke asked.

"Nay, laddie. He's a mountain maun. He can read an' write, but he's not one fer learnin' oot the books. He can hunt a coon like a maun."

"Will you tell me about mountain men?"

"I'll hae a long wag wi' ye aboot the mountains afore I leave," Rory promised.

"If you will excuse me for a few moments, gentlemen?"Joanna said. "I will take this young man to the cookhouse for some tea cakes, and see to our evening meal. "Pray do not rise. Enjoy the fire and good company."

"Nae tae fuss o'er me," Rory said. "I'll make mysel' tae hame. One mair thing. Barika is a free man. Should he not be sharing our table? He does on the Trace."

"I shall certainly extend the invitation," Joanna said. "He is welcome to eat with David – or to join us."

After Joanna left the room, Luke in tow, Rory spoke to Timothy. "You are the Bushnell tha' was in Charles Town wi' Showcroft. Mairi spoke o' you. She was vera' sweet on ye at one time. I tho' you'd kirk her. I dinna mention Mairi in front o' Mrs. Showcroft."

"Why are you here, MacKinnon?"

"Well, lad, that I waul tell in my ain time," Rory said.

"You'd best leave immediately if you intend any harm toward Mrs. Showcroft."

"I dinna come tae argue wi' the lady," Rory said. "I mean the lassie nae harm. I gie' you my word."

"As a gentleman?"

"As a Scotsman." Rory offered his hand. "Whauraboot is tha' Barika?"

"David and Jento have him in hand," Timothy said. "There is no need to worry about Barika."

Riverview
7 October 1756
My dear Katie,

How delighted I am to hear you are well and that your life now includes Two Children. I can think of nothing better for them than to have you as Mother. 'Tis my understanding Mr. Sherrie is in good Health and finds the mountains to his liking. Oh how I do envy you, my dear Katie. You appear so content in your rustic life. And, by freeing Barika, you have accomplished what I've not yet been able to.

How I do miss you, Terribly, my dear Friend and Sister.

I have no cause for happiness in these times. Lately, Mr. Bushnell has become very morose and does spend much time by himself, between the account books and his paintings. Rarely do I see him but for taking meals. He does spend much spare time with David, Barika and Mr. MacKinnon, leaving me to my own devices for companionship.

Two days from now, the menfolk and Luke do travel to Richmond to seek out Talbot, I suspect, though Mr. MacKinnon has not told me the nature of this errand. I will be left alone to my thoughts for I was not invited to travel with them. I must forgive him, for he did give me news of your young family.

I will keep David close at hand. But David does not need my attentions as he is now an intelligent young man who does speak his mind — and deserves his Freedom. He has no further use for my brand of schooling — yes, I do have a free school at Riverview.

Luke too has grown into a young gentleman who has little time now for his mother. He is forever with David, or in the gang quarters with his African friends. He has become a very independent little man. But given certain circumstances, I do — fear for his safety and future. I have given serious thought to visiting England in the spring. Hapchance he will find life at Willowbank to his liking, although I fear he is fast becoming a little Virginian.

I have had no contact with Captain Makem, so cannot tell you how he fares. He has abandoned Riverview and this does give rise to bothersome thoughts.

We did speak once of giving up all for love and your words do now more than ever have a ring of truth about them. Katie, my dear, there is nothing but true love can overcome loneliness when it comes creeping into one's heart. This thing of darkness has me beggared. Was ever woman in this humour woo'd?

When the dreadful loneliness does visit, I do go to the cookhouse where Sukie reigns — and Willow — and Kudie — and Cansu. In their presence I am somewhat comforted. What would my people do if I were no longer here managing Riverview? I have given much thought to such a circumstance and have taken steps to protect them from the cruelty of such people as Flanagan and Talbot.

I shall end this letter by stating that you took the correct route many years ago and that I must heed Shakespeare's words — to thine own self be true — if indeed I am to have a remnant of the happiness that you enjoy. I must find that route ...

I am so unhappy at this moment. But, dearest, I must not visit my feelings on this happy reunion and do apologize for rambling. My love to you. Greetings to Allan and hugs for your dear children.

Your loving friend,
Joanna

CHAPTER THIRTY-TWO
MAKEM'S RANT
11 October, 1756

TWO people stood on the vine-covered stoop awaiting for an answer to their knock at the low wooden door. A cold rain lashed across the windswept bay and swirled around the cottage. Water ran from its eaves onto cobblestones around the foundation. It took a second knock before the door finally opened. Caliganto stood barefoot, a candle in hand, and had just enough time to recognize David before the wind extinguished his light.

"Ndamma, why are you out on such a night as this? Has Mrs. Showcroft sent you? Come in, warm yourself at the fire," Caliganto said, a note of surprise in his voice.

David, with a companion directly behind him, stepped into an entry hall, lit only by glowing embers of a hearth-fire.

Caliganto moved into a room to the left. "The dining room is warmer. Please, come in here." He stirred the coals in a larger fireplace, threw a dry log into their midst, lit the candle again and stood to properly greet his countryman. Only then did he see the second person behind David, a young man.

David stepped aside so his companion could step closer to the fire.

"Mrs. Showcroft!" the fitful firelight gleamed on Caliganto's wide eyes."Please step closer to the fire, warm yourself. Accept the hospitality of Makem's Rant."

"You are all kindness," Joanna said. She untied her cloak, keeping up a stream of talk to mask her nervousness. "I did ride to see the Captain. I have been informed the *Black Wing* sailed into home-harbour a fortnight ago."

"If you would give me leave, I'll go wake him, Mrs. Showcroft." Taking the candle with him, Caliganto strode through the keeping room. A door opened. A loud *"Hell and Damnation!"* in Makem's voice, and urgent whispers could be heard, and then the scuffling of feet on floor.

Warming her hands over the fire, Joanna glanced around the cozy room. Decorations and furnishings were fanciful, belying the fact that two bachelors shared the house. A dramatic sea mural dominated three of the room's walls: the *Black Wing* with its red sails, prominent on the wall opposite the fireplace. Ivory carvings and Chinese bowls graced the carved oak mantel. In a corner, an ornate inlaid cabinet held glassware and fine china. The room was not at all what she had expected – a pleasant chamber with elegant refinements.

"Mrs. Showcroft!"

Both turned to greet Makem as he stepped from the keeping room. He strode to take her hands. "My girl, what has happened? Why are you dressed so?"

Joanna laughed at the apparition approaching her. Makem had dressed hastily. His feet were bare, his hair tousled, a coat thrown over a night shirt stuffed into trousers. "Perhaps, Captain Makem, the horses might be seen to?"

"Caliganto, take David and tend the steeds. We do need a few moments alone."

With David and Caliganto out of the room, Makem took Joanna's hands and drew her closer to the fire. "Sweet lady, do you not understand what scandalous rumours will come of your escapade? Why do you risk a visit to Makem's Rant? Why are you dressed in man's breeches?"

"'Tis a disguise, Sir, so that I could travel without detection. I did come to speak with a long-lost friend, one who has forgot where I live."

"How did you know I had returned – or where to find me?"

"Juba told me the *Black Wing* was in harbour. Mr. Bushnell told me about Makem's Rant and its whereabouts some time ago. When you forsook Riverview, I was determined to find you."

"But, Mrs. Showcroft, 'tis best for us both that I stay away from the plantation."

"Do not, Sir, pretend to know what is good for me. I have been fully instructed in what is expected of a lady of quality."

"Who knows you have come?"

"David is my only accomplice. We left for Williamsburg in proper dress. I did effect this change in a barn along the way. Sukie believes I am Williamsburg. Mr. Bushnell has taken Rory MacKinnon to Richmond for four days, and Barika and Luke with them. Mr. MacKinnon has taken a liking to my wee man and says that he has a grandson – of his daughter Mairi – who is the almost the same age."

"Thunderation! Rory MacKinnon at Riverview?"

"Please, Sir, you are hurting my hands. Mr. MacKinnon arrived this week past to speak with my husb ... with Talbot. Of course, Talbot is not at Riverview and I do not expect him soon. As MacKinnon must be home by the Yule, 'tis his plan to leave before Talbot returns."

"Did MacKinnon state his business?"

"He did not. And I've no right to ask him if it be Talbot's affairs. What does it matter that Rory MacKinnon visits Riverview? 'Tis pleasant company for me. He is no bother. I rode to see you, not to talk about a MacKinnon."

"And ... Mr. Bushnell?"

"I've no desire to include him in this secret." Joanna drew closer to Anthony, close enough that her hands, shaking though they were, touched his face. "Pray hear me, Captain Makem, we have known each other for more than five years and I must speak in clear candour."

"Then in candour, I must say that we have become much more than friends," Makem said.

"And I care – so much for you, Anthony Makem. I am not a young woman; nor am I beautiful. But I am truly ... truly in love with you. And I hope you return my affection."

When Anthony turned his face from Joanna's searching eyes and gentle hands, she cried out in despair, "How came I to this? I have misread your advances." She removed her hands, her eyes wide with startled dismay. "How foolish of me! You already share your bed." Flustered, she turned from him. "Truly, I have been quite stunningly stupid," she murmured, "A gormless fool."

"A fool? No, Jo – Mrs. Showcroft." Anthony placed his hand on Joanna's shoulders and turned her around. "Foolish perhaps, but never a fool. No other woman shares my house or bed."

"Then your advances were mere dalliance. I was a pigeon for plucking."

Anthony ran his fingers along Joanna's high cheekbones. "Nay, by my very soul, I am besotted with you. But you are another man's wife, with a marriage contract that you cannot wish to break."

Joanna smiled past tears. "Ah, that confounded marriage agreement! I count the Turnbull fortune well lost for you, for my love."

"Mrs. Showcroft ... Joanna ... Nay, this cannot be. I am at sea more than I am on shore. I have not always conducted myself as a gentleman. I do not believe I am a – marrying man."

"Hush! Attend me," Joanna said. "I seek unbridled affection from a man who desires naught but affection in return."

"You seek unbridled passion? Or is it unbridled revenge you seek? Is it love or vengeance brings you here? Do not play games with me, Mrs. Showcroft!"

"'Tis no game, Anthony. I stand before you a woman in love, a woman in *need* of love. You must have known for a long time that I care for you. Do you not see me?"

"You must know another man adores you as I do."

"Mr. Bushnell? Perhaps; but I love him only as I should a brother."

Anthony drew Joanna close. "We both know what may come of this."

"What matter? Should we be found out, we shall meet the consequences together."

"You have so much to lose ... so much you hold dear. The marriage agreement –"

"Ah, the Devil take the marriage agreement!" Joanna searched Anthony's face. "What would you have me do, Captain? Play my father's game with a man whom – with good reason – I despise? Or take the love of a man I admire?"

"I would have you love me. Since gazing at the Vision-in-Blue at Horta I have wanted to claim you as my own." Anthony tenderly kissed Joanna's face and then her hands, over and over.

"My dear ... Anthony ... in but three days, I must return to Riverview."

"And on the fourth day?"

"Never think on the fourth day, my love. Let us enjoy what time we might have, and be true to each other. I only ask that, whatever my fate, you will never abandon me."

"Nay, but I am a rogue ... a wanderer –"

Joanna hushed him with a kiss. "And a shocking flirt, I've heard. But you have ever been a gentleman to me. Journeys end in lovers' meeting, Sir. You can be better than rogue, wanderer – aye, better even than a flirt."

"Your love is truly blind, my Joanna. Sweet creature! I've heard liaisons born of passion are doomed," Anthony whispered, stroking Joanna's hair.

"Not all," Joanna said. "Anthony, whatever you decide, I shall always cherish you."

"Achuslo, my angel." Anthony, with his arm around Joanna's slender waist, led her through the keeping room to his bedchamber.

CHAPTER THIRTY-THREE
RIVERVIEW
November 1756

A FIRE burned on the hearth, its flames creating fingers of shadow that bounced off whitewashed walls and the two men seated at the big table. David and Barika — warmed by the fire, surrounded by the smells of cured ham, onions, peppers and dried herbs — were enjoying Sukie's sour milk biscuits and apple spread. David's stones were spread, glowing like golden nuggets in the firelight, on the table in front of him. "You see Barika, I still collect history, even in America."

"I've waited a long time for this," Barika said. "I've missed your story telling. Whom will you choose first?"

David searched the pile for Jento's stone. "Jento gave it to me on the road to Riverview. He had no idea where he was being taken, but trusted me to care for him and to bargain for his freedom."

"And is he free?"

"Teacher Bushnell bought Jento from Mrs. Showcroft and promised that he would be free when he has learned to read and write."

"And you trust Bushnell to keep his word?"

"Perhaps." David chose another stone, rubbed it gently between his thumb and forefinger. "This woman rules with a gentle hand but she is like her stone, delicate yellow, hard white – two people in one. She brings giants to their knees. She has given me great opportunities. I am now not the African who walked to the sea."

"You are not of her race, either, if you are talking of Mrs. Showcroft," Barika said. "Do not deceive yourself, Ndamma. Look at me. I am free. I have a black skin. I am respected for my strength, and my knowledge of the mountains. Yet, I still circle the white world, readily accepted within by some, begrudgingly by others and shut out by many."

"There are exceptions," David set the stone on the table in front of him, the second in his ring. Choosing another, he said, "This man took us from our homeland then brought us here, because he knew the women were compassionate. See, Makem chose a pebble that is as complex as himself. It is black and white, banded with grey." Makem's stone was set beside Joanna's.

"You have placed him as husband to Mrs. Showcroft," Barika said, eyebrows raised in surprise.

David did not move the stone but searched his pile for Caliganto's. "This man is even harder to understand. He is one of us and persuaded us to give up our fast. By his sheer strength he is respected. Yet he has devoted his life to a man who trades in Africans."

Barika gently touched the stone held in the palm of David's hand. "It was he who persuaded Makem to bring us to Riverview. He is not an enemy."

"Not an enemy," repeated David. "He will use the whip against his own people, yet he is ready enough to use his bare hands to kill those of Makem's race who endanger Makem."

"The woman who belongs to this warm place." Barika reached for an apple. "Where is her stone?"

David found it easily. "Sukie is strong in spirit. She has stood up to her masters, even if it meant punishment. She speaks for the slaves and is respected. She is devoted to the Missus." David placed Sukie's stone in the middle of his ring. "She is the heart of the plantation."

"You placed Sukie in the right spot in your history ring," Barika said.

David next retrieved Timothy's stone. "This man opened my eyes to book knowledge. He says there are places that will accept a man for his knowledge and not his colour. He was easily influenced by Showcroft until he found dignity and kindness, near the Missus. He is loyal to her now, but once he was not such a good friend."

"Is the stone double-edged?" asked Barika.

"No. But see, it has the shadow of a tiny leaf in it. Teacher Bushnell calls it an etched stone," David said, setting the stone close to Joanna's. Barika raised his eyebrows once more."You have placed him as husband to a wife."

"'Tis a place he desires," David said. "But that is not to be."

David held a small blue stone up to the candle. "Kudie," he said, "the woman I would marry if we were not slaves. I will bring no children into this world to belong to someone who will sell them on a whim, treat them like animals. Children must never be born into bondage. Remember that, Barika."

"That is admirable," Barika said. "But it is something I will not promise. I will marry and have children. You are Ndamma, the Griot. In Africa, you were ready to take a wife."

"Now I am David duPont, the thinker. If we returned to Africa, we could not live the old life. We have come too far along this path. We must place our hopes with America."

"I will not forget Africa." Barika rolled the apple in his hands. "Neither will you. But I have spent too much time in this country. Look at you now. You read English. You write English. You use an English name." Throwing the apple at the fire, he said, "Just as the fire consumes that apple, America consumes people, whatever their colour. 'Tis such a vast land. There must be a place for Africans here."

"We must think past the colour of our skin, Barika. We have brains to think as they do, to learn what they do. Knowledge must be my stepping stone to their world. I will become educated, then they will have to accept me as an equal."

"Should Mrs. Showcroft take a scunner on you, your learning days will be over." Barika leaned back in his chair and stretched his long legs beneath the table. "You will have to bend that back against a load quickly enough."

"My fate in her hands."

"You do not seem concerned."

"I have no reason to be. I trust her as she trusts me." David turned his attention to the stones again. "Listen carefully. See how this stone is rubbed smooth? I have touched it at least once a day for the last five years. This plain, smooth pebble belongs to the braggart, Barika."

Barika pulled himself up and leaned across the table. "It is the one I gave you," he acknowledged. "What stories does it tell you?"

"This man shared my childhood and youth. He was with me through the terror of captivity and the long voyage. He was taken out of my life, never to be in touch. He never visited, even though he could have, as a free man. He has caused me heartache, yet it's good to see him now so that he might explain himself."

Barika laughed. "Such a gentle chide," he said, poking David's arm.

"If you were free, why did you never come back to Virginia?"

"I made a promise to Mrs. Sherrie," Barika said. "And she made the same promise to Rory MacKinnon."

"A promise?"

"That there would be no contact with Mrs Showcroft until he did corner her husband at the watering hole."

David set the stone down to concentrate on what Barika was saying. "You are here now. Did he finally catch the lion?"

"He did," Barika said. "Katie Sherrie did track it here for Rory."

David gripped Barika's arm. "What is this visit to accomplish?"

Barika got up, looked out the door, then, quiet as a cat climbed the ladder to the loft to make sure they were not heard. Satisfied, he clambered down, sat and, lowering his voice, said, "He has proof that Talbot Showcroft is the father of his daughter Mairi's son, Andre. We journeyed north to confront him. But the man is not here to receive us."

Only the crackling of the fire broke the silence that followed. "He has absolute proof. It cannot be disputed?"

"Absolute. And Rory has decided to stay here until Showcroft returns. He feels uneasy about accepting Riverview's hospitality in such circumstances, so he will arrange to stay in Williamsburg."

David stood so quickly he bumped the table, breaking his ring. "MacKinnon must tell the Missus ... Mrs. Showcroft, why he is here. She must have this news, Barika."

"Rory does not wish to embroil the lady in his scheme."

"Barika, listen to what I have to say. But we ought not to talk here. The walls have ears. We shall walk."

An hour later Rory was wakened from a deep sleep. Barika stood on one side of the high, canopied, bed, and David stood on the other. He struggled to sit up, groping beneath his pillow at the same time.

"Are you looking for your pistol, Rory MacKinnon?" Barika held it in his hand.

"Confoun' deevil," Rory sputtered. "Why you two be standin' afore my bed?"

"To talk." David said, pulling a chair up to the bed.

Barika sat on the side of the bed. "Are you fully awake?"

Rory rubbed his face vigorously with his hands and pulled himself up. "Gie a man a fricht," he muttered, "an' ask if he be awake. Aye, I ken ye."

David took the lead. He described Joanna Showcroft's life at Riverview with Talbot and ended by telling the little he knew of the marriage agreement as he had overheard Mr. and Mrs. Showcroft discussing it, leaving out any mention of her recent visit to Makem's Rant. "You do understand, MacKinnon that Mrs. Showcroft must be informed."

Rory, now clearly alert, eyed both men. "You mean tae tell me Showcroft loses everythin' cause o' Andre?"

"Possibly. If I understood correctly, yes."

"That's nae what I want for Andre. I expecket the laddie tae hae his share o' the man's wealth."

"Is that what Andre wants, my friend? He could not live like this. He is going to be a man o' the mountains." Barika fingered the richly woven bed hangings. "He would not be happy here."

"That is fer him tae decide," said Rory.

"If you approach Showcroft," Barika said, "he may take the opportunity to kill you so you will not tattle to his wife. As soon as he gets word you are in Williamsburg, you will have to mind your back every moment of the day."

"Other MacKinnons waul see justice be done if I canna."

David shifted his position in the chair so that the moonlight fell directly on Rory's face. "Certainly, your sons could kill Showcroft, but they would hang for it. Barika could do the deed and he would hang for it. Andre still would not receive his share, because Showcroft would make sure your evidence was destroyed. You could lose your life, your family. Showcroft would win again."

"Wha' can Mrs. Showcroft do fer me?"

"Let her use the evidence to destroy her husband," David said. "Let her use the courts to find justice for both of you." He watched Rory carefully as he spoke. "The Missus ... Mrs. Showcroft will not see you cheated, Mr. MacKinnon. She will be your ally."

"She is a lady," Rory said. "She will nae take what I hae to say vera' well. I dinna want tae destroy her life, only that o' her husband."

"She may at first be upset," David said. "But do you not think this news will load her gun? 'Tis proof that her husband, after their marriage, had a child by another woman."

"The agreement says she gets everythin' if Showcroft has a child by another woman after kirkin'– yer sure o' that?" Rory said, looking from Barika to David.

"That is my understanding of the talk I overheard."

"I am sure that all she oucht tae do is visit his Carolina Plantations tae see the proof o' his virility."

"Nay, a *European* child is the key," said Barika. "Even Mr. Turnbull would turn a blind eye to slave-children. I should say that in his day he enjoyed the company of a few women and maybe has a child or two running around China or India. Doubtless he has not thought of including them in his fortunes."

"Showcroft is an animal, decripit an' dotteral too." Rory closed his eyes and lay back against the pillows. "Who kens the wordin' o' the marriage agreement?"

"Mr. Bushnell might know more than I," David said.

"Run. Git the maun. Send him tae my room, then leave us alone. Help me oot o' this confoun' bed, Barika. I canna understand anyone sleepin' four feet off the groun'. They be daft in the heid." Rory detected a smile on Barika's face. "Tell Roderick an' Alex aboot this an' I'll toss ye out on your arse, kizzen," he threatened.

"Do that and I'll tell them I sneaked in and lifted your pistol right out from under your pillow without your knowing I was in the room." Barika handed him the pistol, grip first.

"Livin' like this is makin' me soft in the heid," Rory said. "Git oot, both o' ye. Wheest, tha' the lassie doesna' find ye sneakin' doun the halls. Dunna get yoursel' shot when you wake Bushnell. I'll tell ye both in the mornin' what I have decided."

David and Barika left Rory's room as quietly as they entered.

"Cat-feet! They maun hae cat-feet." Rory said wrapping himself in a quilt to wait for Bushnell.

Riverview Plantation
12 November 1756
Dear Dearest Katie:

I have entrusted this Letter to Rory to ensure you receive it in good time. Rory MacKinnon is a gentle man. That he finally brought the information about the birth of Andre and death of Mairi to my Attention speaks well of him. Although the man enjoyed my hospitality for nearly a month, that Revelation came but one week ago. Rory did want to face Talbot up with the truth, but was persuaded to forego that course of action. Rest assured the Situation will be taken in hand. I do now understand your Allegiances to Allan and Rory, and in no way blame you for not writing. Blood ties are strong.

I cannot think why Mr. Bushnell, who knew about Talbot's affaire du coeur with Mairi, did not mention it to me. And I do believe that Captain Makem may have known, too. Mr. MacKinnon knows the terms of my Marriage Agreement and promises to give you the Details. Of course, Mr. Bushnell is devastated. I have not spoken with Captain Makem recently.

Rory has much other News for you – about your father, and Major Straight, and the incidents in Williamsburg. I have spent many pleasant evenings giving him details of those you will remember and wish to know about. You must make plans to visit Virginia, my dearest Katie. My Home is open to you and yours. Can you come this way with your family next Yule season? Of course, Luke will not remember your Role in his first year, but he will, no doubt, be interested in meeting his half-Brother. Such things we have to talk about! You must write immediately to Jackson Shand, so that he might take steps to establish you as Heir to your father's British estate.

If this is any comfort, I believe that your Father became acutely conscious of Major Straight's faults before his death, which is Vindication for your actions. But, my dear. I dictate to you when I should just be happy that you are once again back in my life, however it may play out. The winds of Change are at my back. I will close now, so that Rory may tuck this Letter in his Pack. He and Barika – Richard perhaps – leave after breakfast tomorrow.

I do apologize for my previous rant. There is no cause for worry. All is in hand, my dear. If 'tis not, fate will play the hand.
Your most faithful Friend,
Joanna

CHAPTER THIRTY-FOUR
RIVERVIEW
December 1756

DESPITE the fact that the fire in the hearth was kept at full blaze in Timothy's bedchamber, it gave little comfort from the fingers of cold that licked under doors. A raw wind whipped bare branches of shrubbery into a fury causing them to dance and scratch against window panes etched with delicate frost patterns that sparkled like diamonds when they caught the fire light. Flakes of snow, interspersed with icy rain, swirled through the air. Three quilts covered Joanna and still they were not enough to keep her warm.

Elizabeth Shand sat near the canopied and curtained bed, threading coloured wool through a canvas, glasses partway down the bridge of her nose. She stopped work occasionally to push them back into place and to pull her shawl closer round her ample figure.

"'Tis old age," she said. "Eyes are failing. Teeth are falling out. Joints are sore." She smiled at Joanna. "But I must not complain about my problems when you are so ill. If word had gotten to me sooner, I should have arranged that you be in the Capital with me. Luck made me decide to accompany my husband. Has Dr. Smith bled you yet?"

Joanna, pale and tired, was propped up with a half dozen pillows. "I will not allow such a barbarous practice," she said. "The body takes so long to heal. 'Tis unmanly to draw blood from a weak person."

"My dear, how will you be well if you do not take heed a doctor's orders?"

Joanna waved her hand. "In an insane moment, I allowed myself to be moved to Mr. Bushnell's bedchamber to make it easier for Sukie to nurse me, and for the gentleman to consult with me on plantation matters. As I do have Cansu in the room when Mr. Bushnell is present, there should be no scandalous whisperings. If I do hear any from house slaves, they will be taken to task and put to the fields. You must believe that I am only suffering from severe collywobbles and an ague. A little rest will restore me to proper health. Do not fret so."

"When my husband first laid eyes on you, he felt that you had called him to write your last Testament."

Joanna laughed, which triggered the coughing once more. "It has been my curse to be so well that when illness does strike, all think the worst and are ready to give me the last six feet of ground."

"Jackson seemed perturbed when he left you." Elizabeth dropped her needlework on the bed and went to the door. "My word on it, if the fire is not kept high in this hearth, we will turn to ice." Her summons brought Henkle with an armload of wood. When she sat down again, Elizabeth handed Joanna a glass of whiskey, honey and water. "Take a hearty sip. Jackson does swear by this elixir."

Joanna took a sip and gagged. "The cure is worse than the illness. What a pitiful existence! I have been bed-bound for more than seven days. Poor Luke is restricted to one visit a day, lest he contract the fever. Even then, Sukie keeps him well away from my bed. I do desire to put my arms around him, to reassure him I will regain my health."

"Best you not hug the lad," Elizabeth said. "There is much illness around. Mrs. Campbell died from the malady this past week."

"What news from Williamsburg?"

"The Lieutenant Governor plans his annual New Year's Levee. Of course, the riffraff think themselves welcome, but we do know invitations were sent out. You will be our house guest should your husband be home to accompany you, of course?" Elizabeth looked at Joanna over her glasses. "All are disappointed you do not plan to have your annual fête. With no word from your husband, you must be fretting."

Joanna pulled a blanket to her chin. "Truly, this is the longest he has gone without a word or letter. You know all is not well between us, but that does not excuse his negligence."

Elizabeth shrugged and concentrated on threading bright blue wool through her needle. "To explain any man's actions is futile." She held it up to the light, squinting as she worked. "They are complicated machinery at best, beasts at worse."

"Some men are an unusual breed."

"There is one in this house," Elizabeth said, "as unpredictable as any."

"If the reference is to Mr. Bushnell, you do the man a disservice. He is loyal, wise and kind."

"And Captain Makem." Elizabeth said, examining the back of her canvas. "None is as interesting as that *homme du monde*."

Joanna struggled to sit up. "He does carry an *air de firpouille* about him. What about Anthony?"

Elizabeth snipped at some thread with small silver scissors, pleased that she got a reaction from Joanna at mention of Makem's name. "Have you noted, my dear, that you just called the man by his Christian name? 'Tis a term of endearment that he only allowed his mother, and the old man from whom he took his last name, to use."

"Indeed, 'tis a slip of the tongue," Joanna said.

"Has Makem ever confided his past to you?"

"No, but I am very much interested in what you have to tell me for, I daresay you do have a story on your mind."

"This tale comes from Jackson," Elizabeth said, settling back in her chair. "It seems that this fellow we call Captain Anthony Makem has quite a chequered history. To be sure, he does have an air of scoundrel about him, does he not?"

Joanna nodded and reached for the glass of honeyed whiskey.

"The man was raised by an Irish saltie by the name of Elias Makem. His mother appeared on this fellow's doorstep one stormy night when the east wind was blowing sea spume across the bay. Rumours abounded about where she came from and who she was. The old man kept her secret and sheltered her and the babe. She died when the child was seven years old."

Joanna rolled to her side, the better to breathe and to hear Elizabeth. "Please do continue."

"Elias did raise the boy, paid for his education at William and Mary in Williamsburg. When Makem was eighteen, he was allowed a choice between taking a position with a merchant in Norfolk or taking to the sea. He chose the sea and shipped out on the merchantman *Torbay* for several years. Then, when old Elias became ill, he left the sea for a spell."

"Has he not always resided in Virginia?"

"No. He took Elias to Barbados, engaged the best doctors, and sojourned there for at least four years, working for several British merchants. After Elias died, Makem lost himself by wandering the world. By the time he was twenty-five he was a privateer with his own ship, the *Angel*. Eventually, he turned to the lucrative business of slavery."

"That does explain his capability to be either gentleman or rogue, as he chooses."

"I daresay he associates with the worst of men, and the best, too. Jackson does claim he has run slaves, contraband, guns and gold. But, he also claims the man is well respected in London – the result of the influence of those for whom he worked in the Barbados. Many fear him. He fears no one."

Joanna coughed so violently that Elizabeth jumped to her aid and patted her gently on the back. "My dear!"

Joanna was near tears when she lay back on the pillows. "Go on with Captain Makem's story. How did he meet my husband?"

"Your husband financed Makem's second ship. The *Angel* was crippled in a storm, and Makem ran her up on shore near your husband's holdings north of Charles Town. Your husband needed someone to run contraband and carry rice to England. Makem needed a ship. I do suppose a friendship developed over time."

"Could it be my husband persuaded Captain Makem to become involved in slavery? If his ship was sailing to England, 'tis a small step to make the triangle – England, Africa and the West Indies. Talbot needed slaves for his plantations. Makem could provide them."

"I daresay 'tis possible. Whatever the case, their friendship was cemented when your husband furnished proof about who Makem's mother was. And more importantly, who her father was."

"Pray, do not keep me in suspense," said Joanna. A shiver went through her, unrelated to her illness. Her pulse quickened.

"Your husband did invest in a shipyard in Baltimore that had been owned by a merchant named Alexander Sherway. In an old account book there appeared entries of payments to an Irishman, Elias Makem, ship's carpenter, who worked at the yard. The payments were of a goodly sum, and sent to Elias at a place known as Makem's Rant. These payments began with the arrival of Makem's mother at the old saltie's door."

"I am all twilly, Elizabeth. Please do continue," Joanna said.

"Attend, then. Four weeks before Elias Makem's abrupt departure from Baltimore to that cottage, a young man was found dead at the shipyard ... struck over the head. The son of a well-to-do furniture maker in New York had decided not to enter his father's business, but to find his own way – in Baltimore."

"He was murdered?"

"It appears so, but no one was charged with the deed. Several years before *that*, the Sherway family – father, mother and their daughter Christine did visit New York and stayed for a long time while several suites of furniture were designed for them. Account books do indicate payment for lodging and furniture over several months."

"Why is this significant?"

Elizabeth sighed and gave Joanna a motherly look. "'Tis such a simple line to draw, my dear. The daughter was obviously attracted to the young man, who was smitten by her, I fear. When the Sherway family did return to Baltimore, he followed and lodged with Elias while courting the girl. At that time, Elias resided at O'Malley's Boarding House close by the shipyard. It seems that nature did have a hand in the situation. Elias must have been in their confidence. For, my dear, why would she appear on the doorstep at Makem's Rant after being thrown out of her father's house if it were otherwise?"

"Then, her father would not allow a marriage. Did the young man not come from the same social circles?"

"'Tis said that Christine's hand had been promised to a young man in England, or Ireland. If that was the case, the father would not approve a marriage here."

Joanna's stomach churned. "It appears exceedingly likely that Alexander Sherway did have something to do with the man's murder."

"Nothing was proven. Jackson assumes that the young man ventured to speak with Sherway at the shipyard. An argument ensued and the boy was struck on the head. An unlucky mischance perhaps, but the young man died. Elias Makem may have seen the confrontation because, even though he left the shipyard, he did continue to receive money from Sherway."

"My word! Was he bribed to keep silence?"

"Methinks he was paid to keep Christine and the child. Given the girl's delicate condition the fellow possibly went to the shipyard to ask again for her hand in marriage. Perhaps he asked for work to provide for his child?"

"Elizabeth, how came you by this information?"

"Elias had raised the child and wanted to make the adoption of his last name official. He did confide to Jackson, who drew up the papers. I believe Sherway did not deny he had struck the fellow when confronted by Makem – our Captain Makem, who was himself almost killed by a blow to the back of his head, inflicted by Sherway wielding a fire iron. If Caliganto had not stepped in, and –"

"And killed Sherway?" Joanna asked.

"You mistake the matter, it was in defense of Makem. Knowing that no one would believe Caliganto's story, Makem confessed the deed, stating he had struck the man – his grandfather – in self-defense, and he had the wound to prove it. This happened immediately after Elias' death. Shortly thereafter Makem took to sea with a vengeance."

Joanna grabbed a crockery bowl, threw herself to the side of the bed and was violently ill.

"You poor, poor dear! Perhaps the doctor should be in attendance. I must call –" Elizabeth jumped to her feet. "Sukie! Sukie! Come here at once!" Sukie was in the room in moments, followed by Timothy and Jackson, who had heard Elizabeth's shouts from the comfort of the smoking room.

Jackson gave Timothy a quick glance of conspiracy. "We'll move the lady to the day room where 'tis even warmer," he said.

"'Twas that whiskey made me ill," Joanna said. "By my life, I will never again drink honeyed whiskey."

"Is the Missus worse?" Sukie's concern was genuine.

"Nay, Sukie, I suffer less than yesterday," Joanna said. "Mayhap some of your herb tea might help."

When Joanna turned to speak with Jackson, Sukie beckoned Timothy to follow her from the room. He was back a short time later, looking shaken.

"Bushnell? Are you coming down with the ague too?" Jackson asked.

"Sukie tells me that your husband was in Williamsburg this morning." He averted his eyes from Joanna. "He sent word that he will be here before nightfall."

The mantel clock broke the silence, striking two o'clock.

"Is that not good news?" Elizabeth said, looking from Joanna to Jackson.

"I should say 'tis troubling news," Jackson said. "Pray excuse us, Mrs. Showcroft; you must rest before your husband arrives. There is a break in the weather. We will take our leave. 'Tis quite possible we will pass him on the road." He bowed slightly to Joanna. "I will attend again soon, at a time convenient for you."

"Yes. Thank you Mr. Shand," Joanna said without enthusiasm. "After the New Year I will have recovered sufficiently to manage the concerns we discussed.

Forgive me if I do not see you away."

Elizabeth kissed Joanna's forehead. "I hate to leave you in this condition. Promise you will send for me if the ague worsens. I will return to your bedside with all haste."

Timothy saw the Shands to the door and returned to his chamber. "Mrs. Showcroft, we must gird our loins for the battle ahead."

"With great respect for Advocate Shand, I hope he keeps Rory MacKinnon's news in strictest confidence." Joanna said. "He does speak overmuch with his wife."

"He will keep the trust," Timothy said. "He is an advocate first and a husband second. There will be no blabbing to his good wife. I have his word on the Bible."

"Mr. MacKinnon and Barika, where might they be now?"

"If they took the most direct route, they will be close to home."

"God speed them," said Joanna. "The promise to Mr. MacKinnon will be fulfilled."

"Mrs. Showcroft, you cannot face your husband's ire in your weakened condition."

"Then I shall take your advice and try to mend very quickly. I could not have chosen a more trustworthy accomplice than you." Joanna managed a smile. "It does appear we are always scrambling to keep secrets, does it not?"

"To be sure, I am concerned I carry too many secrets."

"I too have secrets, my friend. But everyone should keep a part of themselves hidden. As colours sometimes elude your palette, Mr. Bushnell, we are like the paint and do not fully show everything. As there is never a perfect picture, nor is there a perfect human being."

"Upon my word, some seem to think themselves so."

"They refuse to see their shocking faults." Joanna smiled. "The pompous too shall fall. My husband might view my occupation of your chamber in a much different light from what it actually is. Please ask Henkle to clean the room. I will instruct Sukie to remove my personals."

"I will carry you to your chamber, Mrs. Showcroft."

"You shall do no such thing, Mr. Bushnell. After I have taken some broth and dry biscuit, I shall walk up myself."

"Mrs. Showcroft, have you suffered the ague before?"

"Aye, badly and only once," Joanna said. "Mr. Bushnell? Where is my portrait? "

"'Tis in my office," Timothy said.

Sukie slipped into the room, her formidable figure swathed in a white apron. "De gentleman will be so kind as to leave?"

"Ah, I must tell you, Mrs. Showcroft. Makem's ship left Norfolk harbour a week ago Saturday. I did hear the news from Jackson, who dined with Makem before he left. He is risking a winter passage to England, and then Africa."

"I should have thought ... I never ..." Joanna burst into tears. "Do ... excuse my ... unwarranted outburst, Sir. 'Tis the ... illness ..."

Timothy offered a linen square. "I should not have mentioned it but I thought it was important you know."

Sukie waited until Timothy left before saying, "You can clean de room, Ma'am, but you cannot be a-cleanin' de memory. I don't wish you to git a beatin' from de Massa. Yo' slaves will be told not to say you sleep in Teacher Bushnell's chamber."

Riverview
2 January 1757
My dear Father:
Another year begins with miles between us. I greet you on this most auspicious day. Always the turning of a New Year brings many resolves and this one is no exception

I had determined several months ago that this would be the year for a visit to Willowbank. I now write to tell you that I am home to England as soon as passage can be arranged. Tis a winter crossing will be attempted, not without some trepidation, but I wish to be at Willowbank for spring's awakening. I have not been well and do resolve to return to Willowbank to recover. I will travel with Jonathan Luke and David duPont. My time at Willowbank will depend on circumstances.

Talbot is not in my party. He did return from the south in great form mid-December. Seeing that I was unwell, and not willing to answer his tirades, he did leave again to spend most of his time in Baltimore where he has business interests, coming home to Riverview for only three days over the Yule. I do expect him at Riverview within the week as we have some business to conduct.

While I am away from Riverview, Timothy Bushnell and Advocate Jackson Shand will act as your administrators. A letter to that effect was lodged with Advocate Shand some years ago. Should I not survive the sea voyage-or any circumstance occur that you no longer control Riverview, they are aware of what must be done. I have made special arrangements for your slaves, should bad come to worse and their futures need be addressed. Both will be diligent in their resolve that Talbot not interfere with Riverview in my absence.

If you have received my last letter, either an answer is on the high seas or you chose to ignore it, thinking it the rant of an angry, lonely woman. No doubt you will have many questions upon my arrival which I may – or may not – answer. I will merely say that I am not the same Joanna who left England seven years ago.

This will be my last correspondence until I see you at Willowbank. I will send word once we have docked that you may send conveyances to meet us and to carry us home.

I send my love, Father.
Yours in 1757,
Joanna

CHAPTER THIRTY-FIVE
RIVERVIEW
Mid-January 1757

The Agreement

TALBOT strode into the library, his clothes smelling of stable, his riding boots covered with muck. Throwing his gloves on a side table, he ran his fingers through his hair, retrieved a bottle of whiskey and a glass from a cabinet.

Jackson stood, nervously sorting through some papers spread before him on the table. If Joanna was nervous, it did not translate into her demeanor as she sat beside him, a long shawl over her house-gown.

"I do tender no apology for my tardy arrival," Talbot said pouring himself a drink. He raised the bottle toward Jackson, who shook his head, then set it on the table. "I made a hasty departure from the crossroads as soon as I received your message. Please be quick about this. Of the evening, I must be in Williamsburg." When his eyes fell on the papers, he glanced at Jackson, then at Joanna. "Why, have you finally come to your senses, wife? Does this signify that you relinquish operation of this plantation to me? Attention must be paid to the docks. River's high. They need be secured." Pulling a chair, he sat at the table, opposite Joanna, raised his glass in her direction. "Is that why I have the pleasure of this little tête-a-tête?"

"It seems early in the day for imbibing," Jackson commented.

"Damme if any time is not good for celebratory libation," Talbot retorted. "Is this so important I must be sober to hear it?"

Jackson placed a yellowed document in front of Talbot. "You will have seen this before."

Picking the paper up, Talbot glanced quickly at the writing. The seal had been broken but the remnants still bore the markings of the Turnbull crest. He threw it back on the table. "'Tis the marriage agreement between my wife and me."

"Then you know the terms as set by Charles Turnbull and signed by yourself and Mrs. Showcroft?"

"To be sure, I have memorized them," Talbot said, lounging in his chair. "And I have adhered to them religiously since we wed."

"You lie!" Joanna said.

"Shall I swear my statement on a Bible?" Talbot said, scowling at Joanna.

"Sir, I should not take a vow that far," Jackson cautioned.

Glancing from Shand to Joanna, Talbot played with his glass, a gesture that indicated to both how nervous the man was. "What stupidity has prompted you to call this gathering?"

Jackson reached beneath the heavily draped table to retrieve the saddlebag. "Well, Sir, you are familiar with this."

"I could not say with certainty that I am." Talbot's eyes narrowed as he glanced toward the bag.

"These are your initials, Showcroft," Jackson pointed out.

"T.S.? 'Tis common enough." Talbot topped his drink.

"Perhaps then, these trifles will refresh your memory." Jackson laid ten gold coins on the table.

Talbot reached for the glittering metal and drew the pile toward him. "Gold coins, nothing more."

As Talbot toyed with the coins, he thought furiously. Of course he recognized the bag. It had been tooled for him in Williamsburg twenty years before.

"Do you deny these belong to you?" Jackson asked.

Talbot shrugged, emptied his glass and wiped his mouth with his sleeve. "Please do join me in a drink, Jackson. Imbibing alone is no pleasure and the Wife does not approve of my drinking to stupification. That alone should give you the incentive to have a tip with me."

Jackson answered by throwing a small bundle of papers, tied with red ribbon, before Talbot. "These, with the gold, were found in the saddlebag. Deny they are yours."

Talbot took his time leafing through the papers. Damn! Where the hell did Shand get these, he thought. They, and the saddlebag, were left with Mairi at MacKinnon's Trace.

"I do not deny that they are my papers," he said. "And if they were found in the saddlebag, the bag then must be the one that was ... stolen years ago in Charles Town. Yes, I do recall now ... I was ... robbed of a night –"

"A plausible story from any but you," Jackson said.

"'Tis the truth, damn you!"

"Nay, 'tis a lie," Jackson said. "A stupid lie, to boot. A thief would have taken the gold. This bag was given to your wife by Rory MacKinnon."

Talbot, startled to hear Rory's name, sat up in his chair, drummed his fingers on the table then laughed, "Utter codswallop! Rory MacKinnon's land is over the Trace Cut, hundreds of miles from here. If you tell me that my wife was there, by God, I shall believe elephants live in Virginia."

"Do not speak so lightly, Husband." Joanna said, her voice quiet but firm. "Rory MacKinnon did come to Riverview and enjoyed my hospitality for some weeks. When your return was delayed, he did impart his information and left for the Trace, accepting our promise that it would be acted upon."

"That dotard nincompoop was here?" Talbot glanced at Jackson, looking for a sympathetic ear. Seeing no change in the Advocate's face, he turned back to Joanna, who was looking at him through narrowed eyes. "So. He did find my saddlebag and returned it," Talbot said. "An honest Scotsman's a rarity, especially where gold is involved. The old man's actions do surprise me."

"An honest Scotsman he is, Husband and not interested in gold coin," Joanna said.

"What is his interest?" When Talbot reached for the bottle, Jackson pulled it across the table beyond his reach.

"He seeks justice," Joanna said

"Justice?" echoed Talbot.

"He demands recognition," Jackson said.

"Recognition for returning a saddlebag?" Talbot sneered, and played with his empty glass.

"Rory MacKinnon demands recognition for your son, Andre, born to Mairi MacKinnon in December 1750," Joanna said.

Talbot rejoined, "Why, there is a joker at this table. A child by the daughter of Rory MacKinnon? Trumpery! Nonsense!"

"Jackson said, "In truth, you not only have a son, but he was conceived after your marriage vows were pronounced."

Talbot struck the table with his fist and leapt to his feet. "A damned untruth! I do know Mairi MacKinnon, but I know no child called Andre."

"Your very actions declare you are a liar, Husband," Joanna drew Mairi's Bible from under her shawl and opened it to a page marked with an embroidered ribbon. "The birth of your son is recorded in Mairi's handwriting in this Bible." Joanna set it on the table, but kept one hand on it.

"For heaven's sake, sit down, Showcroft. Theatrics will not advance your case." Jackson's authoritative voice brought Talbot up short.

Talbot did as he was told but ignored the Bible. His mind worked furiously, trying to conjure various plots that might fit the new evidence laid before him.

"Baldercock! Cozening rascal that he is, MacKinnon hopes to extort money from me. Damn him, how much does he demand?"

"Unlike my husband, who will try anything for financial gain, Rory MacKinnon asks no money for himself. He came to Riverview to ask for what is rightly due his grandson, Andre Showcroft."

"I tell you the man is a scoundrel." Talbot's face was red. His hands trembled as he toyed with his glass.

Jackson placed one more paper before Talbot. "This paper is all a court will need to act. Read it, Sir. You are well and truly caught."

Talbot feigned difficulty reading the fine handwriting on the document. After several minutes, broken only by the crackling of the fire, and a clock's ticking, he laid the sheet down. "Am I to understand there is an alliance between Mrs. Sherrie and Rory MacKinnon? Her name is on this testament."

Joanna answered, "After we received Major Straight's venomous letter in Williamsburg, Katie and Allan Sherrie quitted Riverview to live near Allan's kin, who was, in an interesting turn of fate, the clansman Rory MacKinnon in the Carolinas. Mairi is dead. Katie has raised Andre as her own son. It was she who found the Bible not four months ago." Joanna watched her husband closely while she spoke.

Talbot sat, temper barely under control, head bent, fingering the folds of his cravat, lest he begin to bash fist into hand. "So. I do appear to be caught," he said. "You have won the game, Wife. Does the victory satisfy you? Is this what you have wasted years to achieve, what your father has prayed for? You have brought me to my financial knees, proven that you are more virtuous than I." He glanced up. "What more do you ask?"

"Recognition for Andre," Jackson said. "You must provide for your son."

Talbot threw back his head, laughed, then reached across the table to grab the bottle and pour himself another drink. "Go to the Devil! Speak with my wife about money. By the terms of the agreement, everything I do own now belongs to her."

"Do you wish to give reason for your indiscretion, Talbot?" Joanna hadn't moved from her seat.

"You have the effrontery to ask for details? Well enough. If it will please, why be silent? Bushnell introduced me to Mairi, innocently enough, in Charles Town. She was attracted to Bushnell, but a few charms and gewgaws changed her mind. You were in England. She was flesh and blood in Charles Town. We dallied."

When Joanna kept silent, Talbot stood to pace back and forth behind his chair. "Before my return from Willowbank, after your son's birth, Mairi left Charles Town and returned to MacKinnon's Trace. You decided to come to America, and so I had to confront her. I rode to the Trace where I found my predicament complicated by the arrival of this child – Andre. I had no desire to be parted from my money, or the Turnbull fortunes, by a bastard child. I refused to admit paternity and rode away from Andre and from Mairi."

"And you never returned to the Trace, never saw Mairi again?"

"Never."

"Yet, you showed no surprise when I told you that she was dead," Joanna said.

Talbot stuttered, "I ... was advised of her death in ... Charles Town." He turned on Joanna. "Good God, what matters that now! I had no love for her, no more than I have for you. She was a cheap bit, a whore."

"You are nothing but disgusting."

"Say truth, Wife, I have disgusted you mightily for years," Talbot replied. "Pray do not suppose that some silly agreement gives you the right to all I possess. You are in utter ignorance of what I do own and where. I have no intention of listing it all for you."

"You are not listening, Husband. Advocate Shand and I only insist that you provide for Andre. I make no serious claim to your possessions and properties."

Talbot grabbed the document. "What are you prattling about? You *forgive* me? All will be righted? We will live a lie forever?" He slapped the paper. "This paper is the very reason that you are in Virginia."

"'Tis only one of my reasons, Husband. I had hoped to make a proper marriage. You could never understand that. You did refuse me affection, or even respect. Truly, you were incapable of giving your heart to Jonathan Luke or to me."

"Our marriage agreement makes no mention of affection or respect." Talbot's eyes narrowed. He stopped pacing. "This is not like you, Wife. Why does this agreement now mean nothing to you? Are you not bound for revenge? Why do you not now take your rights under the terms?"

Joanna's eyes remained fixed on Talbot's face. "Because I, too, have broken the agreement."

"You!"

"I am with child, Talbot. And 'tis none of yours."

Talbot stared at Joanna, then turned his back on her. "This I have difficulty believing."

"'Tis the truth," Joanna said.

Talbot whirled around. "If this is true, who is the father? Who took my wife?"

"Crudely, 'tis I took the man," Joanna said.

"You, the lady of such high morals, such integrity!" Talbot shouted. He started around the table toward Joanna.

Jackson shot to his feet, Timothy's loaded pistol in his hand. "Stay where you are, Showcroft. I have taken precautions."

"You would shoot me, Shand?"

"If need be, in defense of your wife."

Talbot backed away, hands in sight.

Jackson laid the pistol on the table by the Bible, close to Joanna, and well out of Talbot's reach.

"'Tis Timothy Bushnell – the traitor!"

"Do not even suggest that Mr. Bushnell is involved," Joanna said. "To do so is an injustice to that gentle man. You are beating the air, Husband. I have not been your wife in the true sense for many months. You surprise me with this bluster. Is what is good for the gander not good for the goose?"

"Then, 'tis Makem, is it?" Talbot hissed. "He came snooping, looking for a bird to pluck when I was away from home. The man has barked after you for years."

"The captain has not visited Riverview since the morning after Major Straight's murder," Joanna said in a steady, clear voice.

"And Makem has not been seen in Williamsburg since the murder," Jackson said.

"Who is the beggar? Who?" Talbot banged the table with his fists. "God damn it, Wife, I have a right to know whom this misbegotten comes from."

"By the gods, that information shall not come from me," said Joanna.

When Talbot came too close, Jackson placed his hand over the pistol.

"I see." Talbot's eyes blazed. "Let me understand this. You will forgive my indiscretion if I accept yours. There will be no argument from you if there is none from me. I could have you whipped publicly for this affront to my name, woman!"

"There is no request for acceptance," Jackson said. "Mrs. Showcroft asks nothing of you for herself. She only requires that you acknowledge Andre MacKinnon as your child."

"And my wife will strut like a peacock, pregnant as a cow, proclaiming the child she is carrying is mine. Tongue do wag. Calculations will be made. Scandalous gossip will place me far away when the misbegotten was conceived."

Joanna's voice, level and calm, broke into the shouting match. "I've no wish to be a scandal for you. I shall return to England. This child shall be born at Willowbank."

"You are leaving ... no regrets ... no apologies ... no explanation."

"No regrets; certainly, no apologies; and no more explanation than I have already given, Talbot."

Grabbing his glass, Talbot made to pour himself another drink.

"Sir, you have imbibed enough," Jackson said.

"You dare preach to me?" Talbot threw the glass at the marble fireplace, where it shattered into pieces and fell to the hearth stone. "Who knows of this pregnancy?"

"Mr. Shand, you, and I."

"And the father?"

"The question does not warrant an answer."

Talbot grabbed the whiskey bottle and hurled it at the fireplace. It missed Joanna's head by inches. The liquor-fuelled fire flared, consumed the alcohol and died back. "There is some humour to this," he hissed. "With you gone, I run Riverview."

"On the contrary, Sir," Jackson said. "Papers have already been drawn up, and signed, giving the responsibility of Riverview to Mr. Bushnell and to me, until Jonathan Luke, Mrs. Showcroft, and the baby return to America."

"You hold high hopes that meal-mouthed turncoat will run this place efficiently?"

"Mr. Bushnell has managed very well so far," Joanna said. "You shall not interfere with this operation, Husband. Mr. Bushnell has full charge. You may return to the property only when I reside at the plantation, or Advocate Shand has given you permission to visit."

"What rubbish do I hear now?" Talbot eyed Jackson. "Such balderdash! And you, Shand, acting as my wife's mouthpiece, resorting to a weapon to control me."

"What must be done, is done, Sir," Jackson said.

Talbot pointed a long, dirty finger at Joanna. "Whom did you bed?"

Joanna pulled the shawl around her shoulders. "Three moons will appear in the same month in the summer sky before I give you a name, Husband."

Talbot paced again, one hand pounding into the other, but kept himself well away from the table. He placed no trust in Jackson or Joanna. Her right hand was hidden under her shawl, and it had never moved. She too might be armed.

"You leave Virginia, and then ... ?"

Jackson struck the table with a fist to make each point. "Sir, you shall bargain with Rory MacKinnon to ensure official recognition for Andre. If he does not hear from you in three months, steps will be taken. I act as Andre's advocate to ensure you keep your promises. If he hears nothing from you, correspondence will be undertaken between Mr. MacKinnon and me."

"Not bloody likely that will happen," Talbot said.

"You shall leave Riverview immediately and not return for your goods until your wife's party has left. She has graciously given you four-and-twenty hours to allow removal of your small possessions. The law will evict you if you tarry longer. Should Mrs. Showcroft feel the need to get word to you, she will write through me."

"The book is closed? No good-bye kiss? No wifely embrace? Aye, so be it." Talbot glared from Joanna to Jackson then, knocking the chair to the floor, seized his coat and strode from the room.

Neither Joanna nor Jackson spoke or moved until they heard him ride down the carriage road, away from Riverview Plantation.

"Splendid restraint, my dear!" Jackson exclaimed. "You always exhibit such command, my girl."

"Truthfully, I am terrified of my husband. Knowing that he is monstrously crazy when angry, I cannot leave soon enough. Mr. Shand, do you think that with the agreement nullified, I need no longer fear for Luke's safety? You know the terms of the contract and know that it was to Talbot's benefit if Luke was ... dead, for that would have been one less ... Oh my dear, and I too ... dead, for that matter."

"Mrs. Showcroft, the man has been cursed with a terrible temper, quite beyond his control once it has been sparked. I do not know what your husband might do now. He is a vindictive man, not of a forgiving nature and may seek revenge. I should be ... watchful."

"Will he stay here ... in Williamsburg?"

"For his own good, he should leave for the Carolinas. I'll remain at Riverview to see you safely away. I do fear for Mr. Bushnell. I doubt he can stand his ground when Talbot is in a rage." Jackson gathered the papers. "I advised him to journey to Richmond for several days. If he obeys, there is nothing to fear."

"Mr. Bushnell will not ride away from Talbot now," Joanna said. "He has vowed to meet the man and have it out over some personal circumstances. He has stated that he will remain at Riverview to protect it."

"Then he will suffer the consequences."

Joanna touched Jackson's hand as he worked. "I must ask for your strictest confidence in this situation, Mr. Shand. I do know you share good tales with Elizabeth. But I insist on complete secrecy. Only three people know I am with child – I, you, and now Talbot. 'Tis the way it must remain."

"My oath on the Bible, Mrs. Showcroft. I assure you that I do keep secrets from my wife. Now I must ask you a question?"

"I'll answer if I can."

"Who is the father?"

Joanna smiled. "That is not information you need be privy to, my friend."

The Leave-taking of Ndamma

WHAT snatches of sleep David managed were interrupted with periods of wakefulness when he lay, eyes fixed upon the ceiling, mind replaying the events of the previous evening. He rose when the first rays of the pale January sun reached over the eastern horizon. After Master Showcroft had quarrelled with the mistress and spent most of his time away from the plantation, Kudie slept in young Luke's room and he in the loft over the weaving house. When Master was home he once again lay before the boy's door.

David made his room comfortable with a cot, a table, a trunk, a few pieces of stoneware and several bookshelves, all given by Mistress Showcroft. The loft was heated from below by the hearth. On cool evenings, if he banked the fire properly, he was warm enough. Midwinter nights, he slept on the floor, close to the fire, amidst spinning wheels and baskets of colourful wool but always was up before Kudie arrived for her day's work.

David threw cold water on his face then drew the trunk from a corner. He hadn't changed his mind. He was going. Piling belongings on the cot, he sorted through them, discarded some and folded others before placing them in the trunk. The last items to be packed were writing supplies, books and a blanket.

When he finished, he left the loft with a small sack, passing Kudie at the outside door. She noticed the bundle in his arms and said, "You are leaving, Ndamma?"

He nodded and walked to the main house. He knocked on the door of Teacher Bushnell's bedchamber.

Timothy, head covered with a nightcap, a nightshirt to his knees, opened the door. He too noticed the bundle. "Good, David. You have decided to go."

"Yes, Teacher Bushnell." David said.

"It is a great relief to me to know you will be with Mrs. Showcroft."

"Is Jento in attendance yet?"

"I dispatched him to the slave quarters to find Henkle," Timothy said. "Would you talk with Luke, please? Mrs. Showcroft has spoken with Kudie, who will pack his trunk."

David took the back stairs three at a time. When he entered Luke's room, a trunk had already been brought down from attic storage. Luke sat in the middle of his bed, surrounded by clothing.

"Why must we go, My-David? Why was I wakened late last night and told we were leaving Riverview? How long will we be gone? What will happen to my pony?"

"Jento will care for your pony, Young Luke. You know that your mother is ailing. She wishes to return to her home in England to get well. Your mother has not seen her father for a long time. You must become acquainted with your grandfather. You may not wish to leave Riverview, but, Young Luke, you must not remain here without your mother."

Luke scrambled from the bed and went to the window overlooking the court-yard. "Why does Father not journey with us to England?"

David didn't answer, knowing that Luke would eventually find the reason by his own considerations. The boy was wise for his age.

Luke circled the bed and stood beside David. "Why are you traveling with us?"

"'Tis a question I asked of myself all night. Not for the journey across the sea. After the voyage from Africa I vowed never to step foot on a sailing vessel again. But ... circumstances change."

"If you are afraid of the ocean, you must stay here, My-David."

"I will face my fears. Young Luke, I did promise to undertake the journey to be servant to you while your mother rests. I will attend her needs when necessary and protect both my charges. You must understand that I need to leave Riverview and America to decide what I must be and do. Look, there will be room for schoolbooks, so you can do lessons. Teacher Bushnell trusts me to help you with them."

"Why must I do lessons on the ship? Do you remember anything about the sea?"

"I did not see much because I was confined to a stinking black hole for much of the time. I will not travel in the same conditions on this voyage. But let me tell you, the ocean was many shades of blue. *Black Wing* was constantly shadowed by sharks. When a captive died, the body was thrown to them, and they ate it. Near land, gulls and sea hawks found the ship."

"My-David, I do not know about England," Luke protested.

David laughed. "I have little knowledge of it myself, but for the books I have read. It will be an adventure for both of us. But I will be more at a disadvantage than you."

Luke glanced around his comfortable room. His mother had made sure he had every convenience. He knew every nook and cranny in the house, every hiding place in the gardens, every stump and tree in the woods. "Will we ever return to Riverview? Promise me that we will come home again."

"If 'tis within my power, you and I will return one day. I too have pleasant memories here and good friends. I must go find one now," David said. "Break your fast in the cook house, Young Luke, then stay with Kudie as your mother instructed."

"I won't see Father again. I saw him ride down the carriage road yesterday."

It was good, David thought, that Talbot Showcroft did not try to see his son. He gathered his bundle, left the mansion and took the path to the gang quarters. He would miss Riverview and his people.

Henkle and Jento joined him near the north gate, the sadness on Jento's face mirrored in Henkle's. Knowing the two wished time to speak, Henkle embraced David then left the two Griots to talk.

"I heard from Master Bushnell," Jento said, "that my countryman is sailing to England."

David placed his arm around Jento and led him to a boulder, where they sat and looked over the river. Flocks of geese, wintering over, sounded their displeasure at being disturbed by a small boat heading upriver toward Richmond. Gnarled trees, their branches stark against the grey blue sky, lined the far shore. This was a scene David would miss.

"Jento, I did consider well my choices."

"Mr. Bushnell did not say why you are going?"

"Learning is my magnet, Jento. Its pull began the day I was given bits of paper with pictures drawn on them. I must go to England where there are beautiful things to see, and much more to learn."

"The mistress said this to persuade you to travel with Luke."

"Nay, hear me out. Teacher Bushnell speaks of hills so high one cannot see the top, of buildings so large one can never imagine living in them, of worship houses so beautiful they bring tears to the eye —"

"You believed him?"

"Yes."

"This is not your way, Ndamma. These are not your people. You will not be accepted. You are the wrong colour."

"When I asked what I might do, and how I should be accepted, Mistress Showcroft said that the way would not be without trials. But if I stood firm and believed, I could do whatever I wanted, be whatever I wished. She gives me freedom, Jento! In her eyes, I am now free. But under law I must leave Virginia to receive it. I will be freed by law in England."

"The mistress dangles false hopes."

"We must learn to trust, Jento, or we will be lost. As I have faith in Mistress Showcroft, you must put confidence Teacher Bushnell." David put his arm around Jento. "We leave in the late afternoon. I brought you some things that I hold close to my heart. Will you accept them and think of me when you touch them?"

"Will you return?"

"That I do promise," David said. "I will return as the free man, as *Mr.* David duPont. Teacher Bushnell says he will keep you at Riverview until I come back. If you are not here, leave word as you go so that I might find you. Look, I have given my papers so that you can practice. You must learn to write and do sums. I've given you a china plate and cup; a silver fork, a neck charm."

Jento, a lump rising in his throat, accepted the gifts without a word.

David looked fondly at Jento then toward the river, tears coursing down his cheeks. "You must understand, Jento, even without freedom, Mistress Showcroft must not travel alone. Young Luke needs help too. I made a promise to Captain Makem that I should guard them — always. In truth, when I return to America I will be better able to help my people." David placed his arm around Jento's shoulder again. "What can I do to ease this leave taking?"

"Nothing. No words can soothe the pain," Jento said. "I look upon you as my brother. I always will."

David took the leather pouch from his belt, caressed it, and said, "Then the last thing I give you is the most important. Accept it as a brother. You must now take on the work of the

Griot. This responsibility was mine to give, and yours to keep, and pass to the next."

"Am I worthy of this?" Jento reluctantly reached for the bag.

"More worthy than I. Do you remember the stones ... the stories?"

Jento nodded. "You have taught me well."

David reached into the sack. "There is one pebble to add," he said handing Jento a beautiful golden object. "My pebble. Attach what you must to it."

"I will," Jento managed to say, as he turned the stone in his hand.

"'Tis amber," David said. "I purchased it at the Yule market in Williamsburg. See, there is an insect in it. This is I, caught between two ways of life, unable to escape either one."

Jento held the stone up to the sun. "A winged creature, caught between two suns. Some day it will fly away and a sun will burn it."

"Not that insect," David smiled. "'Tis frozen in time. Think of me every time you touch the stone." David dug into the sack again then gave Jento a handful of coins. "If the coins are kept in the pouch, they will not be seen ... unless you show them. If some know you have this much money, they will kill you to get it.

"How did you come by so many coins?"

"I did stash the pin-money that Mistress Showcroft gave me so I could buy freedom if it was not given."

"I will keep these and my own for the same purpose," Jento said.

"Teacher Bushnell says he will arrange your freedom; and for you to leave Virginia at the right time. Trust him. I will write, but you must learn to read the letters." David rubbed Jento gently on the back, a gesture of love and concern.

"I can accept the responsibilities, but I will never accept you being so far away."

"You must understand, I have no choice but to embrace freedom. And when the time comes for you to make the same decision, you will choose freedom too, Jento."

"Although we will be separated by miles," Jento said, "we will also be separated by learning. I fear when I see you again, you will no longer be of our people. You will no longer be African, and I shall still be a slave."

David's arms encircled Jento. "Whatever I become, I can never change the colour of my skin, or the feeling in my heart for my birth-land and birthright. I will begin another ring of history and stories. Only they will be written on paper, not kept in a pouch. They will be about other people and other places. But, I will never forget this place – and you Jento."

Jento's sobs were uncontrollable.

"Look at me, Jento. With tears flow sorrow and pain. If we weep together, our burden will be lightened."

Arms around each other, heads together, David and Jento shared their last hour together at Riverview.

Leave-taking, Joanna

"MR. Shand, could I ask for a moment, please, to look at my home?" Joanna said as Jackson's carriage pulled away from the mansion. "One last look."

Jackson instructed his coachman to rein in. The sun, low on the horizon, silhouetted the plantation house against a pale blue winter sky. As a final farewell, Sukie had lit candles at every window in the front facade. Smoke from chimneys mingled with a thin fog that rolled through the pasturage. Trees stood like bare awkward sentinels. Geese called plaintively from the river.

How had she fallen so deeply in love with Riverview, Joanna wondered, that the ache in her heart had the same intensity as that she had experienced when she had left Willowbank?

Now, Riverview's slaves were coming down the front steps. A sound, similar to that of wind wailing out of a fireplace of a stormy night, rolled like a wave down the carriageway. The horses pranced in their traces, nervous of the sound and anxious to be away.

"That is your people mourning our departing," David said from his seat beside Jackson. He kept his eyes averted. He could not look at the house, his fellow slaves, for fear he would break reserve and weep.

"Such a haunting lament. I will carry it in my heart for a very long time." Joanna shivered. Indeed, the sound penetrated to her very soul.

Luke looked from David to the woods, to the house and back to his African companion. He had put his trust in his friend that they would return to the plantation, so he had no reason to cry.

"I do now understand 'tis not what you bring to life but what life brings to you," Joanna said. "Oh, I will miss them so. Look, Mr. Bushnell is waving a white cloth from the high portico. How I will miss Sukie, Henkle, Juba, Jento, Kudie. Cansu, Willow ..."

"'Tis not too late to have a change of mind," Jackson said adjusting a rug around his knees

"Well you know that I must leave for a while," Joanna said. "I will not miss the shameful quarreling. But, I leave my dreams of bettering ... On my word, I did try Mr. Shand. Truthfully, I will return and try again."

"Do not carry the fault, my dear. That your husband was a grasping, uncaring man did not bode well for your marriage. You arrived with high expectations and ideals to a country whose people hold many different views, a country that wrestles with its own complicated troubles – perhaps a country that will one day ... Mrs. Showcroft, to be sure, you cannot redress everything you might wish to, no matter how hard you might try."

"Aye, 'tis over for the present." Joanna took one last, fond look at her plantation – her people – her Virginia. Finding a handkerchief, she waved it vigorously. "By my faith, I have such an overwhelming attachment for this place and these people. What lies ahead, Mr. Shand?"

"If Juba, Mr. Bushnell and your husband obey instructions, there should be no severe consequences. 'Tis not good for you to worry, my dear." Jackson called to the driver and the carriage moved again. As it rounded the last bend in the carriageway, the mansion was lost from view.

"Be truthful, Mr. Shand. Does Talbot listen to anyone?" Joanna put the handkerchief to her mouth. If the rocking motion of the carriage ride could make her ill, how would she survive the sea voyage in her delicate condition?

Jackson was thinking of her situation too. He had already noted that she looked pale. "Did you bring enough medicine?"

"I brought all that Sukie and the good doctor could provide. They, of course, know naught of my condition, so I am unsure that I should swallow some of their more vile powders and potions. Truly, the next eight weeks will be a trial."

"With good winds and luck, you will be home in four. A winter crossing ... But we must not dwell upon that. I daresay you will arrive before your letter to your father."

"We may sail on the same ship." Joanna managed a laugh. "Do we know when we embark?"

"You were fortunate, Mrs. Showcroft. I did manage, with much ado, to secure passage on George Scott's *Larg Doogh,* but only because the land is at war. Scott risks a winter crossing to bring papers from Lieutenant Governor Dinwiddie to Secretary of State Pitt at Whitehall, and Mrs. Scott travels with her husband and has agreed to help you dress. 'Tis a dangerous endeavour they, and you, undertake."

"I cannot stay here, regardless the danger, Mr. Shand. I must convey my thanks to the Captain for allowing us to sail with them."

"You'll board the *Larg Doogh* at midnight and sail with the first tide. Mrs. Showcroft, do not allow David to be treated as an inferior. A proper cabin passage has been tendered for three. The receipt is in your possession. It will be assumed he is your slave, and not a free man. Once *Larg Doogh* is on the high seas, David is a free man under law."

"I am all happiness for David. He has waited too long for his freedom." Joanna said.

Blinking back tears, she turned to watch the buildings by the side of the road. Many of the occupants were known to her. The keeping room window of Mr. Glen's home was bright with lantern light. His large family were having their evening meal. The Widow Black's place was in darkness. The Grey Fox Inn was brightly lit, with horses tethered outside. The porch was empty but for one solitary figure leaning against a support post. The person, recognizing Jackson's carriage, raised his arm in salute. He held a glass in one hand, a bottle in the other.

"To my wife." Talbot Showcroft toasted the retreating carriage. "The trollop." His toast went unnoticed. Nursing the bottle he staggered into the inn and up the narrow stairs to the room he had taken for several nights. He threw himself on the bed, and muttered profanities between drinks until he lapsed into a drunken stupor. The bottle crashed to the floor, spilling its contents onto the boards.

Below, in the taproom, the keeper's wife felt the drops run down her neck and onto her bodice. She glanced up and stepped aside as the whiskey ran through a crack between the boards. She climbed the stairs and opened the door. Kicking the bottle into a corner, she peered into Showcroft's bloated face.

"Damned drunken fool," she said. "You'll pay for my dress, you will. Blubbering into your glass, you were, that your wife deserted you. Blame lies not wi' th' lady. I can't face your sort either. Lucky lady, she is, to be free of you."

CHAPTER THIRTY-SIX
RIVERVIEW
Late January 1757

Talbot's Revenge

TIMOTHY was in his office when he heard the approaching horse. He set down his quill, removed his reading glasses, rubbed his eyes, then went to his bedchamber where windows looked over the front yard and carriage way. Talbot's horse was tied out front.

He'd expected a confrontation for several days. Timothy now braced himself to face the man. He looked for his pistol in the top drawer of his dresser then remembered he had left it on the mantel in the library, loaded, ready to fire. Running from his bedchamber, Timothy came face to face with Talbot. One glance told him the man was drunk and very angry.

Best to keep Talbot's back to the mantel, Timothy thought. I'll manoeuver toward the bell cord by the door. "Showcroft. I did expect to see you sooner." Timothy edged carefully between Talbot and the wall, keeping his back to the windows and his eyes on his adversary.

"To be sure you did," Talbot snarled, his eyes narrow slits in a filthy, unshaven face. He clenched and unclenched his fists. "Where do you think you are sneaking off to?" Like a cat, he jumped to block Timothy's progress toward the door.

"I came to receive you," Timothy said. Taking several steps backward, he managed to pull a chair between himself and Talbot.

"Did you enjoy bedding my wife? How long did it take you to persuade her?"

"Sir, what do you mean?"

"What do I *mean*?" Talbot mocked Timothy. "Hell and the Devil confound it, I *mean* your dalliance with my wife."

"My dalliance? Are you mad?" Timothy moved away from the chair, this time circling to the right. He'd have to take his chances that Talbot would not see the pistol. "How did the two of you intend to explain away the consequences ... a virgin birth?"

"Virgin birth! In God's name what are you chattering about?"

"My wife – your child." Talbot moved toward Timothy, teeth clenched in jaw, livid face twisted in rage.

Timothy froze in astonishment. Talbot's first blow struck him on the cheek. Timothy spun toward the library table.

"Do not dangle me on your innocence-strings. You have lived in my wife's house for years. Was it a small step to take, from bookkeeper to bedfellow?"

Talbot's second punch caught him squarely on the jaw. He fell against the table. The next blow hit him in the stomach. He was no man for fisticuffs. Why had he thought he could face Talbot Showcroft without a weapon in his hand? I am done for, Timothy thought, clutching his stomach.

"'Tis not my child," he managed to say before Talbot struck him again. Timothy reached to the table for support and caught the cover cloth as he fell. The candle fell with him, its flame igniting the cloth's fringe. Eyes closed, Timothy rolled away from the table, clutching his chest.

"You dare sleep under my roof and take my wife!"

"You are one to stand in judgement, Sir. " Timothy said between gasps for breath. "You took the love of my life. You got her with child. You killed her. You deserve to burn in hell."

Fire leapt from table cover to thick rugs, to window curtains. Talbot gave Timothy one more vicious kick to his head. "'I'll not burn." Throwing his arms in the air, he spun in a circle like a madman. "My wife's house shall burn like Hell."

Talbot grabbed a chair and flung it through a window. In a frenzy, he grabbed another and broke the glass in all the windows, one after the other. The fire, whipped by the heavy draft, spread rapidly around him.

With all the strength left in him, Timothy pulled himself up and felt along the mantel for the gun. Blood blinding his sight, his hand closed around it. He cocked the hammer, aimed for the shadowy figure, squeezed the trigger and screamed, "This is for Mairi!"

There was the explosion as he fell to the floor, then silence, but for the crackling of the flames.

Timothy fought for consciousness. "The bell cord," he muttered. He rolled along the floor moaning at the pain of his ribs. Gripping his chest, he rolled again and again, panting to suppress the pain. The fire's heat was intense.

When Timothy's back hit a doorframe, he gripped the molding and tried to pull himself up. Find the cord, he thought. Was he on the right side of the door? Was it the right door? Where was the cord? Fire licked at his feet. His head swam. He screamed. At last his hand found the cord. He held on and pulled it ... five times, he counted each before black relief engulfed him and he slid to the floor.

Jento, carrying wood to the cookhouse, recognized the scream. He had heard it many times in the Fula Jallon. It was the cry of an animal in its death throes. Throwing his load to the ground, he ran for the main house. The fire smell reached Jento before he opened the door. Inside he felt the heat. Smoke billowed from the library, filled the hall and crept up the grand stairway.

Jento threw himself on the floor and crawled toward Teacher Bushnell, lying half in and half out of the library's doorway, his face streaked with blood. Jento leapt like a leopard to Timothy's aid. Arms under back and knees, he lifted the body from the floor with one movement and backed away.

"*Fire! Fire! Fire!*" Sukie ran down the servants' stairs and out the door to the carriage house to sound the alarum bell. Jento ran too, Timothy's body limp in his arms, never stopping until he was in the rose garden, well away from the mansion. The big bell tolled over and over, calling the workers from the fields. Its peal resounded up and down the James River, summoning neighbours and boatmen plying the river.

Black smoke rose over the mansion and rolled down the pasturage toward the water, where several row boats were already pulling to the dock. Juba came running, men and women behind him. Henkle shouted the orders – "Use the servant's door! Carry the silver from the dining room! Take to the stairs! Throw bedding from the upper windows! Put it all in the garden!"

Sukie panted to Jento's side. The bell still tolled, rung now by Kudie. The knelling echoed now in the bells on neighbouring plantations.

"Teacher Bushnell breathes," Jento said, his cheek to Timothy's mouth.

"Was there another?" Sukie asked.

Jento shook his head.

Henkle circled the house and came up the side to the office door. Peering in the window he saw no flames. Cautiously he felt the knob then pushed. Slipping inside, he crossed to the door of the bedchamber. The metal latch felt hot. He heard the fire crackling on the other side. Smoke oozed under the door. Quickly Henkle gathered journals from Teacher Bushnell's desk. He found the cash and document box and ran outside with his arms full. Placing his load a safe distance from the building, he ran back again. This time the smoke was heavy and the heat more intense. He grabbed paint box, easel, glasses, some clothing and a small basket of prized etched stone specimens. He spotted the painting on its easel in the corner closest to the bedchamber but his arms were full. Henkle ran from the room again.

The third time Henkle entered, flames were licking through the door. Fire burned overhead; the smoke was thick and black. He scrambled across the floor to the painting. Lifting it, he rose and ran for the door. Fiery debris fell as the ceiling collapsed behind him. Gasping for air, Henkle threw himself out the door. He placed the portrait of Mistress Showcroft beside the other articles and, clutching his chest, fell to the ground, panting. The office was filled with flames, but Teacher Bushnell's most important possessions, and Riverview's papers, were safe.

CHAPTER THIRTY-SEVEN
WILLOWBANK
Late August 1757

TO keep her mind active during her convalescence, Joanna wrote in her diary, making entries in the privacy of her sitting room. That is where she was on a warm day in August, reflecting and writing while she watched for the return of her father and David, who had raced across the hills on their hunters several hours before.

As she leafed through the pages, reading a passage here, a sentence there, the thoughts of the first few days after returning from America came to mind. Despite her father's initial show of scepticism about David, he was afforded a room on the guest floor and a place at the table, as befit the son of any duke, baron or king. Within a matter of days, after Charles found him to be an articulate scholar, an excellent horseman, and a devotee the number twelve, he warmed to the young man. They became constant companions, which did turn some heads and cause gossip in the village. But no matter, Charles Turnbull set precedent, never followed it. Business associates who accepted invitations to Willowbank were curious to meet the exotic young African, thinking him the newest Job ben Solomon and compatriot of Prince William Ansah Sessarakoo of Annamaboe, whose book, *The Royal African*, was all the rage.

From her comfortable chair, Joanna could watch Luke taking riding lessons in the paddock. "*It is a pity,*" she wrote in her diary, "*that Father does not bother more with Luke. With Talbot's blood running through his veins, I fear my father may never fully accept his grandson. By all measure, I believe Luke is meant to return to Virginia, to make his mark in America.*"

Christine's birth date, July 8, 1757, had been duly recorded. The wee babe slept in a lace-and-satin-swathed cradle next to Joanna's bed, under the watchful eye of a nursemaid who knocked timidly each time she entered to check on both. With delight, Joanna made a notation by the date that the child had a thick shock of red hair, and a turned-up nose, features that did resemble those of her father.

The menfolk must have returned by the deer run, because Charles' heavy knock on the door roused Joanna from her reflective mood.

"Awake?" Not waiting for an answer, Charles entered, followed by a maid carrying a tea tray. Accustomed to enjoying afternoon tea with everyone gathered round her, Joanna asked after David and Luke.

"My dear, I must see you privately." Charles peeked into the cradle. "She is a beautiful baby, Joanna. But she has not my looks and the birth date is wrong. Had you waited ten minutes, she would have been birthed on the ninth, making her a perfect thirty-six, a much more auspicious figure. And why the name Christine?"

"Christine is her own wee thing," Joanna said, quite exasperated by his constant prodding for facts. "I daresay she will make her way without any of your nonsensical numbering."

"Nay, daughter, such a harsh riposte." Charles made himself comfortable in a chair opposite Joanna and pulled a thick letter from his coat pocket. "We caught up with the post-chaise along the way. Among other papers, he was carrying this."

"I have been in a high anxiety, having received no word." Joanna examined the envelope. It bore Riverview's seal and the handwriting looked like Timothy's. She turned it round and round in her hands. "Eight months. Such a long time to hear naught. Why so long to write?"

"Pray do not keep yourself in suspense."

Joanna broke the seal and unfolded several closely written pages. She scanned them, then began to read aloud ...

Riverview Plantation

21 July 1757

Dear Mrs. Showcroft:

My dear Lady, you have, no doubt, given up hope of hearing from me. Advocate Shand and I were of the same opinion - that we must not write until we knew there was a goodly chance you were delivered of your Child. We had no wish to cause you distress before your Travail. You were accurate when you said people do not reveal all of themselves, as I did not know you were in a Delicate Condition when you made your departure.

We are managing at Riverview. But, let me start at the beginning. I have used the word Distress and I must explain. A dreadful Melancholia fell over the plantation **after you left,** *heightened by the appearance of your Husband a few days after your departure. He was drunk and foul, which resulted in a fight that had disastrous Consequences for your Home and for me. A candle was knocked over during an altercation and set a fire that burned the mansion to the ground. Through the heroic efforts of Jento and Henkle, my life and the plantation's Records were saved, along with sundry household effects - glass, silverware, some furniture and bedding - that are now stored in the carriage house.*

After my convalescence, I took up residence in the Weavery which Sukie made habitable, and Riverview carries on the best it can under the circumstances.

Everything is in confusion concerning MacKinnon. I was not in any condition to see, so do not know if Talbot left the building. His Body was not found in the burned shell. But he has not been seen since the fire.

I am telling you, dear Mrs. Showcroft, that you may be a widow. Until your husband presents himself or is recognized somewhere, we must assume the worst; yet we know the man has devious ways. I saw his Horse at the front before the fire, and it was not on the grounds afterwards. Advocate Shand claims he is still alive and has made it his Campaign to prove it.

Your people fare well. Jento reads now. He sat by my bedside day and night until I healed. He pores over the drawings you made for David. I sense that, like David, he is very clever.

As for Captain Makem, no word has been heard from, or Sign seen of him. Has the Gentleman arrived in England?

With no house to keep, Sukie has sent some of the house slaves to Juba in the Fields. Kudie spins to replace your linens and wool. Her Looms are now in the loft of the carriage house. She does ask about David.

On receipt of this letter, Jackson Shand and I hope you are safely delivered of a healthy Baby. You must let us know your good Fortune - boy or girl? Would Mr. Turnbull be so kind as to send word on whether we should rebuild - or not? There are good craftsmen about. You must have a home in America to return to.

Forgive my handwriting. I do poorly with one eye; yet, with Practice I should improve and be able to Paint again. I look for a letter at your earliest convenience.

Your servant

Timothy Bushnell

Postscript: Henkle risked his life to save the Painting of you in your beautiful Blue Gown. The painting of your mother was consumed by the fire, an unfortunate circumstance because, although I did not read it, I assume the finely written message on the pages of the Bible was important to you.

Joanna, hands trembling, tucked the letter in her diary. "Could it be so?" she said. "My Virginia home is no more. Talbot may be dead. Mr. Bushnell is partially blinded. What plague has befallen Riverview?"

Charles looked with speechless consternation at his daughter.

"Why does Mr. Bushnell deem the message on the pages of the Bible important to me?" Joanna asked.

"Did you not pay attention to the portrait?" Charles said.

"I had it hung immediately upon its arrival. Mr. Bushnell did once mention the detail around the hands and Bible but, truth be told, I did not look closely."

"Dear child," Charles said. "The message is merely one of your mother's favourite ... Biblical passages. I sent this particular picture with Captain Makem because ... you did have great love for your mother and were so far away ... from her burial crypt which you visited frequently. I did wish to ... cheer you with her likeness on canvas."

"I am agog with curiosity. Where is the Bible? If it was her favourite passage, the book will open to that page. I may take some comfort from its content."

"That will not be possible, Joanna. The Bible was buried with your mother." To change the subject, Charles said "I should think the information that Talbot is dead would prime your pistol, my dear."

"Pay particular attention to what I say, Father. Talbot is not dead."

"Joanna, show sense, now. His death does mean that the marriage –"

Joanna interrupted, "The confound agreement! You hated the Showcroft family so much that the contract was your revenge."

"Talbot Showcroft did hate the Turnbull family to the same extent. The document was drawn up to pit your business sense against his greed."

"I was a pawn in a game you played, Father, so schooled by your brand of hatred that I stupidly played to your plan. I was used mightily by Talbot – and, I daresay, by you."

Charles rose and came to stand by Joanna's chair. Were his plans coming un-done – all he had worked toward – all that he had done to ensure his daughter would inherit his fortunes and Showcroft's, as well?

"Joanna. Daughter, listen to me!" He reached a hand toward her. "Give some respect –"

"As God is my judge, you do ask *me* for respect?" Joanna looked away from her father's hand.

"Joanna, by my word, by my very actions, I felt that I was doing the right thing for you and what children would be born of your marriage. Had the marriage been of a good repute, by the gods, we would have commanded a mercantile empire! Showcroft did not see the possibilities, because he could not love; he could only claw and grasp. What matters it now? He is dead. You have won! All will be well."

"I tell you the man is alive! Mr. Bushnell is no fighter. Talbot thrashed him to within an inch of his life and left him for dead. To use your words, Father, my husband is playing the game very well indeed. I hazard that he is in hiding for his own reasons – among them, Rory and Andre MacKinnon."

"Who might these MacKinnons be?"

"'Tis of no consequence." Joanna said. "I ask a question, Father. Have you heard news of Captain Anthony Makem?"

"There was talk that he made a winter crossing and was in London in the early year conducting business with several merchants connected to ... Barbados trade. I believe I received the news from ... a member of my London club who corresponds occasionally with me," Charles said. "But why do you not believe that Talbot is dead?"

"My revered Husband is devious enough to be very much alive. Anyone who thinks otherwise does not know Talbot's true nature and intentions. *When* Talbot appears again, you must take steps to annul my marriage."

"Joanna, my dear –"

"Oh botheration! Do not try your warped reasoning on me. If you do, I shall make arrangements to leave for Virginia at once."

"Do not be twilly with me, daughter." Charles sat down again, looking older than his sixty years. "Greed does drive the heart and mind to great measure. If I have wronged you, please to believe I was doing it for your sake. Can you believe that I am truly sorry?"

"Would I could believe you, Father! But I can see well that you still desire Talbot's fortune. Money is your personal avarice. Oh, I am fortune's fool! I have been stunningly stupid, and far too headstrong in what I did."

"Nay, you were only being my Joanna. Do accept my sincerest apology, from my heart."

"I should dearly like to believe you are sorry. Let that suffice."

"I am a man of overbearing opinions, and I will state one now. You should remain in England, at Willowbank – not in Virginia at Riverview."

"Ay, there's the rub, Father. My love for Willowbank has diminished. Virginia has won my heart. The place has such a beauty, newness, challenge ... My concern now is for Mr. Bushnell. He resides in uncomfortable circumstances and does appear to have lost the sight in one eye. The dear man took the brunt of Talbot's anger against both you and me."

"Aye, the lad certainly showed a bit of ginger!" Charles said.

"You must see that the saga in the Colonies is not over. You may still lose. I must return to America."

"Do not say that, daughter."

"I must, Father."

"I shall authorize Mr. Bushnell and Mr. Shand to begin to rebuild immediately. The letter shall go on the morrow on the Liverpool packet, direct to Norfolk. You do credit that I am happy to have you home, Joanna?"

"That I do believe!"

"I will be honest with you, beginning today," Charles said. "Promise me to stay at Willowbank over-winter, that I may enjoy the company of David – and of Luke and Christine."

"If nothing intervenes, that I might promise," Joanna said. A loud knock at the door heralded the arrival of Luke and David.

Joanna would show the letter to David later. She really had no hold over the handsome young man, now that he was free. Yet by his choice, he stayed close to Willowbank, fascinated by her father, his penchant for the number twelve and the trappings of a proper gentleman.

CHAPTER THIRTY-EIGHT
ABOARD THE *BLACK WING*
Summer 1757

MIDMORNING. Caliganto stood beside Makem studying the western sky, a rolling, boiling cauldron of grey-black cloud. The eastern sky, on the other hand was eggshell blue, deepening to purple on the horizon. The wind was up – too strong, too quick – after three days of calm.

"Beggar me, I've seen nothing like this in my days of sailing," Makem said. "'Tis the devil's kettle. If we had half this wind a day ago, we'd be in safe harbour now." He studied the charts, then looked once more at the sky. "Rather than lay-a-try, we'll run for Dominica. 'Tis full sail and tricky but we'll run afore the wind as long as we can. She's a sturdy ship. She'll take a lot afore we have to trim back." He turned to shout, "Ye scurvy sea rats! To the lines!"

By late afternoon the seas were running at twenty feet, but the *Black Wing*, true to her master's commands, ran close-hauled, swift with the wind, pushing through the relentless sea, north and west, toward land. Caliganto pulled himself along a storm line to Makem, who'd been five hours at the wheel, trying to bring the ship to safe anchor before the centre of the storm struck.

"Runnin' true. Land isn't far off the horizon now. It will be lee-shore or grind reef," Makem said taking a bottle of rum and loaf of black bread from Caliganto. "If she lasts that long. Give a hand with the wheel. She's buckin'!"

The *Black Wing* heeled to starboard, wind ripping through the rigging then back-winded, quickly heeled to port. Makem shouted, "Hell and damnation! A maelstrom!"

"Cut off the sails! All of 'em!" Caliganto bellowed orders to crew struggling on the ratlines.

Doctor Petrie pulled himself along the storm line, lost his footing when the *Black Wing* lee-lurched as a massive wave struck the ship. Ducking flying ropes and tackle blocks, he shouted to Makem, "There's naught north, south, east or west to these buggers. We are in the squall from hell!"

The *Black Wing*'s bow plunged into a massive wave, sending a wall of water over the deck and coaming, down into the hold. She bucked, shuddered and unexpectedly swung forty-five degrees and keeled, showing rudder.

"Shallow reef-sea. Too much sail! She's lost!" Makem shouted. "Out o' the ratlines! Open the hatches, Petrie. Caliganto, give him the keys to the coffles."

"You're going to set them free?" Petrie shouted.

"It's every man for himself now, including the slaves. I'll be damned if I'll leave 'em to die in chains."

"That matters that? They can't swim," Petrie said.

"They'll stand a better chance if they're not coffled. You're capable of extraordinary feats when death stares you down. We'll not come out this with a ship under us. I'll beach the *Black Wing* – or run her close as I can."

"They're already loose," Caliganto said. "They never asked to be on middle passage; didn't ask to drown like rats."

Makem smiled grimly at his companion. They seemed to read each other's minds at times. Why the hell had he let Manesty persuade him to make one last slave run?

"Ship will be overrun," Petrie said.

"Hell, the *Black Wing* won't be around much longer to *be* overrun. She can't take much more o' this pounding. Do what I say! "Get those hatches off and free 'em."

Petrie struggled down the deck, now dangerously heeled to port, shouting on the way. In the rigging, the wind caught a shinny-man, whipped him round and tossed him like a rag onto the deck near Petrie.

"Leave him!" Makem shouted. "Out of the rigging, men! Save yourselves!" Half his words were lost to the wind. He beckoned with his whole arm, calling the men down from the yards.

"Rogue wave on the bow!" shouted one of the shinnies handing down the line.

The bow of the *Black Wing* disappeared in a wall of water that washed down the deck like a river in full flood.

Makem and Caliganto wound their arms around the wheel. "Can you bring her into the wind!"

Black Wing's rudder groaned and shuddered but responded.

"Wind's dying," Makem said. "The vortex! Look-a-there!" Water and sky joined in a grey boiling ugly mass. Then, suddenly, blue sky and calm sea, the eye of the storm! "Hell to heaven without leavin' earth!"

During the short calm, Caliganto dragged a hatch cover and coils of rope toward Makem. "Hell might win this round," he said, tying a rope around Makem's waist and threading the loose end through the hatch cover. He did the same for himself then stood ready to help fight the wheel again when the wind back-sided. "Captain goes down with his ship, so does his mate. What's chances we'll get out of this alive?"

"Damned little. Here we go!" Makem felt a tremor on the wheel as the wind once again struck his ship. She dived into the storm, pitched and yawed, then valiantly crested a wave. As she topped the crest, Makem shouted. "Land! Quarter league off! We're catchin' the reef wave!"

"Dominica?"

"Nay – naught but a key, but 'tis land just the same! Haul hard!"

The *Black Wing* nosed into a deep trough then drove on the next mountain of water. Makem and Caliganto, hoping for one last response, hauled the wheel to port. The rudder moved reluctantly. The ship yawed to port, then shuddered as her bottom scraped over coral reef, and she ground to a halt.

Petrie appeared on deck, grabbed the line and slithered his way toward Makem. Behind him, Africans streamed from the hold. Caliganto shouted, gesturing they should jump. The stream of humanity became a river, tumbling and falling down the deck, shrieking with fright. The first were pushed overboard by the last.

"Poor devils. We're close in to land. Some might make it," Makem muttered.

"Coral reef will get them first," Caliganto said. "By the land they lived and by the sea they die, just like us, boss-man."

Makem put his arm around his companion's shoulder. "My prophetic friend, I'll be damned if I'll die when I've so much to live for. And if it be in my power, you won't either."

"You might not have much say over your life – or mine – this time," Caliganto said. "Hades might look good after this."

Petrie worked his way to the wheel. "Keel's grinding coral. 'Tis her end."

The ship lifted on a swell, ground again across coral then lurched sharply to port. Caliganto grabbed for Petrie as he tumbled, and snagged his sleeve, letting go of the wheel. The rope tightened around his waist and knocked the breath from him. On the next surge, the rope held him from being swept overboard, but Petrie was torn from his grasp. The cover, Makem tethered by one rope, Caliganto by another, floated free of the deck dragging the men with it.

The ship rose one last time and then with a sickening crack landed atop the reef, breaking her back. There she stuck and gasped her last as the waves washed over the wreck, giving the *Black Wing* a last ablution.

The hatch cover rode the crest of the boiling, angry sea, pulling Makem and Caliganto with it. Their bodies rolled, tumbled and scraped across sharp coral. As Makem lapsed into unconsciousness, he saw Joanna, beautiful Joanna, his Vision-in-Blue, with a baby in her arms.

CHAPTER THIRTY-NINE
SOUTH CAROLINA,
Autumn 1757

Planters Hall

FLANAGAN rode in by the coastal track, keeping his eyes to the underbrush. There was nothing he enjoyed more after a hot day's work than the sport of running down an errant slave. Closer to the compound he noticed the tracks of at least four horses in the soft sandy soil and spurred his mount. Unwanted company? He followed the prints until they melded with the tracks of plantation wagons.

Flanagan stopped in the shelter of a stand of scrub pine to look over Planters Hall. The large, sprawling one-storey house, surrounded with porches, appeared quiet. There were no horses tied out front. He cautiously circled the area under the cover of the brush, but saw no increased activity around the dependencies.

Returning to the front again, he approached the house by the main carriage way, one hand on his pistol. The other had the horse reined tight and ready to wheel.

A slave-boy ran from under the front porch and stood at attention.

"Possum. Seen anyone round here?" Flanagan dismounted and threw the reins to the little fellow.

"No, Massa."

Flanagan entered the house, still wary and on guard to any unusual movement. He walked the length of the centre hall, checking bedrooms to the left and common room, office and dining room to the right.

A slave met him at entry to the keeping room. "De meal's a-comin', Massa."

Flanagan made his way through the dining room and out French doors to an open porch. Seated at a table set for one, he poured a generous drink.

"Company come," Cook said, putting a roast chicken on the table, unusual because she hated Flannagan and avoided serving him. "Not be a-stayin' Offered a room to de lady to rest awhile. She said dey not stop as dey be a-ridin' ober de mountains."

Flanagan stopped eating. "Did she say where, over-mountain?"

"Yaus, Massa. Said they was a-ridin' over de Trace Cut."

"How many?"

"Fo' – a lady nice-dressed – a chile – older feller – a slave-man."

Flanagan took a long drink. "The woman. How old?"

"Young, Massa. Pretty lady."

"Did she say where she came from?"

"Far 'way. I give dem meal. She say Big Massa would want it so. She know'd Big Massa well-nough."

Flanagan drummed his fingers on the table. "The boy's name," he demanded.

"Ah dunno."

"The others?"

"Slave-man be a-speakin' little. De oder man say nothin' but to de woman."

Flanagan, deep in thought, continued his nervous drumming. "Did she say why she came?"

"Dey come to be a-talkin' wif Big Massa. She say that she libed wid him, once, longtime 'go. Said dat she must talk wif Big Massa."

Flanagan helped himself to a glass of whiskey. "Did she say anythin' about a ship?"

"She say she come from Charles Town. The lady spoke peculiar."

"Did she use the word husband?"

"No, Massa."

Flanagan pushed his plate aside and left the table, glass in hand. "When did they leave?"

"Afer de meal. She say I should be a-tellin' Big Massa she would be a-seein' him at de Trace." Cook handed a paper to Flanagan. "Said 'gib dis to de Big Massa.'"

"I am gone, then. Pack food for two days. What did the woman look like?"

"Brown hair ... thin ... high colour in de cheeks ... voice of de lady but hands dat be used to work."

An all-night ride brought Flanagan to the door of a cottage up the coast. The building was isolated by a swamp on three sides and a thick bush of scrub pine on the fourth. Flanagan shouted a greeting as he entered and stomped through the cottage. He found Talbot eating oatmeal gruel at a table in the keeping room.

"You'll not have so much of an appetite after you hear me out," he said, sitting down. He tried not to stare at the ugly scar across Talbot's lower jaw and cheek, and the lack of a right ear.

"You appear to have ridden with the Devil himself, Flanagan."

"Maybe, I have."

"Coffee?" At Talbot's sign, a comely young African woman appeared from the back hall. "Strong coffee for Flanagan. He's a little piqued."

Flanagan threw the letter on the table. "Read this," he said, "then listen carefully to what I'm gonna say."

Talbot read, his brow furrowed in thought. "How came you by this?"

"From cook, who got it from your wife."

"Impossible!"

Flanagan shook his head. "Your wife, Luke, that African of hers, and Bushnell came to the plantation yesterday. They rode in afore the noon meal and left mid-afternoon."

"Where were they headed?"

"O'er the Trace Cut."

"To MacKinnon's!"

"Appears so."

"The devil! She came back to America. Did she have a baby with her?"

"Cook didn't mention a baby."

"Maybe it was stillborn. Maybe she miscarried. That be the case, the agreement stands. Maybe that's why she is headed for MacKinnons."

"Cook says she came a long way – was in Charles Town."

"From England? From Virginia? Maybe she left the baby with Shands and came after me. What did cook tell her about me?"

"Cook hasn't laid eyes on you in months."

"There's no doubt it was my wife?"

"Who else? There ain't much high-class company visits the plantation nowadays."

Talbot read the note again. It wasn't dated, but the message did congratulate him on the birth of his son.

"This is a copy of a note written by Mairi MacKinnon. It was sent to me where I used to collect my mail in London. It was diverted and delivered to Willowbank. My wife is clever enough to surmise that I did not perish in the fire. She is devious enough to make a copy. You weren't followed, were you?"

"I am not that much a fool," Flanagan said. "Doubled back a couple of times. Checked in the village before I left. The party of four went through before dark. They're miles west of us and headin' over-mountain."

"So, I shall assume that my wife is on her way to the Trace." Talbot reached for his pipe, tamped it well, then lit it. "The woman will expect me to meet her there. If she is traveling with Bushnell, she knows I did not get in touch with MacKinnon. She would also know that Bushnell has accused me of attempting to murder him in Virginia. My wife left this note to bait me."

"What're you goin' to do now?"

Talbot blew smoke rings toward the ceiling. "I've been living in isolation since the fire and confounded disfiguration. 'Tis sick I am of the whole charade. We know the sons rode north, reckoning I might hide in New York or Baltimore. They did leave word in Charles Town that they were looking for me. I'll take the risk and visit Rory MacKinnon. The Trace would be the last place they would think to see me."

Flanagan stopped eating. "You're crazy enough to ride into their territory?"

Looking down the dingy hall of the cottage that had been his hiding place for months, Talbot laughed. "Good God, man! Anything is better than this hell-hole. Why not tempt fate? My life is not at risk as long as my wife is at MacKinnon's. I cannot live in a swamp like an alligator forever."

"I'll ride with you. Bushnell would love to spy you in his gunsight again."

Talbot laughed again. "I should love to get him in mine, for what he did to me. 'Tis better you do not accompany me. Someone might recognize you from the last time you went that way. I will pansy before the wife, swear that I am sorry, beg her forgiveness. I will become a chastened man."

Flanagan roared and slapped his knee. "You lie as good as you drink, Showcroft!"

"I shall say that I have taken much time to think. I'll admit that I am not without faults. Rest assured, Flanagan, I do not intend to come out of this a poor man."

Flanagan pushed himself away from the table. "You'd better let me ride with you."

"I must take up the reins again, soon," Talbot said. "Business matters in Charles Town and the West Indies have been neglected. I'll see to them after I have made a startling appearance once again before my dear wife."

Flanagan took a pipe from the mantel as he watched Talbot's latest woman clear the table. "You sure can pick 'em, Showcroft."

"Years of experience," Talbot said. "And she is not particular about my appearance. I do wonder if my wife knows the fate of the *Black Wing*? Any sign of Makem?"

"Nothin'," Flanagan said. "The wreck was recognized by its figurehead. Lots of bodies on the beach, but all black, so I hear."

Talbot pulled pensively on his pipe. "'Tis a pity about Makem. Good man."

"Sharks fed good," Flanagan said. "Can't say I liked him myself. Old sailors say they can't remember a storm like it. Came outa nowhere and blew like hell for a day, then left a calm that lasted a month. Made land south of Charles Town. Tore through a couple of plantations."

"Would have helped if the ship had foundered off an inhabited island," Talbot said. "It would be hell starving to death on a streak of sand."

He stood in the doorway, looking over the desolate swamp. Lightning bugs flew bright patterns above the tall grass. Frogs chirped their night song. Bats swooped low to feed on the incessant swarm of insects. After his months of self-imposed isolation, the scene had begun to wear on his nerves. "Bring my grey mare," he said. "She's the only one I trust to ride over-mountain."

"She is a bit jumpy," said Flanagan.

"I have my spies, Flanagan. You've been riding her pretty hard up the beach, using your crop, too. That's why she's skittish."

"Just havin' a bit o' fun," grumbled Flanagan.

"Well, have it at the expense of my slaves, not good horseflesh." He leaned against the doorframe deep in thought.

"What're ya thinkin'?"

"What a piece of work life is. It does have its amusing times, does it not?" Talbot turned to Flanagan. "Come back with the horse and any provisions you think I will need. And Flanagan, there is money for you to keep your mouth shut about this."

"It's been shut like a trap so far," Flanagan said. "Money talks to me an' I don't talk to anyone."

"Then see that no one else baits the trap, Flanagan."

CHAPTER FORTY
THE TRACE CUT

TALBOT dismounted and entered a dark, dirty tavern on the eastern side of the Trace Cut. Tavern and keeper were new since he had last traveled the area.

"An ale," he said.

"You travelin' through?" The Innkeeper brought a wooden cup of foaming amber liquid and tried not to stare at the disfigured face. The fella's rough-dressed, he thought, travelling fast and light.

"Yes. On my way to the MacKinnon Trace."

"You're headin' in the right direction," the fellow said. "But ride careful. Tinker Forbes in the corner says there's heavy fog up top." The innkeeper pointed to a table behind Talbot.

When Talbot turned to look, a tall man was leaving by the back door. "Have you a room for over-night? Damn it man, don't stare. I was shot by a madman."

Innkeeper averted his eyes. "There's a bed with no other body in it."

"Do you recall a party of four, recently from England, who came through here last week?"

"Nope," said the innkeeper. "But if they wuz goin' over- mountain, they'd stay this side the last couple a days, heavy as the fog's been. Mountain people would go on over."

Talbot finished his ale and went for his saddlebags. He knew the mountains only too well. They brooded around him, their brilliant autumn foliage folding gently toward the western ridges until a blanket of grey dense cloud covered the crest of the range. Streamers of fog trailed from cool deep ravines. The sun cast fingers of light over everything, causing the mist to shimmer like liquid gold. There was no sense continuing the journey today. Perhaps the wind would rise in the night and dispel the fog.

Talbot carried his bags inside but was in no rush to see the bed. He had chosen his lodgings carefully, knowing Joanna would not stop at cheap, dirty taverns. He sat near the fire eating a meagre meal of corn pudding and pork stew, watching for someone from over- mountain who might know MacKinnon, and tell him who was on the Trace besides Rory.

When no one else entered the tavern, Talbot asked the innkeeper, "Know the MacKinnons?"

"Heard of them," was the reply. "Lot of respect in the valley for 'em. Big family. Boy married into a big family, too. Heard the menfolk rode out a while back, goin' north."

Talbot smiled. Hearing the rumour again carried some reassurance. Flanagan had encountered Roderick and Alex looking for him in Charles Town in June.

Talbot slept poorly. Mairi's face kept appearing in his dreams. The next morning, haggard from lack of sleep, he hung around the tavern until ten o'clock, watching the peaks.

"You know the mountains, Sir," the innkeeper said, watching Talbot saddle the grey. "You've been readin' them all morning. Fog's lifted enough to try the crossing', has it?"

Talbot rode west up a dirt track, just wide enough for an ox cart. Mature trees that lined both sides created a colourful canopy over the trail. The higher it wound up-mountain, the more prominent the rock face became on Talbot's right. Through the trees, he could look south and east. In places, the track hugged the mountainside; sheer cliffs fell away to the left.

The further Talbot traveled from his swampy hide-away, the more uneasy he became about meeting Joanna. By the time he reached the inn below the cut, he had reconciled his fears by thinking that he was past the point of turning back. A touch of the crop threw his horse, usually sure-footed and confident, into a nervous sidestep. "Damn Flanagan!"

Around two o'clock Talbot dismounted in a small glade beside a cold spring to feel the remains of a campfire. Still warm. Someone camped overnight, he thought.

He blew on the coals, added dry grasses and bits of dead branch until he had a flame. For the past hour he had heard the creaking of cart wheels ahead of him, coming down-mountain. There was a pot ready when the ox cart loaded with corn came into sight. Talbot hailed the driver and invited him for tea and dry biscuits.

"What's it like up-top?" he asked the portly wagoner who introduced himself as Alex Grant.

"'Tis fine now," Grant said. "But I dinna' guarantee it fer later. Where you headed?"

"MacKinnon Trace," Talbot said.

"If I be you, I'd ride o'er the cut an' take the valley road in. 'Tis longer but nae so foggy."

"I don't recall there being a valley road," Talbot said.

"Just a trail. But you can tak' the horse on it."

Both heads went up at the sound of a horse coming up-trail. The wagoner waved as the rider went by. The fellow tipped his hat and rode on. Talbot thought he recognized the stranger as the man in the tavern.

"Know the fellow?" Talbot asked.

"Stranger ta me," Grant said. "I'd best be on my way. Wifie's expectin' me back tomorra." He climbed up into his cart. "Dinna' lose your senses tae the mountain spirits," he said. "They can turn you roun' in a minute. Thanks for sharin' your pot."

Talbot gathered his belongings, kicked dirt on the fire and mounted. He followed Grant's cart tracks up the mountain, watching for the stranger. His horse was odd-shod and easy to track. Just below the Trace Cut, Talbot dismounted, tied his horse to a tree and followed a path through the woods for several hundred feet. He stepped out onto a ledge of rock overlooking valleys and ridges, undulating to east and south, vivid in their autumn plumage. The range's highest peaks wore clouds like white blankets.

From Talbot's vantage point, every valley seemed to have its share of miniature buildings and animals. The sounds of civilization carried upwards on the breeze. Talbot heard dogs bark, children laugh, a woman singing; yet all were a quarter mile or more away and below him. He looked with concern at the brooding humpbacked mountain he had to traverse. Already mist was rising from the deeper hollows, rills and creeping over higher ridges. Mounting, he rode the half mile up the cut to the turn-off.

Take the valley road, he recalled Grant's advice, but he felt compelled ... no drawn, to ride the ridge that led to MacKinnon's Trace. Talbot did take time to follow the stranger's track a little further than the trail point to make sure he had ridden off. Then he doubled back and turned the horse south, down the high mountain track he had last ridden six years before.

The fog was thin at first as it tumbled over-ridge. Talbot noticed nothing until all ahead of him swirled in grey mist. He looked for familiar landmarks. Damn! he thought. This is the worst part to manoeuver through in a fog. No chance it will burn off now – too late in the day.

The fog enveloped Talbot in a damp, blind haze. He dismounted and led the horse, trying to feel the trail through the soles of his boots, keeping to the inner track. A rustling, rattling noise followed him. It was nothing Talbot recognized, not leather against horse, not wheel against gravel – just a soft relentless rustling like that of a rattle snake, about to strike. Whatever it was, it grated on his nerves.

Talbot checked his saddle and load. The sound seemed to keep pace with him. Once when he thought he heard the scraping of a horse's shoe against stone, he stopped and listened intently. Was it coming behind him? Or in front? As he could not risk riding, he led the horse and walked, the fog blanketing both. He could neither see the sides of the trail nor four feet ahead.

The sound of water not far off brought him to a halt. Yes, he remembered a waterfall that tumbled off the cliff above the trail, not far from the narrow passage at the Trace overlook. Shivering, he remembered the overlook ... Mairi ... the frightened look on her face. It was the same look that had haunted him last night. Now, the rustling was closer, surrounding him, making it impossible to think.

"Stop!" Talbot shouted. "Whoever you are, come forward." He waited for a horseman to appear. No one came out of the fog.

As the trail slanted steeply, Talbot concentrated on where to place his feet but couldn't feel the familiar track. I am near the overlook, he thought as he remembered the lay of the land. Talbot peered through the fog, then extended his hand. He couldn't see past his palm. Wait! An apparition appeared through his open fingers. A woman dressed in grey stood before him ... now in sight ... now lost in the fog.

"Mairi," he whispered.

The figure appeared again. "I have come for you," she said. "Stay where you are."

"Mairi," Talbot said again.

The horse, sensing a presence, pranced sideways. Talbot worked to control the animal, his eyes on the apparition that was walking slowly toward him.

"I came for you," she said again. "Stay where you are. Take my hand."

"No!" Talbot shouted. "Go away!"

Nostrils flaring, the grey reared and pulled Talbot off balance. The reins ripped from his fingers as he fell to the ground. A woman's skirts swished around his outstretched hands. Talbot rolled to the right, away from the hooves – from the skirt – from the rustling.

"Go away! Go away!"

"Your hand, Sir," the woman said as she reached for Talbot.

Talbot felt cold fingers touch his. In fear, he pulled himself into a ball and rolled away from the apparition. He felt himself go over the edge.

"No! Mairi, no!" he shouted as he fell to the rocks below.

CHAPTER FORTY-ONE
MacKINNON's TRACE

CONSCIOUS moments came with waves of pain in his head. Someone was always at his side ... a man ... a woman. When he cried out, a bitter liquid dribbled onto his lips, and then he slipped into blessed, painless darkness again. He opened his eyes when a cool wet cloth was applied to his forehead.

"Mr. Showcroft, do not try to speak," a woman spoke close to him.

"Mairi," he whispered hoarsely.

"I am Katie Sherrie."

Talbot tried to focus on the woman's face but couldn't. "Joanna ... is ... here?"

"Your wife is not here," Katie said, gently wiping Talbot's face.

"Joanna ... is ... coming?"

A man's voice mingled with the woman's. "He be awake?"

"Just opened his eyes. He doesn't know ..."

"MacKinnon?" asked Talbot.

A rough hand touched Talbot's fevered cheek. "Aye, 'tis MacKinnon. I'll sit wi' ye a wee."

Talbot felt a curious sense of floating. His head seemed disconnected from his body. He told his hands to move. They did not obey, but lay inert and unresponsive. He lapsed into a feverish state, the pain in his head carrying him by turns into a stupor, into glaring clarity, then drifting somewhere between the two. Once he had a sense that someone was holding his head and talking quietly to him.

When he opened his eyes again, the wet cloth was gone from his forehead and a woman sat by his side, her sad eyes on him. When he tried to raise a hand, nothing responded to his commands.

"You are ... Katie," he managed to say.

"Mr. Showcroft, the fog was so thick. You should have held still and taken my hand."

"The rustling," Talbot said, focusing on his last moments on the trail.

"Winds in the valley, blowing round the dry leaves. The sound echoes up the mountain. Allan heard you were at the tavern and waited at the valley trail to ride in with you."

"And I chose the ridge trail."

"'Tis woman's wisdom that I knew you would come the upper trail. Wisdom, and knowing that trail was the only one you knew. The fog was thick. I walked up to wait for you at the overlook. I heard your horse long before I saw you. And perilously close to the edge you were! I walked toward you and put my hand out to guide you away from it."

"How did you know I should come?"

"Why, the copy of the letter. Joanna sent it from England. I felt for her plight and decided to deliver it. You, Sir, knew what you must do – but you did it not."

"Then you were at Planters Hall, not my wife." Talbot sighed heavily then moaned as pain shot up the back of his head.

Rory brought a small brown bottle and a thin sliver of wood. As the pain intensified, he dipped the stick into the bottle and, holding Talbot's jaw, dropped the nectar into his mouth. Talbot resisted, but the darkness engulfed him.

Rory took Katie's place for the bedside vigil, his patient old eyes watching Talbot for signs of lucidity. He gently washed the face, but left the blanket that covered Talbot's body from chin to toe.

"Why do my arms not move?" Talbot asked in a one of his better moments. "Why can I not feel my legs?"

Rory hesitated, then answered, his voice low. "When you went tae the rocks ye fell on yer back. Ye canna' feel pain but in yer heid."

"I won't walk again."

"'Tis worse than that, I'm a'feared." Rory bent his head.

"Spare me the gruesome news," Talbot said. "I'm dying."

"Aye," said the old man, no regret in his voice. "This waul be on MacKinnon hands an in oor herts fer generations. We brought ye o'er- mountain. 'Tis us that killed ye."

Talbot was too weak to ask if Rory meant the statement in anger or jubilation. The rattling in his chest grew louder. Like the rustling leaves on the mountainside, he couldn't escape it.

Once Barika sat with him, clear brown eyes never leaving Talbot's face. There was no fear in them – no hatred either. His hands were as gentle as Katie's when he wiped a fevered brow.

"Not much time left," Talbot said out loud once.

Barika agreed. "Make peace and you will be at peace."

These words Talbot kept in his mind. He waited until Katie was at his side again. "May I – see my son?"

Andre was brought to him. Did the boy look like Luke? Talbot tried to remember Luke's features but his memory forsook him. He began to cry, tears of frustration and finally tears of anger. They let him cry until he was at peace.

"Does he know that I am his father?" Talbot asked Katie.

"He does."

"Is he angry?"

"No. He does pity you."

The rattling filled Talbot's throat, reminding him there was little time left. "Tell Joanna she won. Tell her not to hate me."

"Hush," Katie said. "'Tis not a game. There is no one that wins or loses."

"Please ... Katie ... tell her to see to Andre."

"She will do what is right for him. Mr. Showcroft, I am sorry."

"Sorry? For what?"

"It was my fault you fell over the edge. I frightened your horse."

Talbot managed a smile. "Please, do not hold yourself responsible. It was Grant's mountain spirits caught up with me. It was Mairi's last words to me years ago. It was the ghosts of my mistakes. I would not choose to die this way, but 'tis better than being shot in the back – or drowned at sea."

On a clear, starlit night, Katie, Allan, Rory, Andre and Barika kept deathwatch.

Talbot, propped up with pillows to make his last moments easier, breathed laboriously. He knew that people sat by him, but his mind was years and miles away. He was living every moment of his violent, angry life. Peace and happiness had always eluded him. Greed ruled. Everything carried a price. Death's price was his life. It came silently, painlessly. "Lord," he whispered at the end. "Forgive me the deeds I have done. Joanna ... Mairi ..."

Talbot Showcroft was buried beside Mairi. Katie laid out the body. Allan and Barika made the rough pine coffin. Neighbours came for the short service, led by Rory, not because they knew Talbot Showcroft, but to show respect for the stranger who died in their midst. A simple wooden cross was erected to mark the spot.

Several days after the burial, Katie wrote to Joanna. With Allan by her side she put pen to paper ...

My dearest Joanna, friend ...

CHAPTER FORTY-TWO
WILLOWBANK
Late November, 1757

JOANNA spent many hours in the Pavilion looking west over the hills toward America and Virginia. Her easel was set up near a bank of windows by the hearth where, depending on her mood, she could paint, read or write. Here too, she had privacy to think without constant rattling from her father. His arguments that her best choice was to forget Virginia, stay in England, began to grate.

Katie's letter arrived a fortnight before, and made Joanna's heart soar like the birds she saw from the windows, skimming the waters of the River Wharfe. She had read the letter a dozen times, yet she still could not believe the news it brought. Her father gleefully repeated, "The glue has finally come undone; justice has been meted out."

Although Joanna did feel pity at the way Talbot died, she could find little affection in her heart to mourn him.

Joanna carried a second letter in a silk purse next to her heart, from Timothy Bushnell, telling of the wreck of the *Black Wing*, and the loss of everyone on board. For the sake of custom, she wore mourning dress. But the truth was, she wore it for Anthony Makem more than for her husband.

Joanna stood by one of the pavilion's windows to gaze out at the winter's snowy mantle on the river valley and hills beyond. The stark greys and whites were suddenly relieved by a moving figure. Her gaze became a stare of disbelief. The man who walked through the winter garden was –

"Anthony! Anthony! Ah, my dear Lord, 'tis you!"

Anthony Makem favoured one leg as he walked, using a cane. "My darling Joanna! Aye, come to me, sweet creature." As she ran to him, he threw his arms open to receive her.

Joanna threw her arms around his neck. "By the gods, you are alive!" she cried.

"Aye. Barely." He seized Joanna and kissed her long and tenderly.

"My poor, dear Anthony."

Anthony held her close, kissing her with each word: "Passage – has – been – difficult – my – pretty –"

"Mr. Bushnell wrote that you were lost at sea."

"He would have good reason to believe so. Pray, may I be seated?" Anthony held Joanna around the waist and limped to a bench. "'Tis me now, crom aboo. My leg was broken and did not set right – healed in a crooked and rather painful fashion. There." He lowered himself to the bench and sat, the crooked leg stretched before him, then drew Joanna down to the bench beside him and held her close. "Joanna, I cannot live without you. My thoughts on that island were of you. It was the need to see you again that kept me alive. But, never did I think to see you in England. I journeyed to Willowbank to speak with your father."

"My love, so much has happened since you sailed away." Joanna lay against Anthony's shoulder, holding his hand.

"Sweet lady, after my appeal to your father, I shall approach your husband."

"You've no need, Anthony." Joanna could not contain her smile. "I am a widow. We need not proclaim our affections to anyone but ourselves."

"Showcroft is dead?" Anthony held Joanna away from him to look at her.

"Indeed. He cannot come between us. Katie Sherrie has written, relating the details of his passing. Believe me, Father will not object now."

Anthony gathered her close. How good it was to feel the woman he loved in his arms once more! "Joanna, Do you think I can learn to be a tiller of the earth? By the Gods, I have little desire to return to the sea. Caliganto is dead."

"No! Ah, my dear! I am exceedingly sorry." Joanna moved from Anthony's shoulder.

"'Twas a tragedy. He was so badly hurt – I could not save his life. I did comfort him during his last hours. My great companion died as he lived, courageously."

"Dear, noble, loyal Caliganto."

"He was. To the end." Anthony buried his face in Joanna's fragrant hair. Moments passed before he spoke again. "He tied me and himself to a wooden hatch. We were tossed about and drawn over a coral reef then drifted toward the shore of an island close on Dominica. Even though he was in pain, with all his strength, Caliganto did push me toward land."

"So heroic!" Joanna said. "He loved you as a brother."

"And I did him, in the same way. We did make shore. He had a broken head and he bled excessively from a deep gash in his right thigh. I bound it tightly; did what I could, but there was too much bleeding and no way to stop it. I did bury him away from the beach."

"Poor brave man," Joanna said.

"But for the bodies of some crew and slaves that washed up on shore, with pieces of the *Black Wing*, I was alone on the island. I had far too much time to repent my ways, surrounded by rotting, stinking corpses. Damnation! It was ... Well. I did finally come to believe my fortunes do not lie with the slave trade. Perhaps I took John Newton's message to heart, but I do believe that it was you, Mrs. Showcroft, who had great weight with me – and Caliganto, who stayed always by my side hoping that I would change my ways."

"You do believe that you can quit the sea?"

"By my presence here with you, I truly believe that I can turn my back on the sea – and on the trade in slaves."

"But, who rescued you? How came you here?"

"The island was a layover for a privateer – off the main shipping route, with fresh water. I found signs that someone stayed there not long before. I did not know how long I might wait for rescue, but luck was with me. The same storm that sank the *Black Wing* brought a ship running under a Portuguese flag in for repairs. The island was their little hideaway."

"The sight of a ship must have been overwhelming," Joanna said.

"Aye, 'twas a blessing, sweet lady. The captain was a reasonable sort of fellow. He worked the waters of the Carribean. Been shipwrecked at least once himself. He took me aboard. No one that could call himself a doctor was at hand, so the captain and I did what we could with the leg. Five days out we crossed the path of the slaver *Barlborough*, under Captain Dodson Foster, on its way back to England, so we hailed her. I tell you, 'twas by no mean feat we rigged up a hand-over from ship to ship. So it was that I made my way to Foster's home port, at Lancaster."

"The luck o' the Irish was with you this time, my dear."

"That, a silver tongue in my head and the promise of a bag of coin."

"Mr. Bushnell wrote to say that shortly after the storm a ship sailing to Barbados found the wreck of the *Black Wing* on the reef, and knew her by her figurehead. The island was searched but your body ... Oh my dear – "

"Hush, sweet one, hush. They would not have found Caliganto's body. I dug his grave deep, using my hands and a scrap of wood from the *Black Wing*. The man meant too much to me to leave his body unattended. I tell you, it took the devil of a long time to dig the grave. And the pain – ! Caliganto would have the last laugh, I had just dug the hole when the ship hove over the horizon. Sailors helped me bury him and buried some o' the others too – Petrie, Harley the cook-man, George, a shinny-man ..."

Anthony held Joanna at arm's length. "Enough about the wreck. Have I ever mentioned that you are beautiful, my love? Do you understand that I wish to marry you?"

Joanna studied Anthony's tired, lined face. The tribulations of the last six months showed clearly in his eyes. She reached to stroke his hair. "I do believe you want to marry me. Perhaps the deed could be done directly after a proper period of mourning for my husband. We are not young, Anthony, and 'tis more than six years since we first met."

"My beloved!"

"But, I do have difficulty believing that you can leave the sea. Does not salt water run through your veins? And we must discuss slavery. Anthony, you do know my views on that abomination. You must promise that you will never, ever trade in slaves again."

"I promise, my dearest, I'll never captain a ship again. I'll be content to watch from shore."

"And the slave trade? Would you do what you can to abolish the despicable practice? And do not, Sir, make promises you cannot keep."

Anthony struggled to his feet, then went down on his one good knee before Joanna. Taking her right hand in his, he kissed it and said. "Does my loyalty to Caliganto, which persuaded me to give him learning, not tell you that I can change? Did giving you Ndamma and Barika not say that I have a conscience? Joanna, I do promise to wed you and to leave the sea. Achuslo, my darling, I swear on my mother's grave – nay, on the sea which is ... was my mistress, that I will forsake the trade in slaves, and that I will assist your efforts to abolish the practice."

With the veriest hint of amusement in her voice, Joanna said, "Perhaps you would be agreeable to a marriage contract?"

"No, my darling," Makem said. "I should be more agreeable to having your trust."

Joanna bent to kiss Anthony's forehead. "Off your knee, Sir. I have trusted you before, and with interesting consequences. Anthony, dearest, do you perhaps think that you may be Lord of this Manor? I am still Father's heir, and must assume that obligation should it come due. But, I must say, there may yet be many a twist to the plot ..."

"We shall live each day to its fullest. Should I feel the need to be within the sound of the sea, I can appease that urge at Makem's Rant."

Anthony struggled to his feet and gave Joanna a hand to rise from the bench. "I have always had an agreeable affinity for England."

"I do know that you have business interests in London that require your attention. You perhaps could assist Father with his various business endeavours."

Anthony laughed. "Joanna. Joanna. 'Tis a small world we live in. What puppets we are! The strings are pulled and we dance across the stage ... this way ... that way. Someone above plays the game much better than you and me. Marry me before another string is pulled and we are parted forever!"

"Sir, I am in mourning," Joanna demurred. "A grieving widow."

"Nay, my dear, your kisses tell me otherwise."

Joanna laughed and stood beside Anthony, her hand to his heart. "A quiet marriage ceremony; then we travel to Virginia in the spring."

Anthony put an arm around Joanna's shoulders. "A question, my love. Do my eyes deceive me? Or is that Ndamma galloping by on a fine steed in the lane leading to the village? He has come to England?"

"You do see *Mister* David duPont. With no disagreeable consequences, he has learned to sweep the chapeau and make the leg, to navigate through a silver table setting and to dress as a gentleman. He is forever at Father's side, learning the business. I do believe that David's future may eventually lie in England and very close to Willowbank. In truth, David's presence provides Father with a clever assistant who does hold to the Turnbull eccentric affinity for the number twelve."

"And Luke?"

"My dear wee man is with me. I believe his fortunes lie in America. That is why we must return to Virginia. That, and we must settle my late husband's estate – and his debts. I must ensure that Andre and Luke are recognized as his heirs and do receive what is rightfully theirs. You can assist me, Anthony. You do know more about Talbot's business affairs than I."

"Ever the schemer, Mrs. Showcroft?"

"I must fulfill obligations and promises made, and find a life away from Father's continual harping. We must return. My word on it, I have always tried to obey the man. But no more! My father shall not interfere in the business of Andre, or in Talbot Showcroft's estate."

"Come to me," Anthony said. "As God is my judge, you are full of surprises, my Joanna. Life as your husband will never be blancmange." He stroked her hair and sighed. "My dear, our time together begins so late ... so late. 'We are such stuff as dreams are made of.'"

"Do you know the time and date, Anthony?

Makem looked at the sun then said, "Near noon on November 5th."

Father would say, "A very good day indeed. Your fortunes and good luck will triple." Joanna took Anthony by the arm. "Come with me," she said. "I do have someone that you must see ..."

Willowbank

1 December 1757

Jento & Kudie c/o Mr. Bushnell, Riverview - near Williamsburg, Virginia

This is the first time that I have set pen to paper in way of a letter to my Friends. It is no small feat to do so, as there is much to say to each of you.

The passage to England was doubtless one of the worst that Captain George Scott ever undertook. But we did, after two months, reach the

Thames River Estuary. My first step on land did buckle my legs. Mrs. Showcroft, with Luke holding her hand, was carried from the ship but regained her Health quickly once at Willowbank.

Life is good for me, as a free man, when I am within the confines of the estate. But I will always be seen, by some, as an odd man - someone to fawn over as long as others see a need to do so and to brush aside when that need is over.

I have taken the opportunity to read <u>The Royal African</u> and, while on a visit to London, discoursed at length with the Young Prince of Annamaboe. He did relate his sad tale of being sold by an Englishman trusted very much by his Father. I do have some hesitation when traveling as England does still recognize slavery, and I fear that some rascal will kidnap me and take me to the West Indies for sale. I am assured by Mrs. Showcroft that this is unlikely to happen; but indeed it does, and has. I travel with my own manservant who has become as close to me as Caliganto to Captain Makem. Should the worst happen, we are two to be dealt with, I can assure you!

I have been introduced to a number of Friends, called Quakers, who do not believe in slavery and are beginning to organize against it. I have given my word that I will assist them in their Endeavours, and have spoken several times on the subject. My early life did not follow the trials and tribulations of most slaves, but I can talk eloquently about conditions surrounding slavery in the Colonies. Caliganto did speak about it many times during his efforts to change Captain Makem's opinion of the abhorrent practice. The great man's death did have some benefit as Captain Makem has become a changed man - perhaps. He does say that true freedom can only be found when one has a ship under them on the high seas. Mrs. Showcroft states that even then there can be no freedom because the sea is one's Mistress and demands much. I do hold to the belief that minds cannot be sold and therefore I am free because I think - read - write - Question.

I am treated with great respect by Mr. Turnbull, Mrs. Showcroft, Mr. Makem and many of the house-servants at Willowbank. Their lot is somewhat improved to that of the slaves at Riverview. But, they are not Free people. They are - for the most part - unschooled and know no other Skill but what they do for a pittance.

Mrs. Showcroft assures me that she has written to tell you that Captain Makem is alive and residing at Willowbank. If ever there was a man at a loss for words, it was the Captain when he was handed his Daughter, Christine. There will be a wedding before the year is over.

Mr. Turnbull, who I do greatly admire, is teaching me the rudiments of his various Business endeavours that I might assist when the new Mr. & Mrs. Makem return to Virginia. He was much taken aback by baby Christine's parentage. But then, he became all reason and said that life always does present surprises - that the game is never over.

Certain Freedoms are not to be slighted, my friends. I wear most beautiful clothing - somewhat resembling a strutting peacock on occasion - and have been taught to be a proper gentleman of the first class. It is not always to my liking, but I must learn to endure. I am given the benefits of Willowbank's Library and do read, of a night, keeping two books open at the same time so that I can turn from one to the other at will.

Luke is a fine young lad who loves Horses. We do try to ride the estate several times a week. He is a true American lad and wishes to return to the Colonies as quickly as may be. He does not like the rigorous rules-of-decorum that must be followed in England. As I become more an Englishman, he becomes more a Virginian. His mother tutors him now and does try to be both mother and Grandfather to her child. She gives him and babe Christine such love and affection!

Jento, I have begun another bag of stones. In it, I have pebbles from Mrs. Blakesome, the Housekeeper - Mr. Hobson, the Head Gardener - Henry O'Brien, my manservant and Companion - I do refuse to refer to these people with anything but their proper names! I did find that I had the need to feel their stones before the stories could be written on paper. I have your stone in my bag, and also that of Kudie. They did come across the sea with me.

Kudie. I did make my feelings for you known to Mrs. Showcroft and she has said that when she returns to Virginia, she will begin the task of giving you Freedom which will be dependent on your learning to read and write. Please borrow my drawings from Jento and begin to learn. Mrs. Showcroft has stated that when she returns to Willowbank - which would be after she has been in Virginia for one year - she will bring you with her and give you freedom - freedom to wed me, in proper church fashion, should that be your desire.

Teacher Bushnell, I reserve my fondest words for you. Without your attentions and tutoring I should not be the educated man I do see in the mirror today. You hold a high position in my esteem. I have your etched stone also. Rest assured that your story is the first that I penned, and do revise even as new chapters unfold. Take care, my friend.

If this letter is to reach you in good time, I must close. Please, Mr. Bushnell, write on behalf of Jento and Kudie. Have him pen a few words that I might see he is learning.

And the last for Kudie - until we See each other Again ...
Sincerely,
David duPont

The End and New Beginnings

Author's Note

In *No Choice But Freedom* I have taken the liberty of weaving threads of truth through a fabric of fiction. The looming began while I was doing research on African freedmen and slaves who came to Canada prior to, and after, the American Revolutionary War. Fascinating strands of many lives wove their way across three continents—Africa, Europe and North America. Those threads that formed the fabric of Virginia and the Carolinas, c1750 through c1760, proved too compelling to forget. They demanded a story be told.

The physical settings for *No Choice But Freedom* were chosen for their unique landscapes, and the role each played in forging the country known today as the United States of America. The story begins in the pastoral countryside of the Yorkshire Dales in England where the wealthy lived like kings on baronial estates. It expands to encompass slave castles on the beaches of West Africa. Scenes are set in Williamsburg, Virginia and at a plantation on the James River, west of the capital town.

A most intriguing locale is the beautiful highlands region of the Carolinas, in particular, the area now known as western North Carolina. Scottish emigrants were attracted to this rugged, wild land. Their desire for freedom and their independent, hard-working spirit lead them to survive, and prosper, in the mountainous region.

It is not my intention to dilute the horrors of slavery. I have attempted to show that in a land gone mad with the domination of one race over another, one being over another, there were people on both sides of the power imbalance who tried to make a difference. Sometimes they failed miserably. But when they did succeed, it was one more little step on the road toward freedom. You see, there is more than one form of slavery. As the story unfolds, you'll find that every character is enslaved in one way or another, be it to a master, work, money, an ideal, an eccentricity.

Ndamma's character is loosely based upon the true story of William Servos Hult, an African who rose from slavery to a position of note in the British and Dutch spice trade before he emigrated to Canada. Joanna's character is fashioned on the true story of one highly-principled English woman by the name of Elizabeth Bagley Morrison, an ardent admirer of Shakespeare's writing, who tried to make a mark in the British North American Colonies with her far-reaching ideals. The Bagley family's eccentric belief that the number twelve was lucky for them was "the stuff of legends" in Leicester, England, until the early 1840s when the last of the family emigrated to Canada. Captain Anthony Makem's character mirrors the life of Captain James Dyce Watt, a highly educated man who needed to feel the deck of a sailing ship under his feet. The fictionalized Caliganto has his roots in Aquino Tota, Captain Watt's African cohort.

Writing set in distant times or places always broaches the question of differences regarding speech. To give a book's characters a distinct dialect—or not to do so—is a difficult question. I have made no attempt to colloquialize speech among the African characters: Ndamma, Sukie, Barika and Jento. Readers must assume that when these characters are talking among themselves, they are doing so in an African language. Their speech would be as eloquent in their language as that of Joanna, Timothy, Makem or Charles Turnbull in English.

On the other hand, I have taken the liberty of giving my Scottish characters the fullness of the Scottish "tongue". With the exception of the Gaelic influence, it is a derivative of the English language and lends itself well to colloquialisms. I have also given Sukie a "plantation dialect" when she is speaking with non-Africans. My thanks to immortal bard, William Shakespeare, for the inclusion of his eloquent quotations.

Meet the Author:

Pat Mattaini Mestern has always called the small town of Fergus, Ontario, home. During her youth, Pat was surrounded by books, stimulating conversation and visual history. This background melded with her love of history to create a writing style that focuses on attractive settings and strong characterizations.

Pat Mestern is the author of four published works of fiction: *Magdalena's Song*, 2003; *Clara, 1979; Anna, Child of the Poor House 1981; Rachel's Legacy, 1989.*

Non-fictional works include *"Looking Back" a 2 volume history set, 1983; "Fergus, a Scottish Town By Birthright" 1995, "So You Want to Hold a Festival, A-Z of Festival & Special Event Organization", 2002.*

Mestern's books have been chosen for newspaper serialization, considered for movie production and nominated for awards. When she's not penning book length works, Pat writes travel, life style and local history columns for a variety of national and international publications..Pat is the mother of four children: Andrew, Celeste, Julia and Cecile, and shares her life with husband Ted and ten grandchildren.

Magdalena's Song

Pat Mattaini Mestern

ISBN:0971394580
Trade paperback, pp 276
High Country Publishers, 2003

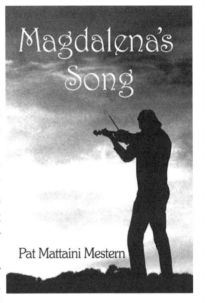

Pat Mattaini Mestern

When the mysterious Count Daniel Vincent Cudzinki visits this industrial village in the Saugeen Valley of Ontario, the tightly woven fabric of its traditional culture unravels. Is he the ghost of an old gypsy, lover of a daughter from one of the town's founding families back for revenge against his tormentor? Or is he simply a labor organizer with a very slick cover story?

Set in the turbulent period just after WWII, this historically and culturally authentic fantasy weaves the fantastic and the mundane in an intriguing web.

Highly recommended ... supurb job of keeping the reader guessing ... [characters] carefully drawn and the reader cares about their outcomes ... romance, mystery and a very satisfying outcome. – *News Express* (Fergus, Ontario)

Pat Mestern's deeply evocative historical novels are among the most rewarding, and the most pleasing, being published today. While they conjure a time long gone and imagine characters long dead, they never fail to embrace the sorts of scandals, dreams and secrets that can haunt nearly every family in every walk of life for many tomorrows. – J. **Marshall Craig**, film director, author of the *Eric Burdon memoir Don't Let Me Be Misunderstood*

Remains with the reader long after the last page is read and Daniel has vanished. Good Conquers evil, tho it takes more than a wee bit of the supernatural to do. – **Margaret Baker**, *Glencoe Wordsmithing*

Marvelous. Congratulations. That is just what any writer hopes to do with writing, and yet so few of us achieve it. – **Ryan Taylor**,author: *Across the Water, Routes to Roots*, radio show host, Fort Wayne IN

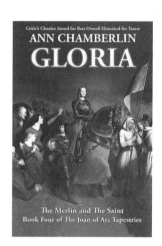

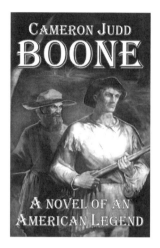

High Country Publishers &

Ingalls Publishing Group, Inc.

invites you to visit our websites to learn more about our books and authors. Visit Pat Mattaini Mestern's site to learn about her other works, and her many other projects in historical fiction and travel writing.

ingallspublishinggroup.com
highcountrypublishers.com
www.mestern.net

HCP/Ingalls Books are distributed to the trade by Biblio Distribution and are available through bookstores and on-line retailers.